STORM OF DESIRE

The two of them sat huddled together while the rain beat down. Shane's heat radiated through Dani like a Caribbean sun. Slowly her teeth stopped chattering. With a long sigh she relaxed against him.

"Better?" Shane asked from behind her.

His mouth was so close to Dani's ear that she felt the warmth of his breath. The shiver that went over her had nothing to do with cold.

"Yes," she said, biting her lower lip. "Thank you."

With a hunger she was just admitting to herself, she put her hands on Shane's forearms. Arms crossed over her chest, she smoothed her hands over his arms from wrist to shoulder and back. Her palms drank in his heat. In a silence broken only by rain, she traced the outline of his biceps again and again, measuring his strength.

Shane's arms flexed, hardening beneath Dani's touch as he drew her closer. A shiver of desire went through her.

He leaned forward a little and brushed his lips against the soft, damp skin of her neck. Then he tasted her with the thoroughness and delicacy of a cat licking cream from a spoon.

"Shane?" Dani whispered.

"I'm right here."

"Is this a good idea?"

"No," he said. "Want me to stop?"

Closing her eyes, Dani tilted her head to one side, offering him more skin to kiss . . .

Turn the page to see what the world is saying
about this extraordinary author . . .

Everybody loves Ann Maxwell!

Writers love Ann Maxwell!

"Ann Maxwell's voice is one of the most powerful and compelling in the romance genre. She writes intense stories, and her readers are equally intense in their response. She has contributed much to the definition of the modern romance novel."

—*New York Times* bestselling author Jayne Ann Krentz

"No one has a voice like Ann Maxwell. She is stellar!"

—Stella Cameron, author of *Sheer Pleasures*

"Ann Maxwell may be *the* most talented, evocative writer in the genre. I pick up her books for more than pleasure. I pick them up to be inspired."

—Suzanne Forster, author of *Shameless*

Critics love Ann Maxwell!

". . . Weaves together past and present, tosses in tidbits about archeology without impairing the story's non-stop action or putting a crimp in the romance. Maxwell's control of her material and unabashed willingness to entertain make this book a success."

—*Publisher's Weekly* on *The Secret Sisters*

"Only Ann Maxwell could have brought this story to such explosive life. . . . An unforgettable sensory experience, this splendorous tale of adventure is everything a reader could wish and much, much more."

—*Rave Reviews* on *The Diamond Tiger*

You'll love Ann Maxwell, too!

Also By This Author

Writing as Ann Maxwell

The Ruby
The Secret Sisters
The Diamond Tiger
Fire Dancer
Dancer's Luck
Dancer's Illusion
Timeshadow Rider
The Jaws of Menx
Name of a Shadow
The Singer Enigma
Dead God Dancing
Change

Writing as Elizabeth Lowell

Winter Fire
Autumn Lover
Enchanted
Only Mine
Only His
Only You
Forbidden
Untamed
A Woman Without Lies
Forget Me Not
Lover in the Rough
Tell Me No Lies
Desert Rain

SHADOW AND SILK

Ann Maxwell

Zebra Books
Kensington Publishing Corp.

http://www.zebrabooks.com

ZEBRA BOOKS are published by

Kensington Publishing Corp.
850 Third Avenue
New York, NY 10022

First Printing: January, 1997
10   9   8   7   6   5   4   3   2   1

Printed in the United States of America

Chapter One

Lhasa, Tibet
October

You can't put it off any longer, Danielle Warren told herself forcefully. It's now or never.

Taking a deep breath, she stepped once again into Lhasa's random, narrow streets. The stone city was infused with the weight of time and the silent pleas that fluttered up from prayer flags fading into the late-afternoon light.

Dani felt like sending up a few prayers herself. She was afraid that she was being followed by more than the chill wind sweeping down from the ramparts of the Potala Palace.

Shoving her hands more deeply into the pockets of her ragged down coat, she bent against the icy air. Her cold fingers curled tightly around two rolls of Chinese currency as though she was afraid that Tibet's wind demons might steal them.

But what Dani really feared were the two-legged variety of demons, the ones she was working so hard to elude in October's chill, slanting light.

Shivering, Dani took shelter in a doorway that was older than Christ. At two miles above sea level, the air was thin and cold as a blade of ice. Because she had been living for weeks in tribal dome tents on the high, dry deserts of Tibet, the altitude didn't bother her.

The shadow Dani thought she had seen out of the corner of her eye did.

Breathing lightly, she waited and stared into the slowly fading light. Nothing moved nearby but prayers strung from ropes, left like laundry to ride the dry wind.

With quick, determined strides, Dani emerged from the cover of the doorway and headed toward the market. Her steps made little noise on the streets and stairs and pathways that had been worn smooth by time and the passage of countless other feet.

Every few minutes she stepped abruptly into the lee of doorways or posts, as though she sought relief from the wind despite her warm clothing. Each time she stopped, she watched her back trail.

Each time she saw nothing but shadows.

I must have gotten away from them, Dani reassured herself silently. They were watching the front of the hotel, not the service entrance at the back.

Letting out a long breath, she hurried toward the market once more. As a field archaeologist whose specialty was textiles, she was accustomed to traveling in Tibet and other rough places around the world.

But she was not used to the feeling of danger that chased her on the cold Himalayan wind.

The spiritual center of Tibet was an occupied city, unwilling captive to the People's Republic of China. What Dani was doing—or would be as soon as she got to the marketplace— was against the law.

It was also against her best judgment and her own scruples. Personally and professionally, she condemned the widespread and immensely profitable international trade in ancient Silk Road artifacts. She was a scholar, not a curator or a merchant. Illegal trafficking in antiquities was something she fought when-ever and wherever she encountered it.

Except for tonight. Tonight Dani was a player for the first time in her life.

And she was afraid.

Stop gnawing on it, Dani told herself fiercely. It's not like I'm buying an irreplaceable piece of a native culture so I can sell it overseas at a thousand percent profit. I'm preventing the destruction of a literally priceless, very fragile artifact.

Grimly she wondered if the expressionless soldiers of the PRC would believe that if they caught her.

Her fingers ached from her fierce grip on the money in her pockets. With those greasy bills she would rescue one of the most extraordinary textile artifacts it had ever been her privilege to see.

Such a simple thing . . . a piece of blue silk that was more than twenty centuries old.

An ancient bit of cloth that, unprotected, would be torn apart by the raw Tibetan wind.

A scrap of silk that was the heart and soul of Tibet.

Don't think about it, Dani told herself. It won't do any good. I've been over it all before a hundred times. I made my decision. Now I have to live with it.

Or die with it.

Stop thinking about it!

Dani loosened her fierce grip on the wad of Chinese currency in her pocket. She carried the equivalent of two thousand American dollars. Even in New York or Tokyo, that amount was big enough to draw a second glance. In a remote, lawless city like Lhasa, two thousand American dollars could buy anything, even a human life.

Yet what really made Dani nervous were the two large, intimidating men who had followed her on and off all day. Neither of them had bothered her directly. In fact, neither of them had even attempted to speak to her.

Dani would have felt better if they had. Like most women who traveled alone, she had become quite skillful at turning aside unwanted male attention.

Unfortunately, these two males were different. They both had pretended to ignore her. They had even pretended to ignore one another.

Yet both of them had been as faithful to Dani's every move as her own shadow.

It wasn't surveillance itself that bothered her. Plainclothes soldiers and agents of the Public Security Bureau were everywhere in Lhasa. They watched Tibetans and foreigners alike. Tourists and trekkers were as common as the wind in Lhasa.

But both of these men were Westerners, not agents of the PRC. Worse, both were big men of precisely the sort who put her on edge.

Once Dani had been attracted to big men, but no longer. Her ex-husband had taught her to fear a man's strength.

Judging by the Vasque hiking boots and North Face Polartec jacket, Dani had decided that the first man she had spotted, while she was changing a traveler's check at the Holiday Inn, was an American.

The man was dark, with a short beard and thick, equally short hair. He had an easy way of moving that spoke of strength and coordination.

Oddly, part of her found him attractive. She didn't understand it. She refused even to acknowledge it. He was entirely too masculine for her comfort.

His eyes were intense. The one time she caught him watching her directly, he seemed to look right down into her nervous soul. She had done her best to look right through him in return.

He hadn't taken the hint. When she stepped out of the American outpost of the Holiday Inn onto the street that led to Potala, the dark stranger came outside right after her.

Dani had expected him to approach her then. Instead, without so much as a glance at her, he disappeared into the teeming crowds of Buddhist pilgrims and worldly trekkers.

She caught another glimpse of him ten minutes later. She was walking into the People's Bank to convert another wad of Foreign Exchange coupons into local currency. This time the dark stranger was lounging in the shade outside the bank.

He looked away when Dani glanced in his direction.

She had taken the opportunity to memorize the big stranger. His face was weathered, as though he had spent a long time in the high Himalayan sunshine. He was lean and hard-muscled.

He could have just come from an extended, high-altitude trek on limited rations.

Despite his American clothing, he was entirely at home in the Tibetan street scene. When a monk passed by, the big man bowed his head slightly. It was an expression of respect usually found only in Tibetans, and devout Buddhists at that.

The gesture could have been intended to shield the stranger's face from Dani's eyes. But there was an automatic quality to the bow. The longer she thought about it, the more she believed that he might indeed be Buddhist.

It was oddly reassuring, the way the stranger bowed to a monk half his size.

The comforting thought vanished as he continued to follow her through the grisly open-air slaughterhouse and meat market called Yak Alley. She was grateful that the thin, cold air didn't carry smells very well. She had been in some Amazon fish markets that would have gagged a skunk.

From Yak Alley Dani slipped into the quiet, shadowed darkness of a small shop immediately adjacent to the Jokhang Temple and waited as long as she dared.

When she emerged, the tall, bearded stranger was gone. In his place was another tall stranger.

The second man was as big as the first man. It was easy to tell them apart, because the new man was pale by comparison. No beard. Fine, almost white hair worn slightly long. He had wide cheekbones and a blank, blue-eyed fairness about him that made Dani decide he was Scandinavian.

Irrationally, Dani found herself wishing that the first man was back. At some gut level, she preferred him to his blond partner.

The second man had a good sense of natural camouflage. He blended effortlessly into one of the inevitable, talkative bands of Dutch trekkers that had gathered outside the main entrance to the temple.

When Dani walked off along the pilgrimage path that circled the temple, the blank-eyed man moved with her. She assumed that the two men were working her in relay.

She caught another glimpse of the American's black North

Face jacket. He had covered his dark hair with a soft Tibetan felt hat. He was lounging against a wall across the market with the hat pulled down over his eyes, as though he was half-asleep.

The next time Dani checked, the American had disappeared completely.

His absence did nothing to comfort her. Even when she could see his blond, blank-eyed associate, she found herself looking over her shoulder frequently for the first man.

When she didn't catch another glimpse of his wind- and sunburned face, she fought a growing uneasiness. She half expected him to jump out of an alley and attack her.

Dani distrusted big men. They were all bullies, whether or not they realized it.

It wasn't that she was small. At five feet, five inches and a well-conditioned one hundred ten pounds, she was just slightly below the average size of her gender. But life—and her ex-husband—had taught her that only a man's personal sense of honor guaranteed a woman's physical safety.

A lot of men lacked that sense of honor.

Shivering, Dani found a sheltered alcove along the street leading to the grand stairway up the front of the Potala Palace. She snapped up her coat collar and buried her nose in it, partly to stay warm but mostly to conceal her Occidental face and hazel eyes.

She waited, watching the last light fade behind the ragged brown mountains that surrounded Lhasa. The shadows deepened. The cold bit through her quilted Chinese coat. Smudged and dirty from almost six weeks of fieldwork, the coat blended well with the rough clothing of the natives on the street.

Even though the open-air markets were shutting down with the sun, the ancient city was still alive with pilgrims and trekkers. The ragged pilgrims moved with ecstatic exhaustion, having prostrated themselves for every inch of their journey. Their faces were transformed by being finally within reach of the holy center of their spiritual universe.

The expensively outfitted trekkers strode upright with eager confidence, ready to prove themselves against the highest mountains in the world. The trekkers who had just conquered the mountains, and themselves, had faces lined with fatigue and an elation that was strikingly similar to that of the pilgrims.

Motionless, Dani watched as a cadre of Chinese security policemen in dark green uniforms marched up the street toward the broad stairway that slanted across the front rampart of the palace. The soldiers walked stiffly, warily. Despite official proclamations to the contrary, the Chinese knew they were in hostile territory.

More than forty years had passed since the People's Republic of China had invaded the mountain kingdom of Tibet. In that time the PRC had tried to break the Tibetan spirit in a thousand overt and subtle ways.

Tibetan cultural practices, most of them based in the country's ancient religious traditions, had been outlawed. Buddhist priests had been persecuted and debased. Tibet's government had been secularized.

Thousands of ethnic Chinese had immigrated into the harsh mountain land. It was a conscious effort by the PRC to break the hold of the indigenous peoples on Tibet itself. Chinese dominated the civic and commercial life of Lhasa.

But Dani had shared the lives of the native Tibetans outside the cities. In the domed tents and barren highlands, the Buddhist religion was still the blood and bone and breath of the people. Their very lives were a prayer offered to their gods.

Even inside the cities, animosity existed between the pervasive spirituality of Tibetans and the determined secularity of the PRC. Within the past five years, the friction had flared into full-scale riots.

Although the infant insurrection had been crushed by the PRC's superior arms, there were still places in Lhasa where the Chinese security police went only in squad strength. There were other places where they went not at all.

No matter how many years the Chinese had ruled, no matter how many promises of prosperity, communism, and community were made, most Tibetans still regarded the Chinese as an army of occupation.

For ten minutes Dani waited at the edge of what was no-man's land for the Chinese. Eyes narrowed against the cold wind, she searched her back trail and the streets.

There was no sign of the two Westerners who had been following her. Nor did she see anyone who looked like he might be a plainclothes agent of the Public Safety Bureau.

Finally Dani turned to confront her uncertain future.

The white wings of the earth-and-stone building that had once been the residence of the Dalai Lama rose up thirteen stories above her. The Chinese army had sent the holiest of all Tibetans into exile and turned his sacred palace into a museum for curious Westerners.

Not that there was a great deal to see except the building itself. The objects of greatest spiritual focus for the Tibetans had been removed to Beijing for "safekeeping."

Yet nothing the Chinese had done could break the hold of Buddhism on Tibet. Loosen it, yes.

Otherwise Dani wouldn't have been standing alone and shivering in the failing light, waiting to buy a very sacred piece of Tibet's past.

Now or never, Dani reminded herself forcefully. If the silk isn't handled correctly, it will be lost for all time. Get moving!

She left the cold shadows and made her way to the sacred palace itself. A long flight of cobblestone steps led up to the stone ramparts. Instead of setting off up the stairs, she stood at the bottom.

A pair of monks wrapped in orange robes against the cold wind were coming down the steps. One of them saw the young, dark-haired woman and called out something in Tibetan.

The words sounded to Dani like a warning that the museums and strong rooms in the palace were already closed. She nodded in respect and kept on waiting.

The monks passed by. They were headed into the city.

For five minutes she was alone at the base of the long stairway. The shadows darkened. From one of the alleys close by came the furtive rustlings of rats. A few hundred feet away a dog howled, startling her.

Dani stamped her feet. The stone steps were cold despite

having stored up a day of sunlight. At this altitude, the heat of the sun was as thin as the air itself.

While Dani waited, the Dalai Lama's former residence took on an eerie radiance in the slowly dying light. Ancient yet timeless, solid yet grounded in transcendence, the holy palace rose out of the land, shining against the descending twilight.

For an instant Dani felt dwarfed, alien, almost overwhelmed by millennia of human lives and prayers whose center had been the palace.

It wasn't the first time she had felt the fragility of human life against the immensity of eternity. In her work as an archaeologist, she had become accustomed to the weight of time and the dust of human bones and dreams.

But this was the first time in Dani's life that she had felt her own human vulnerability while waiting to commit a crime punishable by death.

Yet she held her ground. The silk was more valuable than any life.

Even her own.

Chapter Two

The rat was huge.

It had emerged from beneath a loose roof tile and scuttled down the roof's slope. Its coat was dark gray and shiny in the radiance of the mountain twilight.

Claws clicked softly, quickly. The tiny sounds carried well in the quiet surrounding the base of the Potala Palace.

Shane Crowe, lying spread-eagled and absolutely motionless on the roof, knew the exact instant when the rat caught his scent.

The rodent froze. The black end of its nose lifted and twitched. Eyes like black beads peered toward him.

I'll bet the bastard is hoping for a free meal, Shane thought with grim humor. Sorry, pal. You lose. I may not smell like a rose, and my beard itches from all the tile dust, but I'm no corpse left for sky burial so that the Tibetan elements can pick my flesh and soul clean of my bones.

The rat was cautious. It stayed where it was, waiting to see if the human moved.

I don't smell dead enough for you, huh? Shane asked silently. Well, stick around. I have a bad feeling about tonight.

Damn all amateurs.

The highly academic Dr. Danielle Warren—Dani to her friends—has no business risking her long legs and elegant neck in this business, Shane thought in disgust.

Especially not when a nasty piece of work like Feng was part of the bargain. Shane had been edging very, very slowly down the roof, waiting for Feng to appear.

The four-legged variety of rat had appeared first. The rat waited now with the patience of all predators, trying to decide if it had found a meal to eat or danger to flee.

Shane stared at the rat. To an animal, such a direct meeting of eyes was a threat. He hoped to drive the rat away without making any motion that would reveal his own presence to anyone below.

Unlike the blithe Dani, Feng would be alert to any hint of danger from any quarter, even the roofs above.

Will he bring the silk? Shane asked himself for the hundredth time. Or will he just fleece the pretty little professor and run like hell?

Emboldened by Shane's absolute stillness, the rat skittered a few inches closer.

From below came the sound of other footsteps. The human kind.

Shane listened and prayed to ancient gods that he would be close enough to overhear whatever conversation took place between the Han thief and the American archaeologist.

Bring it, Feng, he demanded silently. I want to meet the man who stole that silk from inside an Azure temple guarded by men I trained myself.

The Han thief was adept. One in a million.

Shane was as familiar with the Tibetan capital as any Westerner could ever be, yet Feng had eluded him in Lhasa for three days. That meant Feng was well connected and very, very cautious.

This would be Shane's best chance, perhaps his only one, to retrieve the silk.

Damn that woman, he thought. She couldn't have picked a worse time or place to get in the way.

Not that I'm ungrateful. She led me to Feng and hopefully

to the silk. But she's so bloody naive that I can't just leave her to the vultures.

When Shane had first seen Dani, the depth of his protective instinct toward her had surprised him. He fought it, for he knew it meant complications at a time when he couldn't afford any.

The feeling had persisted. He must protect the woman.

Shane had shrugged and accepted it as he had learned to accept so many things.

Never argue with Karma, he reminded himself dryly. You always lose.

But his first loyalty must be to the Azure monks. They had retained Risk Limited—and him—to recover their sacred fragment of silk.

That was his primary objective and obligation. He had no doubt of it.

When the sound of footsteps moved past the area where Dani waited, he was disappointed and relieved at the same time.

Disappointed that the silk wasn't within his immediate grasp.

Relieved that Dani wasn't in immediate danger.

He didn't want to see Dani hurt, or even frightened, if he could avoid it.

Not that she couldn't use a good scare, Shane thought impatiently. She doesn't have a clue about how vulnerable she is. A few bribes at the hotel and I had everything about her but her birth certificate.

And if she had brought that with her, he could have had it when he searched her room. She had made no attempt to hide her identity or to have another identity waiting once she bought the silk.

Too trusting, Shane thought. An innocent in a game played by carnivores.

A fool, he summed up grimly.

Even now he could hardly believe that Dani had stood in the middle of the open-air market at the temple, negotiating with Feng. Then she had roamed Lhasa, conducting legal and illegal currency transactions, accumulating her bankroll.

Shane had spent most of the day watching her all to predictable movements. The only surprise was that the Chinese security police agents hadn't swept down and snapped her up in a Beijing minute.

Or the Russian who is following her, Shane thought uneasily, toting up the odds against himself. At least, I'm betting he's Russian.

The pale foreigner had the bullet-headed blond look of an Estonian or Ukrainian. Shane had seen plenty of the type in Afghanistan—Spetznaz troopers, the special operations teams who roamed Afghanistan like packs of wolves in the days before the Soviet empire collapsed.

He knew the look of the Spetznaz well. He had lived for months at a time with the ragged soldiers of the mujahedeen, teaching them how to bring down high-tech Soviet tanks with ancient black powder weapons.

Cursing silently, he measured the extent of Dani's naiveté. Only a blind innocent could have missed the heavy-handed Russian's surveillance.

True, Shane admitted reluctantly, she had showed intelligence in adapting the old service-entrance gambit to Lhasa's Holiday Inn. She wasn't stupid.

But she still was an amateur in a game where professionals died regularly.

Greed could have blinded her, Shane reminded himself. That would explain the risks she takes as though she doesn't even notice them.

The idea of Dani as a greedy dealer in dubious antiquities didn't appeal to him. Nor did it fit with what he had found in her room. She had none of the luxurious items associated with greed. Her clothes had been comfortable, easily washable under primitive circumstances, and well worn.

Her underwear had been the same.

If he had found some alluring bits of peekaboo lace in Dani's backpack, she would have been easy to ignore. Fantasy underwear. Fantasy woman. Irrelevant to Shane Crowe.

But something about her plain, well-worn, painstakingly clean underwear had been relevant. Instantly.

For the first time in almost three years, his self-imposed vow of celibacy seemed confining rather than liberating.

More footsteps came from below. They stopped where he thought Dani was. Voices came.

Her voice and a man's.

Feng? Shane wondered.

Wondering was all he could do. He was too far from the edge of the roof to see directly or hear clearly. If he moved, the rat would squeal and flee.

Dani wouldn't notice, but Feng would, if indeed he was the one talking to her.

The rat and Shane stared at each other in the deepening twilight. The animal was so close that Shane could see a flea crawl slowly across the creature's bald nose, headed for the corner of an eye.

The rat paid no attention to the parasite. Caught between fight, flight, and the possibility of food, the rat waited.

Shane pursed his lips and blew a slow, steady stream of air in the rodent's direction.

The rat withdrew a foot, then turned and scuttled silently toward his lair beneath the peak of the low roof.

Shane resumed his millimeter crawl toward the edge of the roof, testing each tile in front of him as he went. He turned his energy inward, shutting out all distracting thoughts, fearing nothing except betraying his own presence.

Another nine inches to go, then six.

Silent as the night itself, Shane flowed down the roof until the edge was an inch beyond the tips of his outspread fingers.

He could hear the voices clearly now.

"I heard you prowling a moment ago," Dani said, her voice faintly accusing.

"Yes, Miss Warren."

"I told you I would be alone."

"So you did. It was necessary for this worthless one to be certain of solitude."

Shane eased forward again. With one eye, he could just catch sight of the top of Dani's head. She had dark, lustrous hair. She must have been on the road for some time, since her hair appeared to have been cut most recently with dull scissors or a camp knife.

Moving as slowly as a shadow changing in the moonlight, Shane went the last bit that allowed him to see the rest of Dani's face. Her skin was smooth and clear, her features well formed. Her changeable hazel eyes were as dark as night now.

He would have found her attractive at any time, but the intensity of her eyes as she watched Feng step out of the shadows was compelling.

There's real force in this woman, Shane realized. Too damned bad that she's naive enough to have put herself out on the wrong end of a breaking limb.

But not naive enough to step completely out of the shadows. Not yet.

"Do not fear, Miss Warren. It is only I, Feng."

Feng's wide smile revealed three stained, decayed teeth in the front of his mouth, legacy of a lifetime of holding and smoking cigarettes through those same teeth.

Dani wasn't reassured by Feng's smile. It reminded her of childhood jack-o-lanterns and ghosts in graveyards.

It amazed Dani that an Asian with such a gap-toothed smile could have acquired excellent English. He pronounced even the difficult consonants precisely, if slowly.

"I recognize you," Dani said. "Where is the silk?"

She made no attempt to hide her impatience. The longer she waited in such a relatively exposed place, the greater the danger of discovery became.

"Feng is a man of his word," he said.

He turned slightly. There was a metal tube slung across his back, held in place with a leather thong. The tube seemed to glow, gathering light to itself just as the sacred palace had.

"The silk?" Dani asked.

"As you see."

"I see only a metal tube."

Feng stopped a few feet away from her. He cocked his head, examining her from head to toe.

"I see no hands holding money," he countered.

Dani kept her fists shoved into the pockets of her coat. She hadn't like Feng in full daylight with people around. She liked him even less in deepening twilight with no one around.

"I have the money," she said curtly.

"Where?"

"Close by."

Feng hissed through his stained teeth.

"No money. No silk," he said with a bluntness he had learned from Westerners.

"I haven't seen the silk yet."

Feng's narrowed, black glance darted around, probing shadows for any signs of watchers.

Wind gusted, rising with the falling light.

Forcing herself not to shiver, Dani waited as though she had all night and a roaring fire to keep her warm.

Reluctantly Feng unslung the tube and took off the cap. He tipped the tube. When nothing appeared, he started to shake the metal vigorously.

"Wait!" Dani said, horrified. "Do it gently!"

"Less noise, please!" Feng said in a low, urgent voice.

"If this material is what you say," she shot back softly, "you could destroy it in an instant of rough handling."

Feng grunted and looked at the open end of the tube.

Dani had the distinct impression that he hadn't ever seen the contents.

Thank God, she said silently. Maybe whoever packed the tube knew more about handling ancient silk than this dolt.

"May I?" Dani asked.

She held out her hand in a gesture that was more a command than a request.

Feng hesitated, then handed over the tube.

"You destroy, you pay," he said.

Dani shot him an impatient look.

"If it comes out of the tube already destroyed," she said, "I won't pay you a tin penny."

Feng grunted.

Gently Dani tipped and tapped the metal cylinder until its contents slid out into her hand. It was a tube of white silk tied in several places by azure silk ribbons.

A single glance at the weave of the white silk told Dani that the cloth was modern and machine-woven.

She was reassured rather than dismayed. Lacking a climate-controlled museum case, a wrapping of heavy silk and Lhasa's extremely dry, cold air was the best protection she could have hoped to find for the fragile, ancient silk she had seen briefly earlier that day.

With chilled fingers Dani undid the ribbon that bound one end of the roll. Very gently she turned back a corner of the protective fabric, taking care not to breathe directly on whatever the modern silk enclosed.

Inside the roll was another piece of cloth. Even without direct light, she recognized the combination of wild and domestic silk threads. The style of weaving itself was ancient, with a pattern only on the weft threads.

Considering the presumed age of the fabric, the azure dye was remarkably intense, glowing even in the twilight. The radiance of the blue was enhanced by the incredibly fine gold threads that had been spun in with some of the silk.

What a glorious piece this once was, Dani thought, awed. Even what remains is extraordinary.

She rubbed her fingertips vigorously on the inside of her coat, warming and cleaning them by friction. Then, more delicately than a breath, she brushed her fingertips over a corner of the cloth.

Her experienced sense of touch instantly detected the smooth resilience of thrown silk and the subtle variations in texture that were the result of both the silk itself and the weaver's own touch on the loom.

The fabric was just as she had seen it laid out carefully on top of a chest in the back of the shop where Feng had first approached her. The feel of it was unmistakable to her sensitive, trained fingertips.

Quickly Dani covered the ancient silk, wrapped it, tied it securely, and eased it back into the tube. Breathing a sigh of relief, she capped the tube firmly. It was the best she could do to preserve the fragile artifact until she got back to America.

Without warning Feng snatched the aluminum tube from Dani's fingers.

"You are satisfied," he said.

It wasn't a question, but Dani answered anyway.

"Yes," she said. "Completely."

"The money, Miss Warren. Then I, too, will be satisfied completely."

Feng's grin was quick, nervous, and not in the least reassuring.

"In a moment," Dani said.

"Why wait? The night is advancing."

She didn't need to be reminded of that. Yet still she hesitated. The silk was real. She was sure of that.

But an afternoon of being followed by two large Westerners had made Dani more cautious.

"Where did you get this?" she asked baldly.

Feng made a derisive sound.

"You Westerners are interested only in possessing the ancient history woven into the silk," he said. "What care have you for the antics of modern trade?"

"Times have changed since Westerners first came here a century ago," Dani said quietly. "Some of us want to make sure that artifacts and relics are preserved, not merely sold to the highest bidder."

Feng managed to look wounded by her lack of trust. He held up the aluminum tube for her to see.

"I have handled it carefully," he said. "I, too, care."

"That's why there are several dents in the container," Dani said sarcastically.

Feng started to object, then made a dismissive gesture.

"I could not carry it with me at all times," he said. "The police were everywhere in Lhasa today. I had to hide the tube behind some rocks in the wall of my house."

Still Dani hesitated. She sensed that this was the moment of deepest danger for her. Staring at Feng, she tried to read his gaunt, wind-burned features.

Not much bigger than I am, Dani thought, but don't kid yourself. He's stronger than I am.

How can I prevent him from taking the money and the silk, too?

Feng stared back, waiting with growing impatience.

"One more question," Dani said.

"But—"

"Answer me truthfully," she interrupted, "or I'll walk away right now."

Feng nodded an inch in agreement.

"Why did you approach me in the Barkhor market?" Dani asked.

A flickering movement of Feng's eyes was the only betrayal of his surprise.

"You were Western," he said, recovering quickly.

"So were a thousand others today."

"You were interested in purchasing the ancient things."

"So were five hundred others. Why me, Feng? Why did you choose me?"

She waited, watching his face.

Nothing she saw reassured her.

"I, uh, saw you inspecting the Khampas' banners at the temple," Feng said. "You touched them so carefully that I assumed you were interested in silks."

"Is that so?" Dani asked softly.

Feng nodded.

"The Khampas' banners were made yesterday," she pointed out, "yet you knew I had expertise in ancient silks."

Feng's eyelids flinched. He said nothing.

"Are you trying to set me up?" Dani asked.

"Oh, no, no, miss," Feng said quickly. "I have more to fear from the police than you do."

"Then why did you pick me to show the silk to?"

Spread-eagled and exposed on the nearby roof, Shane didn't know whether to swear or cheer at Dani's persistence. Up to now, she had seemed so eager to stick her neck into the noose.

It's about time, lady, Shane thought sardonically. You're up to your lips in yak shit and you're just catching on.

So tell her, Feng. Why did you pick on the innocent little professor?

Shane was rather curious himself.

Then he heard a faint, distant sound, metal on metal He

recognized it instantly as the tailgate of a truck being unhitched and lowered.

Danger.

Shane had heard the sound a dozen times in ambushes and on night patrol in the mountains. PRC troop carriers had those kinds of tailgates. They had to be dropped before the squad of soldiers in back could get out.

Slowly Shane lifted his head and stared in the direction of the sound. Seventy yards away, at the far approach to the Potala Palace wall, he caught a glimpse of a truck.

The truck had not been there a few minutes ago.

Even in the twilight Shane had no difficulty recognizing the military shade of green. Like the sound of the tailgate dropping, he had seen the colors of the PRC all too often, in every kind of light.

The only way the truck could have arrived without being noticed was to roll in with the engine off and brake to a halt with the taillights unplugged.

This is no routine patrol, Shane realized. These are top security troopers on a well-planned mission.

Shit.

Shane turned his head and looked back toward the heart of the city. He saw more headlights moving in his direction.

Feng and Dani are rats in a trap, Shane thought. But then, so am I. The only difference is that I know it.

Shane hoped it would be enough of a difference.

Then he caught another sound, a boot scraping carelessly on a paving stone. The soldiers were closing in.

I'll have to make a grab for the silk, Shane decided calmly. It's my best chance. My only one.

Slowly Shane raised himself on the roof, measuring his distance from Feng and the aluminum tube.

"Well, Feng?" Dani prodded. "Why did you choose me out of all the Westerners in the market this morning?"

Feng sighed, smiled nervously, and gave in.

"You are very quick, Miss Warren. I came to you because—"

There was a soft, muffled popping sound.

Silencer, Shane thought instantly. Christ.

Dani saw a look of surprise on Feng's face as a rip suddenly opened up on his jacket. Blood burst through the cloth as Feng was flung back against the wall.

Instinctively Dani grabbed for the aluminum tube as Feng slumped to the cobbles, but he was already beyond her reach. His body had folded protectively around the tube.

In numb disbelief Dani stared at Feng's surprised face, his twisted body. A strange slackness came over him, but he didn't release the tube.

Blood stopped flowing from the fresh wound.

Abruptly Dani knew that Feng would never answer her question. He was quite dead.

Shane had known Feng was dead from the way he hit the wall. With cool precision Shane weighed impacts and timed sounds and calculated trajectories.

The Russian, Shane concluded instantly. It has to be. Security troopers don't use silencers. They come in with all barrels blazing and jackboots slapping on the pavement.

Shane's years of military training took over. Knowing he was still concealed from the assassin, he slowly turned his head toward the spot from which the shot had come. He caught a flicker of movement.

The Russian, changing positions.

Dani gasped as the blank-faced blond Westerner who had followed her earlier stepped out of the shadows thirty yards away.

The gun he carried was pointed right at her heart.

"Stand back from the silk," he said, "or die."

Chapter Three

Except for Shane's own reactions, the world seemed to shift into slow motion for him. It was always that way for him in battle. It gave him an edge many other men didn't have.

As Shane rolled to one side, he slipped his own weapon out of the holster in the small of his back. The gun was a matte-black small-caliber pistol with a long barrel, a varmint gun of the sort that many backpackers carried in the outlands of Tibet.

Shane valued accuracy over stopping power. In any case, a small pistol was easier to explain to authorities in places like Tibet than a high-caliber man killer with a fifteen-round clip and all the bells and whistles.

Before Shane could bring the pistol to bear on the Russian target, he heard a sudden shout in Chinese.

"Stop! We are the authorities!"

A pair of men in green uniforms appeared between the buildings a half-block away.

The Russian reacted instantly. He switched his silenced pistol for an automatic weapon and fired a short, sharp volley.

The PRC soldiers ducked behind cover. A few seconds later they returned fire with their own automatic weapons.

Shane could see the Russian now. He was well trained and

either brave or crazy. Or both. He fired in short, measured bursts, burning half a magazine of ammunition to pin down the security troops.

Yet instead of seizing the advantage to run away, the Russian turned back and slipped through the shadows. He was stalking the dead Feng.

And the living Danielle Warren.

Dani was reaching for the aluminum tube when the Russian saw what she was doing. He fired a short burst in her direction. Bullets sang wildly off the stone street.

With a muffled, startled sound, Dani leaped back and looked around frantically for shelter.

Shane didn't know whether to be relieved or furious when she flattened herself into the doorway directly beneath his rooftop perch.

Motionless, Shane held his position for a swift three-count, reassessing the situation.

The Russian moved again, using the natural cover of the narrow street. He fired precise two-shot bursts in the direction of the soldiers.

They ducked, then fired back. First it was only a single weapon, then two, then three. Soon it was impossible to tell how many guns answered. Bullets sang off the paving blocks and kicked up puffs of grit from the walls.

The Russian fell back into a doorway long enough to change magazines on his automatic. Then he fired again and moved quickly toward his goal.

He was ten yards from the fallen Feng, twenty feet from Dani.

Calmly Shane drew a bead on the Russian's head with his pistol.

The range was easy, but Shane couldn't fire without drawing the attention of the PRC to himself. From the moment the soldiers spotted him, Shane figured he had five seconds, at best, before they blew him off the rooftop.

That wasn't enough time to save himself, much less the silk.

Shane could see the Russian's goal—the metal tube in the dead man's hand. It was Shane's goal, too, but he was in no position to reach it.

Then Shane saw Dani step out from the cover of the doorway beneath him. She, too, was after the tube.

She has guts, Shane thought admiringly, even if she is a little light on brains.

Softly he called out to her, "Dani. No."

Dani barely heard the thread of sound, but she recognized her own name. She froze and looked up.

The Russian followed her glance. His blond head swung around, scanning the roofline as he analyzed the new factor in this three-cornered firefight.

Shane saw the outline of the Russian's weapon for the first time. An Uzi.

The world slowed even more for Shane. Even as the barrel swung up toward him, he mentally marked the oddity of an Uzi-wielding Russian.

Then Shane saw the muzzle, felt its one-eyed stare, and rolled back out of sight as four bullets shattered the tile at the edge of the roof.

The Russian's shots drew return fire from the Chinese. He ducked back under cover as bullets thudded against the wall above him.

For the moment the PRC seemed unaware of Shane. They poured fire into the Russian's position and began their deadly ballet of shoot and advance.

Shane could see that the outcome was inevitable. The Russian was vastly outnumbered, but he was close enough to grab the tube and retreat.

Dani would have to retreat, too, or she would be swallowed up by the advancing troops. In her position, a trained agent would be moving fast and quiet right now, fading into the night.

But Dani didn't know how. She had never been under fire. She had never seen a man murdered. She had never been the target of a murderer.

She was an innocent, a noncombatant, the kind of person who made an operator like Shane curse.

He could save the silk or he could save Dani.

His choice.

Her life.

No real choice at all.

Fuck it, Shane cursed in silent, savage fury.

Then he rolled back to the edge of the roof and stuck his head over where Dani could see him.

"Come here, Dani," Shane whispered urgently.

Her eyes widened. She stared at Shane as though he was a castle gargoyle that had suddenly broken into song.

The Russian was caught in his own instant of indecision. He couldn't get a clear shot at Shane without exposing himself to the troops.

Like the trained agent he was, the Russian plastered himself against the door frame and waited for better odds.

Shane reached down over the edge of the roof.

"Take my hand," Shane said in a soft voice. "Quickly! It's your only chance."

Dani glanced at the Russian, at the advancing troops, and at the dead Feng folded over the precious silk.

She stepped out of cover and reached up toward the roof.

Shane's fingers locked around Dani's wrist. She was small and light and adrenaline was a storm in his bloodstream. He lifted her as though she was made of straw rather than flesh and bone.

Dani helped. She swung one leg up, caught the edge of the tiles, surged forward, scrambled, and flattened out on the roof.

She must have had some kind of training, Shane thought in relief. She flipped up onto the roof like a trapeze artist catching her perch high above a circus ring.

Holding onto Dani's wrist, Shane dragged her back from danger at the edge of the roof. She didn't fight. She moved with him, then flattened out on the roof again. This time she was on her back instead of her stomach, breathing hard.

Shane wasn't. His breath was slow and steady. He stretched out on his stomach with his gun arm across Dani, covering the courtyard below. As he waited for a target to appear, he realized that he was lying next to a woman in an intimate position, his arm across her breasts.

For an instant he sensed the feminine softness of Dani's

body. She was panting from her exertions. Her breath bathed his face. She smelled sweet.

"Stay put," he said in a very low voice. "The cops haven't seen us yet."

Shane eased forward until he was half sprawled across Dani. Then he peered carefully over the edge of the roof long enough to see the endgame.

There was no warning. The Russian fired most of a clip down the street in a shattering burst of sound. The shots were still echoing when he dove out of cover in a crouching run. Without breaking stride he shoved Feng over, scooped up the metal tube, and raced down the street.

The security troops must have been so astonished by the daring maneuver that they hesitated before bringing their weapons to bear. By the time they recovered and began to fire again, it was too late. Their target had disappeared.

The soldiers fired for ten or fifteen seconds anyway before they gave up.

Slapping, hard-running footsteps faded in the distance.

Silence returned like thunder.

Once more Shane became aware of the woman who lay beneath him. Dani shifted slightly. Her breasts moved against the muscle of his arm. The sensation was pleasant, almost erotic.

Shane flexed his biceps gently. The sensation was repeated. Then Dani shifted slowly, almost like a lover rolling toward him in the night.

He glanced down at her face a few inches from his own. Something of his instinctive masculine reaction to her closeness must have showed in his eyes.

Dani's expression changed.

"I'm only moving," she said softly through her teeth, "because a broken tile is digging a hole in my back."

"So don't get any ideas, is that it?" Shane murmured.

"That's it."

"Don't worry. You're safe for another month."

"What?"

"Time to go," he said softly. "How are you at climbing?"

"Better than I am at lying on my back."

Shane smiled slightly. He rolled onto his side and transferred the gun to his other hand. Then he grasped Dani's hand.

"Crawl," he murmured.

Together they crawled up the low, slanting roof.

Their biggest exposure came at the roofline. Shane hustled Dani over it with a sudden thrust of his shoulder and hip. They slid and scuttled crabwise quickly down the other side.

At the eaves, Dani hesitated. Shane jerked her wrist and dumped her inelegantly over the edge. Other than an involuntary gasp when gravity took over, she kept quiet.

Silently Shane applauded her guts. Most people would have made a lot of noise when they found themselves in apparent freefall over the edge of a roof.

Shane caught Dani's full weight in midair, held her for a moment while she gathered herself, and then slowly released her. She landed with a small grunt on the cobbles.

A second later Shane landed beside her. He grabbed her wrist and started to lead her away.

Dani took one step and groaned.

"My ankle," she said.

"Quiet."

Shane bent down and put his mouth right next to Dani's ear. For the first time he realized how small she was. Not tiny, not delicate, just small.

"There are troops coming in from all sides," Shane murmured. "Do I have to carry you?"

"Don't worry, you big bastard," Dani said just as softly. "I won't slow you down."

The sheer anger vibrating in her voice surprised Shane.

Adrenaline takes some people that way, he reminded himself. Anger, pure and wild. Especially when they aren't accustomed to fighting for their life.

"Leave me here," Dani snarled softly. "I don't know who you are or why those people are shooting at you, but I'm just an American archaeologist. I'll take my chances."

"You don't have the chance of a snowflake in hell. You're right in the center of a first-class Charlie Foxtrot."

"What?"

"A clusterfuck. Now can you walk or do I have to carry you?"

"I don't even know who you are," Dani whispered. "Why should I go with you?"

"My name is Shane Crowe and I'm the only one who hasn't tried to kill you."

"What would you call dropping me off a roof?"

"Saving your life."

"I can walk."

"Good."

With that Shane straightened, took Dani by the wrist again, and started walking.

Dani didn't fight any longer. Limping but still quick, she let Shane lead her away down a narrow alleyway. It opened onto the base of the steps that led up to the sacred Buddhist palace.

Behind them she heard a building commotion. Shouted orders and running feet, angry protests and shrill screams came from the inhabitants of the buildings.

Dani had seen the Chinese occupation forces in action before. She could imagine what was happening.

Angry or not, big or not, stranger or not, she was glad that the man called Shane Crowe hadn't left her behind.

Shane had an even clearer vision in his mind of what was happening behind them. The PRC had reached the dead Feng, but they found no one else. Now they were fanning out into the Tibetan neighborhood, rousting households and searching with rough fists and gun butts for their elusive prey.

Dani's ankle arched and throbbed. She gritted her teeth, determined to keep up with Shane's big, quiet strides. There was a peculiar grace to his movements that made her think of a dancer or a man well trained in martial arts.

Considering the circumstances, she told herself dryly, I'll vote for the martial arts.

With no hesitation Shane led Dani through a maze of alleys that would have confused anyone but a Lhasa native. Four times he stopped and pressed Dani into cover.

Each time she heard nothing that would have alarmed her. Yet each time, troopers passed within a dozen yards of them, searching the streets.

And each time, she felt a heightened awareness of this man's strength. One of his arms was a hard bar across her body, holding her deep in the shadows.

In a corner of her mind she realized that, despite the gun in Shane's other hand, she didn't feel the sense of powerlessness that she had known when her ex-husband grabbed her and held her down. She didn't know why Shane's strength was different. She only knew that it was.

When Shane's arm dropped, Dani followed him. They reached the base of the stairs that led up the ramparts to Potala Palace. Shane stopped to let her catch her breath.

"So you're an archaeologist," he said softly. "What are you doing here?"

"I just got in from six weeks on desert, mapping trade routes. Who are you, some kind of cop?"

"No," he said.

"Then what are you?"

"It doesn't matter. You probably wouldn't believe me if I told you anyway."

"CIA?"

Shane laughed softly.

"Haven't you heard?" he asked. "They're an international joke. I'm strictly private."

Dani shook her head like a dog coming out of water, trying to make sense out of the shattered mosaic of the moment.

"You think you've had a strange day so far?" Shane asked softly, amused. "Just wait. You're going where no woman has ever been before."

Shane took Dani by the hand and led her up the first flight of worn stone stairs to a landing. He knocked on a small, windowless wooden door that was set into the stone wall.

The door swung open silently. A wizened monk in a dark blue robe stood aside to give them access.

Shane drew Dani through the doorway into the darkness.

When Dani realized where she was, she sensed that she had just fallen down the rabbit's hole and life would never be quite the same again.

She was right.

Chapter Four

Harmony Estate, Aruba
October

Katya Pilenkova glanced at the tiny, elegant Cartier watch on her wrist. Quickly she calculated the time difference between Aruba and Lhasa.

Any moment now, she reassured herself. He will call. He must. Without the silk . . .

Anxiety settled unhappily in Katya's chest. It was a feeling she was accustomed to. Vodka, chilled almost to the point of freezing, took care of it.

Too soon for that, Katya cautioned herself. First the men must arrive.

As for Ilya, he will call when he has something to report. Until then, I have much to do. The estate must be in perfect order for this meeting.

Katya would personally see that everything was done as she required, down to the last detail.

It was a task that would have daunted many people. At five acres, Katya's home was one of the biggest oceanfront estates on the island that still remained in private hands.

The twenty cabanas scattered along a quarter mile of private beach were gracious and palatial. Three oversize swimming pools waited in clean turquoise silence for people who preferred not to swim in salt water.

The stone and stucco main house had eight thousand square feet of living space. Originally built by a Dutch trader, it had been refurbished once by a Venezuelan oil man. More recently a Colombian drug lord had spent ten million dollars on the estate before he turned his back on the wrong man and died.

The estate looked like a highly exclusive resort or an expensive corporate retreat. In actuality it was more like a seventeenth-century French salon. Instead of philosophers and poets, the estate's habitués were the leading criminal minds of the late twentieth century.

Its owner, hostess, and mastermind was Katya Pilenkova. Harmony Estate was both her calling card and her refuge.

The courtyard Christmas tree, Katya thought, ticking off a list in her mind. How will it look when the men arrive? First impressions are vital.

At the moment, Aruba's famous white sugar sand covered the estate's courtyard. It wasn't snow, but it was as close as Katya could come in the Caribbean.

October's soft trade winds swept through the courtyard. Branches of a forty-foot Colorado spruce swayed and shivered. Among the branches, countless white lights twinkled and shimmered in the tropical air four thousand miles from where the tree had grown.

Though the trade winds always blew on Aruba, the spruce was still fresh and green. The tree had arrived on a chartered jet less than twenty-four hours after it was cut. The scent of evergreen was heavy on the hot, humid air.

Frowning, Katya looked thoughtfully at the tree. In her mind the freshness of the spruce wasn't the issue. It was the tree's decorations. She had imported a Broadway set designer to take care of the holiday trimmings. At the time it had seemed a good solution.

Now Katya wasn't so certain. But then, she was never certain of any man she couldn't control sexually. The set designer happened to be a homosexual given to extravagant gestures.

Extravagance Katya understood. The gay designer she did not.

Carefully she studied the green spruce. The lights were artistically placed, as were the ornaments. Indeed, there was a surprisingly clever balance among the American Santa Claus effigies, handblown French glass balls, and handmade Italian ornaments.

It is enough, Katya decided finally. It will be sufficient to divert men who are as sentimental as they are brutal.

Turning, Katya gave a sweeping glance to the rest of the estate she had named Harmony.

Tinsel garlands that twisted and glittered in the wind were wound around palms and sea grapes. Dancing, sparkling colored lights were splashed over the torch-shaped divi-divi trees. The effect of the outdoor lights was subtle now, but would be a blazing cascade of color against the tropic darkness.

The cabanas scattered over the grounds and along the leeward beach were decorated with the holiday trappings of twelve different cultures. The entire five acres of the villa's grounds had been transformed into the fairyland of a poor child's dreams.

The illusion of Christmas was complete, right down to a Russian Orthodox Christ Child in a Nativity scene in front of Katya's private cabana.

Katya Pilenkova had a genius for creating illusions. She knew it.

More importantly, she used it.

At thirty, Katya was a striking blonde with green eyes and a figure that was perfectly suited to the strapless Chanel gown she wore at the moment.

When the Soviet Union still existed, Katya was a promising actress in the Moscow Film Institute. Very early in her career, she realized that actors and actresses were pawns. True power lay behind the camera.

Katya set about to become a director. In time, she gained a reputation as one of the institute's most powerful directors.

Unfortunately for her ambitions, the institute's state support had dried up during the collapse of the Soviet system.

Like many of the Soviet *nomenklatura,* the state-sponsored elite, Katya had been forced to scramble for her very existence when the Soviet Union self-destructed.

Survival hadn't been easy. Almost overnight Moscow took on the aspect of a frontier boomtown. Everything was for sale and nothing had value, least of all life. With the Communist Party gone, power went to those who were hard and ruthless enough to grab it and keep it.

Proudly Katya looked around at the tangible results of her success when many around her had failed.

And died.

For Katya, the transformation from film director to whorehouse madam had been natural. Illusions were illusions. As far as she was concerned, the only difference was the size of the audience.

Once I created illusions to please millions of cinema lovers in public theaters, Katya thought with a small smile. Now I fulfill the private fantasies of a handful of wealthy, powerful, brutal men.

The new illusions were costly to maintain. The price of failure was more painful than starvation. Still, Katya preferred the new life to the old. Professional prostitutes were a good deal more realistic about life than professional actors were.

Katya herself wasn't a prostitute. She didn't have to look in a man's eyes and tell him that he was the best ever while she was folding his fee and tucking it into her purse.

The lying wouldn't have bothered Katya. The loss of power would have. What little respect men had for women vanished the instant a female spread her legs for them.

Particularly the men of the Harmony.

Life had taught Katya that a man always valued the woman he didn't have more than the one he did. She maintained her allure and hold over Harmony's men by never surrendering her body to them. Like the literary hostesses of seventeenth-century France, Katya possessed and wielded a great deal of indirect power.

But not enough power, Katya thought coolly as she turned and crossed the courtyard to the pavilion. Not yet. Too much depends upon this little Christmas farce in October.

As soon as Katya's foot touched the marble entrance, a black footman dressed in an elf's outfit opened the double doors to admit the owner of the estate.

A wall of cool air washed over Katya as she entered the pavilion. The shutters were tightly closed throughout, bringing on the night.

Boston, the head of the household staff, met Katya with a broad ivory smile.

"Turn up the air-conditioning more," Katya ordered. "Then add more logs to that fire. This room must feel like winter."

Boston nodded dolefully.

"Yas'am," he drawled.

The butler's accent was lazy Caribbean, but he dispatched houseboys with an efficiency that was unusual in Aruba. Then he fell in beside Katya like a junior officer at a parade inspection.

Katya gestured to sparkling strands of tinsel that cascaded down one wall.

"Those garlands," she said. "Whose Christmas do they represent?"

"Our American guests," Boston said immediately. "I ordered them special from Chicago, Czarina."

Boston's manner with Katya was relaxed and informal, but never too much so. He was the only member of the staff who dared to use Katya's nickname to her face. He did that only when he was confident of her mood.

"The trappings must be right," she reminded him. "Christmas is the most intricate holiday. Everything must be authentic."

"Everything is," Boston assured her. "I know about illusion, too."

"Of course you do," Katya said impatiently. "Otherwise I would not tolerate your smug presence."

She walked swiftly to the fireplace. There she inspected the row of oversize red flannel stockings that had been hung in a neat row from the edge of the cherry wood mantel.

"Excellent," she murmured.

Boston simply nodded. He hadn't wanted to drive nails into a seventeen-century English antique, but Katya had insisted.

She eyed the intricate embroidery on the cuff of each of the twelve stockings.

"The names," she said.

"Checked twice for spelling."

"Such a bother, so many cultures, so many proud and prickly men . . ."

"That's what the estate is famous for."

Katya stopped at a stocking emblazoned with an intricate Chinese ideograph rather than Roman letters.

"Triple-checked that one with the manager at the Shanghai Trading Bank in Oranjestad," Boston said, anticipating Katya's question. "It's proper Mandarin."

"Is not Tony Liu Cantonese?" Katya asked sharply.

"He speaks Mandarin. He couldn't do what he does in some back-country dialect."

"You do."

"I know several dialects, including Oxford English. That's why you hired me, Czarina."

"Yes."

Smiling thinly, Katya walked on. As she did, she made a note to check Boston's background again.

An intelligent personal assistant is like having a pet wolf, she reminded herself. Quite useful, until the inevitable betrayal occurs.

Katya turned her attention to the glistening twenty-foot-high indoor Christmas tree.

The evergreen was a model of multiculturalism. Russian icons, Colombian *Penas,* Italian candles, and elegantly fashioned Chinese ideograms on white rice paper, all scattered through the branches.

A vast, carefully designed buffet lay ready off on the far side of the room, away from the unnecessary fire. The tables were laden with holiday foods from twelve countries. Each item had been selected to suggest to one or more guests that it was Christmastime, rather than a week before Halloween.

The bar had been stocked with holiday whiskeys and liqueurs and a rich, dark Mexican beer that was intended as a substitute for the December bocks of Italy, France, and Russia.

Only after Katya was satisfied with the other arrangements did she spare a glance for the girls who stood at desultory attention in front of the buffet tables.

There were fourteen beautiful young women for an even dozen guests. The extras were for Jose Gabriel de la Pena, the Colombian, and Salvatore Spagnolini, the Mafiosi who oversaw the Chicago Mob's interests in Las Vegas.

De la Pena and Spagnolini were the fiercest personal rivals in the Harmony. They played out that rivalry in the bedroom. If one man claimed to wear out one girl and therefore required two at a time or three, the other man automatically increased his order.

Such foolishness, Katya thought. Spagnolini is a drunk who usually passes out before he has even one girl, much less two.

Katya knew every man's sexual predilection and dereliction. She had seen the tapes from cameras hidden behind overhead mirrors in all the cabanas.

Ostensibly Katya used the tapes to monitor her girls, ensuring that they earned their $25,000-a-week salary. In truth, the tapes were most valuable as a source of intelligence.

Beautiful sluts were easy to find. Accurate information was not.

The first girl Katya inspected was Magda, a tall, slender model from Mexico City. She smiled sweetly, showing off the tiny beauty mark that recently had been tattooed at the corner of her surgically altered mouth.

Katya had learned that Giovanni Scarfo, the Sicilian envoy to the Harmony, had once offered Cindy Crawford a million dollars to spend the night with him. She had refused. Magda, with her new beauty mark and lips, would be an adequate replacement.

"Very nice," Katya said nodding.

"Gracias."

Coolly Katya inspected the Mexican woman's makeup, her

amply augmented breasts, and her thigh-length evening dress. Obviously Magda wore nothing underneath but her own skin.

"Do remember to keep your knees together when you sit down," Katya advised curtly.

"All night?" Magda asked, wide-eyed.

"Of course not. But you must not distract all the men in the room. You are a special favor, just for Signor Scarfo."

Katya raised her voice so that all the girls could hear.

"Some of our guests may have business they want to discuss first. Therefore, do not start your work too quickly. Tease them only. Wait for the signal, after we have passed out the gifts."

"I thought we were the gifts," said Galina Tereshkova, the ethereal blonde from the Caucasus.

She had been the female half of the sixth-ranked Soviet figure-skating pair until her partner died of AIDS. Now Katya was grooming her, intending to turn her into a permanent member of the staff at the estate.

Katya smiled thinly. "You are not the gifts. You are merely the party favors. Do not forget it. Ever."

With that Katya went to one of the Asian girls, a runner-up as Miss Thailand. Recently the girl's almond-shaped eyes had been surgically altered.

After a close inspection, Katya nodded her approval of the results.

"Excellent work." She glanced at Boston. "Make a note of the surgeon's name."

"Yas'am."

"Pay attention, girls," Katya said. "Remember the estate's rules. You are not common prostitutes. No one is allowed to accept any gratuities from our guests. You are well paid and you are paid solely by me."

Holly Trent, the voluptuous blonde from Los Angeles who had been assigned to Tony Liu, mumbled something as she plumped her breasts inside the confines of her push-up bra.

"What was that, Holly?"

Holly grimaced. She was still smarting over her assignment to the Chinese gangster.

"I want my money ready by eight o'clock in the morning,"

Holly said. "I'll need the Lear jet, too. I have a heavy weekend date in Newport."

"Do you need any extras?" Tawni Lee broke in.

She was American of Asian descent, small and slender, with the face of a flawless China doll.

Holly looked the Amerasian girl up and down, then shook her head.

"No exotics, I'm afraid," Holly said matter-of-factly. "These guys are California real estate developers. They like the cornfed look."

"Cornfed?" Shari Cyrus asked sarcastically. "Breast-fed is more their style."

Shari was a sweet-faced Texas girl with a tiny waist, slender hips, and breasts that defied gravity beneath the sheer silk of her blouse. Her nipples were drawn and erect, as though she was either aroused or cold.

Katya knew those nipples were another carefully constructed surgical fillip.

"Stop this vulgar bitching," Katya said, raising her voice. "Remember your training."

Shari Cyrus laughed out loud.

"I'm not sure what kind of training you all go through over there in Russia," she drawled, "but here in America, a girl just learns to spread her legs and let a man do what comes naturally, so to speak."

"A man may believe he is doing what comes naturally," Katya said coolly, "but the trick lies in the part that does not come naturally."

"Huh?"

"My job," Katya said crisply, "is to make every one of the men in the room want me. Your job is to make your individual client settle for something less."

A soft whisper of surprise passed through the room. It was followed by laughter.

Shari smiled slowly.

"I'll have to remember that," Shari said, "when I have my own place."

Katya smiled sweetly. "Not on Aruba."

"You bet," Shari said.

She meant it. Shari had quickly figured out that Katya was the most dangerous of all the people who came and went from the estate.

"One last thing," Katya murmured. "I have heard that several of you flew in early, and that you were tricking—is that the correct term?—at the Aruba Hilton Casino."

Several of the girls looked sideways at a lush, red-headed Irish girl named Imelda, who maintained apartments in both London and Paris.

"That will stop," Katya said flatly. "Your dates tonight are some of the most important men in the world."

"I never saw them in the *Times,*" Imelda muttered.

"Only social climbers and politicians appear in the news," Katya said. "These men are much too rich and powerful to permit such publicity."

"So?" Imelda asked, shrugging.

"So these men must never be able to pick up a young woman in a casino one night and then encounter her the next night here at the estate," Katya said.

"None of our dates were here yet," Imelda objected. "I checked. I'm not a total twit, you know."

"None of our out-of-town clients were here," Katya said distinctly, "but there will be several local men in attendance tonight. One is the head of the local branch of Bank Leumi, as well as the regional director of Seven Oaks Bank, London."

"Bankers? I thought this was a party for international, uh . . ." Imelda paused, searching for a neutral word. "Businessmen, I guess you could call them."

"Bankers are why the Harmony comes to Aruba," Shari muttered to Imelda. "The waters of the Caribbean do a wonderful job of washing the blood from gold."

"Really?" Imelda replied.

Her tone invited a fuller explanation, but Katya cut Shari off when she would have spoken.

"The background of our guests is not your concern," Katya said coldly. "Just make sure that they enjoy themselves."

Even as she spoke, Katya made a mental note to drop Imelda

from the estate's roster. The girl was naive or she was fishing for information.

Either prospect was dangerous.

Especially now, when so much depended on her carefully wrought silk strategy.

Ilya, Katya thought urgently, where are you? Do you have it yet?

There was no answer. Nor would there be until Ilya Kasatonin finally called.

If he called.

He will call, Katya told herself firmly. He must.

None of Katya's turmoil showed on her face as she continued on down the row of women, adjusting a neckline here and checking an effect there. She was nearly finished when Boston made a small motion to catch her attention.

"The limousines just turned into the driveway," Boston said.

"Places, girls," Katya ordered, clapping her hands sharply. "The play begins."

Chapter Five

The first white stretch limousine swept into the Harmony compound in front of the pavilion. With smooth expertise the driver brought the vehicle to a stop so that the passenger door was centered precisely at the entrance to the pavilion.

The back door of the limousine burst open before the valet reached it. A thick, paunchy, yet muscular Latin stepped out wearing a maroon silk suit. His white silk shirt was transparent with sweat despite the limousine's air-conditioning. His dark, rough-featured face was beaded with moisture.

He was swearing in Spanish and English, describing the weather and his surroundings in words that would have made a seasoned streetwalker flinch.

Katya smiled brightly to conceal her distaste.

She was used to tutoring unschooled criminals and thugs in semi-civilized behavior, but Jose Gabriel de la Pena was slow to learn. He was exactly what one would expect in a man who had begun his criminal career stealing gravestones in cemeteries, sanding off their inscriptions, and selling them to newly bereaved customers.

"I am so regretful that the trip was difficult, Jose," Katya said.

"Hijo de la chingada," was de la Pena's only response.

Katya smoothed her fingers over de la Pena's arm. Smiling with the familiarity and indulgence of a mother or a lover, she straightened the maroon jacket over his paunch. Her fingers came near his crotch, but never actually touched him.

"Come inside where it is cool, *mi corazon,*" Katya said. "The rest of our guests are arriving."

"Let them wait. I want a drink first. Two drinks."

She glanced over at the line of a half-dozen limos discharging their passengers beneath the arches of pine boughs. The girls had gathered like bright falcons, each ready to cut her particular prey from the preening flock of men.

"The Americans, they are here?" de la Pena asked.

Katya looked up at him from beneath artfully darkened eyelashes. He was unusually belligerent.

"They are here," she said as she led the way toward the pavilion. "What is wrong, *mi corazon?*"

"I must spend some time with that swine Spagnolini," de la Pena muttered. "The payment for a load was supposed to reach our man in New York today but it never arrived."

More anxiety coiled beneath Katya's serene surface. She suspected that the payment was just another in a long row of excuses for trouble between the Colombian and the American mobster.

"It was a major payment?" she asked calmly.

Despite his chunky build, de la Pena shrugged with Latin grace.

"A million and a half," he said.

"American?"

"Canadian, for a change."

Katya made a murmuring, soothing sound. A few million Canadian dollars shouldn't be enough to ruin her carefully planned party with a brawl.

"But the number of dollars is not important," de la Pena said curtly. "I will have the payment or that bastard's balls. He will learn that he is not man enough to match cocks with me."

Katya made another soothing, admiring sound.

The doorman swung the big glass doors of the pavilion open as soon as Katya and de la Pena arrived. Katya put her hand over his and squeezed gently.

"Of course no one is powerful enough to intimidate you," Katya said.

De la Pena grunted.

"You will not quarrel with Mr. Spagnolini here, will you?" Katya asked gently. "This is a special celebration."

"He will pay me."

"Of course he will. But the place to remind him is not here and now. This is Harmony Estate, *mi corazon,* not some back alley in the Bronx or Bogota."

De la Pena grunted again and allowed himself to be led to the estate's well-stocked bar.

The bartender was already prepared for the Colombian's arrival. Two crystal shot glasses full of raw, cheap aguadiente stood on the bar. The open bottle was nearby, ready for immediate use.

De la Pena slammed down one glass of the liquor. Impatiently he set the glass on the cherry wood bar and reached for the second shot glass. He started to drink, then paused. He was shrewd enough to know that too much liquor too quickly would dull his mind.

It did not pay to be stupid around the beautiful, untouchable Katya Pilenkova.

"Any news from the Japanese?" de la Pena asked. "Is Kojimura going to be here? Or that cheating bastard Ishida?"

Katya shook her head, taking care to present de la Pena with a view of her shining hair and fair-skinned cleavage even as she carefully planned her answer. Kojimura and Ishida were heads of powerful Japanese Yakuza organizations. As such, the men were very important to Katya's plans.

Perhaps more important than de la Pena.

"Mr. Kojimura and Mr. Ishida were here last week," Katya said indifferently.

De la Pena sipped at the fiery liquor in his glass.

"Together?" he asked.

"Yes. They had a pleasant time, although I believe Mr. Ishida lost quite a lot of money in the casinos."

"He always does," de la Pena said. "He is more interested in gambling than in doing business these days. That is why Kojimura will drill him a new asshole."

"My assessment exactly. Either way, the Yakuza will remain part of the Harmony."

More important to Katya, through the Yakuza she would cement relations with the most powerful man in Japan, Yukio Koyama. He was the respectable interface between the Yakuzas and the vast wealth of Japan. With Koyama on her side, Katya would have what she had long sought: an eager outlet for the art and artifacts that her connections in Russia provided by the trainload as they raped the remains of the Soviet Union.

De la Pena finished off the rest of his drink in a gulp and slammed the glass on the bar in a wordless demand for more.

The bartender looked at Katya.

She moved her head in a tiny, negative motion that the Colombian didn't see. Aguadiente was the drink of choice among Colombian *cartelistas*. De la Pena could consume great quantities of it before his shrewdness was overwhelmed.

But aguadiente made him irritable to the point of irrationality. Katya did not want to see the Harmony blow up in an ugly fight.

"That is why I invited Mr. Kojimura and his patron to our little conference in Seattle next month," Katya said. "I suspect Mr. Ishida will no longer be a factor by then."

"*Verdad?*"

"Yes," Katya said with quiet satisfaction. "Apparently he has contracted a painful and debilitating sexual disease. Even with extensive treatments . . ."

Delicately Katya left the rest of the sentence unsaid.

De la Pena laughed harshly. With an impatient sweep of his hand he gestured to the bottle and the hovering bartender.

"Remind me to have my whores checked for infection next time I sleep over at your estate," de la Pena said.

"I would never do such a thing to you, *mi corazon,*" Katya murmured.

She took the bottle from the bartender before he could fill de la Pena's glass.

"It is clear," Katya said, "that Mr. Kojimura is the most powerful Yakuza leader in Japan at the moment."

De la Pena gave Katya a look from clear black eyes.

"Mr. Kojimura's patron seems willing to discuss participation in the accords that have been concluded here," Katya added.

She poured the shot glass on the bar half-full of clear, oily liquid.

"Seems willing?" de la Pena asked.

He grabbed the glass and shot the aguardiente down his throat. Abruptly he held out the glass for more, continuing scornfully, "Is that the best you can do, my lovely Madonna?"

Katya smiled like the actress she was.

"Kojimura's involvement is vital," de la Pena snarled. "Without it, the Orient will remain closed to our drugs. The agreement you call the Harmony is useless if half the world is cut off."

Katya's smile not only stayed in place, it softened with apparent admiration for the Colombian's intelligence.

"You are so correct," she murmured. "I have given it much thought."

De la Pena grunted. He didn't really approve of women thinking, but he did approve of the enormous leap in his personal wealth that had come on the heels of joining the Harmony.

"Mr. Kojimura's patron," Katya said, "is just like the rest of us. He wants to be assured that we properly appreciate his position within his world, and ours."

With growing impatience de la Pena held out his shot glass, waiting for Katya to pour more of the fierce liquor for him.

Katya touched the neck of the bottle to the glass. Deftly she spilled a few drops into the shot glass. Then, like a mother with her son, she set the bottle back on the bar with a firm thump, making it clear that de la Pena would get no more.

"Be assured that Mr. Kojimura is both interested and willing," Katya said. "His patron will be the same, as soon as he receives our little gift."

As she spoke, she caressed de la Pena's hand and slipped the crystal shot glass from between his fingers.

''We just need to—how do the Americans say it?—blow in his ear with the proper force,'' Katya said.

''Try blowing his cock instead.''

''Naughty boy,'' Katya said.

Her smile said the opposite.

De la Pena forgot about the drink he hadn't yet gotten. Each time he came to the estate, he was certain he was closer to getting between Katya's long white legs.

Each time he had come away from the estate thoroughly sated, but not by the fire-haired Madonna.

''I found out,'' Katya said, ''that only one passion moves Mr. Kojimura's patron. Mr. Koyama is an avid collector.''

''Of what? The tips of his men's little fingers?''

De la Pena laughed shortly and glanced at his own hands. For a man who had cut more than his share of throats, he was oddly squeamish about the Yakuza soldier's tradition of severing the tip of one little finger as a sign of loyalty to his leader.

''Silk,'' Katya said succinctly. ''Mr. Koyama has the most extensive collection of ancient and contemporary silk fabrics in the world.''

''Silk? I fart through silk.'' De la Pena laughed. ''He can have my shorts for his collection.''

Katya made a disapproving sound.

''Silk and steel are the principal metaphors of Japanese culture,'' she said.

De la Pena shrugged. He had a total lack of interest in anyone's culture, including his own.

''Mr. Koyama is obsessed by ancient silk,'' Katya went on. ''He has scraps that date back to the time before the first Christmas.''

''So bury him in silk.''

''Something a bit more subtle, I think,'' Katya said dryly.

Bored by the conversation, de la Pena glanced toward the young prostitutes who were smiling and swaying with practiced allure for their assigned clients.

''It's a pity Koyama isn't here tonight,'' de la Pena said. ''We could wrap up *las putas* in silk tights and give him a Christmas present to remember.''

"He has many women. His present must be very special."

"What is it?"

"Silk, of course."

Katya smiled and slipped her arm through de la Pena's.

"Come," she murmured, "it is time to pass out the presents."

When Katya entered the room, every man's eye went to her. At a silent signal, each girl excused herself from her assignment and went to the big cherry wood mantel. One by one, in predetermined order, the girls returned to their men bearing the elaborately embroidered Christmas stockings.

Katya appeared to watch everyone equally, but most of her attention was on Tony Liu. He sat on a chair in the corner of the estate's pavilion. He mixed with no one, including his assigned woman.

Grinning and nodding and picking his teeth with a slender piece of ivory, Liu watched the other members of the Harmony receive their Christmas presents. Once in awhile he sucked air noisily through the gap between his front teeth. The rest of the time he watched, quietly, as though he was content to wait until someone spoke to him.

Katya knew that Liu's demeanor was an act as carefully constructed as her own.

Liu was an oddity at the Harmony. Most of the men in the room were big, robust male animals, charismatic if not handsome, muscular if sometimes gone prematurely to fat. The slightly built, self-effacing Liu seemed out of place, hardly worth including in such a gathering.

The Chinese gangster worked hard to sustain that illusion.

Katya saw through illusion to the reality beneath. She had made a careful study of the large-toothed little man and his culture. She knew that, to an Asian, picking one's teeth in public was a deliberate insult, something akin to farting at the dinner table.

Liu enjoyed insulting Westerners, but he did it only in ways he thought they would not recognize. In that manner, he was able to laugh at them twice.

It was a very Asian pastime, like tai chi chuan, the graceful, slow calisthenics that seemed harmless but could be used to break a man's neck.

Katya recognized the usefulness of seeming too weak or amusing to be a threat. In her mind it was a feminine tactic. Subtlety rather than brawn.

That was one of the reasons Katya had lobbied long and hard to include Liu in the Harmony. In fact, he was the reason for the whole Christmas charade. He was to receive a gift that would impress him without insulting the more volatile male egos in the room.

There was far more to Tony Liu than he ever showed to the rest of the world. He headed the Earth and Sky Tong, an organization more than three centuries old. It operated an immigrant smuggling apparatus that pumped thousands of Overseas Chinese into the West.

In addition he had amassed significant legitimate wealth through his family business, which produced and processed fruits and vegetables popular in Chinatowns around the world. The combination of technical skills and a global, legitimate distribution network would be extremely useful to a criminal association such as the Harmony.

What the male principals of the Harmony didn't realize— and Katya did—was that Liu was the touch point between a vast international network of Chinese gangs and the West.

Earth and Sky supplied expensive automobiles and other contraband to regional strongmen on the Chinese mainland. Mainland commissars welcomed him to their offices and to their tables. Even Hong Kong's triad societies paid Liu respect, for they had learned that his ruthlessness and cunning equaled their own.

Tony Liu could inflict great pain or bestow great profits upon the Western crime lords of the Harmony.

Yet even six months after his provisional membership in the Harmony had been ratified, Liu maintained a grinning, toothpicking distance from the rest of the members.

To Jose de la Pena and Giovanni Scarfo and the rest of the men in the pavilion, Tony Liu was a clownish little Asian with a network of gambling rooms and opium dens in Chinatowns around the world and a stranglehold on the Asian vegetable business. As far as the men of the Harmony were concerned, Liu was a peon among the demi-gods of the underworld.

Katya almost smiled at the thought of what was coming next. When it came Tony Liu's turn to receive his gift stocking, it was Katya herself who went to the mantel and delivered the stocking to him.

"Mr. Liu," Katya said, smiling and bowing gracefully, "this is a small token of the Harmony's esteem for you."

For a second Tony Liu looked uncomfortable. The deliberately self-effacing smile froze on his round, beardless face. With odd reluctance he accepted the stocking.

Liu had seen the other gifts. Giovanni Scarfo, the Italian who always dressed formally, had received a three carat, D-flawless, blue-white diamond stickpin which he immediately placed in his four-in-hand tie.

De la Pena, who loved to fish, gleefully jingled the keys to a new Grady White offshore cruiser which was parked in a slip at the estate's private marina.

Sallie Spags, the Chicago gangster, could hardly keep his eyes off the garish, overbearing oil portrait of himself that Katya had commissioned from a set of photographs.

The rest of the gifts were similarly expensive and carefully calculated to please the men who received them.

Liu had a keen appreciation of the befuddling power of flattery. He regarded himself as well inoculated against such infections.

But Katya Pilenkova was an extraordinarily beautiful Caucasian female. Liu wasn't quite immune to her smile. He was still virile enough that he wondered what kind of gift she had selected just for him.

The stocking seemed nearly empty.

Deep inside, lodged in the oversize red flannel foot, there was a small, flat packet. Liu fished and groped and finally had to turn the stocking upside down to shake the gift out into his lap.

The packet was wrapped in handsome blue and gold foil. It was tied with a rich blue velvet ribbon. The design on the wrapping paper was official and somewhat familiar, but Liu couldn't place it immediately.

Then it came to him.

Almost unwillingly, Liu's fingers caressed the velvet ribbon.

He looked up for an instant at Katya. His dark eyes showed an expression of faint surprise.

Katya's green eyes sparkled like a delighted mistress whose only pleasure lay in pleasing her master.

As though still unwilling to commit himself, Liu turned the flat package over and looked at its back. Then he slipped the blue velvet ribbon off with his small, deft fingers and broke the seal on the wrapping. The blue of the foil was a perfect match for the blue cover of the small booklet inside.

Tony Liu knew what the booklet was, even before he turned it over and read the gold block lettering on the front.

Passport, Commonwealth of Canada.

Silently Liu traced the ornate seal on the front cover. He flipped open the front page and stared at a square photograph of himself affixed to the inside cover and embossed with an official stamp. There was a blank signature line beneath the photograph.

For a few seconds the grin vanished from his face. He looked bluntly skeptical. With seeming casualness, he examined the passport's cover, its binding, its front page. He fanned the blank visa pages.

"This is an excellent forgery," he said.

"The government of Canada doesn't issue forgeries," Katya answered calmly.

Liu glanced at her, trying to read a joke in her words.

She smiled her most charming smile.

"The passport is as real as the Harmony's esteem for you," Katya said. "The applications have all been approved. The requisite files have been created in Ottawa."

She produced a Mont Blanc fountain pen the size of an expensive cigar and handed it to Liu.

"Put your signature on the blank line and you will become a citizen of Canada," Katya said.

"Canada?"

Sallie Spagnolini laughed and wandered over to look at the cover of the new passport.

"If I'd known you wanted new citizenship," he said, "I'd

have talked to one of my senators. You could have been a red-blooded American.''

Katya's sideways glance was cool.

''American citizenship is not quite the prize that it once was,'' she pointed out. ''A Canadian passport bestows the same benefits without the accompanying problems.''

''Yeah, Sallie,'' de la Pena cut in. ''An American aboard a hijacked airliner is a hostage, but a Canadian is an ambassador of good will.''

Before the derisive remark could cause trouble, Katya made a discreet signal. There was a soft explosion of perfume and sighs and quick, clever hands as the whores came to claim their clients.

The men of the Harmony were busy, leaving Katya alone with Tony Liu.

Though Liu's expression hadn't changed, when he looked up at Katya, his intelligence showed through the cover of his bland features for the first time.

''How was this accomplished?'' he asked quietly.

''How did this application win approval when your others have been rejected?'' she asked.

''Yes.''

''That is unimportant.''

''Ah?''

''What matters,'' Katya said gently, ''is that you will be able to walk right past the immigration inspectors and customs agents at Vancouver airport next time you want to visit that new grandson of yours in Burnaby.''

Liu's black eyes widened fractionally at the mention of his grandson.

''You will be able to cross the border into the United States, as well,'' Katya added. ''Canadian citizens are allowed to do that whenever they wish.''

''Not when their name is Tony Liu,'' he said softly, succinctly.

''There will be no embarrassing delays,'' Katya assured him. ''A friend of ours removed your name from the watch list on the U.S. Immigration Service's computer system.''

A flicker of something that could have been dislike or respect showed in Liu's eyes.

"How did you know about my grandson?" Liu asked.

Deliberately Katya let her charming smile slip for an instant. In that moment the ruthless intelligence beneath her beauty showed clearly.

She wanted Liu to be quite certain who was the power behind the Harmony.

"It is my pleasure," she murmured, "to attend to the comforts of all my friends here at the estate."

"And to administer to their discomforts, as well?" Liu replied softly.

"Only when it is necessary, Mr. Liu. An intelligent man would never need to worry about discomfort."

Katya was smiling again. Charming again. Beguiling with her exotic, round green eyes and sunset-colored hair.

Liu could hardly believe it was the same woman who a moment ago had looked at him with the intelligence of a human and the emotions of a snake.

"You are very clever, aren't you?" he said thoughtfully.

"Women must always be clever, for men are always strong."

Liu looked at the passport again. He wondered how Katya had learned of his previous and unsuccessful efforts to obtain one. He also wondered how he had underestimated her so completely.

Then he wondered why Katya Pilenkova had chosen to reveal herself to him tonight.

"Excuse me," said Boston.

Katya glanced up at Boston with a look that told him there had better be an excellent reason for interrupting her.

"A phone call for you," Boston said.

An odd, expectant expression flashed over Katya's face. There was only one caller who merited such attention.

Ilya, she thought fervently. At last!

Chapter Six

Katya hurried out of the pavilion to her office, which was in a remote wing of the house, connected only by a lanai to the much larger estate house. Her personal quarters were also there.

When Katya worked, or entertained her dangerous lover, she wanted complete privacy. The isolation of her quarters provided that.

The light on her private phone was blinking. Hands shaking from excitement, she fumbled the Russian diamond and Colombian emerald earring from her right ear and laid it on the table next to her computer.

Automatically Katya turned on the tape machine. When she picked up the receiver, the hollow hum on the line told her the call came from a great distance.

She tried to still her eagerness, but couldn't.

"Ilya?" she asked huskily. "Is it you?"

The name echoed over the lines.

"No names, woman," Ilya Kasatonin said coldly. "The computers in the United States are listening always."

Katya flushed. She shouldn't have needed the reminder. She knew very well that international long-distance phone calls were monitored by the American National Security Agency, and probably by local authorities, as well.

"I am sorry," she said quietly. "I will not forget again."

Fundamentally Katya was like Tony Liu. She concealed her real emotions carefully. She felt little but contempt for all men in the world, save one.

That one was on the other end of the phone line.

"All right, then," Kasatonin said. "I did not think my woman was a fool."

"Only for you, my love. I was worried. You expect me to worry, do you not? Where are you?"

A hard, deep male laugh echoed across the continents.

"Just where I need to be," Kasatonin said.

"Then you have the . . . it?"

He laughed heartily again.

"Of course," Kasatonin said.

"Of course," Katya mimicked. "Then why were you late in calling, my darling?"

"There was a small difficulty."

Katya's breath caught.

"You are all right?" she demanded.

"Do I sound otherwise?"

She sighed. "No. I simply worry. What went wrong?"

"I suspect our old friends from the deserts of California."

"Sacred mother," Katya muttered. "Not again."

"I was successful. That is all that matters."

"Are you out of danger?"

"Not yet, but I expect to be shortly."

"The normal route?" she asked.

"No. I will have to improvise. It seems that the local officials have become irritable."

Katya's heart turned over. Kasatonin always was most calm when danger was the greatest.

"Is there anything I can do?" she asked.

"Nothing, unless you have a chartered jet on the runway."

"Of course."

"And a secure landing strip on my end."

There was silence. Both of them knew there was no such

thing as a secure landing strip in Tibet for anything but PRC-approved flights.

"What will you do?" Katya asked.

"I will take a slow boat."

Katya frowned. She had been hoping to see Kasatonin soon. Very soon.

"Arrange to have someone meet me at the place we discussed before I left," Kasatonin said. "I would prefer that it be someone with excellent local connections. Is that possible?"

A relieved smile spread across Katya's face.

"As a matter of fact, yes," she said. "I know just the person to manage it."

"Good. I will count on you, then."

"As I count on you, my love," Katya said softly.

"What? I can't hear you. This is a bad connection."

"Nothing," she said.

"Good. I thought you might be getting sentimental on me." Kasatonin laughed harshly. "Ah, my little one. Do you miss me?"

"Only as I do life," Katya said.

"Foolish child, what am I going to do with you?"

Katya closed her eyes.

"I can think of many things, my love," she murmured.

Kasatonin made a rough sound.

"How many times do I have to tell you not to attach yourself to me?" he asked. "Eventually one of these little adventures of mine will go wrong."

"No."

"Yes. You know it as well as I. Then where will you be, foolish one?"

"I do not know," she whispered.

There was an echo of despair to Katya's voice that would have astonished anyone in the Harmony. She had only one weakness in her armor, and his name was Ilya Kasatonin.

"You have been warned," Kasatonin said, his voice gruff and dismissive. "We use one another and we prosper. But do not talk of love. It is for peasants and fools."

Katya was silent for a time. The hum of the long-distance lines welled up between them.

Finally Kasatonin broke the silence.

"I must go," he said.

Katya swallowed hard. When she spoke, her voice had regained its customary crispness.

"When will you be in the town we discussed?" Katya asked.

"Four days."

"Expect someone sent by a Canadian named Tony."

"Tony. I have it."

There was a click on the line. Ilya was gone.

Katya stood for a long time, staring at the dead phone receiver in her hand. Then she hung up the instrument and drew a deep breath, composing herself.

She didn't understand her need for Kasatonin. She merely accepted it and tried to control the damage as best she could.

At the moment, Katya needed to conceal her very personal, very female reaction to the danger her elusive lover was in. Any strong emotion she had could be turned against her by the men of the Harmony.

Just as she used the men's individual weaknesses against them.

Katya turned off the tape machine and rewound the tape so she could listen to the conversation again. She would indulge herself later, when the Harmony's dangerous men were occupied by their skilled, impersonal whores.

Slowly she sat down at the computer table. As always, the machine was up and running, ready for her command. She put her fingers lightly on the keyboard and called up a special file.

It was Katya's coded private file used to log all her calls, and where she recorded all her thoughts while her mind was still untouched by the icy vodka that called to her almost as compellingly as Kasatonin did.

But unlike her yearning for Kasatonin, she could control her desire for vodka's potent oil oblivion.

She typed for less than a minute, noting the contents of the call in her own personal shorthand. Automatically she copied the file to her permanent storage disk.

When Katya picked up the diamond and emerald earring from the lacquered top of her desk and slipped it back onto the lobe of her ear, her fingers were steady.

Coolly she turned to inspect herself in the mirror at the door. A beautiful, enigmatic woman in an icy green dress stared back at her, composed and ready to face a hostile world.

When Katya returned to the pavilion, the party had begun to degenerate into drinking contests and whoring exhibitions. Recognizing that she had only a short time to work, she went directly to Tony Liu.

The short Asian sat alone before the roaring fire in the stone fireplace. He was staring thoughtfully at the dark blue passport he held in one hand.

At Katya's approach, Liu glanced up. The steady look he gave her conveyed respect.

"You are a very clever woman," he said. "I had not noticed before how clever."

"The gift? It was a small thing."

"Not the gift alone."

Katya waited, hoping she hadn't somehow offended the proud, secretive Chinese.

"Most women," Liu said calmly, "can control a single man with the contraction of their vagina. But Katya Pilenkova controls a dozen men with an untouched vagina."

Liu spoke without rancor, as though he was genuinely amused.

Perhaps he was.

Still Katya waited, sensing that he was reaching some kind of decision.

For a moment longer he tapped the passport against his palm. Then he slipped the gift into the inside pocket of his jacket.

"I thought I was beyond that weakness," he said, "but strangely, you have managed to gain a measure of control even over me."

Katya was gracious in her victory. She smiled at Liu as though he truly was a valued friend.

At the moment, he was. For Kasatonin's sake, if for nothing else.

"Let us speak of friendship, rather than control," she said gently.

Liu's smile was ironic.

"It is fitting, I suppose," he murmured, "that your control over me goes back to the time when I showed weakness in the arms of a woman. Were it not for that weakness, I would never have had a son and he would never have had a son and I would not find myself in your debt."

"The debt goes both ways," Katya said. "That is why the Harmony exists."

Liu remained silent.

At that moment Katya was almost relieved that she was about to ask a favor of the discreet Tony Liu. Like all the men in the Harmony, like all the men in the world for that matter, Tony Liu had great pride. He could be a dangerous enemy.

Katya needed a dangerous friend.

"Mr. Liu," she murmured, "I believe you are related to the leader of the Karens, the man they call the Generalissimo of the Poppy Flowers?"

Instantly Liu changed from an intelligent, contemplative man to his former mask. A broad, obsequious smile spread across his face again.

"We are related, yes," Liu said.

"There is a small town called Baoshan in the upper reaches of the Lancang Jiang, the Mekong River, just where it comes out of the Himalayas," Katya said. "I believe it is under your relative's control."

Liu nodded. "The Karen people control all that area, even though it is within the borders of the People's Republic."

"Could the Karen people move a valuable parcel from that town to, say, Hong Kong?"

Liu nodded again. "If the parcel was small enough, and valuable enough, for the risk."

"It is small. It is more valuable to the Harmony than all the raw opium the Karen armies could grow in a year. In ten years."

Surprise flickered for just an instant beneath Liu's mask.

"It could be done," he said.

"By you?"

He nodded.

"On behalf of the Harmony," Katya said, "I would like someone you trust to be in Baoshan in four days time. He is to contact a man named Ilya Kasatonin."

"Kasatonin? One of your countrymen? What does he look like?"

Katya brushed the question away.

"He will be the only Russian in Baoshan," she said. "He will have a small but very important shipment that must be moved through Hong Kong."

"It is possible."

"Is it also possible to send the package on to a city called Seattle in the northwestern part of the United States?"

"Yes. How much time do I have?"

"A month."

Liu thought for a moment.

"In one month," he said, "you will be meeting with the honored and reticent gentleman from Japan?"

Katya knew she had nothing to gain from lying to Liu—and much to lose.

"Exactly," Katya said.

"Will special handling be required?"

"Quite possibly."

"I will need to make some phone calls," Liu said.

"Your usual cabana is prepared. I have retained a chef from Taipei to await your needs."

"And a woman with tiny feet from Fukien, no doubt," Liu said with a small bow, "as well as the generously endowed blonde."

"Your pleasure is also mine."

"Your hospitality is overwhelming, as always."

Liu bowed again, more deeply, and left for his cabana.

Katya returned the bow with Chinese precision, just deep enough to return the respect she had been shown.

No more. No less.

When Liu left the pavilion, Katya turned and walked over to de la Pena, who had been watching from across the room. The heavy-set Colombian was sprawled in a chair in front of the fire. Two girls were fondling him and hanging on his every word.

"Some iced shrimp would be pleasant, yes?" Katya asked.

De la Pena grunted. At his curt gesture, the girls who had been entertaining him went to the buffet and waited to be recalled.

"What is your interest in Tony Liu?" de la Pena asked bluntly.

Katya would have preferred to say nothing at all, but de la Pena was the duly elected chairman of the Harmony.

For the moment.

"There was a difficulty with a previously selected shipping route for Mr. Koyama's gift," Katya said. "Mr. Liu was able to supply us with a better route."

"You should have come to me. I could have arranged for a shipment through Thailand. One of the Triad leaders there owes me several favors."

"Mr. Liu needs to feel that he is a valued part of the Harmony."

De la Pena grunted, unconvinced.

"This shipment," Katya pointed out, "is far more fragile than heroin. Mr. Liu will have the necessary contacts to see that it is properly prepared. The immigrants he smuggles into the West also smuggle art for him."

De la Pena shrugged and accepted Katya's decision. His eyes wandered toward the buffet.

Katya eyed the Colombian's bulging crotch and spoke quickly. Obviously neither business nor food was on de la Pena's mind at the moment.

"Do you still have that Washington lawyer on your payroll?" Katya asked.

De la Pena glanced at her irritably.

"Demosthenes is reserved for very important matters," he said coldly.

"But of course."

"After the *cagada* of the Bank of Credit and Commerce International, Washington attorneys are being much more careful about the kinds of matters they will handle."

"This matter is vital," Katya said.

"Bribery again?"

"No. A different kind of message."

The Colombian smiled, showing two rows of sharp, crooked teeth.

"My six-year-old son is a better assassin than the lawyer," de la Pena said.

Katya smiled.

"Nothing that bloody," she said, amused. "Just a simple warning to a group that has caused us too much trouble recently."

De la Pena's focus returned to Katya.

"Trouble?" he asked.

"Yes."

Katya knelt next to de la Pena so that she could talk without fear of being overheard.

"Do you know," she murmured against his sweaty hair, "of a group of American private investigators who call themselves Risk Limited?"

Chapter Seven

Tibet
October

First it had been the silence that had gnawed on Danielle Warren's nerves. Eighteen hours alone, listening for any sound in the lifeless air of a tiny stone cell deep beneath the Potala Palace.

Now it was the piercing, penetrating roar of an unmuffled motor two feet away from Dani's head that was driving her crazy. Or would have, if she had allowed it.

At least I'm not alone now, Dani thought.

On the other hand, she wasn't convinced that having company was an improvement. There certainly would have been more room in the box without Shane Crowe wedged in next to and beneath her.

Since before dawn, the two of them had been crammed into a smuggler's trap concealed beneath the front seat of a Jiefang cross-country truck. The trap was a metal box approximately the size of a coffin.

The hidden compartment hadn't been constructed for smuggling people. It boasted no human comforts, save the mattress-like effect that was achieved for Dani by Shane's body.

Some mattress, Dani thought. He's only slightly softer than steel.

She knew, because she was in a position to appreciate every hard inch of Shane Crowe's body.

Well, not *every* inch, Dani admitted wryly.

Her own humorous acceptance of the situation alternately amazed and appalled her. Their bodies had been wedged into forced intimacy, chest to thigh, for hours.

Not that there was anything personal in the arrangement. It was simply the only way both of them could fit in the secret compartment.

Yesterday Dani couldn't have imagined being crammed in a box with a big stranger for hour after hour, unable to breathe without feeling his body against her breasts, practically tasting his every breath. The thought of such unwilling intimacy would have given her cold chills.

But then, yesterday she couldn't have imagined a lot of things, including having a man shot to death at her feet.

Live and learn, Dani told herself. At least I'm alive to learn. Feng isn't.

Without Shane, I'd be dead, too.

Owing the big stranger her life was unsettling. Even more distressing to Dani was the fact that a deeply buried female part of her was enjoying Shane's body and his complex male scent in her nostrils.

Maybe it's just that Shane smells better than the exhaust, Dani told herself. And much better than whatever weed the driver smokes.

Then she wondered what Shane was thinking, if he noticed her scent.

The thought was disturbing, but Dani pursued it anyway. She would think about almost anything rather than the exhaustion, nausea, and fear that lay just beneath her gallows humor and tightly held self-control.

This is an adventure she told herself for the hundredth time.

This is why I went into fieldwork. I wanted adventure instead of a desk in academia.

But not this much adventure.

The truck hit an unusually big bump. Dani jolted hard against the box and then back into Shane.

At first the noise had been an even worse torment for Dani than being stuffed into a metal coffin with a strange man. But after five hours, sound had numbed Dani's ears.

The change in her feelings toward Shane was more subtle. His strength no longer made her nervous. The fact that he had saved her life, and seemed as determined to ignore their physical intimacy as she was, reassured Dani on a primitive level that went deeper than words.

Whatever else Shane Crowe might be, he wasn't a sexual bully like her ex-husband.

The highway resumed its long, tortuous climb into the Himalayas. The engine noise went from deafening to merely labored. Gears clashed viciously. Great puffs of smoke from the truck's rusty exhaust system mixed with tobacco smoke from the cab above Dani's and Shane's heads.

Grimly Dani breathed in through her nose and out through her clenched teeth. As she fought nausea, she reminded herself that the only other choice had been a real coffin rather than a smuggler's hidden box.

Without the truck, there was no way they could have escaped the police and army dragnet that had spread from Lhasa to the surrounding countryside. Even knowing that, she had started to argue when she saw the size of the metal box that was supposed to be their ticket to freedom.

Without a word Shane had simply climbed into the box and settled onto his back. His shoulders were too broad, so he had been forced to wedge one arm beneath his body.

Silently Dani had climbed in on top of Shane, scrunched to the side, and tried to touch as little of him as possible. However uncomfortable she was, she knew it had to be worse for him.

Yet Shane hadn't moved throughout the long hours.

If Dani hadn't felt his regular breathing, she would have

thought he was dead. His eyes were half-closed. His body was utterly relaxed.

She had seen nothing like it except among monks who were highly adept at a form of meditation that was close to self-hypnosis.

The truck lurched up and then slammed back down onto the road again. Gears clashed.

Shane noticed the noise and stench only at a carefully disciplined distance. His left arm was sending pain messages to his unresponsive brain. His right arm had long since gone to sleep beneath Dani's weight.

Physical discomfort wasn't real to Shane. His mind was focused on the round surface of a bolt in the metal roof a few inches above his head. It was the only object that he permitted to exist in his personal universe. He examined it with relentless interest.

Nothing was real except the bolt and the mind that meditated upon it.

Through all the jolts and lurches, the thunderous engine and grinding of gears, the choking smoke and the much more distracting female scent of Danielle Warren, Shane contemplated the central reality of the bolt's existence.

He thought about the history of such bolts.

He thought about all the various technologies that were required to make the metal bolt.

He thought about the invention of that technology by a series of clever primates.

He even spent some time trying to imagine what would happen if all the bolts in the world were to vanish at the same time.

Shane thought about anything that would take his mind off the fetid air, the abrasive noise, and the enticing scent of the woman whose head lay on his shoulder.

He carefully didn't think about the rest of Dani's body, lying on his with the intimacy of a lover.

If Shane turned his head, he could see a pinprick of light through a gap between the cab and the truck bed, which carried eight tons of mixed freight.

He knew the truck had already passed through two army checkpoints. The first was a permanent fixture on the Katmandu Road. He suspected the other was an auxiliary post, probably thrown up to look for Dani and himself.

Such reminders of why they were wedged into the box had helped Shane to maintain his disciplined focus. But now he was beginning to feel restive.

At first he blamed himself for the failure of his concentration.

I'm tired, he told himself. Too tired to dominate my own thoughts, much less to guide them in the Buddhist way.

Even as that explanation came, he rejected it. He had meditated for hour after hour under circumstances far more physically uncomfortable than the cramped box he rode in now.

It's Dani, Shane admitted. I could ignore having her all over me like a rash, but I can tell how uncomfortable she is.

Dani's body had lost its resilience. She was stiff with trying to hold herself away from him and brace herself against unpredictable bumps.

Shane could have told her that the first was unnecessary and the second impossible.

Maybe it's fear that is making her stiff, he thought.

They had spent no time together in the catacombs beneath the Potala Palace. Shane had suspected that being locked in a cell with him would only have made Dani more upset.

Maybe I was wrong, he thought. Maybe she didn't dislike me on sight.

Maybe pigs fly.

Shane might have spent a lot of time with Buddhist monks, but he hadn't forgotten the way a woman looks at a man who interests her.

The first time Dani spotted me in the hotel in Lhasa, her eyes sent a clear signal.

Drop off, as Cassandra would say.

Cassandra had perfected the look during her years as an ambassador. Shane had been on the receiving end of that look more than once in his time with Risk Limited.

Not that Shane had been trying to get physically close to Cassandra. Far from it.

I'd have to go through Gillie to do that, Shane thought wryly, and my mama didn't raise any fools.

Except lately.

Very lately, Shane admitted. A certain hazel-eyed woman whose hair smells sweet is playing hell with my concentration.

Relax, Dani, Shane advised her silently. We'll get out of this in one piece.

Deaf, maybe, but otherwise intact.

Since they had climbed into the smuggler's box, the noise had made talking impossible. Otherwise Shane would have reassured Dani that claustrophobia not only was normal under the circumstances, it was almost inevitable.

See that pinpoint of light? Shane silently asked Dani. There's still a world out there. We'll be out there with it soon.

I hope you're still as game now as you were yesterday.

Shane knew what Dani didn't. In many ways, the most demanding part of the journey was yet to come.

The truck reached the top of a grade. Suddenly the world was quiet again.

Dani understood why. It didn't comfort her.

She had ridden with Tibetan truckers before. She knew about their practice of coasting in neutral, free-wheeling down the most horrifying grades with nothing to hold them back but brakes whose lining was as thin as the air at sixteen thousand feet.

The sudden, total rigidity of Dani's body scattered what little concentration Shane had left.

"Are you okay?" he asked.

They were the first words either of them had been able to speak in several hours.

"I'm fine," Dani said through gritted teeth.

Shane wasn't convinced.

"Back down the road, before my arm went to sleep," he said, "I could feel you trembling."

"I'm fine," she repeated. "I just hope to hell all this is necessary."

"It is. Tibet is alive with armed men looking for us."

"Why? Do they think we killed Feng?"

"They don't care about one more dead smuggler. They think we have the silk."

"How do you know?"

"I have good sources in Lhasa," Shane said. "Can you lift your head for a minute?"

Dani raised her head and promptly bumped into a sharp metal corner. She stifled a sound of pain and annoyance.

"Sorry," Shane said.

He shifted his arm a little. Sensation began returning, first as sharp pain, then as needles and pins.

"Okay," Shane said. "Back to normal."

"Normal?" Dani grumbled, but rested her head on Shane again. "What's normal about this?"

"Can I do anything to make you more comfortable?" he asked. "Besides vanishing entirely?"

Shane's concern for her was so unexpected that Dani laughed aloud.

"Vanishing wouldn't help," she said, "You're softer than the metal box. Barely."

The bit of light leaking from the cab into the box revealed Shane's quick smile.

"Besides," Dani added, "you're the one who should be complaining."

"Why?"

"You're on the bottom."

Shane's chest moved with silent laughter.

Dani felt it in every cell of her body. She wondered if he had felt her laughter in the same way. The thought was as intriguing as it was unnerving.

"How long are we going to be here?" she asked quickly.

"Three more hours," Shane said. "Maybe—"

The rest of his words were drowned out by clashing gears and the renewed roar of the engine as the truck started up the next slope.

Dani sighed and wondered how long three hours could be.

A long time, she decided. Centuries.

Shane went back to concentrating on the bolt that stuck out

into the trap. He memorized every nick and pit that time and harsh use had put on the metal.

Twenty minutes crawled by.

Gradually Shane became aware that Dani's body had stiffened again.

Suddenly the world was quiet.

"Three more hours, maybe four," Shane said quickly, picking up their conversation in midstride.

Dani tried not to groan.

"Breathe only through your mouth," Shane said. "Slowly. The fumes aren't so bad that way."

What he didn't add was that concentrating on her breathing would help the time to pass more quickly.

Carefully Dani began breathing through her mouth.

After a few minutes Shane felt the tension begin to ease in her body. He turned his head enough to look at her.

Dani lay with her eyes squeezed shut so tightly that she had little crow's feet at their corners.

"Open your eyes," Shane said. "Find something to look at."

Reluctantly Dani opened her eyes.

Looking at the box wasn't comforting. She settled on the rumpled fabric of Shane's khaki shirt, which was close enough to be out of focus.

"Think about what you're seeing," Shane said. "Let your body worry about balance instead of your mind."

"Easy to say."

"Try it."

Why not? Dani asked herself. It might work. God knows Shane is relaxed enough.

With a little effort, Dani could imagine that Shane's shirt was actually the desolate mountains and valleys of Tibet's lunar landscape. She was lying on a flying carpet, looking down on sweeping distances.

Suddenly the box seemed much bigger.

Unconsciously Dani took a deep breath and relaxed against her own personal magic carpet.

"Better?" Shane asked.

Dani nodded slightly.

Shane sensed the motion of her head against his biceps. He also sensed her increasing relaxation.

Good, he applauded silently. You'll need your strength for what's ahead.

"Who are you, anyway?" Dani asked after a time. "CIA?"

Shane made a sound that might have been a laugh.

"So we're back to that, are we?" he asked.

"You told me to find something to look at. It's you or the box, and I've seen enough of the box to last me a lifetime."

"What makes you think I'm CIA?"

"You know a lot about the sneaky, underground life."

"Yeah?"

"Yeah. No normal civilian type would have been able to get me out of that place alive."

Shane didn't argue. He remembered all too keenly the decision he had made.

Save the silk or save the woman.

"You're pretty unusual yourself," Shane said.

"As in stupid?" Dani retorted.

"I thought so at first."

"Thanks."

"You're welcome. Then I changed my mind."

"Why?" Dani asked.

"A stupid person would have started screaming before we left the city limits of Lhasa in this box."

"Is that a compliment?"

"It's a fact."

Dani thought that over through a few more bumps and lurches. Then she realized that Shane hadn't answered her original question.

"So, are you CIA?" she asked bluntly.

"No. I'm a civilian. I work for an organization called Risk Limited."

"Never heard of it."

"That's what we pay our PR people big bucks for," Shane said, "to keep us *out* of the news."

"Is Risk Limited based in Asia?"

"United States."

"You're a long way from home."

"We have—had—a contract with the Azure Sect of Buddhism, to provide advice and security. They'll probably terminate the contract now."

"Like I said, CIA," Dani replied skeptically.

Shane drew a deep breath and blew it out, trying to get rid of his irritation along with it.

"What difference does it make?" he asked finally.

"None, I suppose," Dani said. "At least you aren't trying to pass yourself off as one of us."

"Us?"

"Some covert types use academic backgrounds as cover stories."

"Shocking," Shane said dryly.

"You're damned right it is," Dani shot back. "Archaeologists have a tough enough time in the third world as it is. We don't need spooks and spies hiding behind the artifacts."

Shane started to say something, but his words were overwhelmed by a sudden blast of noise from the truck's engine.

Dani stiffened.

After a few moments Shane felt Dani's body relax again. He wondered what she had chosen to focus on. He turned his head slightly to see where she was looking.

Her eyes were open, but veiled by long, dense eyelashes.

No mascara, Shane thought idly. Shiny and clean. From this angle, all she can see is my shirt.

Wonder what she sees in it? Sweat? Dirt?

Mentally he shrugged. Whatever Dani was seeing was relaxing her.

He stared back at the bolt overhead. It had lost its mystery. He looked down at Dani's eyelashes.

Black butterflies, he decided. Resting.

Then Shane thought of the ancient Asian riddle: *Last night I dreamed I was a butterfly. Then I awoke to find myself a man. Or am I a butterfly dreaming I am a man?*

The riddle was more interesting to Shane than a rusty bolt and less disturbing to his peace of mind than Dani's eyelashes.

For a long time they lay alone together in their private worlds, ignoring the roar and stench and claustrophobia of reality.

Abruptly the pitch of the engine changed. The driver pumped the accelerator roughly three times.

The butterfly decided it was definitely a man, and the man was in deep kim chee.

Dani rolled her head toward him and started to say something, but he cut her off with a curt jerk of his head.

The driver began downshifting and braking with unnecessary force.

"Soldiers," Shane said in a low voice.

Dani froze.

The truck stopped. The engine settled down to a rough idle.

Above the sound, Dani could just make out a harsh command in Chinese and a mumbled response in Tibetan.

The tiny crack of light in their coffin vanished. It was blocked by a dark green curtain. A soldier's chest. He wore a lacquered red star.

People's Republic of China.

Oh, God, Dani thought. They've finally found us.

Chapter Eight

Instinctively Dani held her breath and tried to shrink into nothingness. As she did, she sensed the tension in the man who lay beneath her.

Oddly, it reassured her. Shane seemed so powerful, so controlled, so utterly self-assured, that she hadn't thought of him as vulnerable to the same fears that assailed her. Sensing his tension made her feel less alone.

Dani didn't know enough Chinese to follow the conversation between the truck driver and the soldiers.

Shane did. He listened intently, wanting to know how much trouble they were in.

Their driver passed around cigarettes. It was expected of truck drivers at each official road block, a small "courtesy" rather than a bribe.

The driver and the soldiers stood outside smoking and talking in the knife-edged wind. As the chatter dragged on and on— cold weather and hot liquor, stubborn bosses and willing women—Shane relaxed.

The soldiers weren't sniffing after two escaping Americans. The men were simply bored by their lonely post high on the shoulder of the Himalayas.

Finally the truck's engine started up again. With a backfire, a roar, and a blast of vile exhaust, the truck passed through the checkpoint. After several bumps, the engine shifted into neutral, free-wheeling down an incline.

Tension seeped out of Shane. They weren't home free by any means, but they were closer.

"Finally," Dani said. "I missed the exhaust."

"You're kidding."

"Nope. Without the engine running, I was getting cold."

"Open your coat," Shane said matter-of-factly. "I've got enough body heat for both of us."

Without thinking Dani jerked her head back so that she could see Shane's face. She got a rap on the skull for her efforts. Her head thumped back down on his chest.

Gears clashed. The engine revved loudly and stayed that way as the truck accelerated on the rough gravel road.

Talk was impossible again.

The truck climbed higher and higher, until finally even the engine exhaust wasn't enough to keep Dani warm.

Open your coat. I've got enough body heat for both of us.

It was a battle in the small box, but Dani finally got her coat unbuttoned so that the down wasn't insulating her from Shane's body heat.

Very quickly she discovered that Shane was right. He was warm enough for both of them.

With a long sigh, she relaxed against him and let her mind wander over the peaks and valleys of her warm magic carpet.

Shane felt the warmth of her breath against his throat, the vivid softness of her body, and cursed his stupidity at suggesting she open her coat.

I'm a butterfly dreaming I'm a man, Shane decided.

Under the circumstances, he had little choice. If he was a butterfly, Dani had to be a flower, or her weight would have crushed him.

Logic, Shane told himself. That was the key to self-control. Butterfly and flower. A butterfly's luxurious, gentle, repeated probing of silken petals until warm nectar flows . . .

Abruptly Shane went back to concentrating on the bolt.

He didn't know how long it was before the bedlam inside the metal box stopped. He blinked, focused on reality, and looked at the quality of the light coming into the box.

Early afternoon.

The truck driver turned onto a little track beside the main road. He cut his engine, got out, and pissed by the rear of the truck. Then he walked to the front of the truck and began cursing the engine in words that a monk never should have known.

"Get ready," Shane whispered.

"For what?"

"Can you walk or should I carry you?"

"Haven't we had this conversation before?"

"Yes. Answer me."

"I can walk."

"If your knees buckle, I'll carry you."

Dani didn't doubt it. Shane's voice was as flat and impersonal as the metal coffin surrounding them.

Harsh, screeching sounds came as the monk lifted the hood of the truck. He came back into the cab, muttering in a mountain dialect about tools and a balky demon-yak made of metal.

When the driver leaned into the cab, he spoke soft, concise English.

"Quickly," he said. "There is a small shrine beside the truck. The knapsack is behind it. When I lift the seat, take the gear and be gone."

"Are we clear?" Shane asked softly.

"There is an army patrol two miles back."

"Shit."

"I will lead them away, but you must hurry!"

When the driver lifted the seat, bright afternoon sunshine almost blinded Dani. She blinked repeatedly. Groaning, she tried to force her stiff body into an upright position. She got far enough that she saw the driver heading toward the front of the truck again, wrench in hand.

Shane's free arm closed around her. She made a startled sound as he lifted her into a sitting position.

"Can you move?" he asked.

Dani didn't answer. She simply began pulling herself out of the box.

Cold air hit her like a knife in the lungs.

Off to the right side Dani saw a small stone shrine. Wind-shredded silk prayer flags snapped in the air, sending their silent, endless pleas for safety to the mountain gods.

"Go through the door on the passenger side and get behind the shrine," Shane said. "Stay low. A man can see a hundred miles in air like this."

Biting back a groan as stiff muscles knotted, Dani scrambled out of the smuggler's trap and across the passenger seat of the truck. Her knees buckled when her feet hit the ground. She knelt there, trying to regain her balance while she buttoned her coat.

Before Dani got one button done, Shane landed beside her. A big hand closed around her upper arm, steadying her.

Rather bitterly Dani noted that he moved with remarkable ease for a big man who had been stuck inside a sardine can for hours.

"Quickly, quickly," the driver ordered in a low voice.

Shane started forward, lifting Dani to her feet. He moved fast despite his crouched position and the fact that he was dragging Dani along with him.

"Thanks, Dorjee," Shane called softly. "May the demons smile."

"On you as well, revered master," the driver called after them. *"Hurry."*

When Dani and Shane vanished into the shadows behind the shrine, the driver slammed down the truck's hood. Very quickly he was back in behind the wheel. He revved up the noisy engine, backed onto the main road again, shifted into first, and ground off down the road.

Dani sat with her back against the stone wall of the shrine, gasping deeply in the thin, clean, icy air. While Shane rummaged through the worn leather knapsack that was waiting for them, she finished buttoning her coat.

From the road behind them came the sound of another engine laboring toward the shrine.

Shane cocked his head, calculated distances and options, and made a decision in less that two heartbeats.

"There's a gulch thirty yards over there," he said quickly, pointing. "See it?"

Dani nodded.

"That's where we're going," Shane said. "Now!"

With no more warning than that, he yanked Dani to her feet and began running across the broken ground. Boulders and stones were everywhere, like a huge shrine shattered by a careless god.

Shane didn't slow down when he reached the edge of a gully. He simply dragged Dani after him down the steep bank and pointed up the dry streambed.

"Run for your life!" he said.

A thrust of his arm reinforced the order.

Dani ran.

Shane followed right on her heels. The sound of their feet pounding on the gritty, pebbly ground was soon overwhelmed by Dani's sawing breaths. She felt like she had run a mile already, but she knew it was barely a hundred yards.

Suddenly Shane spun her to one side and hauled her into the shelter of a small dry cave that had been dug out of the bank by the runoff of spring snow.

"Stay here," he said between rapid breaths. "This is—as good—as it gets."

Dani simply nodded. She was too busy dragging at air to waste any on words.

"How's the ankle?" Shane asked after a moment. "Can you keep going?"

Again, Dani nodded.

Shane touched her cheek in quick caress and smiled.

"I knew you were tougher than you looked," he said.

Absurdly, Dani smiled back even though she resented the ease with which Shane had caught his breath.

"What—now?" she panted.

"We wait."

"For a guide?"

"For the PRC," Shane said, jerking his thumb back toward the shrine. "Stay put. Promise?"

Dani nodded.

Shane slid along the rough wall of the streambed until he could look back toward the shrine without being visible himself.

Instants later a heavy green Chinese Army truck rolled along the gravel highway toward the shrine at thirty miles an hour.

Shane breathed easily, waiting for whatever the Tibetan demons had in store for him.

The truck roared past the shrine without slowing.

Shane mouthed Tibetan words of thanksgiving. Then he went back to find Dani.

As promised, she hadn't moved.

"Well?" she asked.

"PRC soldiers from Lhasa," Shane said succinctly. "They're still tailing Dorjee. He's in for it if they catch him."

"Why would they be interested in a truck driver sitting on an empty box?"

Without answering, Shane stole another glance over the edge of the bank. Both the Jiefang truck and the army patrol were out of sight. He sent a silent prayer after the truck and turned back to Dani.

"Dorjee isn't just a truck driver," Shane said. "He's a priest, a monk from the Azure Sect."

Dani stared at him.

"He's one of my best men," Shane added. "He'll be dead meat if the army catches up with him."

For a second Dani couldn't breathe. She remembered what Dorjee had called Shane. *Revered master.*

"Can't we help him?" she asked urgently.

"Dorjee made his peace with himself and his gods when he volunteered to drive the truck."

"But—"

"All we can do is make sure his sacrifice isn't wasted," Shane interrupted curtly. "Let's go."

Dani looked around. The barren landscape stretched away on all sides for hundreds of miles. There was nothing to indicate that one direction was better than any other.

"Where?" Dani asked.

"Trust me," Shane said ironically.

"Do I have a choice?"

"On your feet or over my shoulder."

Dani stood up.

"Right," Shane said. "On your feet it is. If you change your mind, let me know."

"I've been walking all but a year of my life," Dani said through her teeth.

"Not at this altitude."

"I've been living with the herders for months."

"That explains it."

"What?"

"Your coat. It looks like you mugged a Chinese rag picker for it."

Shane wrapped his hand around Dani's upper arm.

"Come on," he said. "We have two hours to cover five klicks. Some of it is uphill."

Dani pulled loose from Shane's grip. There was something almost proprietary about it, something she resisted instinctively.

"I'm not a piece of luggage," she said. "I don't need to be dragged over the landscape."

Shane gave her a quick look. Then he turned away and started walking.

She didn't waste any time following.

For the first hour Shane set a hard pace across the dry, barren plateau. His legs were long, he was used to the thin air, he was physically fit, and he knew that every step was one closer to safety.

Dani was used to the altitude, but her legs were shorter. At times she almost had to run to keep up. Her stiff ankle eventually loosened, but she knew she would pay later, when they stopped and the cold set in.

Along the mountain ramparts, clouds were gathering. Shane watched them with a growing sense of unhappiness, but he said nothing.

Dani estimated they had come four kilometers when Shane crested a rise and stopped just below the ridgeline on the other side. Without a word she sat down on a nearby rock and simply breathed.

Shane glanced at her. She was pale and panting, but still game. He nodded, turned away, and climbed up the ridge just enough to look back over to the road they had abandoned.

From where Shane stood it would have been easy to believe there were no other human beings on the face of the earth. Or anything else, for that matter.

The gray-white track of the gravel truck road snaked across the barren landscape. The sky was as empty as the road. Not even a vulture. The sun was balanced just above the rim of the mountains.

In half an hour the sun would set behind the snow-covered peaks. Then the cold would be brutal.

When Shane came back to Dani, her breathing had slowed. He took her wrist and felt for her pulse beneath her gloves.

"What in—" she began.

"Quiet," Shane interrupted.

Startled, Dani obeyed.

"Not even eighty," Shane said, releasing her wrist. "You weren't kidding about living with yak herders, were you? We've climbed nearly a thousand feet in four clicks."

Dani felt a sudden surge of pride. She had kept up with a large, exceptionally fit male, and she had done it despite her ankle.

If only Steve could see me now, Dani thought. I'd run his arrogant ass right into the ground.

"What a nasty smile," Shane said. "I'm glad you're still so full of piss and vinegar."

"Why? We've only got one more kilometer to go."

"Yeah. That kilometer."

Shane gestured toward a rock wall that loomed in front of them.

By squinting and making free use of her imagination, Dani could just make out a trail winding up the steep, rock-strewn slope. Her heart skipped a beat.

"Bloody hell," Dani said.

"Gillie couldn't have put it better himself."

"Who's Gillie?"

"There's a hermit's cave up above," Shane said, ignoring Dani's question. "It's in a cirque with a small lake and a bit of graze for yaks."

"I don't see it."

"Evening comes early there," Shane said, looking up the slope, "and the stars are a permanent glory. No one will be there now."

Dani gave Shane a sideways look.

"You sound quite familiar with the place," she said.

"I lived there for six months."

"Herding yaks?" she asked in disbelief.

"No. Meditating on becoming an Azure monk."

Before Dani could think of anything to say, Shane shouldered the pack and set off up the slope. He didn't look back.

After going up the first hundred yards of trail, Dani didn't care where Shane looked or didn't look. She just cared about breathing and walking at the same time.

The wind rose as the sun set. Cold bit into the landscape like a living thing.

By the time Dani reached the shelter, Shane had a small fire burning in the one-room hut and water steaming in a small kettle. Dani ducked through the doorway with a profound sense of relief at being beyond the reach of the wind.

The sun still shone on the snow-covered peaks several thousand feet above the hut, but in the hidden valley the air was like breathing shattered ice.

When Dani looked at the flames in the small, stone-walled stove, she understood all the way to the marrow of her bones why primitive man worshipped fire.

For several minutes she simply caught her breath and warmed her numb hands over the flames. She would have liked more heat, but only a small pile of sticks lay nearby.

"I don't think that will keep us warm all night," Dani said.

"If you were my *sang-yum,* I would put you to work shagging in some dried yak dung."

"Forget it," Dani said. "You're not a monk and I'm certainly not your consort."

Shane smiled slightly.

"You don't seem the type to be a monk," Dani added.

"What makes you say that?"

"I think my first guess about your occupation was the best one."

"You mean the CIA?"

Dani nodded

"I worked for them once," Shane said, "back when there was a nasty little war in Afghanistan. We had a parting of ways, as they say."

Shane's tone suggested the parting hadn't been happy.

"So," Dani said. "You've been a spook and a hermit. What else?"

He shrugged. "I was with a private charity for a while, working on community development and cleanup."

Dani laughed out loud.

"Community development?" she asked sardonically. "You? With a CIA background? What were you doing? Training guerrillas?"

Shane pulled a metal tube out of the knapsack and went to work opening it.

"I was digging holes in the ground," he said.

"Mining?"

"Nope. De-mining. The Russians scattered antipersonnel mines all over Afghanistan. The mujahedeen did the same."

"So?"

"So once the fighting stopped, somebody had to go in and dig the mines up before the kids in the neighborhood did."

Dani froze in position over the flames and stared at Shane in disbelief. His nonchalance was chilling.

"You made a living digging up and disarming live land mines?" she asked finally.

"Digging them up, and teaching civilians how to do it."

"My God."

"God had little to do with it," Shane said. "The UN figures there are five million live land mines scattered around the world. The pay's not real good but you'll never run out of work."

"Why did you quit?"

Shane glanced up from the metal framework he was assembling. His eyes were hooded and blank.

"You ask a lot of questions," he said.

"Considering what you've put me through in the past day," Dani shot back, "I haven't asked many questions at all."

Shane's expression softened. He went back to assembling the framework.

"I quit because I lost my nerve," he said simply.

"You? I don't believe it."

"Believe it. I had three assistants, bright young Afghanis, killed in eight months. I decided I wasn't such a good teacher."

"Maybe they weren't such good students," Dani said. "Bright young men can be thick-headed sometimes. I know. I've taught a few."

Shane didn't answer. He concentrated on adjusting the alignment of the metal rays he had erected on the little stand. When he was satisfied, he set the antenna outside the door of the hut. Then he dug a small radio transmitter out of the knapsack, checked the battery, and connected it to the antenna. He flipped a few switches, checked a dial, and set the radio aside.

"Now what?" Dani said.

"We wait for our ride."

"Flying yaks? Magic carpets?"

"Nothing that exotic. We're only a hundred miles as the crow flies from Nepal. There's a high-altitude helicopter waiting for our signal. He'll be along tonight if there's enough light. Tomorrow at the latest."

"You produce satellite beacons and high-altitude helicopters and you expect me to believe you aren't CIA?" Dani said.

"The Agency has okay equipment, but Risk Limited is a private enterprise. Our stuff is better."

Shane looked directly at Dani for the first time since the subject of land mines had come up.

"Now, about that yak dung," he said.

"What about it?"

Shane glanced up at the golden light on the mountain peaks above.

"We have a very small window tonight. If that chopper

doesn't come in the next half-hour, it won't come until morning. So it's either bundle with me or start gathering dried yak shit."

"I'll take the yak dung."

"Your choice."

A red light on the radio transmitter flashed on and the radio gave a squawk of static.

Shane reached for the radio, punched a button to acknowledge the signal.

"They must have been airborne, waiting for the signal," he said. "You'll be in Katmandu for dinner."

Shane stood up and went to the door of the hut. Silently he scanned the sky.

Dani went and stood beside him. Far off in the distance, they both heard the familiar faint whirring of a helicopter.

"That's one I owe you, Gillie," Shane murmured. "A big one. Bigger than you know."

Then he laughed quietly.

Dani looked at Shane's face. Even in the twilight of the valley she could see that the hard planes of his face were softer. He was grinning with relief.

Knowing that safety was at hand made Dani feel like a balloon whose air was running out. The past twenty-four hours had been an adrenaline roller coaster. Now it was over.

Abruptly she felt lightheaded. The pain that she had been ignoring in her ankle stabbed through her whole body. She groped for the door frame, needing something to lean on before she fell. Her hand connected with Shane's arm.

"Dani?"

"Ankle," was all she could say.

The world shifted suddenly as Shane put one arm behind Dani's back, the other beneath her knees and lifted her against his chest.

"Easy, honey," Shane said against her hair. "It's almost over."

Dani felt his strength and warmth like an electric current passing through him into her. She let out a long breath and simply absorbed the fact that she was safe.

A helicopter flashed in low over the peaks, shattering the

small valley's peace. The chopper headed straight down the slope toward a flat spot fifty yards from the side of the hut and landed without hesitation.

Shane headed for the helicopter, still carrying Dani.

"Wounded?" asked the pilot.

Dani was startled to hear a woman's voice.

"Ankle and exhaustion," Shane said.

"Right. Hand her over."

Shane boosted Dani into a seat and fastened the safety harness.

"Clear," he said, stepping back.

Suddenly Dani realized Shane wasn't coming. She felt sharp disappointment, as though somehow she had been cheated.

"Wait!" Dani cried. "Where are you going?"

"After the silk."

"You mean all this was just to get me out of Tibet?"

Shane nodded and made a twirling motion with his hand.

The rotor speed increased.

"But why?" Dani asked. "You don't even know me!"

"My choice, Dani, not yours. You don't owe anyone anything. Remember that if they come after you."

"Who? What are you talking about? Damn it, who *are* you!"

The chopper roared and leaped into the darkening sky, drowning out Shane's answer.

If he answered at all.

Somehow Dani doubted it.

Chapter Nine

Aruba
November

Moist, silky night air swirled through the open doors of Katya Pilenkova's personal quarters. A full moon hung over the rippling Caribbean waters like beaten gold over hammered silver.

As always, following an evening with the bankers of Aruba, Katya was soaking in a sunken tub of perfumed water. After a time, the hot bath would loosen the coils of her distaste for the men she had entertained. Scented oil would purge the stink of their sweat and crude sexuality from her nostrils.

Animals, Katya thought disdainfully.

Will they never learn that I am not a whore for their lust? Bankers are clerks, bureaucrats, ciphers.

Hot water swirled around Katya, urging relaxation. A subtle, expensive scent rose from the bath to soothe her.

Katya was not appeased. Ever since she had obtained her own wealth and power through the Harmony, Aruba's bankers had little to offer her. Therefore, she loathed them.

The bankers are even more reptilian than the men of the

Harmony, Katya thought with icy distaste. At least gang chief-
tains and accomplished criminals have their own wealth and
power. The bankers have nothing but a title.

Yet, she admitted grudgingly, they have a use, like scrub
women. They launder money very efficiently.

The thought soothed Katya more than any perfume or hot
water could. She hadn't put herself on display tonight for nothing. Scrub women might be beneath her, but they were still
necessary.

With a sigh, Katya gave herself to the swirling bath.

When she finally emerged, her pale skin glowed pinkly from
the residual heat of the bath. She toweled the last drops of
scented water from her breasts and legs and back. Languidly
she slipped into a nightgown of sheer, red silk. It felt like a
lover's breath settling over her body.

Where is Ilya? Katya thought. Is he safe? When will he come
back to me?

Nothing answered her but the random movements of the
bedroom curtains in the wind.

Katya snapped off the lights in the bathroom and went toward
her bed. The bedroom was shadowed, but the moonlight was
bright through the glass doors from a side patio.

How good it would be to step out into the night, she thought
restlessly.

But she didn't. She stayed in her dark bedroom. She was
unable to shake the feeling that someone might be watching
her windows from outside. It was a feeling she often experienced when the men of the Harmony were around.

A sensation like cold fingers chilled Katya's neck.

Her heartbeat quickened with fear in the instant before she
realized what had happened. Tendrils of her hair were damp
from the steam of the bath. They were curling down over her
neck, tickling her sensitive nape.

Impatiently Katya retied the black velvet ribbon that was
supposed to keep her fine blond hair up away from her skin.
Still, a spectral shiver went over her, like cold fingernails caressing her nape.

A combination of fear and sexual hunger went through Katya.

For her, the feelings were one and the same. She had never been sexually drawn to any man she could control. And she feared any man she could not. Especially one.

Ilya Kasatonin.

A shudder that was both hot and cold shot through Katya. Swiftly she walked through the villa to the wet bar with its special freezer, opened it, and pulled out a bottle of vodka.

The frozen neck of the bottle rang against a crystal whiskey glass. The vodka was so cold that a sheen of frost formed on the outside of the thin, carved crystal as she poured.

Before Katya allowed herself to so much as sip the liquor she hungered for, she capped the bottle and put it back in the freezer. Each gesture was controlled, almost ritualized.

She would rule the vodka. It would not rule her.

Katya sipped the double shot of liquor. Then she knocked half of it back in a single gulp. A flush of heat radiated out from her stomach.

"Ahhhh," she murmured.

After a night with timid, greedy-eyed bankers, she needed a warmth inside her to match the satin softness of the Caribbean night.

Icy glass in hand, Katya stood and thought about the dinner party she had just conducted for the benefit of the Harmony. Exactly one dozen of the most important bankers in Aruba had been at her table. Exactly one dozen of them had stared at her breasts so cleverly half-concealed, half-revealed in emerald green damask.

But there is not a real man among them, Katya thought scornfully. Each one of them is afraid to touch me, much less try to take me.

They were deathly afraid of that moment of male weakness when they lost control in a woman's arms.

That is why they plunge themselves into whores, Katya thought. With a whore, they are always the master, even at the most vulnerable of all moments, when their bloated cock spews its miserable seed.

Smiling coldly, Katya stood in the darkness. She had learned very young that most men feared the loss of sexual control almost as much as they feared death itself.

"To the little death, as the French say," Katya whispered, lifting her glass in mocking toast.

Even the brutal masters of the Harmony were wary of dying that way.

With her.

They shared that fear with the bloodless bankers and the passionless lawyers and the spineless politicians of the world.

Wise men, Katya conceded. They know how I killed my Chechen patron when I finally allowed him to seduce me. So simple . . . a needle into the head of his cock, a shot of poison, a very big death. Heart attack, as the police said.

The men of the Russian Thieves World knew otherwise. They respected Katya for her cleverness in stepping into the Chechen gangster's shoes.

They also feared her.

Katya had made certain that the Harmony's men heard the story.

"To fear," Katya said scornfully. "The only aphrodisiac that truly works."

She upended the glass.

Sometimes it seemed that the whole world was peopled with corporate eunuchs, bureaucrats, and bean-counters. Creatures with no inner strength. Insects with great fear and small vision. The very thought of letting one of them inside her body chilled her even as the vodka heated her blood.

Katya went to the freezer, opened it, and poured herself another shot. She closed the freezer with a firm push.

Just one more, she told herself. I have earned it tonight.

She drank it fast and hard, as though speed somehow denied the act of breaking her own rules about how much and when she should drink vodka.

What does it matter? Katya thought bitterly. I am alone. I flaunt my unlocked doors, but none are brave enough to try the darkness inside.

Restlessly Katya went back to her bedroom. The sheer inner curtain beside the sliding glass door shifted in the moving air.

There was a different scent on the breeze. A man's scent.

He was in the room with her.

Even as Katya tensed to scream, a hard arm encircled her body just beneath her breasts. A callused hand muffled her startled cry. He held her tall body against his own with one arm, controlling her easily, making a joke of her struggles.

Katya tried to fill her lungs to scream, but his hand was over her mouth and nose. He was suffocating her. His arm tightened around her ribcage, bruising her breasts, squeezing the life's breath out of her.

"I could kill you, you know," he whispered softly.

Katya froze. Uncertainty and fear shuddered through her . . . and another emotion that was as elemental as fear of death.

"You know that, don't you?" the man whispered hoarsely.

She nodded.

"Maybe I will," the man whispered.

His lips were against Katya's ear. Casually he flexed his biceps beneath her breasts. He was powerful enough to crush her ribcage if he wished.

Katya shivered.

Is this finally *the* time?

A thrill of fear and arousal shot through her.

The man drew a deep breath through his nostrils, as though he had just caught the scent of Katya's bath and her fear and something else, something elemental.

He laughed silently.

"Then, again, maybe I won't kill you," he whispered. "Maybe not this time. As long as you do what I want."

The grip on Katya softened. Hesitantly she breathed in.

His hand slid up the sheer silk of her nightgown until his palm rested on her ribcage just under the uplifted curve of her breast. He raked the soft skin beneath her ear with the point of his chin.

His beard stubble was thick and spiky, as though he had not shaved in a week or more. His breath smelled of old vodka with a hint of exotic spices. Curry, perhaps, or Asian chilies.

Katya stood on tiptoes and held her breath against the smell. Her body trembled with strain but she made no noise.

"Are you alone?" he demanded.

She nodded her head.

Slowly he lifted his right hand from her mouth, still holding her close with his left arm. He was weighing her reactions, waiting for any sign that she would scream.

There was none.

"Ah," he said. "You learn."

When Katya remained silent, he lowered his hand. Slowly he stroked over the skin along her breastbone and then across the tip of her right breast.

The skin on his fingertips was rough. It caught on the sheer silk. And on something more interesting.

In spite of herself, Katya felt her nipple harden.

His fingertips closed on her with a force that hurt. She gasped. He ran his palm over the silk and the thrusting nipple beneath.

"Don't bother screaming," he said in a low voice. "I will kill anyone who comes. But first I will kill you."

Katya didn't doubt it.

The hand over her breast moved. She heard a faint rasping sound, metal against stiff fabric. A knife appeared in front of her face. The knife had a sharp, straight point and a deep blood gutter along the spine of the blade.

Moonlight gleamed on metal, as cold as frozen mercury.

"I will do what you want," Katya whispered, trembling. "Do not cut me."

"Of course you will do what I want. The knife makes women very obedient."

He loosened his grip around her ribcage, then drew the flat of his hand across her taut belly.

Katya sensed an opening, a moment when he would free her. She coiled to spring away.

He was too quick for her. He always had been.

He caught her arms behind her back with one of his hands and yanked her to him. Then he held her pinioned there like an elegant, long-winged bird.

The terrible, exciting freedom of helplessness turned Katya's bones to water.

"You will do what I want," he said softly, "because it is

also what you want. The only question is, when do I sheathe the knife, and where?''

Katya shivered again and stared at the gleaming metal.

He laughed. With a flick of his hand, he put the blade along the line of Katya's breastbone. The point of the knife darted beneath the thin right strap of her gown.

Katya felt silk slither away from her right breast. The knife flicked again. She gasped. But it was only silk, not flesh, that met the blade.

This time.

The nightgown slid down to Katya's waist when he jerked her hard against his body. She trembled. A low, hoarse sound came from her throat.

''Quiet,'' the man said against her ear. ''You haven't been hurt yet, have you?''

Numbly Katya shook her head.

They stood locked together, he with the knife in one hand and Katya's wrists in the other. She could sense his eyes on the tips of her breasts. She willed herself to remain unmoved.

Her nipples puckered and thrust out.

This time the man's laughter was real.

This time.

The punishing grip of his hands softened. Dizziness took what remained of Katya's strength. Her head lolled to one side and she sagged against his strength.

''Did you think it would be that easy?'' he whispered.

Still holding Katya's arms behind her, he laid the cold steel knife between her breasts. The needle point pressed against the skin at the base of her throat.

Katya gasped and lifted herself, shrinking away from the sharp tip of the blade.

''You understand what is required?'' he whispered.

''Yes.''

''I don't trust you. Walk with me.''

For a moment, the only sound in the room was the soft, ragged slide of Katya's feet over the carpet as she edged toward the bed. When she moved too slowly, one of his feet pushed against her.

He, too, was barefoot.

When they reached the edge of the bed, the only sound Katya heard was the rasp of her captor's breath. Her own breathing had fallen into his pattern, tense and fierce.

"Hold still," he warned.

He released Katya's arms.

She felt his rough hand settle on her neck. His callused index finger stroked the fine hairs. She shivered and drew a swift breath as he jerked the velvet ribbon free. Cold hair fell against her neck.

He laid his face against her neck and bit her nape with a care that was more warning than caress.

"Turn around," he ordered.

Hesitating, Katya slowly turned toward him. Her head was bowed. She was afraid to look at his face, afraid that this time she would see only the killer and not the lover of her dreams.

And nightmares.

He was tall. Too tall. And strong. Too strong. She was a willow pitted against an oak.

"Your hands," he commanded softly.

"No," Katya whispered. "Please."

"Your hands."

Katya lowered her head to hide her small, triumphant smile. Even this man was afraid of her.

But unlike the bankers and gangsters, he would take her anyway.

Slowly, Katya offered her hands.

The knife vanished into its sheath. With a swift motion he wound the black velvet ribbon around her wrists. Before she could breathe, her hands were tightly bound.

Triumph and helplessness racked Katya, arousing her as nothing else could.

"Lie on the bed," he ordered. "You know how."

Slowly, Katya sank onto the bed, taking care not to look at his face as he moved toward her. The silk was cool against her flushed body.

She slid across the sheets and lay back against the pillow.

Despite being tied at the wrists, her hands covered the pale hair of her pubic mound.

"Is this what you want?" Katya asked.

Her voice was soft, oddly innocent.

"No," he said curtly. "Shall I refresh your memory with blood?"

Katya watched his hand move to the hilt of the knife. As soon as his fingers touched steel, she raised her bound hands and rested them languidly above her head.

Only then did she lift her eyes and look at her captor's face. Relief, fear, and sexuality whipped through her.

"Like this, Ilya?" she whispered.

"Open your legs wider."

As Katya obeyed, Kasatonin peeled off his soiled shirt. His chest was pale, smooth, and hairless, like white stone in the moonlight. His arms and shoulders were well-muscled and deeply scarred.

He threw the shirt aside. His hand rested for a moment on the handle of the knife in his waistband. Suddenly steel gleamed in the moonlight.

"If you don't satisfy me, I may kill you," Kasatonin said. "Then, again, I may kill you anyway."

Katya said nothing. He spoke the exact truth. That was the secret of his control over her.

She never knew whether the little or big death awaited her in Ilya Kasatonin's arms.

He dropped the knife at the foot of the bed, undid his belt, and let his clothes fall to the floor. As he walked to the head of the bed, moonlight shone on the smooth, raised scars that covered most of his groin.

Katya made a sound that was half sighing, half sobbing. She rolled over and reached out with her bound hands. She caressed the scars as though they were the sum of her happiness.

A small sliver of flesh stirred beneath her hands. It was all that remained of Kasatonin's genitals. Caressingly she pressed her palms against the cold warmth of the scars.

"I have missed you so much," she whispered.

Kasatonin said nothing. He simply stood and let her run her

hands across his scars and the remnant of his manhood. He wondered as he had a thousand times before if the Afghani devils had been extremely clumsy in their surgery.

Or extremely deft.

Slowly Kasatonin closed his eyes and allowed himself to enjoy Katya's skilled hands.

"I was afraid you would never come," Katya said, sighing.

"Why would you care?" he asked, his voice rough with arousal. "You know you will get nothing from me."

"I will get exactly what I want."

Katya slid closer and lifted her face to kiss the scars all around the slender bit of flesh that remained.

"Not that way," he said.

Kasatonin turned his back on her and headed for the freezer where vodka always waited.

For an instant, Katya's glance slid toward the knife at the foot of the bed.

No, she told herself. With my hands bound, he is too quick, too strong.

She had learned that the first time Kasatonin had taken her. She had the scars to prove it, fine lines radiating beneath her pubic hair.

It had been the first climax Katya had ever known, more addictive than vodka and more dangerous.

Kasatonin returned with the bottle of frosty vodka. He looked at the untouched knife and smiled slightly. He took a swig from the nearly empty bottle. Then he ran the icy, smooth neck down over Katya's breasts.

She gasped and sat bolt upright. "Pig! That is freezing!"

"Only a pig would be allowed into your bed, little mink."

Casually Kasatonin held Katya wrists down with his left arm while he used his right hand to rub the neck of the bottle around her nipples.

Katya flinched at the touch of the freezing glass, but she made no effort to escape. When Kasatonin moved the bottle down her ribcage and across her warm belly, she bit her lower lip in anticipation.

"The bottle is delightful," Kasatonin said softly. "So like you."

"What do you mean?"

"It is icy, smooth, and transparent. As with all glass, it inevitably breaks. But until it does, a bottle has many uses."

"Uses?" Katya whispered.

Kasatonin laughed, lifted the neck of the bottle to his lips, and drank until there was only a mouthful left. Then, watching her, he resumed his exploration of her body with the bottle's long, frozen neck.

Katya held her breath. Cold fire slid down her belly and stopped at the spot where her fine, blond hair began again.

"Many uses," Kasatonin said in a low voice. "That is how Tony Liu is moving the silk."

"What?" Katya asked, dazed.

She never knew what to expect next from her lover.

Kasatonin tipped the bottle. Thick, nearly frozen vodka spilled out into a small puddle on Katya's skin.

"His man brought a glass-blower up from Bangkok," he said.

"Bangkok," Katya repeated numbly.

It was all she could think of to say as she watched the vodka vanishing into her hair.

"The glass-blower is a heroin addict who produces laboratory equipment in return for his daily ration."

Katya gasped and arched her back as the icy vodka seared a path between her legs.

"They sealed the silk inside a glass capsule," Kasatonin added, watching her, "so the fiber would not rot in the tropical air."

Knowing that his lover's attention was finally focused between her legs, Kasatonin released his grip on Katya's hands. Like the vodka, he raked his cold mouth over her until he could suck the warming liquor from her skin. But that was all he sucked.

Shuddering, Katya lay back, vibrating with the sensation of Kasatonin's mouth. She wanted more of it, of him, of the icy glass and the vodka and his teeth scoring her into life.

"My idea," she said in a thin voice. "The bottle."

Kasatonin's tongue strayed in the pale forest of Katya's hair.

"Why?" he asked.

"The silk must be perfect for the Japanese lord."

"It nearly got me killed."

As Kasatonin spoke, he poured the last of the vodka over Katya's pubic hair.

"Is that why you are so wet?" he asked. "You like the idea of my death?"

Before she could answer, his mouth was all over her. Teeth raked her until she writhed and pleaded for the release that he held just beyond her reach. His tongue stabbed her but could not satisfy her.

He knew it. He enjoyed her torment, so like his own had been since the mujahedeen had carved him up as a warning and sent him back to Russia.

Then the cold Katya had come to him and he had learned that even ice could burn under the right conditions. He had learned something else, too. Satisfaction of a kind was still possible for him. Barely.

It was why he hadn't killed her when she tried to cut his throat.

Katya made a hoarse sound as ice penetrated her roughly, repeatedly. It was what she craved, yet it wasn't enough.

They both knew it.

Kasatonin put his head between her legs. Recklessly he raked her aroused skin with his teeth, tasting vodka.

Ice inside her, fire outside, Katya tried not to scream at the intense pain. And the pleasure. She pushed at Kasatonin's head with her bound hands.

"Stop," she said harshly.

"No. I like it this way."

"It is too rough!"

"Poor little mink," Kasatonin mocked. "Is it really too rough? Or not rough enough?"

His teeth closed, tearing sensitive flesh until he tasted blood and vodka. Katya bucked and writhed against him. Then he tasted a different liquor as she climaxed. He laughed aloud.

"I am good only for the rough work," Kasatonin said, lifting his face. "That is why you come for me and no other."

Then he toyed with and tormented her some more until she lay spent and gasping, begging him to stop. After a time, he did, but only when he was certain that he had aroused her yet again.

And not satisfied her.

Calmly he picked up his knife and sliced the velvet bonds from Katya's wrists.

"Like me, you are good only for rough work," he said.

He pulled himself up her body until he lay heavily against her. Then he rolled over onto his back, dragging her with him.

"Rough work," Katya repeated raggedly. "That is what I have in mind for you."

"You mean this?"

Kasatonin thrust his scarred groin hard against her. Just enough of him remained to torment both of them.

Katya's breath caught, part from pain and part from pleasure.

"Yes," she said hoarsely. "That rough work and then another kind."

With a practiced motion, Katya reversed her position until she could hold the remnant cock in her mouth and offer her own bruised flesh in return.

Kasatonin's fingers tightened around the knife. This was his time of greatest vulnerability. He knew it.

He craved it.

"What rough work?" he asked.

"You should have killed those fools in Lhasa," she said, sucking lightly, teasing him.

But she didn't tease him too much. The knife in his hand was as much promise as threat.

"The one from Risk Limited?" Kasatonin asked, his voice a bit strained.

Triumph flicked at Katya as delicately as Kasatonin's tongue. Nothing but her clever, dangerous mouth could call the maimed remnants of her lover's cock to life. Or half-life. She was never certain.

It was the one question Katya knew would bring her death at Kasatonin's hands.

"That American," Katya said, "and also the woman."

"She is nothing."

For a moment Katya was too busy at her work to answer. When she knew Kasatonin was close to his limit, she released him.

"There must be no—how do the Americans say it?—frayed ends," Katya explained.

Kasatonin frowned, then nodded curtly.

"You are right," he said. "No loose ends."

Katya rewarded him with a swift suction that was just short of pain.

He thrust against her mouth, moving more and more rapidly until he jerked like a puppet on a string.

Relief curled through Katya. Tonight she would survive.

But tomorrow?

Shivering with dread and anticipation, Katya's mouth moved over Kasatonin's scarred body, loving him in the only way she could.

Chapter Ten

Washington, D.C.
November

*My choice, Dani, not yours. You don't owe anyone anything.
Remember that if they come after you.*

As Danielle Warren climbed into a taxi, she wondered if the
invitation to meet Elmer Johnstone and discuss preservation of
historic fabrics came from the enigmatic "they" Shane had
mentioned.

Of course it didn't, Dani told herself briskly for the tenth
time in as many minutes.

After several weeks back in Washington, D.C., it seemed to
Dani as though her summer in the high desert of Central Asia
and her brush with illegal trading in artifacts and death was
only a dream.

Granted, it was an unsettling dream at times. Particularly
when Dani remembered the man with the dark hair, dark eyes,
and dangerous smile.

A dream, that's all, Dani insisted.

Sometimes she even believed it.

Yet the bite in D.C.'s air kept nibbling at the edges of Dani's memories. The wind whispered to her of Tibet's chill and a hut high in a hidden valley where a man who moved like a warrior had once meditated upon being a monk.

This is D.C., not Tibet, Dani reminded herself. Look at the elms and oaks. Tibet doesn't have trees worth mentioning.

As Dani had been instructed by the polite, enigmatic note from Mr. Johnstone, she stopped the cab in front of the new wing of the National Gallery of Art. When she got out, leaves stripped from elms along the mall swirled around her. In the distance, the big oaks in front of the Capitol building stood regally bare against the gray sky.

The subtle tension that had built since Dani had received the invitation eased as she looked around. She loved the long mall that marched down the heart of her adopted home. Each change in season renewed her pleasure in the city and in life.

A stout man in a gray overcoat glanced up from his copy of *The Post* as Dani paid the cab driver and turned toward the museum. She wondered if the man was Johnstone.

He had no such doubt as to her identity.

"Ms. Warren," he said, offering her a soft, pudgy pink hand. "I'm Elmer Johnstone."

Dani smiled with the automatic civility of someone who has attended too many faculty teas. Despite her smile, her hazel eyes measured Johnstone as though he was a piece of fabric presented for her evaluation.

"Mr. Johnstone," Dani said, taking his hand.

Beneath the well-cut, half-buttoned topcoat, Johnstone was dressed in a conservative blue suit, white shirt, and a yellow bow tie that had been shaped by human fingers rather than a production line machine. The bow tie was the kind of individualistic touch that could have been the trademark of a Southern senator, a wealthy lobbyist, or an eccentric member of the Washington press corps.

"Good of you to come," Johnstone said, his voice warm.

Politician or lobbyist, Dani decided silently. No reporter would bother to butter me up.

"I'm always willing to come to the National Gallery to talk

about the 'proper preservation of historically meaningful and archaeologically significant fabrics,' " Dani said.

Johnstone's smile changed slightly as he recognized her precise recital of the letter he had sent by messenger yesterday.

"Ah, yes," Johnstone said, his round face suddenly downcast. "Well, that's what I need to explain to you. In this particular instance, there's a problem to be overcome before we get to the 'preservation.' That is, um . . ."

He paused as though searching for the correct phrase.

Dani smiled frostily, waiting.

Johnstone sighed.

"I'm afraid you have caught me out," he said finally. "I'm not with the National Gallery—"

"Who are you with, then?" Dani interrupted.

"—but I wanted to speak with you privately for a moment," Johnstone continued without a pause, "and there's no place quite as private and yet as safely public as Pennsylvania Avenue on a cold fall day. Shall we walk?"

"Does this have to do with ancient fabrics or not?"

"Yes."

Still, Dani hesitated. Johnstone looked harmless enough, but she wasn't a fool. Washington, D.C. was home to many a scoundrel, whether elected or simply self-appointed.

"Don't worry," Johnstone said, smiling. "Not only am I happily married, I'm no match for a fit young woman who climbs rooftops in Lhasa and walks mountain trails off the highway to Katmandu."

For the space of several heartbeats, Dani simply stared at him.

She hadn't discussed Lhasa with anyone. Period.

"Tibet?" Dani asked calmly. "I was there with the hill tribes recently."

"And with a thief called Feng."

"Feng? You must be mistaken. My translator wasn't called Feng. Nor was he a thief."

Johnstone nodded approvingly.

"As he said, an innocent, but not a stupid one."

"He?"

"Shane Crowe, of course."

This time it was harder for Dani not to show a response.

"I work for Risk Limited," Johnstone said. "Shane is an old friend of mine. Saved my life, as a matter of fact. Just as he saved yours."

Dani didn't miss the light stress on the last sentence.

You don't owe anyone anything. Remember that if they come after you.

Apparently "they" had.

Shane had been right about that, but wrong about the rest. Dani owed her life to him.

In truth, she owed Shane even more than that. He had taught her that at least one big man could be trusted not to use his strength against a woman.

Of the two debts, Dani wasn't sure which was bigger.

"Did Shane send you?" she asked bluntly.

"No. His boss did."

"But not Shane."

Dani didn't know why she was disappointed, but she couldn't deny that she was.

"No," Johnstone said. "Shane was against the idea. He was rather tedious about it, if you must know the truth."

With that, he glanced at the fat stainless-steel Rolex Oyster on his wrist. The watch looked remarkably utilitarian for a man in a yellow bow tie.

"I'm afraid we're on a rather short clock, as Gillie would put it," Johnstone said.

"Gillie. Shane mentioned him."

"Did he? Unusual. In any case, Gillie thought it would be instructive for you to see what Risk Limited is up against in regard to the silk Shane lost in Lhasa."

My choice, Dani, not yours.

And he had chosen to save Dani rather than the silk.

"Shall we walk?" Johnstone asked.

"Yes," Dani said abruptly. "I think we shall."

Johnstone led the way up Pennsylvania Avenue toward Capitol Hill three blocks away. He moved with a springy step that was surprising for a man of his weight.

While Johnstone walked, he talked.

"As you might have guessed from my accent, I'm Canadian," he said. "I was the Iranian correspondent for the *Toronto Globe and Mail*."

Now I recognize the name," Dani said. "Several years ago you were taken hostage by rebel Kurds, weren't you?"

Johnstone nodded. "I'm impressed by your memory."

Dani shrugged.

"I've spent time in Kurdistan myself," she said. "They have a long history of marvelous fabrics."

Johnstone smiled rather grimly.

"My memories of the Kurds are not as, um, esthetically pleasing as yours," he said.

"Understandable." Dani frowned. "Come to think of it, I never heard about you being rescued. You just sort of disappeared from the news."

"My company wrote me off publicly, claiming they would never pay ransom as a matter of principle."

"Charming."

"Intelligent," Johnstone corrected. "My company already had hired a private security firm specializing in kidnap and ransom cases."

"Risk Limited," Dani said.

It wasn't a question.

Johnstone nodded. "Precisely."

"Private, not government," Dani said.

But there was skepticism buried in her bland words.

"Very private," Johnstone said. "In the postmodern world, large units—be it governments or multinational corporations—simply aren't capable of putting out small fires before they become conflagrations."

Dani didn't argue the point. She had watched hostage negotiations go on interminably. Too often, the results were headlines and dead hostages, all of which was instantly forgotten with the next act of terrorism.

"What, exactly, is Risk Limited?" she asked.

"An international consortium of men and women who have

proven their ability to operate in hostile and unstructured environments.''

"Try it in plain English."

Johnstone smiled.

"Risk Limited," he said, "gets the job done in places where nobody awards points for style."

Dani couldn't help smiling.

"Oh, I don't know," she said. "Shane had a very distinctive style."

"Umm?"

"Integrity matched with strength and intelligence," Dani said succinctly.

"Integrity," Johnstone said, tasting the word. "Interesting."

"You don't think Shane has it?"

"Oh, I'm quite certain he does. Most people misjudge him, however. They assume he is a brute rather than a gifted negotiator."

"Negotiator? I suppose you could call a gun a negotiating tool," Dani said dryly.

"I didn't say Shane was Mother Teresa. When negotiations don't work, he falls back on other skills. That's how he rescued me."

"Talking?"

"Actually, he never made a sound. He knocked out a guard in the courtyard below my window, climbed the rock wall barehanded, and came through the window."

"Then a long ride under a smuggler's seat, right?"

"Not in my case. A brisk five-minute walk and a waiting helicopter."

"Shane always does seem to have one of those on hand," Dani said.

"Easy enough, as long as you don't mind paying a thousand dollars an hour for standby time," Johnstone said.

Dani blinked. "Risk Limited must have a ferocious overhead."

"They make up for it by charging ferocious fees. Rescuing me cost my company nearly a million dollars."

You don't owe anyone anything.

Like hell I don't, Dani thought bitterly. I got myself into trouble. Shane and Risk Limited got me out.

And an Azure monk called Dorjee. I can't forget him.

He made his peace with himself and his gods when he volunteered to drive the truck. All we can do is make sure his sacrifice isn't wasted.

"How much money did I cost?" Dani asked.

Saying nothing, Johnstone looked both ways before he guided Dani across Pennsylvania Avenue and up the sidewalk along the south edge of Capitol Hill. The Senate Office Buildings loomed.

"If there had been someone to charge," Johnstone said, "such as your archaeology department, your rescue might have cost several hundred thousand dollars."

"A hundred thousand a day or any part thereof?" Dani asked tightly.

"It depends on the location and circumstances."

Dani said nothing.

She couldn't. It would take a lifetime to pay off that kind of debt.

Johnstone glanced aside at his suddenly quiet companion.

"Don't look so dismayed, Ms. Warren. Shane was already working on the case for another client. He insists that your rescue was, um, a 'charitable contribution' on the part of Risk Limited."

"Corporations don't run on charity."

"That's why Risk Limited isn't a corporation." Johnstone smiled winningly. "In any case, Shane said you didn't weigh enough to matter on the fuel consumption."

Dani remembered being carried to the helicopter. The feeling of safety had been overwhelming.

"I was very lucky," she said softly.

"We both were. We both owe our lives to the same man and to the same organization."

"Yes."

"My debt to my rescuer is why I am what I am today."

"Which is?" Dani asked.

"Since I met Shane Crowe, I've been a public relations consultant for Risk Limited."

"One of the ones paid *not* to get their name in the headlines?"

"Succinctly put."

"Shane's words, not mine. But it still sounds like the CIA to me," Dani added.

"Innocent, but not trusting. An interesting combination."

"Innocent or not, a woman alone in the world develops a lack of trust very quickly," Dani retorted.

"Then I'm doubly surprised you reached out in Lhasa's darkness and took Shane Crowe's hand."

Dani's breath came in with a rushing sound.

"So am I," she whispered. "I still don't know why I trusted him."

"Perhaps the dead man at your feet had something to do with it," Johnstone suggested wryly.

"I didn't know who shot Feng. I still don't."

"Amazing. No wonder Shane is so protective of you."

Silently Dani shook her head, but she knew she couldn't deny what had happened.

She did owe someone.

"What does Risk Limited want in repayment?" Dani asked baldly.

"We employ a great many specialists on a part-time or consulting basis."

Dani waited.

"Ah, here we are," was all Johnstone said.

"Here" was the side entrance of the New Senate Office Building on the south rampart of the Hill. Johnstone escorted Dani through the metal detectors and down a hallway to a small guard station in front of a blank pair of double doors.

The uniformed Capitol policeman at the desk compared Johnstone's ID card to a list in front of him. After a moment he nodded and produced two security badges on long chains.

Johnstone put one around his own neck and looped the other over Dani's head.

She picked up the badge and looked at it. Bold print stated that she was an "Invited Guest."

"Invited to what?" Dani asked.

"This way," Johnstone said.

A few moments later he gestured to a discreet bronze plaque mounted on the marble slab beside a nearby door.

Hearing Room, Senate Intelligence Committee
No Public Spectators

Dani started to say something.

"No more questions for now," Johnstone said. "If anybody asks, say you're a consultant for Risk Limited."

"I'm not a—"

"We'll work out the terms later," he interrupted. "But for now, we really must be quiet."

Giving Dani no chance to back out, he opened one of the double doors and led her into the corridors of power.

Chapter Eleven

The hearing room itself was small. There was no public seating, no press gallery. The Intelligence Committee was one of the few legislative groups on Capital Hill that was allowed to do its work in private.

At the moment just five senators were present. One of them was the chairman, a courtly Southern gentleman named Horace Sumpter.

Dani recognized only one other senator, the celebrated John Fitzroy, scion of one of America's oldest and most powerful political families. He occupied one of Connecticut's two Senate seats, a position that would probably be a lifetime tenure.

The other senators seated in their leather chairs seemed faintly familiar if only because they were so similar—large, forceful, commanding, and male. No matter their individual politics, they all wore conservative wool suits.

The textile historian in Dani took note of the senators' sleek wool uniforms. Fine wool suits were the mark of the Washington elite, just as silk togas had been the uniform of Rome's most powerful men.

Dani wondered whether the senators' expensive, hard-woven wool would stand up to time as well as the gold-shot silk she had seen in Lhasa. On the whole, she doubted it. For Tibetans, the ancient silk was an object of reverence and holiness, a tangible bridge to transcendence. The wool suits were merely clothes.

The furnishings in the hearing room consisted of a handsome elevated dais with fifteen high-backed leather chairs, a small seating area for staff members, and a witness table. The horse-shoe shape of the dais had the effect of focusing the room on the witness table where two men and a woman now sat.

Dani's breath caught as she recognized one of the men.

Lhasa was half a world away, yet Shane Crowe looked no less lethal in a dark suit, white shirt, and dark green tie than he had in trekker's technical clothing and a week's beard.

Grimly Dani forced herself to look away from Shane. The other man at the table was tall, with a strict military posture even while seated. His hair was black and very close-cropped.

At first Dani thought the man was heavily tanned. Then, when he turned toward the woman at his side, Dani realized that man was black. Though well past youth, he was one of the most handsome men she had ever seen.

If Michalangelo had gotten a look at this one, Dani thought wryly, his David would have been done in black marble rather than white.

The man murmured something to the woman who sat in the center seat. Her bearing was erect and confident without being in the least military.

When she turned to confer with the man, Dani saw that the woman was fully mature, her finely drawn features somewhat softened by time. She had a look of fierce energy and intelligence. Her cheeks and green eyes were lightly accented with makeup, effective without being obvious.

Dani noted approvingly that the woman was confident enough of herself to let her red hair go gray at its own pace, rather than endure endless, unconvincing dye jobs.

"Cassandra Redpath," whispered Johnstone in Dani's ear.

That explains her confidence, Dani thought.

Redpath had been the first woman deputy chief of the Central

Intelligence Agency, an ambassador to the United Nations, and a highly respected historian.

"What is she doing with Shane?" Dani whispered very softly.

"She's his boss. Quiet, please."

While Dani was digesting the fact that Cassandra Redpath ran Risk Limited, a sixth senator entered the room from a door behind the dais. He waved genially to Redpath as he took his seat.

Redpath returned the greeting with a smile and a nod. She turned to confer with Shane, who sat on her right.

As he bent to whisper something in Redpath's ear, Shane glanced over his shoulder and saw Dani with Elmer Johnstone. Other than a slight narrowing of his eyes, he didn't react.

Still, Dani had the clear feeling that he wasn't happy to see her again.

You don't owe anyone anything.

Nice try, Dani thought angrily, but I pay my own debts.

With a light touch on her elbow, Johnstone led Dani to a single row of chairs arrayed along one wall of the chamber.

No sooner were they seated than the chairman nodded toward the witnesses.

The hearing had begun.

"Ambassador Redpath, it's a delight to see you here in Washington again," Sumpter said. "Your wisdom and insight are always welcome."

He paused to clear his throat and stroke his tie as though to be certain it was in place.

A nervous gesture? Dani wondered. Or is he simply one of those men who is always fussing with his clothes?

"This is an unusual hearing, Ambassador Redpath," Sumpter said, "so you deserve some explanation of its purpose."

"I appreciate your kindness, Senator," Redpath said, "but I can assure you that we know exactly why we are here. Not everyone in this room is enthusiastic about Risk Limited's existence."

Sumpter touched his gold tie bar.

"Ah, hem," he murmured. "Be that as it may, your private organization has performed acts of public benefit."

Senator Fitzroy shifted and tapped a pen on the table. The noise was slight, but enough to distract from Sumpter's words.

"Your unmasking of the nasty relationship between the Defense Minister of Mexico and Colombian drug traffickers was a stroke of intelligence genius," Sumpter said, raising his voice slightly.

"Thank you," Redpath said distinctly.

"So was your successful recovery of Ferdinand Marcos's hidden assets," Sumpter said, "and your confiscation of Russian fissionable materials in Zurich."

Redpath simply nodded and waited. She knew that underneath the butter would come the rebuke.

"Frankly, you have irritated a few professionals in government intelligence services with your efficiency," Sumpter added.

"Risk Limited is not in competition with government agencies," Redpath said. "We are an entirely private enterprise."

Fitzroy's pen beat an increased tattoo.

"With global connections," Sumpter pointed out.

"Multinational corporations aren't illegal."

"Of course not."

"Judge Risk Limited by our enemies, Senator."

"I beg your pardon?" Sumpter said.

"As the result of Risk Limited's assistance to Italian magistrates investigating corruption," Redpath said, "the Sicilian Mafia has offered $100,000 reward for my death."

Sumpter slid a sidelong look at Fitzroy, whose tattoo was becoming insulting.

Redpath ignored Fitzroy.

"An amalgamation of Russian crime syndicates killed a Risk Limited investigator last year in Brighton Beach," Redpath continued, "and another of our investigators was ambushed as he interviewed a witness last year in a case in Cambria, California."

"I presume there's a point to this litany?" Fitzroy asked.

Redpath glanced at Fitzroy.

"Yes, Senator," she said crisply, "there is. Our enemies are the enemies of all civilized peoples. Yet, as private investigators, we do not enjoy the kind of professional courtesy that is usually extended to special agents of legitimate governments."

"Such as?" he challenged.

"Officially sanctioned secrecy."

With that Redpath turned her attention back to Sumpter.

"Therefore," she said, "Risk Limited keeps as low a profile as possible. We are very much concerned about the potential danger to our employees from hearings like this."

Sumpter nodded. Then he leaned forward and looked down the dais at his New England colleague.

"Just to make certain that the record is clear," Sumpter said, "as with most of the hearings of this committee, our proceedings are off the record in their entirety."

Fitzroy looked bored.

"Ambassador Redpath and her colleagues are here today voluntarily," Sumpter continued. "There are to be no leaks of testimony, no stories planted with reporters about Risk Limited's actions, nothing of that sort."

Fitzroy looked at his watch. An aide leaned forward and began whispering in the senator's ear.

"With that understood," Sumpter said, "I yield the floor to my good friend, Senator Fitzroy, who personally requested this appearance by Risk Limited."

Fitzroy continued his hushed discussion with his aide for a few moments more. He calculated the time with a precision that had been honed during a lifetime in politics. The pause was just long enough to be rude without being outright offensive.

Dani smiled thinly. It didn't take a Washington insider to realize that Fitzroy wasn't a fan of Risk Limited.

The senator's face, so familiar on both the news and society pages of national newspapers, looked puffy and flushed in person. He had a private reputation as a drinker and a womanizer.

Nothing new there, Dani thought. Most of the politicians in Washington have the same reputation.

The well-scrubbed young man with round eyeglasses and a

hard, preppie polish continued his hushed briefing of Senator Fitzroy. The aide fanned several pages of a short document, pointing to specific passages, and handed them to the senator.

Irritably Fitzroy pulled out a pair of half-glasses and peered at the sheaf of papers. After a few moments more he swiveled his chair away from the aide and faced the witness table.

"Thank you, Mr. Chairman," Fitzroy said. "Let me assure my esteemed colleague that any leaks of material from this committee have not come from my side of the Mason-Dixon line."

Sumpter nodded indifferently.

Despite the carefully mannered discourse, it was clear to Dani that the two men had little respect for one another.

"At the same time, Mr. Chairman," Fitzroy said in a rich, yet clipped voice, "I am concerned about the privatization of international law enforcement. I believe matters of life and death ought to be left in the hands of duly constituted governments."

Sumpter looked uninterested. Obviously it wasn't the first time he had heard Fitzroy's views.

"Specifically," Fitzroy said, turning to Redpath, "I have questions about the operations of private security organizations like yours."

"That's why we're here," Redpath said.

"Isn't it true," Fitzroy said, "that private security has been corrupted by discredited intelligence operatives and ruthless privateers who got free training from legitimate governments and then sold their services to anyone who could pay for them; multinational corporations, for instance, who hire private armies in foreign countries to protect their profit margins?"

Redpath smiled to herself, obviously amused.

"Senator Fitzroy," she said, "your statement is riddled with loaded adjectives and flawed assumptions."

Fitzroy shifted and faced her more squarely, as though surprised by the directness of her rebuttal. He opened his mouth, but she was still talking, giving him no chance to speak.

"Risk Limited hires former soldiers, intelligence officers, and law-enforcement investigators," Redpath said. "I myself am a former public servant of unblemished professional and personal reputation, which is more than can be said of many elected officials.''

''The point—'' Fitzroy began.

Redpath ignored him.

''As for the rest of your monologue,'' she interrupted, ''Risk Limited does indeed work for private corporations around the world. We also work for foreign governments that need international investigations and for individuals who find themselves in need of specialized services.''

''Specialized services,'' Fitzroy cut in sarcastically. ''Precisely which of your specialized services might an *honest* individual need?''

''Advice about how to deal with the kidnapping of a loved one by terrorists or criminal gangs somewhere in the world. Over the years we've handled a number of those cases.''

''For whom?'' Fitzroy demanded.

''You know full well that we promise anonymity to our clients.''

''So you say. *Convenient* is what I say.''

Redpath simply looked at Fitzroy with the attentive patience of the diplomat she once had been.

''Anonymity cloaks criminal deeds,'' Fitzroy said.

''I will defer to your greater experience in that area,'' Redpath answered smoothly.

''But yours is much greater,'' Fitzroy shot back. ''An anonymous group hired Risk Limited to assassinate political activists in Northern Ireland.''

Pointedly, Fitzroy looked at the tall black man sitting beside Redpath.

She leaned closer to the microphone. Though her voice was soft, her green eyes were as hard as gemstones.

''I don't know what you are talking about,'' she said.

''I'm referring to your associate, Sergeant-Major Gillespie,'' Fitzroy said.

The man with the military bearing straightened even more.

''Mr. Gillespie,'' Fitzroy said, ''is a former member of the notorious Secret Air Services of the British army, the rogue unit that has operated so disastrously in Northern Ireland for years now, murdering innocent political activists and destroying civil order.''

"Notorious? Rogue? Disastrous? Murdering?'' Redpath repeated in a clipped voice. Then, coolly, "Preposterous, Senator. As preposterous as calling the Irish Republican Army 'innocent political activists.' ''

"Not at all preposterous," Fitzroy snapped. "Isn't it true that Mr. Gillespie is the man who was identified in the British press as Soldier Three during an official governmental investigation of political assassinations by special British operatives?''

Dani sensed as much as saw the tension that went through both Shane and Redpath. Gillespie's bearing was unchanged.

"I didn't realize that this hearing would involve a discussion of British military tactics," Redpath said neutrally, "or I would have brought along experts to testify.''

"This is a hearing into the activities of private security services and the kind of outlaws they employ," Fitzroy retorted. "You are the only so-called expert required.''

Gillespie leaned forward and whispered in Redpath's ear. She turned to him. For an instant, a look passed between them that was more personal than professional.

Redpath moved her head in a slight negative.

Gillespie whispered again.

Clearly unhappy, Redpath shielded her mouth with her hand and whispered something to Gillespie.

An oddly gentle smile and a negative shake of his head was Gillespie's only answer.

Finally, reluctantly, Redpath slid the microphone toward him.

Gillespie leaned forward and spoke in a deep, rich voice that was haunted by the accents of the Caribbean, Britain, and America.

"I am Ranulph Gillespie, a retired non-commissioned officer in Her Majesty's 22nd Special Air Services Regiment," Gillespie said. "I am also the man publicly identified as Soldier Three during the hearings you mentioned.''

Redpath's mouth tightened.

"I committed no act that could be considered improper,''

Gillespie said. "That was the precise finding of the inquiry you mentioned."

"A *British* inquiry," Fitzroy said.

"The 'innocent political activists' involved in the incident under inquiry," Gillespie continued, "were two young Irishmen carrying an Armalite AR-15 assault rifle, three hand grenades, and a Browning Hi-Power nine-millimeter pistol."

Fitzroy tapped his pen on the table.

"I will concede, Senator," Gillespie added, "that the two were naive if not innocent. We later discovered that they had been set up by their comrades in the Irish Republican Army."

"I doubt that."

"Doubt whatever you wish," Gillespie said. "The proof is incontrovertible. In an effort to create an international incident, the IRA deliberately staked those boys out like lambs for the slaughter."

"You admit they were boys."

"Senator, at our age, half the world seems boyish."

Sumpter snickered.

Fitzroy merely looked annoyed at being reminded of his age.

"If I am guilty of anything," Gillespie added, "it is simply of being a better shot than either of the two young men who tried to kill me."

With a sharp movement, Fitzroy looked at his aide, who was flipping quickly through documents.

Redpath leaned over and spoke into the microphone she had ceded to Gillespie.

"What should interest you, Senator Fitzroy," Redpath said coolly, "is the fact that the two young Irishmen were armed with weapons purchased with money that was raised in the United States."

Fitzroy spun back to face Redpath.

"Most of the money," she said, "was ultimately traced to Irish Republican bars in the Northeastern part of the United States. The owners of those bars are among your most faithful political contributors."

A deep red flush spread across the senator's face.

"Are you suggesting some connection between myself and terrorism?" he thundered.

"The Ambassador would never do that," Gillespie replied calmly. "She is merely establishing two discrete facts. Conclusions are for others to draw."

Fitzroy glared at the cool, deliberate soldier.

Gillespie smiled.

Finally Fitzroy turned his glare on the young staff aide who hovered at his elbow.

The aide had an East coast polish and well-tailored appearance that spoke of ambition, schooling, and family connections. His eyes were fixed on Gillespie, as though he didn't quite believe what he had just heard.

Belatedly the aide realized that the senator was waving the sheaf of prepared questions in his face like a flag. He turned to his boss.

Behind his hand Fitzroy hissed a sibilant question. The young aide's helpless shrug was eloquent. He took the papers from Fitzroy, riffled through them, and pointed to another passage.

Fitzroy ran his eyes over the section quickly, shook his head, and shot the young aide a look that could have melted glass.

"Mr. Chairman," Fitzroy said, glancing at his watch, "My aide has just reminded me that a critical matter is being heard in the Commerce Committee, of which I am also a member. If the chair has no objections, I would ask that my questioning of these witnesses be handled by my aide, Sidney March."

Sumpter made a show of looking puzzled.

"But," Sumpter said, "it was my impression that you specifically requested this hearing and discussion. Are you saying the subject no longer interests you?"

Fitzroy flashed the telegenic smile that was his trademark.

"Not at all, Mr. Chairman," he said. "My interest originated in Mr. March's research. It is only fair that he have the experience of questioning the ambassador."

With that Fitzroy handed the prepared questions back to his aide, stood up, nodded solemnly to Sumpter, and walked out of the hearing room.

Sidney March stared blankly at the papers in his hand, then

at Sumpter, and finally at the three people seated behind the witness table. For a moment, the aide was speechless.

He had just realized his boss had thrown him to the wolves.

"When you're ready to proceed, Mr. March," Sumpter said.

March swallowed hard and tried to regain his composure. He shuffled through the papers again, looking for a fact or a question he might use to redeem himself.

"Ambassador Redpath," he began, his voice a little shaky. "Is it not true that your organization operates as a kind of vigilante force, that is to say, without the support of law?"

Redpath took the microphone back from Gillespie.

"Not at all," she said. "Risk Limited operators work within the legal structure of whatever country they find themselves in. If we didn't, we would run the same risk of prosecution as any private citizen of that country."

"But what if the country has no effective legal structure?" March challenged.

"If law exists, we act within it. If not, we act according to the dictates of common sense."

"Your operators are trained in violence," March pointed out.

"Yes. Sometimes it is the only alternative to capitulation."

"Then you approve of the private use of deadly force," March said triumphantly.

Gillespie leaned forward and touched Redpath's arm. She yielded the microphone.

"Few people who use deadly force approve wholeheartedly of it, much less enjoy it," Gillespie said. "Part of my job is to see that no one who enjoys violence is employed by Risk Limited."

Sidney March started to speak, but Sumpter cut him off.

"Mr. March, we are wasting valuable time discussing philosophy rather than facts. What specific incident or incidents have you discovered that led Senator Fitzroy to suggest that Risk Limited acts unethically?"

March's mouth opened and closed twice.

"That's what I intended to develop in these hearings," March said finally.

"That wasn't what I was told at the time Senator Fitzroy suggested this hearing," Sumpter said. "Clear proof was mentioned. Is it forthcoming?"

"I—I—that is, I had hoped—"

"Thank you," Sumpter interrupted. "You have cleared the air admirably."

March flushed and looked around for support from the other senators.

Only one was left. The others had simply slipped out once they saw the way the political wind was blowing.

"I assume that no one else has any questions for these witnesses," Sumpter said.

Silence rang in the hearing room.

"In that case," Sumpter said, "I will thank all three of you again for joining our wild goose chase."

"Our pleasure, Mr. Chairman," Redpath said.

"I'm sure it was."

Sumpter picked up the gavel at his elbow and rapped it firmly on the rich cherry wood dais.

"I hereby declare this committee hearing to be in recess," he said. "Mr. March, I'd like a word with you, please."

"He's not the only one," said a voice in Dani's ear.

She jumped and looked at Shane. She had been so involved with the hearing that she hadn't even heard him approach her. Gillespie was standing beside Shane.

Dani felt like a shrub in a forest. She stood hastily.

"Talk to her later," Gillespie said to Shane. "Right now, Ms. Warren has a meeting with Buddha's heirs."

"Do I?" she asked.

"Yes," Gillespie said crisply. "At fourteen hundred hours."

"I don't salute worth a damn, Sergeant-Major, sir," Dani said with a smile.

Shane chuckled.

So did Gillespie.

"Welcome aboard, Ms. Warren," Gillespie said, "and if it wouldn't inconvenience you too greatly, could you move your charming bum toward the door? We're expected in twenty minutes."

"Buddha's heirs," Dani said. "This is about the Lhasa silk, isn't it?"

Gillespie and Shane both looked around quickly, seeing if anyone could have overheard.

No one was near.

"Yes," Gillespie said in a low voice.

"I have a seminar in forty minutes," Dani said.

"You're covered."

"Excuse me?"

"The ambassador has many former students. Some of them are in academic positions. You're covered."

"Just like that?" Dani asked.

Gillespie nodded. "Are you coming?"

"You don't have to," Shane said quietly. "Remember?"

"Very clearly," Dani said. "Lead the way, Sergeant-Major."

Chapter Twelve

Another, larger Senate hearing had just recessed. The hallway was jammed with reporters and camera crews. Their target of the moment was a senator who was holding forth on the evils of taxation and the necessity to do more for the nation's poor folks.

If the reporters noticed anything contradictory in the senator's statement, none pointed it out.

"Go with Shane," Gillespie said. "We'll be along in a bit."

At Gillespie's signal, Shane took Dani's arm. Moments later he was going through the crowded hall like an ice-breaker through packed ice, leaving an opening for Dani in his wake.

The discreet power of the hand around her arm was hauntingly familiar to her. It reminded her of Shane's disciplined strength and the way he had placed himself between her and whatever might harm her.

Even as she enjoyed the feeling of being protected, it irked her.

This is Washington, D.C., not the wilds of Tibet, Dani thought with irritation. I'm not likely to be attacked in the corridors of the Senate office building.

When Shane reached the revolving door that led to the street, he let go of Dani and stepped into the first compartment. She took the next. Very quickly she was out again in the brisk fall afternoon with the scent of burning leaves in the air.

Shane stood on the sidewalk, waiting for her. His right hand was extended toward her but his attention ranged up and down the street. Somewhere between the hearing room and the sidewalk he had unbuttoned the jacket of his dark suit.

Dani caught a glimpse of a matte-black pistol in a holster on Shane's belt.

For a dizzying instant Dani was back in Tibet. The cool sharpness in the air became bitter cold and the smoke came not from leaves but from a thousand cooking fires.

"Dani?"

She blinked and saw that Shane was standing very close to her.

"What is it?" he asked urgently. "Did you see someone you remember from Tibet?"

"Not someone. Some*thing*."

"What?"

"Your gun. For a minute, I thought we were back in Lhasa."

The subtle tension went out of Shane's stance.

"You heard the ambassador," he said. "Lhasa's a suburb of Washington. Our small blue planet is getting smaller every day."

"If you're trying to scare me, don't bother," Dani said. "I live in Adams Morgan, along with half the cab drivers and all the foreign terrorists in the District of Columbia."

Shane blinked and laughed out loud. Then he looked startled, as though the sound of his own reaction was unexpected.

And out of place.

With a seemingly casual glance, he looked all around before he touched Dani's shoulder lightly.

She wasn't fooled by the ease of his manner. She knew that his clear, dark eyes had missed nothing.

"This way," Shane said.

He led Dani toward a black limousine that was parked nearby. For all Shane's politeness, she was acutely aware that his left hand was never far from the holster beneath his open jacket.

While he opened the door and steered her onto the plush back seat, his attention never left the pedestrian traffic and the street.

Uneasiness slid over Dani like a ghostly caress. Shane was every bit as alert and deadly in Washington as he had been the night he pulled her up on a roof in Lhasa and dropped her into a dark alley.

His knee brushed hers as he slid into one of the two jump seats facing her. The brief contact made her aware of her fashionably short skirt. When she was sitting down, the hem of the skirt stopped inches above her knees.

Shane noticed it, too.

Their eyes met for an instant. He gave her a quick smile that was startling in its frankness.

To Dani the smile was as unsettling as the fact that Shane was armed.

"No wonder you flunked out of monkhood," Dani muttered.

Shane memorized the elegant line of Dani's legs before looking back at her eyes.

"That's not why," Shane said, "but you're still safe for a little while longer."

"From what?"

"Me."

Dani opened her mouth. No words came out.

"I warned you," Shane said. "Remember? You don't owe anyone anything. So if you came along because of some cock-eyed notion that you owe me or Risk Limited, open that door and run like hell."

"But—"

"Last warning," Shane interrupted. "Gillie will be here in a minute."

"I'm here because of the silk," Dani said. "Aren't you?"

"There's silk and then there's silk," Shane said, looking at Dani's legs again.

"Damn it, stop that."

"Surely I can't be the first man who has noticed your legs," Shane said calmly.

"No, but . . ." Dani's voice died.

"But?" Shane offered helpfully.

Dani's teeth clicked together. She was hardly about to admit that Shane's glance bothered her because she was attracted to him.

"Go to hell," she said.

"Already have. Many times. Can't recommend it. That's why I'm telling you to get out while you still can."

Dani gave Shane a cool look and switched her attention to the darkly smoked glass of the limousine's windows.

Shane stretched his long legs out into the area in front of the vacant seat. He slouched down in the jump seat, obviously at ease.

Yet his left hand was never far from his belt.

The limousine door opened. Cassandra Redpath slid into the jumpseat next to Shane. The ambassador moved with confidence and grace. Obviously she was thoroughly at home with limousines and herself.

As the door closed firmly behind Redpath, she dropped a leather bag onto the floor. It hit the thick carpet with a thump, as though full of heavy books.

Gillespie opened the other door and took a seat next to Dani. The door closed behind him with a solid, final sound.

You should get out of this limo before it's too late.

Dani suspected it had been too late since the instant she had put her hand—and her life—in Shane's.

"I'm Cassandra Redpath, and I do apologize for all this hush-hush routine," the ambassador said cheerfully. "It's probably not necessary, but one can never be too sure, given the circumstances."

While she spoke, she took Dani's hand and gave her fingers a companionable squeeze, as reassuring as an aunt with a favored niece.

"And this is Ranulph Gillespie, British Army, retired," Redpath added.

"We met in the hearing room," Dani said automatically.

"Yes, well, sometimes Gillie forgets little formalities when he's on the job," Redpath said.

Gillespie nodded curtly. "Ms. Warren, very happy to meet you and all that."

Then he leaned forward, reached past Redpath and rapped on the bulletproof glass behind the driver. Instantly the limousine started forward.

"Pass it over," Gillespie said, settling back.

Shane picked up the heavy leather bag and handed it across the opening to Gillespie. As they merged with traffic, the big soldier opened the bag.

Dani caught a glimpse of a lethal-looking submachine gun and several clips of ammunition.

"Don't mind the sergeant-major," Redpath said with faint humor to Dani. "He is one of those professional men of arms I was telling the committee about. That means he is aware of enemies you and I never notice."

"I feel so much better," Dani said ironically.

"Gillie is also still a bit puffed up," Redpath added. "He's not used to demolishing U.S. senators."

"Actually, guv, I'm entirely too used to leveling stupid politicians, present company excepted," Gillespie said. "The little sods who work for them are the ones that give me gas."

Gillespie turned and pinned Dani with black, clear eyes.

"What did you think of that act?" he asked.

"I'll have to watch C-Span more often," Dani said blandly. "I had no idea Senate hearings were so interesting."

"It could have been a royal Charlie Foxtrot," Gillespie said.

Dani tried not to show that she understood what he was talking about.

Shane winked at her.

"That sod was going to set up Risk Limited to look like Ollie North's secret army," Gillespie continued. "Then he was going to leak the hearing transcript to a former chum who is now a reporter for the Washington *Post.*"

Dani's dark eyebrows rose.

"What does the aide have against Risk Limited?" she asked.

"Nothing personal as far as I could find out," Shane said. "We didn't get much warning before the hearing."

"So he's just another Washington power junkie?" Dani asked.

"Maybe." Shane shrugged. "From what I found out about

March, he's so ambitious he probably didn't even care that he was being used.''

''Used?''

''Yeah.'' Shane turned to Redpath. ''Did you find out who was pulling March's strings?''

Redpath's smile was almost feline.

''We had a short chat with the young Mr. March,'' she murmured. ''He is really a polite, helpful young man, once he knows on which side of his croissant the jam is spread.''

Gillespie snorted.

''The idea of singling out Risk Limited,'' Redpath said, ''was suggested to him by one of the senior partners at Demby, Kravitz, and Shorr over on Pennsylvania Avenue.''

''Demby, as in George Demby, former chairman of the Democratic National Committee?'' Shane asked.

''One and the same,'' Gillespie growled. ''Officially, they are just your average influence-peddling Washington law firm—''

''—but they are also formally registered agents of a half-dozen holding companies in Luxembourg and the Bankers' League of the Isle of Aruba,'' finished Redpath.

''Aruba?'' Shane asked sharply. ''Then you've confirmed it's the Harmony?''

Neither Redpath nor Gillespie answered, which was enough confirmation in itself.

Shane turned and looked at Dani.

''Jesus, lady,'' he said softly. ''When you decide to step into the shit, you pick the deepest pile on the planet.''

For a moment Dani simply stared at Shane. Nothing in his eyes or the grim line of his mouth suggested he was joking.

''The only harmony I know is musical,'' Dani said. ''How could I have gotten in their way?''

''You tried to save the silk,'' Redpath replied.

''In Lhasa?'' Dani asked.

Shane nodded.

''Of course I tried to save the silk,'' Dani said impatiently. ''That's what I do for a living. I find, acquire, and/or preserve ancient textiles. I've been doing it for years without stepping into the shit, as you put it so delicately.''

Shane's smile was cool, as though he was enjoying a small and very dangerous irony.

"I keep telling you," Shane said. "The world is a tiny little place."

"Meaning?"

"Meaning that the bullet-headed son of a bitch who killed Feng and tried to kill you is a Russian named Ilya Kasatonin."

"How do you know?" Dani demanded, feeling cornered.

Shane sensed it. He shook his head.

"Too late, honey," he said. "You're in it up to your beautiful lips now."

"Kasatonin," Gillespie said, "is a cashiered veteran of Spetznaz."

"Soviet special forces," Shane translated.

"So?" Dani asked.

"In plain words, Ms. Warren," Gillespie said, "Kasatonin is one of the most dangerous men in the world. He is the director of security and all-purpose assassin for the Harmony."

"The Harmony again," Dani said. "What is it?"

Gillespie glanced at Shane and shook his head slightly. Even so, Dani saw it.

"Later," Gillespie said.

"Yeah, right," Dani said in a voice that made a lie of the words. "How do I know that this Kasatonin is who you say he is? Shane never mentioned his name in Lhasa."

Shane looked sideways at Gillespie.

"I told you she was innocent, not stupid," Shane said. "Remember?"

Gillespie grunted.

"You asked for it," Shane said relentlessly. "Hell, you *demanded* it. Well, here it is, Gillie. Enjoy it."

"Bloody, *bloody* hell," Gillespie muttered.

Redpath gave both men a cool look, but said nothing.

The sergeant-major straightened his long legs and propped them on the seat between Redpath and Shane. He laced his fingers behind his head.

For a minute no one said anything.

"There aren't a great many international phone calls made from Lhasa," Gillespie finally, reluctantly, said.

Dani nodded. She knew how difficult it was to get a reliable line down the street, much less across the ocean.

"Some big blond Westerner made several international calls in the week before you met Feng," Gillespie said. "He made one more shortly after Feng was killed. All of the calls went directly to the Caribbean Basin."

"So what you're telling me is that someone saw a blond man with a calling card," Dani said skeptically.

"It wasn't that simple," Redpath said.

"I'm relieved," Dani said.

Redpath smiled faintly. "You must understand, Gillespie is quite reluctant to talk about the ways in which he and Shane work their magic."

"Methods and resources, guv," Gillespie said irritably. "Never discuss methods and resources."

"Parlor tricks," Redpath said.

"Parlor tricks that cost ten thousand dollars before I was through," Gillespie retorted.

Dani winced, adding up the bill for her own rescue.

"Expensive parlor tricks, then," Redpath said shrugging.

Then she smiled, reached over, and touched Gillespie's knee.

"Talk to her," Redpath said gently. "We need her."

The hard, handsome lines of Gillespie's face softened for an instant. But plainly he was still reluctant to discuss the details of his "parlor tricks."

"I once spent a day with an African shaman," Dani said casually. "He explained every sacred amulet and potion in his zebra-skin pouch. I've never broken that confidence, Sergeant-Major. I won't break yours."

Gillespie looked at Dani intently, seeking some sign that she was joking.

"She's serious," Shane said. "You can try keeping her in the dark about everything, but I'll bet the need-to-know approach will get you nothing but bloody shins from this one."

Shane didn't say *I told you so*. He didn't have to.

Gillespie was hearing the message loud and clear.

"After Shane found out about the calls," Gillespie said, "I ordered out one of our Hong Kong operatives. He posed as a communications salesman, dropped in on the purchasing agent for Tibet telecomm, and bought a log of all overseas calls for a one-week period."

"Just like that?" Dani asked. Then, "Scratch the question. Hard currency is rare in Tibet."

Gillespie smiled briefly.

"Once we had the log," he said, "it was tickety-boo. There were something like six thousand calls on the list, but the pattern was as plain as print on the page. Six calls went to a familiar number in Aruba."

Dani digested that. Then she turned to Shane.

"How did you know he was Russian?"

"I told you I spent some time in Afghanistan with the mujahedeen years ago," Shane said.

Dani nodded.

"You only need to see a Spetznaz team in action once," Shane said simply. "If you survive, you remember their fire-and-move tactics for the rest of your life."

Redpath pulled out a blown-up photograph from a file in her leather bag. She handed it over to Dani.

"Is this the man you saw in the alley in Lhasa?" Redpath asked.

The photo showed a tall, well-muscled man poised on the end of a low springboard over a large swimming pool. The shot was grainy, obviously blown up from a picture taken at long distance.

Even so, considerable detail survived. Dani could see the man's face without effort. The three deep scars on his torso stood out clearly. Because he was completely naked, she could see that his genitals had been excised.

"My God," Dani said faintly.

"The Afghanis had an interesting kind of torture that was reserved for Russian special forces troops," Shane said. "Just the threat was enough to break most of them, but apparently not Ilya Kasatonin."

"What I'm still trying to figure out," Gillespie said, "is

how he manages to keep up with our own sweet Katya between the sheets.''

"Use your imagination," Shane suggested.

"I have. No good."

"Let me suggest a few movies for you."

"Suck eggs, mate."

"Who is Katya?" Dani asked.

"Katya Pilenkova owns Harmony Estate," Redpath said. "She also seems to be the glue that holds that group of thugs together. I suppose that little triumph of the feminine collaborative management style ought to gratify me, but it doesn't."

"Thugs? You mean men like Kasatonin?"

"Not quite," Shane said dryly. "The rest are fully intact, if only marginally functional in some cases."

"Kasatonin must have found some way of functioning," Gillespie said. "Katya has her needs, odd though they may be."

Dani gave both men a wide-eyed look.

"I take it the two of you are from the tight-lipped, look-Ma-no-hands school of sex?" she asked.

Gillespie's jaw dropped, then he laughed richly. So did Redpath.

Shane just gave Dani a speculative look.

He's too damned quick, Dani thought. When will I learn to keep my mouth shut around him?

Dani handed the photo back to Redpath. Then she met Shane's eyes calmly.

"That's the man from Lhasa," Dani confirmed.

She looked at Redpath. "I assume Shane was trying to steal the silk, too?" she asked pointedly.

"No more and no less than you were," Shane said, his voice clipped.

"I was trying to buy it for a good reason," Dani said.

"Academia?" Shane retorted.

"Preservation. Ancient silk is incredibly fragile. Despite the tensile strength of the gold woven in with the silk threads, that Feng creature would have destroyed the fabric, even if it was only half as old as he suggested."

"Ah, but it is that old," Redpath said.

"Seventh century B.C.?" Dani said sharply. "I doubt it."

"The legitimate owners of the silk are quite certain of its age and provenance."

Silently Dani considered her own memories of the silk. Then she shrugged. "Perhaps," she said neutrally. "In any case, the silk I saw was quite old. Despite that, the cloth was in excellent shape. Obviously its previous owner knew how to care of it."

Shane looked at Redpath. She nodded slightly.

"That silk is the property of the Azure Brothers," Shane said.

"Azure . . ." Dani said, frowning. Then, "Dorjee. Our driver. Was he an Azure monk? Was that why he risked his life for us? Because the silk was sacred to him?"

"Yes," Shane said.

"Did he make it?" Dani asked starkly.

"He got scuffed up some, but he made it."

Dani let out a long breath.

"Thank God," she said in a low voice. "The thought that he might have died because of me was . . . unbearable."

Gillespie shot her a quick look that was a mixture of surprise and approval.

Redpath simply nodded, as though the words confirmed an opinion she already held. She reached into the folder and produced another photo.

"Was this the silk Feng showed you the night Kasatonin attacked?"

For a time Dani simply looked at the photo. It showed a piece of azure silk in a glass case. The photo had been shot with hard artificial light, but even that couldn't flatten the rich luster of the mixture of silk and golden thread.

The case rested on an altar painted with Buddhist symbols. The room itself was of dark stone. It reminded Dani of the cell where she had hidden for endless hours before Shane came and freed her.

"The silk in this photo looks quite similar," Dani said finally, "but unless I can see—and touch—the weaving itself, I can't be positive."

"But it could be the same silk?" Redpath asked.

"It could be. Or it could be something else entirely."

Gillespie grunted. "Not what I'd call a positive ID."

"Would you rather I lie?"

"No," Shane and Gillespie said together.

"But it would help if you could give us odds for or against," Shane added.

"Have you seen the original silk? The piece in the case?" Dani asked Shane.

"Yes."

"Is it the same color as the silk in the photograph?"

Shane frowned. "Close, but the real thing is more . . . radiant, I guess. There is no other blue quite like it."

"Then the odds are that this is the same piece I saw in Lhasa," Dani said.

Gillespie grinned. "Good news."

"Is it?" Dani asked. "Colors eventually fade. It's unlikely that this silk is as old as the monks say."

"You're the expert," Gillespie said, shrugging. "Old or new, the monks lost it and they want it back."

"The cold, dry air of the Tibetan desert preserves things remarkably well," Shane said with quiet intensity.

"Yes, but—" Dani began.

"This piece of silk has been attended by generations of devoted monks," Shane continued. "It is the linchpin of their system of beliefs. It is as holy to the tribal people as the Shroud of Turin is to faithful Christians. *It was the Buddha's own robe.*"

"I'm not disputing the silk's holiness," Dani said carefully, "merely its probable age."

Shane looked as though he was about to object, then shrugged.

"I've heard very little about the Azure Sect," Dani said, changing the subject.

"They're far more reserved about publicity than the Dalai Lama's Yellow Sect," Shane said. "But the Azure Sect is no less powerful when it comes to the loyalty of the Tibetan people."

"The Azure monks," Redpath added, "are believed to

embody the ancient traditions of the mountain and desert kingdom that built the now-ruined cities along the Silk Road. You
have lived with some of the tribes, I believe?''

"Yes," Dani said.

"Are they profoundly spiritual peoples?"

"Very much so," Dani said. "Their religion is so deeply
woven into their lives that to remove it would be to destroy
their society."

"Precisely," Shane said. "Yet you were trying to buy the
silk anyway."

"Only to save it," Dani said hotly. "And I didn't know that
it was a holy relic."

"Then you should have stayed the hell out of—"

Redpath cleared her throat sharply.

Shane shut up.

"Buddhist Tibet," Redpath said in a mild voice, "is more
a theocracy than a nation-state as we understand it in the West."

"Certainly in the hills and mountains, religion rules the
people's lives," Dani said.

"The city people are more circumspect about their religion,"
Shane said. "They have to be to survive. But they are devout
Buddhists."

"Relics such as this piece of silk are instruments of state,"
Redpath said. "They are focal points of national pride and a
rallying point for political as well as religious sentiment."

"I'm aware of that," Dani said. "It's one of the reasons
that the PRC executes people who traffic in artifacts."

"Except when the thieves are from the Chinese government," Shane said. "Then they just sack up all the sacred
Buddhist icons they can get their hands on and haul them off
to Beijing for 'safekeeping.' "

"Are you saying that Feng was an agent of the Chinese
government?" Dani asked.

"It occurred to us," Shane said. "It should have occurred
to you, too."

"It did."

"Finally," Shane muttered.

"Mr. Crowe," Redpath said.

"Yes, guv. I'll shut up."

"Excellent." Redpath turned to Dani. "You have had several weeks to think about your experience in Lhasa. Have you come to any conclusions about why you were approached by Feng?"

"I think . . ." Dani hesitated, then shrugged. "I think that whoever gave the silk to Feng wanted to make certain that the silk was preserved. Somehow they knew I had the expertise to do so."

"Interesting," Redpath murmured. "You don't think Feng himself was the original thief?"

"No," Dani said flatly. "Feng knew nothing about handling ancient silk. If he had been the one to steal it, the silk would have come to me as a handful of disintegrating shreds."

Gillespie grunted. "You were right, guv. We need her. None of our assets or experts thought of that."

Shane's mouth flattened but he said not one word.

"Will you help us?" Redpath asked Dani.

"How? I'm an academic, not a warrior."

Redpath laughed. "Risk Limited uses far more experts of various kinds than, er, warriors."

Dani didn't answer. She simply waited and watched the intent, emerald eyes of the other woman.

"You have unique knowledge of ancient silk in general," Redpath said, "and of the stolen silk in particular. You have proven your ability to think analytically. Shane tells me that you handle yourself well in situations of physical danger."

Surprised, Dani glanced at Shane.

"I said you could keep your mud in a ball," he muttered.

"Thanks, I guess," Dani said.

"It's the truth," Shane said, shrugging.

The limousine began to slow. It turned up a long, fenced lane. Ahead, up on a wooded hillside, was an elegant antebellum mansion. There was a feeling of peace in the pastoral scene. It seemed far away from the violent world where sacred relics were stolen for reasons of greed, politics, or temporal power.

The limousine pulled into a portico and stopped before massive double doors. The mansion was a bright, recently painted white that made the blue of the front doors all the more striking.

Dani recognized the color instantly. She had seen it in the robe of the monk who had hidden Shane and herself after the silk disappeared.

"Azure monks?" Dani asked. "Here?"

"As the ambassador pointed out," Shane said, "the silk has secular as well as spiritual value. D.C. and its suburbs are the Mecca of the secular."

As Gillespie reached to open the limousine door, Redpath stopped him with a touch of her hand.

"Ms. Warren?" she asked. "Have you decided?"

"I decided when I learned how much it cost to keep a helicopter on standby," Dani said.

"You don't owe—" Shane began.

"Bullshit," Dani interrupted savagely. "If Risk Limited needs me, I'm ready."

Redpath smiled.

"We do need you. Now more than ever."

"Why?" Shane demanded.

"Because I'm afraid we can no longer trust our clients completely."

"The monks?" Shane asked in disbelief.

Redpath's short, well-manicured nails drummed briefly on the leather folder in her lap.

"Why?" Shane demanded

"Call it intuition."

"Call it horseshit," Shane retorted.

Gillespie's head swiveled around. He gave Shane a hard look.

Redpath simply smiled.

"Open the door, Gillie," Redpath said. "We have a lot of ground to cover and a very short clock."

Chapter Thirteen

The doorman wore a black business suit, but his weathered skin and short-cropped black hair marked him as Tibetan. After he opened the doors of the limousine, he gave the emerging occupants a deep bow.

When Shane greeted the man in his native language, he grinned broadly, answered quickly, and returned to English.

"Honored it is that Prasam Dhamsa be to know you here, Ambassador," the doorman said, bowing again.

"I wouldn't bet on that," Gillespie muttered so that only Redpath could hear.

Ignoring the sergeant-major, Redpath smiled and bowed very slightly to the doorman.

"The honor is mine," she said.

The doorman escorted the four people to the azure doors, opened one, and ushered them into the foyer.

It was like being taken back in time and space, to a place where machines didn't exist.

Only gods did.

Above the door leading to the inner house, two stylized golden deer supported a wheel. It was familiar to both Shane and Dani, for the same motif appeared at the entrance to all Tibetan Buddhist temples.

The deer symbolized the site where the Buddha gave his first sermon, telling men the four noble truths—suffering, the cause of suffering, the end of suffering, and the path to that end. The wheel itself represented the complex truths and their relationship to man and to the endless cycle of birth, death, and rebirth.

Painted Buddhas sat facing the visitors, hands curled in graceful meditation. Beyond them, partitions had been removed or reshaped to create a great room with a warren of smaller rooms surrounding it on three sides.

Prayer wheels were everywhere, ready to be swept into motion by a passing hand, sending their sacred words spinning up into the void. The air itself was infused with incense and vibrated with the distant, guttural chanting of monks.

To the Western ear, the sound was more primal than spiritual. It was like the rapid breathing of an immense beast rather than the deliberate elegance created by Gregorian monks. There was something hypnotic in the Tibetan chants, something that reached past the individual mind to the elemental tribal awareness beneath.

Belatedly Dani realized that the doorman had vanished. No one else was in sight.

After a minute of waiting, Gillespie assumed a position of parade rest that radiated impatience.

Shane's position was more casual, but every bit as impatient beneath the surface.

"Not your usual greeting?" Dani murmured to him.

"Not by a long shot," Shane whispered very softly. "Prasam Dhamsa must be well and truly pissed off at me."

Gillespie said something in the musical patois of Jamaica.

Redpath shot him a sidelong glance and answered in the same language.

"I don't like being summoned like a bleeding servant, guv," Gillespie said in clear English. Then, much more softly, "Particularly if this is a set-up."

"Nonetheless," Redpath murmured, "we will go softly, softly, here and mebbe catchee monkee, don't you see?"

"If this is a set-up," Shane put in quietly, "I doubt that Dhamsa was part of it."

Gillespie snorted.

"Possibly," Redpath said. "If so, his hold on the Azures must be tenuous, which makes it all the more imperative that we walk softly."

Shane paused, thought about it for an instant, then nodded.

After muttering a few more Jamaican phrases, Gillespie fell silent.

Dani watched the interchange with interest. Redpath might be the boss, but Dani knew that wasn't why Redpath got the last word. Both men clearly respected her intelligence. Both men deferred to her because of that respect.

Yet either man could have broken Redpath like a matchstick. Gillespie was even bigger than Shane. Redpath barely came up to the sergeant-major's breastbone, yet she acted as if it made no difference.

Perhaps it doesn't to some men, Dani thought. Very unusual men.

The thought tantalized her. Experience had taught her that at some point in puberty, the average male became stronger than the average female. Period. All the protestations of sexual equality couldn't change that stark fact. In a pure state of nature, man could take what he wanted from woman if he was willing to use his physical superiority.

Dani still remembered her shock when the grammar school boys she had dominated with her fast reflexes and intelligence suddenly became stronger than she was. Some of the males became even quicker.

Like Shane. Dani had never seen a man move as fast as he had on the roof at Lhasa. He had moved intelligently, as well. Most of all, he had moved with restraint.

Maybe that's all that matters, Dani thought. Men and women coexist successfully when men voluntarily suspend their physical advantage over women.

Steve never learned that. He never wanted to. He relished the fact that he was stronger than me.

He used it.

No, Dani admitted grimly to herself. He *abused* it. And me.

After Steve, Dani had believed that in all male-female relationships, women ended up with the short, bloody end of the stick. Yet watching Redpath, Gillespie, and Shane suggested that there were indeed ways men and women could deal with one another that didn't pivot on brute power.

Dani looked sideways at Shane.

I wonder what basis a woman might use to build a relationship with him? she thought. He is so controlled. Almost obsessively so.

Shane's discipline both reassured her and troubled her.

What would happen if he ever slipped the leash? Dani asked silently.

The idea wasn't appealing to her.

Yet Shane was.

"Gilbert Stuart," Redpath said.

Dani realized that she was staring at Shane—and he at her. His eyes were narrowed, intent, alive with intelligence and speculation.

Quickly she turned toward Redpath, who was examining a painting that hung in the entry hall where they waited.

"Must have come with the house," Shane said. "The monks respect art, even when it isn't their own."

"Why did the Azures come to Virginia?" Dani asked. "The edge of the Beltway is hardly a good place for monks who support the simplicity and spirituality of tribal life."

"Small world, getting smaller," Shane said. "The Azures finally realized they had to reach outside themselves if they were ever to defeat the Chinese."

Something in Shane's voice intrigued Dani.

"Did you help them to realize that?" she asked.

"I don't know."

"It's not a happy realization, is it?" Dani asked.

Shane was silent. In the end, it was Redpath who spoke.

"For better or for worse, the Azures have become quite

worldly," she said. "They use this house to entertain American and European officials whom they want to impress with a taste of the exotic."

"Risky," Dani said. "Politicians are always after the lowest common denominator. The incense, guttural chants, and painted Buddhas are alien to American politicians."

Redpath smiled slightly.

"Agreed," she murmured. "Eighteen months ago, when I attended a seminar here with half the ambassadors in Washington, there was only a whiff of incense and no chants at all. The Buddhas were in shadow rather than spotlighted."

"Dhamsa must figure you're shock-proof," Dani said.

An interior door burst open before Redpath could answer. A detail of Tibetan men in azure robes filed through the doorway, almost at a quick-step, like a well-drilled platoon.

Even in bare feet and a fluttering cotton robe, their leader was large and imposing. He wore round, metal-rimmed scholar's glasses, a black crewcut, and the look of a man who was used to being obeyed without argument.

"Good evening, Ambassador," the lama said carefully. "Difficult I hope was not the journey."

His words were thickly accented, as though English was a trial he endured only grudgingly.

"Prasam Dhamsa, it is always worth a small inconvenience to see you," Redpath said.

She offered her hand.

The Buddhist lama took it with both of his. The gesture might have been intended to be warm and formal, but it ended up merely formal.

"Follow," Dhamsa said. "We eat."

The lama led the way to a comfortable, Western-style dining room. His shrewd black eyes oversaw the seating of his guests and several members of his retinue at a large table.

Dani recognized the food on the table as traditional Tibetan fare—chick peas, freshly baked flatbread, and a rich, greasy stew. She breathed in the fragrances and frowned slightly.

Something was missing.

"Beef instead of yak," Shane said very quietly.

"Oh. Of course."

"But the tea will be made with yak butter."

"Good."

Shane looked surprised.

"I acquired a taste for it in Tibet," Dani admitted.

"So did I. Gillie thinks I'm nuts. So does the ambassador."

"That just leaves more for the rest of us," Dani said, licking her lips in anticipation.

Shane laughed softly.

As the meal progressed, Dhamsa's formality gradually thawed. He particularly approved of Dani's pleasure in the simple food and her obvious familiarity with the small rituals of handling and eating associated with each dish.

Finally the lama turned to Redpath, who was seated at his right.

"My silk?" the lama asked. "Have you word?"

Years of diplomatic training allowed Redpath to hide her surprise at such unusual bluntness.

"We are still pursuing several leads," Redpath said.

Dhamsa hesitated, searching for words.

Redpath could have suggested that he use Shane as a translator, but chose not to. It was a subtle way of telling the lama that she didn't enjoy being summoned like a wayward acolyte into the presence of the divine lama.

"Dr. Danielle Warren will be helping us," she said, nodding toward Dani.

"A female?" the lama asked.

"This female," Redpath said blandly, "is from the archaeology department at American University. Dr. Warren is an expert on ancient Asian textiles."

Probing black eyes reassessed Dani in an instant.

"A scholar," the lama said. "Honored am I."

"The honor is entirely mine, holiness," Dani said, bowing her head. "Although I have heard much of your order, I never expected to meet you in the horse country of Virginia."

"Us you know?" the lama asked.

Dani felt a subtle pressure of Shane's foot against hers. She took it as a warning to say as little as possible.

"I have spent many summers along the Silk Road," she said. "The Azure monks are revered among the tribes."

"Silk Road," Dhamsa said. "The Road of Knowledge. The azure order there was birthed. The spirit it . . . I . . ."

The lama made a sound of frustration.

Quietly Shane said, "Prasam Dhamsa once walked the length of the Silk Road, following the progress of Buddhism from India to China. The timeless spirit of the Gautama Buddha was very clear to him in the vast silence of the land."

The lama smiled and nodded vigorously.

"Yes, my son," Dhamsa said. "Very yes! Again someday the Road of Knowledge I walk, if . . ." He sighed, then smiled sadly. "Complex is the world. Here is my place."

The monk on Prasam's left looked up from his untouched plate of food for the first time.

"Welcome to the Western home of the Azure monks," the monk said in excellent English to Dani.

He was young, young enough to be Dhamsa's grandson. Dani had already noted that his robe was not cotton like the old lama's. The young monk's robe was a fine, sky-blue silk.

"Obviously your expertise will be doubly necessary now," the young monk added.

"How so?" Dani asked carefully.

"The only other Westerner who understood our ways has been ignominiously ejected from Tibet. Is that not correct. Mr. Crowe?"

Shane chewed a mouthful of food very thoroughly, then drank several swallows of yak tea before he made any move to answer the monk.

In America it was good manners not to speak with a mouthful of food. In tribal society, it was a matter of indifference. Shane knew it. So did Dani.

So did the young monk. Shane had rebuked him without saying a word.

"Do I know this youth?" Shane asked the lama.

Dhamsa glanced at the young monk with a mixture of irritation, acceptance, and respect.

"Pakit Rama," the lama said. "A junior monk."

Shane's eyebrows rose. For a junior monk to speak so bluntly in the lama's presence was unprecedented. Shane nodded curtly to Pakit Rama.

"As you have no doubt guessed," Pakit said, "I was educated in the West."

"Your English is excellent," Redpath said neutrally.

"As is yours," the monk said.

Gillespie shot the young man a glance.

The lama said something quick and curt in Tibetan. Pakit's mouth tightened, but he bowed respectfully to the lama and then to Redpath.

"I meant no insult," Pakit said to Redpath.

"None taken," she said.

Dani wasn't sure if she believed either one of them.

"I am afraid Western impatience has infected me," Pakit said. "The silk is so vital to Tibet. . . . There are no words to describe its importance."

"I understand," Redpath said.

This time Dani believed both of them.

"Prasam Dhamsa," Pakit said, "relies on me for advice as to how best to conduct our business with the rest of the world."

Dhamsa's expression suggested that the young monk's advice was not always welcome.

Shane understood the lama's ambivalence. It was hard to straddle the fence between spiritual simplicity and geo-political complexity.

Hard, hell, Shane thought. It's impossible. At least it was for me.

"The Western education that makes my holy leader so uncomfortable was in international politics and diplomacy," Pakit said.

"Stanford or the University of California?" Redpath asked.

Pakit looked startled. "Stanford, but how did you know?"

"Californians have an accent."

"Truly? I hadn't noticed."

"Don't worry," Redpath assured the young man. "Television is leveling all linguistic differences in the U.S. Your accent is, or soon will be, the dominant one."

Smiling slightly, Dani took a sip of tea with yak butter and savored memories of summers spent along the Silk Road.

"Much of what you have written was required reading in my courses," Pakit said to Redpath.

It should have been a compliment. Yet something in Pakit's tone suggested very subtly that if the material hadn't been required, he wouldn't have bothered reading Ambassador Redpath.

Shane sipped tea and looked as relaxed as Dani. He wasn't. He sensed that Pakit resented Redpath's presence.

Probably just pride, Shane thought to himself. It gets young men every time. Pakit wants to be the sole influence whispering in Prasam's ear.

"Some of my writings were done before you were born," Redpath said blandly. "I'm sure you found them out of date."

Pakit blinked, surprised. Then he smiled oddly.

"The world changes quickly and radically," Pakit agreed. "The institutions that survive must change with it."

Dhamsa frowned and shifted in irritation.

"The world may change," Redpath said, "but human nature remains unchanged and unchanging. Ambition, greed, pride, fear, sexuality. They are constants."

"A very old-fashioned outlook," Pakit said.

"Thank you," Redpath murmured. "I find little in postmodernism to recommend it."

Shane hid his smile in his cup of tea. He suspected that the young monk would discover that crossing verbal swords with Cassandra Redpath was a fast way to learn just how stupid you were by comparison.

Pakit grunted. "His holiness shares your views."

"Yes," Redpath murmured. "Through Mr. Crowe, the lama and I have enjoyed many philosophical discussions."

"I see now why he chose to entrust you and your men with the silk relic."

"You sound as though you disagreed with the lama's decision," Redpath said.

Pakit shook his head emphatically.

"I saw no need to post a guard on the silk in the first place," the young monk said. "It merely drew attention to the relic."

Dhamsa spoke softly in Tibetan. Shane translated.

"The Buddha's Robe is at the heart of Tibetan culture," Shane said. "The Chinese government understands the power of such religious symbols, even if some of the younger Azure monks do not."

Pakit rested his elbows on the table, steepled his fingers, and stared directly at Dhamsa. The young man's smile was cool.

He reminded Dani of the lawyer setting his teeth in an argument he had already rehearsed.

"We Tibetans must make our peace, eventually, with the People's Republic," Pakit said calmly in English.

"Must we?" asked the lama.

"Yes. They are the future."

Dhamsa said something in Tibetan.

Shane translated quietly.

"His holiness says that many futures have come and gone," Shane said. "Buddhism remains. It is the enduring essence beneath all change. It is the Great Unchanging."

Pakit shot Shane a narrow-eyed look.

"Is my translation lacking?" Shane asked the younger monk.

"It is excellent."

"You are gracious," Shane said indifferently.

"The fact remains," Pakit said, "that the People's Republic is no more dangerous to Tibet than any other central authority."

"Perhaps," Shane said. "Most Tibetans believe differently. They believe that the warrior-king Gesar will return. Then Tibet will again enjoy the freedom that comes with a just ruler."

"Most Tibetans have never been more than twenty miles from their birthplace," Pakit said.

"That's why they value their religion," Shane said. "It is bred into their very bones. It is the air they breathe, the sky overhead, the stone beneath their feet. It is the transcendent made tangible."

"Religion and modernism can coexist very well," Pakit said. "Look at America."

"In America, the government keeps its hands off religion," Shane said. "The PRC doesn't."

"Superficially, yes." Pakit said, "but in truth, the People's—"

"Enough it is," Dhamsa interrupted bluntly in English. "Silk important. Talk wasted."

He set down his teacup with a distinct thump.

Pakit reached for his own tea, sipped, and spoke again.

"I apologize," Pakit said quietly. "His holiness, as always, speaks of essence while lesser spirits learn."

Dhamsa's expression softened slightly. He gestured for Pakit to continue to take the burden of English conversation from the lama's shoulders.

"I counseled against guarding the silk that had once graced the Gautama Buddha's flesh," Pakit said.

Dhamsa looked less pleased.

"Events have proven my fears were well-grounded," Pakit pointed out. "There are thieves in this world who are too clever even for the renowned operatives of Risk Limited."

Dhamsa grunted.

Gillespie shifted in his chair, calling attention to himself for the first time. He was getting impatient with the well-educated young monk who loved the sound of his own voice.

"Don't bet on it, mate," Gillespie said. "We're pursuing some hot trails."

"Truly?" Pakit asked. "Then why is the famous Mr. Crowe here instead of in Tibet?"

Gillespie looked at Redpath. She was sipping the loathsome yak butter tea as though it was fine wine.

"We follow where the trail leads," she said after a moment.

"In other words, you believe the silk has already been taken from our kingdom," Pakit said.

Then he repeated the same thing in Tibetan, as though to make certain that Dhamsa understood the full extent of the catastrophe.

It wasn't necessary. Although the lama spoke English only with difficulty, he understood it quite well.

"The man who stole the silk from Feng wasn't Tibetan," Shane said. "It's doubtful he would remain in Tibet."

Dhamsa spoke quickly in Tibetan.

"But why would anyone remove the silk from Tibet?" Pakit translated, alarmed. "In Tibet the silk is an object of veneration. Removing Buddha's silk from Tibet would be like removing the Holy Lands from Jerusalem. It is pointless!"

Dani gave the young monk a surprised look.

"Surely you have explained to his holiness about collectors?" Dani said to Pakit.

"I . . ." Pakit's voice faded. He looked deeply troubled. "I had never thought of such collection in conjunction with holy relics."

"Then you are more Buddhist than modern, despite your Stanford education," Shane said.

"Collection," the lama said. "Explain, please."

"There are silk collectors all over the world," Dani said. "Ancient silks can be as valuable as paintings by Europe's Old Masters or Grecian marble statuary from the time of Pericles."

Dhamsa became very still, as though gathering strength for a battle that could destroy him.

"The Japanese are particularly avid collectors," Dani said. "They have the cultural history to appreciate ancient silk, the pride of true collectors, and the money to drive prices into the hundreds of thousands of dollars for certain textiles."

"What might happen if the thief was involved with such secular collectors?" Pakit asked.

"The silk would probably be sold to the highest bidder," Dani said simply.

"How?" Pakit demanded. "It is so fragile . . ."

Shane gave the young monk a look that was more compassionate than impatient.

"The thieves were careful of the silk," Shane said. "Isn't that right, Dani?"

Tactfully Dani decided against mentioning Feng's incompetence.

"Of course," she said. "The silk would have no value as a handful of crumbling shreds."

Pakit looked appalled.

Dhamsa looked twenty years older.

"You mentioned auctions?" Pakit asked faintly.

"Given the history of the silk," Dani said, "and the way it was stolen from your order, I don't think it will be auctioned."

"Why?" Redpath asked.

"Too public," Dani said succinctly. "Too much chance that word of the relic would get out. Then there would be an unholy stink."

"The silk would be confiscated and returned to its rightful owners," Redpath said. "With suitable and abject apologies from all parties involved."

"Yes," Dani said. "That's why the silk probably will be offered discreetly to a very few private collectors. It might even have been stolen to order."

"Explain," Dhamsa said bluntly.

"The thieves may have had a customer in mind before the silk was stolen," Dani said.

"But what of museums?" Pakit asked urgently. "Much of what exists in museums was simply stolen in the first place."

"Some people see it that way," Dani said. "Others don't. In any case, recent thefts are viewed as just that. Theft."

"Then no museum would take the silk?" Pakit asked, dismayed.

"It's possible, but not likely. Why?"

"A museum or university would care for the silk," Pakit said simply. "Thieves and collectors who buy from thieves . . . who knows what level of skill or caring they have?"

"That's why we must recover the silk quickly," Redpath said.

"It would have been better if Mr. Crowe had not lost it in the first place," Pakit said.

"Shane didn't lose the silk," Dani said. "I did."

Pakit simply shook his head, overwhelmed by the magnitude of what had happened.

"Prasam Dhamsa," Shane said, "your order is revered throughout Tibet. You and your tribal brothers hear things that might be helpful, even if they don't seem important at the time."

Dhamsa nodded distantly.

"Did you receive any recent reports of unusual pilgrimages or overland treks?" Shane asked.

At first Dhamsa didn't seem to hear the question. He spoke softly in Tibetan.

"I had never dreamed that the Buddha's Robe would leave Tibet," Shane translated quietly for the lama, "unless it was taken by the Chinese. It is so fragile, so delicate. Sometimes I think it is like the most devout among us, not yet ready for the world at large."

"We must be ready for the world at large," Pakit said decisively, "or it will devour us. That much I have learned in the West."

Dhamsa kept talking.

Shane translated simultaneously, giving Dani the eerie feeling of actually understanding the lama's speech.

"In answer to your question, the Chinese authorities have been unusually vigilant. Nothing moves by road or airplane without being searched."

"There are other ways out of Tibet, holiness," Redpath said.

"I suppose one could sprout wings like the vultures who oversee the sky burials," Pakit said tartly.

"I had in mind escape routes that might be so difficult they would never be considered by the Chinese authorities," Shane said.

Dhamsa looked thoughtful. He spoke curtly in Tibetan to Pakit.

"One of the brothers who had been at a monastery in eastern Tibet," Pakit said, "reported that a band of pilgrims was seen heading into the Tanglha mountains."

"When?" Shane demanded.

"Some days after the theft," Pakit said.

Dani sensed the focus in Shane. It was like a current running through a bare wire, hidden yet vibrant with energy.

"Why weren't we told?" Shane asked softly.

"They were simply European trekkers looking for new mountain peaks to conquer," Pakit said. "We have many such in Tibet."

Shane nodded and said nothing.

But he had changed. The vivid intensity was gone. Now he was turned inward, almost shut down.

Yet Dani sensed the mind at work inside the silence. Abruptly she believed that this Shane had spent six months in meditation. The combination of calm and focus in him was almost tangible.

"Was there anything else reported?" Redpath asked Dhamsa.

"No."

Quietly Redpath took control of the conversation. Though she never seemed hurried, much less rude, she managed to wrap up the dinner in less than fifteen minutes. The necessary exchanges of good wishes on departure took only five.

No sooner had Dani, Shane, Gillespie, and Redpath climbed into the limousine and the door closed than Redpath turned to Shane.

"All right," she said. "Spit it out. Why did you want me to hustle us out of there?"

"You remember how Dani and I got out of Tibet?" Shane asked.

"Bloody right I do," Redpath retorted. "I just paid the helicopter bill!"

Dani winced.

"Well, if that route hadn't worked out," Shane said, "my fallback was a raft trip down the Mekong River to the Karen highlands of Thailand."

"So?"

"The Mekong flows through three different nations in Southeast Asia," Shane said. "In each country it is known by a different name. For instance, at its origins, it is called the Nu Jiang River."

"What is your point?" Redpath asked impatiently

"The closest peaks to the Nu Jiang are in the Tanglhas. There are few peaks of any stature in the Tanglha range. I doubt that mountain climbers would bother."

For a long time, Redpath studied the darkening woods outside the car window thinking "But the Mekong could be an escape route, regardless of what it's called."

Smiling slightly, Gillespie watched her.

Suddenly, she reached for the limo phone. "Gillie?"

"Yes, guv?"

"What's the country code for Thailand?" she asked. "We need to activate another local asset."

Chapter Fourteen

While Redpath was in her private office finishing the series of phone calls she had begun in the limousine, Dani, Shane, and Gillespie waited in the large study of the mansion that was Risk Limited's Washington headquarters.

The building sprawled with quiet elegance across a large lot at the edge of Rock Creek Park in Georgetown. The main floor had been converted into rooms that would have been appropriate for a well-endowed Washington think tank or a wealthy international charitable foundation. There were private apartments on the other floors, where Redpath and other Risk Limited employees lived when they were in Washington, D.C.

Except for the indecipherable murmur of Redpath's telephone conversations, the place was quiet.

"Somehow this mansion seemed familiar when I first saw it," Dani said.

The observation was directed at Shane, who hadn't said three words to Dani all the way back from Virginia.

It was Gillespie who answered Dani's query.

"This was the only embassy designed by Frank Lloyd Wright," Gillespie said.

"That explains it," she said.

Shane said nothing. Since leaving the Azure monks, he had ignored Dani.

Or he had seemed to. Twice she had turned around suddenly and seen him watching her with a cross between hostility and pure masculine interest in his dark eyes.

She wasn't certain which was more unsettling.

To take her mind off Shane, she glanced around Redpath's personal library. It was the size of a small ballroom. Art and books filled the space.

Slowly Dani ran her fingers down the end of a wooden bookshelf. Cool, smooth, civilized, and yet still natural, the feel of the wood pleased her senses.

"Cherry," Gillespie said.

"I beg your pardon?" Dani asked, startled.

"The wood."

"It's beautiful."

Dani looked from the bookcase to the books themselves. Immediately she was lost. Forgetting time, forgetting herself, forgetting everything but the tantalizing knowledge massed in the room, Dani wandered among the bookcases.

Histories, cultural studies, political analyses. Languages both ancient and modern. Leatherbound first editions, illuminated manuscripts, modern hardbacks, university paperbacks. All were present. All were ordered with a subtlety that escaped Dani.

Yet she had no doubt that such an order existed. Cassandra Redpath was a woman who saw connections where other people saw chaos.

"Remarkable," Dani said softly.

"It's a working library, not a showplace," Gillespie said.

"I meant the mind that assembled it."

Gillespie's smile flashed, reminding Dani of just how handsome he was.

"Cassandra is a remarkable woman," he said.

"Obviously. She must read at least five languages."

Gillespie nodded absently. The door to Redpath's private office wasn't completely closed. Most of Gillespie's attention was on the low, soft voice of his boss as she talked to Risk Limited people around the world.

Dani wandered off down another row of bookcases. Given Redpath's background in politics, Dani was surprised to find a wealth of books on art and artifacts among the treatises on philosophy, history, and war.

Islamic decorative art, Chinese bronzes, Celtic art, and late medieval illuminated manuscripts seemed to be particular favorites.

"Amazing," Dani whispered.

"What is?"

She jumped and spun around.

Shane was standing less than an arm's length away. She hadn't heard him approach. Nor had she sensed his presence.

"I'm surprised that there are so many books on art," Dani said.

"Art contains the essence of a society."

Dani grimaced, thinking of what she had seen the last time she strolled through Manhattan art galleries.

"Then we're in deep yak dung," she said.

Unwillingly, Shane smiled.

Dani didn't notice. She had just discovered a first edition of an old French monograph on Persian tapestries.

"I read this in translation," she said, touching the table of contents reverently. "I can't imagine owning the original. It must be worth thousands."

"Probably," Shane said with a total lack of interest.

The volume was well-thumbed and obviously regularly used. It was shelved close to a contemporary study of medieval edged weapons, complete with discussions of the subtle and pragmatic differences between one-hand, hand-and-a-half, and two-hand swords.

"Amazing," Dani said again.

"The money?"

Dani looked up, saw Shane watching her intently, and felt an odd thread of excitement tingling through her body.

"No," she said, reshelving the book carefully. "The mixture

of violence and beauty. It's a recurrent theme in Ms. Redpath's library.''

''It's an accurate reflection of life.''

''I'd like to argue the point, but I can't.''

''No ivory tower for you?'' Shane asked.

The subtly goading quality of his voice irritated Dani.

''I was shaken out of my ivory tower years ago,'' she said flatly. ''I don't spend my days denying the violence of the world around me and then triple-lock my doors every night and never see the contradiction.''

''You just accept violence?''

''Is this a multiple choice test?''

Shane almost smiled.

''Sorry,'' he said. ''Few people can get past violence as a fact of life.''

Dani studied Shane openly. At the moment he looked less lethal, less dangerous, than at any time she had ever seen him.

Yet, she reminded herself, he has a pistol beneath his well-tailored suit coat.

''Always ready for violence,'' Dani said, thinking aloud.

''Always ready for death,'' Shane corrected softly. ''There's a difference. It's the only way to achieve peace in a violent world.''

''Easy enough for a large, fit male to say. You're not likely to meet your match on any street corner.''

''Think so?''

''I know so.''

''You're wrong. It takes only a few ounces of pressure to pull a trigger. Ask any parent who ever left a loaded gun in the wrong place.''

Dani grimaced, but again she couldn't argue the point.

Silver chimes quivered in the silence. It was the second time the crystal clock had sounded the hour since Dani had entered the library.

Grateful for the distraction, Dani walked toward the conference table at the far end of the room, where the clock was a centerpiece.

Ten o'clock.

Dani sat at the long table and studied the unusual clock.

After ten minutes she was no closer to understanding how it worked than she had been after ten seconds.

On the other hand, the fire crackling in the stone fireplace nearby was quite easy to appreciate.

"Crystal technology," Shane said from behind Dani.

She drew a startled breath. The man was unnervingly light on his big feet.

"The whole globe resonates like the crystal inside your digital watch," Shane said. "It was developed by the same people, as a matter of fact. Cassandra did some work for them on a patent infringement case."

Gillespie sat down in a leather chair in front of the leaping flames, warming himself as though it were the dead of winter.

"Ruddy thing's a Charlie Foxtrot, though," Gillespie said.

"What does that mean?" Dani asked innocently.

Shane snickered.

"Totally impractical," Gillespie answered. "Touch it and it loses time. Every new charwoman has a go at it and there's ruddy hell to pay getting the thing right again."

"What exactly is the derivation of 'Charlie Foxtrot'?" Dani asked.

Gillespie looked distinctly uncomfortable.

Belatedly Dani regretted teasing him. Somehow Gillespie was less sure of himself with other women when Redpath was not around.

"Go ahead, Gillie," Shane encouraged.

"It's an American phrase," Gillespie retorted. "You tell her."

Dani turned and looked at Shane as though she hadn't the faintest idea what anyone was talking about. Only the dancing light in her eyes gave away the game.

"It's international radio code," Shane said. "Charlie Foxtrot stands for the letters C and F, which is a polite way of calling something a 'cluster fuck.'"

"Is that related to a circle jerk?" Dani asked, deadpan.

Gillespie looked surprised, then joined Shane's laughter.

"Point taken," Gillespie said. "You may be a little professor, but you aren't an ivory tower type. Bloody good job, too."

Before Dani could ask what Gillespie meant, the door to Redpath's private office opened. She looked tired, but there was a pleased smile on her face.

"One of my old colleagues from Langely is now in drug interdiction in Thailand," Redpath said. "He maintains good contacts in passport control at all the airports in the region."

Any hint of relaxation left Gillespie as he waited. It was the same for Shane.

Redpath yawned. "Excuse me."

"Only if you tell me good news," Shane retorted.

"A large, handsome blond European man tried to board a British Airways plane," Redpath said.

"And?" Gillespie said.

Redpath gave him a feline smile.

"Sadly," she murmured, "the man's South African passport did not contain an entry visa stamp."

"Where was he coming from?" Shane asked.

"The Golden Triangle."

"Karen territory," Shane said. "I didn't know the Harmony had connections there."

"Nor did I," Redpath said. "Apparently Tony Liu has joined the rest of the global thieves."

"Bloody hell," Gillespie muttered.

"I'll second that," Shane said. "Anything else?"

"The local authorities inspected the man's ticket and itinerary," Redpath said. "He was booked to London through Karachi and from there on to the Caribbean."

"Aruba?" Gillespie asked quickly.

"Aruba," Redpath confirmed.

"Lots of people go to Aruba," Shane pointed out. "We have to be sure."

"We are," Redpath said.

"How sure?"

"As certain as it gets, this side of hell. Because the man was coming from a known opium-producing region, he and his effects were searched quite thoroughly."

"Full body cavity, huh?" Gillespie said. "What did they find?"

"It was what they *didn't* find that impressed them," Redpath said dryly.

Shane understood first. He smiled thinly.

"So it was Kasatonin," Shane said. "Did he have the silk?"

"No," Redpath said.

"Was anyone with him?" Gillespie asked.

"No. Not that it would have mattered. For some reason, the local drug officials checked everyone else who had come in with the Russian, regardless of nationality."

Shane whistled softly. "The PRC is really pissed off, if they put out an alert through other nations."

"Agreed," Redpath said. "The searchers found no contraband of any sort."

"Too bad," Shane said. "I'd like to have talked to any passenger on Kasatonin's plane."

"We did lean rather hard," Redpath said, "but no go. The smaller the country, the more touchy the nationalistic pride."

Gillespie grunted. "Did they at least give us a passenger list?"

"No."

"Bollocks."

"We hacked our way into their computer," Redpath said calmly. "A cross-check with intelligence files turned up another passenger."

"American?" Shane asked.

"A Brit," Redpath said. "He's a lab tech of some sort. He's suspected of supplying equipment to the Chinese triads who refine the Karen opium into heroin."

Shane frowned. "So?"

"When the authorities went through his baggage, they found a small vacuum pump and equipment for melting and blowing glass. No opium or heroin though," Redpath said. "Not even the smallest trace."

Gillespie and Shane looked puzzled.

Dani didn't.

"Thank God," she said fervently.

"What's so wonderful about someone hauling a glass-blowing kit up the Mekong River?" Shane asked.

"It means that the silk is being carefully handled."

"How?" he demanded.

"A sealed glass capsule would be a good way to protect the silk," Dani said. "A vacuum capsule is about as perfect as it gets, short of a climate-controlled museum case."

"Excellent," Redpath said. "I'm glad you decided to consult for us, Ms. Warren. Now we know just what to look for."

Gillespie gave Shane an I-told-you-so kind of look. Shane's mouth flattened.

Dani saw, and wondered why Shane had been so against asking for her help in the first place.

"Kasatonin must have been pretty confident, if he didn't have the silk with him," Gillespie said, following his own line of thought.

"The Karens have been smuggling longer than there have been customs laws," Shane said. "If anyone could move a small, priceless shipment through that jungle, it's them."

"Where would the silk be headed?" Gillespie asked.

"Planning on a little theft?" Shane asked.

"One way or another we have to get that bloody rag back."

"Always the pragmatist," Redpath said dryly.

"That's why you keep me around, guv."

"Is that it?" Redpath murmured. "I wondered."

Gillespie winked at his boss, changing his whole appearance from fierce to sensual.

Dani stared in disbelief.

Shane ignored Gillespie and Redpath. He had given up trying to sort out their complex relationship. He simply accepted it.

"Here's the way the silk will come out," Shane said.

He pointed to the crystal globe on the table. Being careful not to touch the subtly vibrating crystal, he traced a route across its luminous surface.

"Gulf of Thailand," Shane said, "then the South China Sea."

His finger swept north and east, pointing to a spot on the edge of the Pacific.

"Hong Kong," Shane said.

Gillespie leaned forward. "Good. We're halfway there."

Shane shook his head. "Do you have any idea how many boats there are in that corner of the world?" he asked.

"A finite number," Gillespie said.

"A *big* finite number," Shane corrected. "Without an informant or some kind of advance knowledge, you might just as well hunt fly shit in a pepper mill the size of the Lincoln Memorial."

For a time there was silence as the four of them stared at the elegant crystal globe as though it held the answer to the only question that mattered.

Where is the silk?

A rush of exhilaration went through Dani. Her intelligence and expertise had never been challenged in quite this way.

It's a global game of chess, she thought.

Then, quickly, she realized that it wasn't. Not quite.

It's more like an international bridge tournament, Dani decided. A game in some ways, but a game where bidding a slam involves something more dangerous than counting trump.

After a time Shane shook his head and swore softly. His expression said that he had worked through all the various combinations only to reach an unhappy conclusion.

"Aruba," he said flatly. "It's all we've got."

Redpath looked at Shane sharply.

"I can't allow it," she said.' 'The Harmony owns that island, down to the last grain of sand."

"I didn't say I liked it," Shane muttered. "I just said that's the way it is."

"We have only one asset there," Redpath said. "Even that one is suspect."

Shane shrugged. "Life's a bitch and then you die. I'll leave as soon as you can arrange transportation."

"No," Redpath said. "You can't go in alone. It's too dangerous."

"Nothing is more dangerous than losing the silk," Shane said almost gently.

Redpath's mouth turned down. She said nothing.

"Why?" Dani asked.

Shane turned and looked at her with hooded eyes.

"Two reasons," he said. "When word of the silk's loss goes out—and inevitably it will—the Azure monks will lose the respect of the tribesmen."

"To them," Redpath added, "Buddha's robe represents the transcendent made tangible. It's difficult for a secular Westerner to accept, but that makes it no less true."

Dani hesitated, then nodded.

"The Azure monks are the glue that holds the Free Tibet movement together," Shane said.

"Somehow I can't see Prasam Dhamsa as a terrorist or freedom fighter," Dani said.

"He isn't," Shane said. "But the very fact of the Azure monks' existence as keepers of Buddha's robe is a potent symbol for Tibetans. A rallying point. A flag, if you will."

Slowly Dani nodded.

"The PRC," Redpath said quietly, "already controls too much of the world's population for the comfort of anyone who believes in individual choice."

"The PRC can't last forever," Dani said. "Look at the Soviet Union."

"The U.S.S.R. disintegrated for many reasons," Gillespie said, "not the least of which was the relentless pressure to produce more and more arms from less and less gross national product. If the pressure hadn't existed, the U.S.S.R. would still be around."

"That's the big picture," Shane said. "Then there's the smaller picture."

Dani turned to Shane. "As in personal?"

"As in professional," he said coolly. "If Prasam Dhamsa spreads the word that Risk Limited can't get the job done, everything Cassandra and Gillie have worked for, everything that we all stand for, won't be worth a handful of warm spit."

"Our reputation can withstand a rude shock or two," Redpath said. "I won't order you or anyone else into the devil's den."

"You're not ordering me," he said. "I'm volunteering.

"But—"

"But nothing," Shane interrupted. "I lost the silk. I'll get it back. If that means expending a small trump or two, so be it. Risk Limited will survive the game."

Dani looked at Shane, faintly shocked at his allusion to cards. She felt as though he had eavesdropped on her own thoughts.

"Trumps?" she asked. "Are they the same as 'assets'?"

Shane nodded.

"People," Dani summarized.

Shane nodded again.

"You're talking about people dying."

"Everyone does, sooner or later."

For a taut moment Dani stared at Shane. He returned her look with absolute calm.

He wasn't just making conversation, she realized with a chill. He meant every word when he said that being ready to die was the only way to live in peace.

But Dani didn't want Shane to die. The depth of her feeling shocked her.

"I'd rather you died later than sooner," she said.

Shane's dark eyes looked at Dani. Again she had the odd feeling that he was seeing into her, judging the emotional truth of her words.

"We have an informant inside The Harmony," Redpath said. "Unfortunately, the informant has not been entirely proven."

"What does that mean?" Dani asked sharply.

"Shane might well find himself with a double agent on his hands."

"My God," Dani said.

"Under normal circumstances, I would forbid Shane from going," Redpath said. "That's my right. I own Risk Limited. I can be an absolute tyrant, should I choose it."

"Do it," Dani said.

"Unfortunately, I may not have that luxury," Redpath admitted.

Gillespie rubbed a hand across his short-cropped black hair.

"I'll go with him," Gillespie said.

"No," Shane and Redpath said instantly.

"Too many people in the Caribbean know you," Redpath said. "You would be a liability."

"No one in Aruba knows me," Shane pointed out. "In fact, damned few people even know I'm a Risk Limited consultant."

"How would you go in?" Redpath asked.

"Five thousand tourists and gamblers fly into Aruba every week," Shane said.

"The Harmony watches every flight," Gillespie countered. "They get their knickers in a twist at the thought of the DEA or the FBI sending intelligence agents in."

"You're forgetting something," Dani said to Shane.

"What?"

"Kasatonin saw you."

Shane's eyes narrowed.

"Okay," he said quickly. "Plan B. I'll get a fast boat over from Curacao. I'll swim ashore."

Redpath glanced at Gillespie, who shrugged. "I can set up a boat run," he said, "or maybe a chopper. No need to take much kit. We'll send Dillman and Souther in as the advance team. They can buy or rent everything Shane would need in Oranjestad."

"They can't rent him a girlfriend he can trust," Dani said.

Shane stared at her, not sure he had heard her correctly.

"A single man is a threat," she said. "A man with a girlfriend is just after a good time."

"No," Shane said instantly. "No way in hell."

"I'm responsible for the loss of the silk, not you," Dani said. "If I hadn't been in the way, you would have gotten the silk from Kasatonin."

"*No,*" Shane said.

Dani looked to Redpath.

"Who's the tyrant here?" she asked calmly, "you or Shane?"

Redpath laughed. "She's right, Shane. You would be less conspicuous with a female draped over your brawny arm."

"Shit."

"Yak or bull?" retorted Dani. "I kept up with you in Tibet, remember?"

"You have the guts," Shane said, "but you don't have the training."

"Oh, I don't know. My ex-husband was the brawny type. I'm told I looked real good draped on his arm."

Shane made an impatient sound.

"Besides," Dani continued, "if you get lucky and actually find the silk in Aruba, how will you know if it's the real thing or an imitation?"

"I've seen the real thing many times."

"Could you tell in the dark, with a touch?" Dani challenged.

"No."

"I can."

"What?" Redpath and Gillespie said as one.

Dani shrugged. "I have knowledge, practice, and very sensitive fingertips. One of my professors said I should have been a safe-cracker."

"Fascinating," Redpath said. "Are there many out there like you?"

"No. Most people rely on scientific analysis. So do I."

"But only as a back-up," Redpath said.

It wasn't a question, but Dani nodded anyway.

"It makes the university or museum or government or whatever more comfortable."

Redpath switched her attention to Shane.

For the space of several breaths Shane was as still and silent as Prasam Dhamsa had been.

Shane knew that sending Dani in made sense. He just didn't like it. The thought of putting her in danger again made him furious.

On the other hand, he didn't have a hell of a lot of choice.

"Can you swim?" Shane finally asked.

Dani smiled triumphantly. "I'm certified as an open-water diver."

For a moment Shane and Dani looked at one another. In that moment, nothing else existed.

"I'll walk you home," Shane said. "If you still want to go with me after that, so be it."

Her breath caught. Then she took Shane's challenge.

"After you, big man," she said, draping herself over his arm.

"Crap," was all he replied.

Georgetown's streets were quiet but for the rustle of leaves on the night wind. Shane strode along the sidewalk quickly. They walked nearly a mile before he slowed.

Dani drew a deep breath and shortened her strides. They were on Pennsylvania Avenue, headed in the direction of her apartment.

"I'm not used to working with anyone," Shane said.

"Anyone, or just me?"

"Anyone. I work better alone. It's why I left the military. It's why I went off to live as a hermit in Tibet. It eats me alive to take responsibility for the rest of the team."

Dani sensed the turmoil beneath Shane's calm surface.

"I've never said that to anyone else," he added. "Gillespie senses it, though. He's never forced a partner on me. Until tonight."

"We did all right in Tibet."

"Aruba isn't Tibet."

"I assume you're talking about more than the climate," Dani said dryly.

"The Harmony is . . . evil. Old-fashioned word, but the only one that gets the job done. If they get a whiff of who we are, we'd be crab bait."

"I won't tell if you won't."

"This isn't a game," Shane said impatiently.

"It wasn't a game back in Tibet. The bullets were for keeps."

Shane tried another tack.

"Why is it so important for you to go?" he asked.

"The silk," Dani said simply.

"You don't believe it's the Buddha's robe."

"Is it required?"

"Why else would you go?" Shane asked.

"To see the silk again. Safe."

The passion in Dani's voice was muted, but very real.

There's only one card left to play, Shane thought. I had hoped not to use it.

Yet even as the thought echoed in his mind, his pulse quickened hungrily.

Shane and Dani walked on for a time, turning automatically onto Connecticut Avenue and then onto her street. Their pace slowed as they got closer to her apartment. She wasn't surprised that he knew where she lived.

A car cruised by slowly on the street beside them like a circling urban raptor. Its interior was dark. Still, Dani could see the outline of a male driver and another male in the passenger seat.

For an instant Dani felt a rush of adrenaline. Had she been alone, she would have quickened her pace, heading for the safety of her building.

Shane glanced in the direction of the passing vehicle. As the car passed beneath a streetlight, there was an instant of eye contact between Shane and the passenger.

The look on the passenger's face changed from cool speculation to uneasiness. He said something out of the corner of his mouth to the driver. The car picked up speed and disappeared.

Shane kept walking as though nothing had happened.

"Weren't you afraid they might be from the Harmony?" Dani asked

"When the Harmony sends for you, they don't cruise your street. They jump out of a closet and shoot your skivvies full of holes."

"Skivvies?"

"Yeah. Shoot 'em low, they don't get over it."

"Lovely."

"Gillie thinks so. It's one of his favorite sayings."

Dani fitted a key into the lock of the heavy security door to her apartment building.

Shane stood with his hands shoved into the pockets of his jacket and stared down at her with hooded eyes.

"What can I say that would make you change your mind?" he asked bluntly.

When Dani looked up from the lock, she was intensely aware of the physical difference between Shane and herself. He loomed over her like a cliff. Faint light from the entry fell across his face in bars, making him seem even more dark, menacing in his strength.

Yet Dani wasn't afraid. Not of Shane.

"There's nothing you can say," she said quietly.

Slowly Shane took his hands from his pockets and reached for her.

Dani held her breath, not sure what was to come, afraid and yet not really fearful. His hands settled on her shoulders, and his arms drew her closer as he bent down to her mouth.

The kiss was more gentle than Dani had expected, and far more hungry. It haunted her in ways that had nothing to do with her fear of large men.

"What about that?" Shane asked softly. "Does that change your mind?"

"Should it?"

"You're damned right it should."

He kissed her again, less gently this time. She sensed the barely restrained passion in him and trembled.

But not with fear.

Suddenly she found herself kissing him fiercely, almost fighting him for the embrace with a passion that demanded more from him than a warrior's restraint.

Shane made a thick sound. His arms closed around her, lifting her, holding her so close there was barely room between them for the heat of their bodies to mingle.

Finally, reluctantly, he let her slide down the length of his body. He made no effort to hide his arousal. He simply looked at her with a raw desire that made her want to be close to him again.

Very close.

"That's what I've been trying to tell you," he said bluntly. "We want each other. There's nothing worse for a covert operation than sex."

For a moment longer Dani savored the warmth of his hands,

the caressing pressure of his thumbs against the underside of her breasts, and the undisguised hunger in his eyes.

Then she drew a long, ragged breath and slowly let it out.

"Then we'll just have to say no, won't we?" Dani said.

Shane said something in Tibetan.

Dani didn't ask for a translation.

"You still insist on going?" he asked, but without real hope.

"Yes."

"It's going to be hell, lady. I promise that you'll roast in the fires with me."

Chapter Fifteen

Curacao
November

Five days later Dani sat in a Risk Limited executive jet and stared down at the cloud-striped blue water below, but it wasn't the clouds she was seeing. It was Shane as he had looked with darkness and light falling across a face drawn taut by passion.

He had barely spoken to her since that night. It was Gillespie who took over her crash course in field training. Gillespie who had been pleasantly surprised that Dani knew some judo and a few other nasty tricks that might slow a man down.

It had also been Gillespie who was scathing on the subject of Dani's ignorance about firearms. By the time he was finished, she knew how to load and fire revolvers and semiautomatic pistols. She had been briefed in the principles of light automatic weapons and had even learned how to fire three-round bursts with an Uzi, the Israeli weapon that Risk Limited operators favored.

Sometimes she even hit her target. Most of the time Gillespie muttered about waiting until she saw the whites of their eyes and then running like hell.

On the other hand, he had praised her natural sense of orientation, and her map skills, ability to memorize faces and names, and to initiate as well as understand orders.

I should have gotten high marks for liking my own company, too, Dani thought wryly. Shane sure has avoided me since he walked me home that night, kissed me, and all but melted the cement under my feet.

She tried not to think about the passion that had flared so unexpectedly and wildly between them.

Unfortunately the long flight to Plesman Airport in Curacao left her little else to think about, except the danger that lay ahead of them.

All things considered, it was easier to think about Shane.

The plane swooped down like a falcon plunging toward the airfield below. Gillespie stirred from his seat next to the pilot, craned forward, and nodded.

Shane didn't bother looking down. He simply sat as he had for the entire flight, wondering how the hell he had gotten himself in such a fix as having Dani for a partner in a covert operation.

Stupidity, Shane decided acidly. Or passion.

Same difference.

A Bell JetRanger sat like an impatient hornet on the tarmac as Risk Limited's Gulfstream II touched down on the runway. Gillespie had the door of the aircraft open almost before the jet braked to a halt beside the helicopter.

Gillespie stepped out into sultry trade winds and stretched blissfully. Dressed in khaki shorts and a black shirt decorated with huge red flowers, he looked the part of a tourist.

"Bless me, I'm home," Gillespie said with a broad smile on his face as Dani descended. "Too bloody hot, but still home."

"With that name, I thought you were some sort of Scottish laird," Dani said.

"I am, but some of my genes came from south of Capricorn."

"Two worlds and at home in both," Dani said.

Gillespie grinned.

"Move it, Gillie," Shane said from behind Dani. "We're on a short clock."

With a sly smile Gillespie saluted Shane and headed for the idling chopper. Shane was barely a step behind him.

Dani hurried to catch up with her reluctant partner.

"I guess this means we don't have to swim to Aruba after all," she said.

"I thought you were up for adventure," Shane muttered.

"Bitch, bitch, bitch," Dani retorted. "I've held up my end of the bargain the last five days. Even Gillie said I'm ready, so belt up, as he would say."

"Gillie gave you a 'marginal' in firearms and an 'adequate' in self-defense," Shane said tersely. "No Risk Limited field operative should be allowed to go to the toilet alone with those scores, much less into the Harmony's jaws."

"Gillie gave me top marks at country orientation and a 'very good' at shared problem-solving," Dani said distinctly.

Shane grunted.

"I can break a man's nose if I have to," Dani said, "but I plan to let you take care of the mayhem while I handle the more elegant tasks."

"Plan, huh? Jesus. I bet you believe in the Easter Bunny, too."

"Don't you?"

Shane shot Dani a sideways look that could have etched stone.

"I'm the senior operator," he said flatly. "I call the shots."

"What happened to democracy?"

"You left it behind. Your choice, remember?"

"Give it a rest," Gillespie said, turning around suddenly. "Did you snarl at each other all the way across Tibet?"

"No," Shane said.

"Yes," Dani said simultaneously.

They gave each other a startled look and laughed.

Gillespie let out a hidden breath of relief. He and Cassandra had had several "discussions" about the advisability of sending a relative innocent like Dani into the field, especially when Shane was dead set against it.

But they were here, together.

Here they would stay.

The helicopter pilot stepped out onto the tarmac and Gillespie went ahead to meet him. The two men shook hands like old friends. They stood in the wash of the slowly turning main rotor, shouting over the massive blow-torch sound of the JetRanger's turbine.

Gillespie walked around the aircraft, inspecting it as though he were personally responsible for its performance.

Amused, Dani watched. After a few days, she had learned to look past Gillespie's unusually handsome exterior to the man beneath. He was meticulous, unbending, sometimes abrasive, sometimes compassionate, and always intelligent. He was completely at ease among machines, weapons, and comrades at arms.

Gillespie and Shane are quite alike in some regards, Dani thought, looking sidelong at the man who stood beside her. They're both warriors. They make good friends and bad enemies.

But Shane didn't share Gillie's fascination and familiarity with modern technology. Shane used what he had to and never fussed about it. All he cared was that the tool was in working order and ready to go when he needed it.

Dani studied the two men through lowered eyelashes and decided that the differences didn't end there.

Shane doesn't carry himself in the military style, she realized. For all his size, he somehow blends in. He's understated. More . . . shadowed.

Sometimes Dani looked at Shane and thought about still waters running deep and swift. Dangerous waters.

The insight was both intriguing and unsettling, attraction and warning at once.

"Gillie would like to be going himself, wouldn't he?" Dani asked Shane.

"Yeah, he'd love to be back in operations, but Cassandra needs him beside her."

"It's odd for a man of his sort to give up what he loves so much."

"He found something he loves better, I guess," Shane said.
"Cassandra?"

Shane shrugged.

"Cassandra or Risk Limited," he said. "Whatever. Gillie was a legend in Her Majesty's Special Air Services. Cassandra is the only one who's ever gotten him to bend his knee or his stiff neck."

"You make it sound like involuntary servitude."

Shane shot Dani a sidelong glance.

"How else is there to look at it?" he asked.

"As a partnership."

Shane made a sound that could have meant anything.

"I haven't heard either of them complain," Dani added. "Have you?"

He didn't answer.

With a final glance at the chopper, Gillespie trotted back to Shane and Dani, carrying a familiar yellow and black paper folder. He handed it to Shane.

"Hertz rental car contract, ignition keys, and room key for a beachside cabana at the Hyatt Regency Aruba," Gillespie said. "The car is a blue Toyota convertible parked in a palmetto grove a hundred meters back from the beach where Miller will drop you."

Shane nodded and pocketed the folder.

Gillespie glanced at Dani.

"You'll find everything you need in the suite," he said. "Beachwear and some frocks for the casino. Remember. You're just two happy lovers on holiday."

"Happy lovers, huh?" Dani asked sardonically. She looked at Shane. "Do keep that in mind when you go into your strong, silent mode."

Shane muttered something under his breath.

"Be an old-fashioned lass," Gillespie said to Dani. "Let your man make all the tactical decisions."

"I never did make very good wallpaper," Dani said.

"Bloody hell." Gillespie sighed. "Five days wasn't long enough."

"Five years wouldn't have been long enough," Shane said.

Gillespie shot him a simmering look before he turned back to Dani. Gently he tapped her forehead with a stiff forefinger.

"You've got a very good head," he said. "Use it instead of your mouth."

Dani smiled in spite of herself. She gave Gillespie a quick hug, surprising both of them.

"Thanks, I think," she said.

He smiled, shook Shane's hand, and waved them aboard the helicopter. As they approached, the main rotor began to pick up speed.

This time the pilot was a man with graying hair, a white mustache, and two fingers missing from his right hand. The old injury didn't slow him in the least. Seconds after Shane and Dani strapped in, they were airborne.

For the next forty minutes they sat in the back seats, their knees almost touching. The relentless thunder of the chopper made conversation impossible.

Back in the noise box again, Dani thought wryly. *Only this time the seat is more comfortable. Sort of. All in all, Shane made a nice mattress.*

The thought made her smile.

Shane handed Dani a set of earphones, pointed to a jack, and put on his own.

"Drill time," he said.

From a folder he drew out a sheaf of eight by ten photos. He held one out to her.

Dani managed not to groan.

"Katya Pilenkova," she said promptly. "Resident whore-master of Harmony Estates. Former member of Soviet Nomenklatura. She helped rape the empire after it fell. In exchange for dirty money from the West, trainloads of rubles went to the Italian Mafia and the Colombian Cartel. The rubles were used to buy everything from art to fissionable materials on the Russian black market, which she then resold legitimately to the West. Presto, clean dollars."

Shane made an impatient movement. He didn't care about Katya's bio. He wanted Dani to concentrate on one thing and one thing only.

"Is Katya dangerous?" Shane asked curtly.

"Only with your back turned. Or in bed. Or if you're a bottle of half-frozen vodka. Lord, but that woman can drink."

Shane smiled thinly. Another photo came out of the sheaf.

"Ilya Kasatonin," Dani said. "Lover and probable partner of Katya. The Harmony's resident assassin. He gave the Afghanis the same kind of hell they gave him. And yes, he's dangerous."

A third photo appeared.

"Kojimura," Dani said. "Suspected to be holding back from full participation in the Harmony, like Tony Liu of China. Katya is still looking for a handle on Liu. She has one on Ishida, who is also a Yakuza biggie."

"If the Karens are handling the silk, Katya found Liu's lever," Shane said. "That leaves Kojimura. Without his support, the Harmony will find itself stymied. The Yakuza will play one Harmony member off against the others."

A fourth picture appeared, then a fifth, then others, and names rolled off Dani's tongue: de la Pena, Spagnolini, Liu, Ishida. The roll call of crimes was finally numbing rather than horrifying. They became just facts, like the number of peaches in a crate or bottles in a case or bodies in a mass grave.

Feeling surreal, Dani looked at Ishida's picture and remembered his competitor, Kojimura.

"What about Kojimura's private life?" Dani asked. "Does he do anything more than drink, whore, and go home to beat the poor wretch he married?"

"He's third-generation Yakuza," Shane said. "He wants to be respected as well as feared. He's big on Japanese culture. So is his patron."

"The interface?"

Shane nodded. "Whoever that is, we haven't been able to find out yet."

Frowning, Dani looked back at Kojimura's picture. Like the Sicilians, the Japanese accepted the presence of organized crime to the point that, at the highest levels, there was an "interface" between the legal world of business and the illegal world of the Yakuzas. Yukio Koyama was such a man.

"Is Kojimura Christian, Marxist, Buddhist, Moslem, Hindu?" Dani asked.

"Satanist, more likely."

"In Asia? I doubt it. Any obsessions besides eight-year-old blondes?"

"Ancient Japanese swords," Shane said. "His family is famous for their collection. But lately he's branched out into . . ."

Shane's voice died. A look of surprise came and went from his face so quickly that Dani wasn't certain she had seen it.

"What?" she asked.

"Silk," Shane said simply. "Kojimura has begun to acquire silk. I guess his father and grandfather collected all the good swords."

"Ancient or modern silk?"

"Both."

"Asian or European?" Dani asked.

"Asian."

"Japanese or Chinese, Persian or Indian?"

"God, woman, you ask a lot of questions."

"Give me answers and I'll shut up."

Shane smiled briefly. "I don't know if Kojimura specializes."

"Find out."

"Is it important?"

"Collectors are weird," Dani said. "Some collect for others to admire. Some collect and keep it in a closet and gloat over it. Some do both. Some won't touch anything that isn't from a certain time period. Others want only Japanese or Chinese or whatever. Some require both time and country and type of weaving and—"

"I get the picture," Shane interrupted. "If Buddha's silk fits Kojimura's collecting profile, we don't need to worry about a private auction. Katya will use the silk to cement relations with him, and Kojimura will fall like a ripe peach into the Harmony's net."

"Like I said. Collectors are an odd bunch."

Shane switched the channel on his headset, spoke briefly to

the pilot, and switched back to Dani. Without a word, he began pulling more pictures from the file.

Faithfully Dani recited the name, nationality, and chilling personal history of the gangsters who met to do business at Katya Pilenkova's ironically named estate.

Shane listened silently. He knew that drilling Dani wasn't necessary, except as a way to keep her mind off what was coming.

Or to keep my mind off of it, he admitted to himself. By Buddha's tears, I wish she had stayed home!

But she hadn't. Now the dangerous time had begun, another life depending on Shane's own skill.

It was one thing to die from your own mistake. It was quite another to take someone with you.

Especially Dani, Shane thought bleakly. Why in hell did it have to be her?

Eleven miles out from Aruba, the pilot took the copter down to within ten feet of the water.

Dani watched while the brown and green lump of land ahead began to take shape. When she wasn't being "debriefed" on ancient silks, silk moths, types of thread, styles of weaving, styles of dying, etc., she had read books on Aruba and had studied maps.

The work had paid off. Landmarks Dani had previously seen only in two dimensions suddenly appeared in three.

The Haystack looks just like one, she thought. More than five hundred feet tall. The rest of the place was flat and sandy. She had expected a kind of Caribbean desert. Even so, the stark mixture of rock, sand, and wind-sculpted divi-divi trees was disconcerting.

So much for dreams of tropical paradise, Dani thought. Oh, well, it's not like we're on a real lovers' getaway. We're going to the world's biggest outdoor laundry. Half the world's dirty money goes in and then comes out as white as the sands.

Not for the first time, Dani thought how odd it was that Risk Limited and the Harmony owed their separate births to the same tectonic shift in global politics—the implosion of the Soviet empire. The collapse of civil order and national borders was an opportunity that had been instantly understood and seized by the various international criminal organizations.

Japanese Yakuza, Chinese tong, Sicilian or American Mafia, Colombian cartel, Russian *mafiya*—the name didn't matter. The result was the same, a takeover or corruption of whatever civil authority existed.

A subtle coolness went over Dani as she reviewed the information she had acquired in the past few days about the entity known as the Harmony.

None of what Dani had learned was comforting.

"Too bad international politicians and cops can't cooperate as pragmatically as international crooks," Dani said. "The Harmony would have been stillborn."

"It wasn't," Shane said. "It's thriving. Aruba is its guts. The Belly of the Beast drawn in shades of white and turquoise."

"We're just happy tourists," Dani said.

"Yeah."

"I hope you're right about Katya and her delusions of grandeur."

"Enough vodka does that to even the toughest mind. The Harmony has grown so swiftly and with so little opposition, Katya thinks she's bullet-proof."

Dani bit her lip and looked down at the island, thinking about bullets and Feng and a killer named Kasatonin.

Swiftly the chopper approached the Harmony's citadel. The leeward beaches of Aruba were harsher and more narrow than the ones on the west side, much less favored by tourists and natives alike. That was why Gillespie had chosen such a beach as an entry site.

The pilot turned the howling helicopter into a graceful sea bird, lifting over a line of palms and then wheeling to follow a narrow dirt road south along the shore. He flew with a fixed, elated grin on his face, like a young boy on a rollercoaster. Only when they approached the landing area did he finally cut back the speed.

The pilot's voice came into Shane and Dani's earphones.

"Looks deserted to me."

"Roger that," Shane said.

"Get the door open," the pilot said. "I'll flare out over the beach. You two bail out and head inland."

"Roger. Out."

Shane took off his headset and seat restraints. Hastily Dani did the same as he slid the side door open. The downdraft of the rotor filled the cabin with howling wind.

A shot of adrenaline surged through Dani.

It's real, she thought suddenly. My God, what have I gotten myself into?

She looked at Shane's calm face and remembered his combination of restraint and lethal skill. The instant of panic passed.

At least I'm not alone this time, she thought. Even if my partner sometimes has the conversational skills of a clam.

Shane caught a glimpse of a blue car hidden in a tangle of brush. He pointed and gave the signal to set down.

The pilot eased back on the collective. The chopper settled toward the beach, stopping a few feet short of the sand.

Shane stepped out onto the helicopter's skid and all but vanished in a cloud of blowing sand. Without looking back, he reached for Dani's hand and inched a little farther out onto the skid.

After only an instant of hesitation, Dani took his hand and let him guide her into position in the doorway.

The helicopter dropped a few inches lower and hovered like a small, stalled tornado. The pilot shoved a small leather shoulder bag at Dani.

Automatically she grabbed the strap. In the next moment Shane drew her out onto the skid and then leaped lightly down to the ground.

As soon as Dani's feet hit the sand, he wrapped his arms around her, held her face against his chest, and turned his back to the helicopter.

Instantly the chopper leaped into the sky, leaving Shane and Dani to face the Harmony alone.

Chapter Sixteen

Aruba
November

Eyes clamped shut, Dani buried her face in Shane's shirt, grateful for the buffer against the sandy violence of the departing helicopter.

Through slitted eyes, Shane watched the chopper swinging away across the beach and over the waves, headed back for a landing pad in Curacao. Within fifteen seconds the noise of the aircraft faded into the softer sounds of wind and sea.

Shane mentally ticked off one hurdle safely passed. Getting in was the most dangerous part of any mission.

Getting out was the second most dangerous.

Dammit, Dani, why didn't you stay where you were safe? Shane demanded silently.

But she hadn't. Now she was his responsibility.

Dani's breath was warm against Shane's chest, warmer than the tropical day. He realized that he was standing like an idiot, holding onto her when he should be moving and moving fast.

She's hell on my concentration, Shane thought savagely. Too much time spent in a monastery. *Damn.*

Abruptly he released her, took the leather bag, and undid the catch. Inside was a cloth-wrapped parcel tied with string. He made short work of the wrapping.

A pistol emerged from the cloth. Shane checked it out with a few quick motions of his hands, found the weapon ready, and dropped it back into the black bag.

"Good to go," he muttered. Then, to Dani, "Stay here until I call you."

"Where are you going?"

"The car."

Dani looked around. The blue convertible had been obvious from the air but was nearly invisible from ground level. Clearly Shane had pinpointed the car's location while he was still in the air.

With a speed and thoroughness that spoke of practice, Shane inspected the ground around the palmetto grove. There was no sign that it had been disturbed since the palmetto screen was put in place and all tracks brushed away.

Shane began tearing the palmettos away.

When Dani realized that the vegetation was an artistically woven screen that concealed the rental car, she started forward.

"Stay put, damn it!" Shane said without looking back.

Dani froze, wondering how he had known she would head for the car the moment it was uncovered.

After a few days, she thought, Shane knows me better than my ex-husband ever did.

She didn't know whether the insight was comforting, maddening, disconcerting, or all three at once.

Quickly, without touching anything, Shane inspected the car itself. He finished on his stomach, staring at the underside of the chassis. Satisfied, he stood up, absently brushed off sand, and grasped the door handle.

The mechanism clicked open.

Two down, Shane thought, and only hell knows how many to go.

He opened the door, got behind the wheel, put the key in the ignition, and turned.

The car started smoothly.

Three down.

"All right," Shane called to Dani. "Let's move."

While Dani hurried over, he opened the glove box and shoved the leather bag inside.

"What was that all about?" Dani asked after she closed the door behind her.

"Gillie's BFO #237," Shane said, as he backed onto the highway. "Lay ambushes around escape vehicles."

"What's a BFO?"

"A blinding flash of the obvious."

Dani laughed.

"A blinding flash of the obvious," Shane continued, "is much better than the blinding flash of a car bomb. That's BFO #1."

The smile vanished from Dani's face.

"If you're trying to scare me, you can stop," she said.

"I'm trying to educate you. A good car bomb goes off within a second after the ignition is switched on."

"I'll keep that in mind."

"You do that. I don't share Gillie's organic approach to operational training. I don't think that doing what comes naturally is always the right tactic."

Tires hit tarmac. The car accelerated swiftly.

Three minutes after Shane and Dani had stepped off the skid of the helicopter, there was no evidence that they were anything other than tourists in tropical clothes.

Shane drove the roads of the little island as though he had been born there, but Dani quickly felt her "country orientation" fading.

Knowing Gillie, she thought, there's a map around somewhere. For me, not for Shane. The Zen cyborg doesn't need one.

There was a map of Aruba in the pocket on the passenger side. It took Dani less than a minute to figure out where they were now on the island and where they were headed.

Fifteen minutes later Shane turned onto the main highway and headed toward Oranjestad. As the car neared the airport, the scrubby countryside gradually gave way to suburbs.

At first the houses were little more than small shacks decorated with pagan talismans. Further on, prosperous bungalows stood side by side with Dutch windmills turning slowly in the constant wind. There was an odd peacefulness in the place.

Dani sighed and relaxed. It would be easy to play tourist in this setting.

Beyond the airport, the city of Oranjestad began to take shape. Dani imagined that they were just what they appeared to be: tourists who had been sightseeing on the island and would soon leave the same way they had come—aboard an American Airlines flight like the one she had seen taxiing toward the airport terminal.

Just lovers on a holiday.

She glanced at Shane beside her. He was an entirely presentable traveling companion; intelligent, good-looking, and engaging when he wanted to be.

Which wasn't often, lately.

"You sure know how to show a girl a good time in exotic places," she said. "First Lhasa, now Aruba."

She gestured toward the town and beyond, to the towering high-rise hotels along the west-facing beaches.

"Just remember why we're here," Shane said.

"Oh, don't worry," Dani said. "I won't forget. If I do, I'm sure the Zen cyborg will be right there to remind me."

"The what?"

"You."

Shane's expression tightened for an instant. Then his face again became the mask it had been since Redpath had told him that Dani was going to Aruba.

With or without Shane Crowe.

Shane had been tempted to call her bluff, but hadn't. If he didn't go, Gillespie would have. That made no professional sense at all.

As for personal sense, Shane reminded himself regularly of his self-elected vow of abstinence.

Two years, eleven months, twenty-two days and counting.

The heart of Oranjestad looked just like the video Gillespie had played for them. There were colonial-era business blocks in pastel shades. The old businesses alternated with glistening new shopping malls, new casinos wrapped in neon, and new bank buildings of smoked glass and stainless steel.

Dani drew a deep breath. Something sweet and flowery was in the air.

"Fruit?" she asked. "Or do they perfume the air for tourists?"

"It's the faint stink of corruption," Shane said.

"How romantic."

"Romantic?" He laughed harshly. "There are three hundred and fifty banks here, and each one of them is willing to be as crooked as the competition. What you're looking at are glass and steel monuments to corruption and raw greed."

"Do smile, darling. We're on vacation, remember?"

Shane shot Dani a look of disbelief.

"A lovers' holiday, to be precise," she said sweetly. "Isn't that how Gillie put it?"

"Shit."

Dani bit her tongue. She sensed that Shane was close to the edge of his considerable restraint.

At the north edge of the city, they turned and followed the main highway out along a beach road. On either side of the route grew a wall of small hotels, casinos, and restaurants. The modest buildings quickly gave way to the high-ticket, high-rise beach area. The wall of buildings became towering cliffs of concrete and glass.

Slits in the manmade cliffs revealed crowded sand that was the color and texture of sugar. The sand was so white it hurt human eyes even through sunglasses. Incandescent, blinding, the sand spread out to the glittering blue water.

"Welcome to the home of the Harmony," Shane said. "Happy holidays and all that."

"I would have been happier if Gillie hadn't briefed me."

"You had a choice."

"Don't you ever get tired of saying I told you so?" Dani asked sharply.

"No. I'm a machine, remember? A cyborg."

Dani winced. It sounded a lot colder coming from Shane's

lips than she had meant it to be. She decided to change the subject. Fast.

"It's hard to imagine so many people vacationing blissfully in the shadow of something like the Harmony," she said.

"Ever been to Rio?"

"No, but I hope to. I've heard it's beautiful."

"Rio is cutting edge," Shane said, "and the edge is a mugger's knife. The beaches aren't safe for tourists. Not much there is."

"You take a rather grim view of the world."

"Comes of living without rose-colored glasses and ivory towers."

"Do you work at being a bastard or does it just come naturally?" Dani asked.

"Naturally. My parents never married."

"So much for that conversation. Gosh, aren't we having fun?"

"No."

"Smile, you bas—hard-headed son of a bitch," Dani corrected hastily. "We're lovers on vacation and this is a convertible. We're on display."

Shane smiled like a wolf looking at a lamb chop.

"Forget it," Dani said. "I'll smile for both of us."

The convertible sped past tall twin-and triple-towered hotels on the ocean side of the highway. Ornate gambling halls were skillfully integrated into the resort complexes, as though the casinos were no more necessary for profit than the swimming pools.

"Not like Las Vegas," Dani said. "In Vegas they do everything but set off an atom bomb to attract attention to the casinos."

"Vegas, huh? Do you like gambling?"

"Why else would I spend summers on the Silk Road?" Dani retorted.

"I meant gambling with money, not your neck."

Dani shrugged.

"Gambling for money doesn't appeal to me," she said. "But I know it's the drug of choice for some people."

"It's no accident that crime, commercial gambling, and civic corruption usually are found in the same bed," Shane said. "The scent of human weakness draws predators like flies to a pus-filled wound."

"Such a pleasant image."

"The flies thinks so," Shane replied.

"Wait," Dani said abruptly. "We just passed the Hyatt."

"I know. Look at the next place."

Dani saw big steel gates blocking a driveway that led down toward the water. A burnished brass sign set in one of the gateposts announced the name of the resort.

HARMONY ESTATE PRIVATE NO TRESPASSING

"Looks like half of Malibu Beach," Dani said carelessly.

"Don't kid yourself, professor. This ain't Malibu."

"I didn't realize we were going to be so close to the estate."

"Close is why we're here."

Shane turned around in the center of the road like a tourist and took a side route onto the Hyatt grounds. Moments later he parked in the shade of a palm grove. He reached into the glove box and pulled out the leather bag.

Before Dani could open her door, Shane was out of the car. She got out fast and hurried to catch up with him.

"Slow down, *darling*," she said.

"Sorry. The heat is giving me a rash."

Dani knew that nothing was giving Shane a rash but her unwanted presence.

"You aren't a gracious loser," she muttered.

"Show me a gracious loser and I'll show you a loser, period."

Dani shoved her arm through Shane's and dug in her heels.

"Stop right here," she said quietly.

Shane stopped in mid-stride and looked down at Dani. She gave him a smile with lots of teeth and no warmth.

"We're lovers on vacation, remember," she said in a low voice.

"The way you keep remind—"

Dani's hand went over Shane's mouth in a gesture that could have been a lover's caress, but wasn't.

She stood on tiptoe and breathed into his ear.

''Stop treating me like a snotty little sister,'' Dani said softly, distinctly. ''Especially while we're under the noses of the people we're trying to fool.''

As Dani settled back onto her feet, one of her breasts brushed gently against Shane's forearm. The contact might or might not have been intentional.

What stopped Shane cold was that he wanted very much to find out.

Eight days to go on my vow and counting, he reminded himself sardonically.

On the other hand, his vow had very specific parameters.

Deliberately Shane bent down and kissed the corner of Dani's mouth.

''I'm glad that's how you want to play this,'' he said in a husky voice.

''That's not what I'm—''

The rest of Dani's words were lost in a quick, hard kiss.

''Don't be so impatient,'' he said, smiling. ''We'll be inside soon enough.''

''You s—''

Shane grabbed Dani's head and pushed her mouth against his neck, cutting off her words.

''We're lovers, remember?'' he whispered in her ear. ''You think the palms have ears, remember?''

After a few moments, Dani's body relaxed. She nodded against the faintly beard-stubbled skin of Shane's neck.

''Until I'm certain that cottage doesn't have ears,'' he said, ''you will keep your mouth shut except to kiss me. If you open those lips again except on direct orders, I'll take it as an invitation for sex. Understood?''

Dani stiffened from head to heels. She nodded curtly.

Shane released her head. As he did, his fingers trailed through her hair in what could have been a warning or a caress.

Or both.

Arm in arm, they strolled down the path toward a group of cabanas. As they approached the one closest to the water—and to Harmony Estate's wrought-iron fence—Shane pulled a room key from the pocket of his shorts. He checked the number on the key tag before he leaned down to Dani.

"Make tourist talk," he whispered. "And remember, we've been here for several days."

"I still can't believe the flowers," Dani said after a moment. "Makes me think of silk."

Shane gave her a look of disbelief.

"Er, satin actually," Dani corrected hastily. "All lush and shiny and soft."

He grunted.

"And all those birds standing around one-legged on the beach," Dani said. "Aren't they cute?"

"Cute," Shane said. "Yeah."

"I can't believe that gorgeous stretch of beach is still deserted. Do you suppose anyone would mind if we sort of snuck over and used it? The fence doesn't go all the way to the water."

Shane followed Dani's glance. She was studying the estate through the bars of the wrought-iron fence. The coils of razor wire across the top and the mechanized cameras sweeping the beach spoiled the feeling of unfettered paradise.

"Sure they'd mind," Shane said acidly. "Rich people give me a pain. They don't use what they have and they won't let anyone else use it, either."

The key turned in the lock with smooth, oiled ease. The door didn't squeak.

Nothing exploded.

With a glance that appeared casual, Shane checked out the room before he stepped in.

Empty.

"After you," he murmured. "Right on your heels, in fact."

As Dani walked into the room, she realized that Shane's left hand was never far from the open flap of the leather pouch that concealed the pistol.

A chill went over her skin that had nothing to do with the cabana's abundant air-conditioning. Sunlight and flowers and velvet tropical air hadn't dulled the razor-edge of his vigilance one bit.

Uneasily she looked around. The cabana had a front sitting room with windows that opened onto the sand. There was a well-stocked wet bar in a small alcove and a bedroom set back from the surf.

"I do like this furniture," Dani said.

"Yeah," Shane said absently. "Real nice."

He had barely glanced at the quality of the furnishings. He was going over the chairs and tables, and the rest of the room, looking for obvious bugs and the not-so-obvious kind.

While Shane examined lightbulbs and wall sockets, Dani went on her own tour of inspection. The whole time she gave chatty updates on how, even after several days, she really loved the furniture, the view, the weather, and the doors that opened onto the beach.

Shane's answers varied from "uh" to "yeah" to "nice."

"Good taste in liquor, too," she said.

"Yeah?"

"Grand Marnier."

"Nice."

"I'll say. A bottle this size would cost fifty bucks at duty-free."

Shane stood up from his inspection of an oddly placed electrical socket and looked at Dani.

"You like Grand Marnier, huh?" he asked.

"Men," Dani said in profound disgust. "You can't even remember my favorite color, can you?"

"Uh . . ."

"Yeah," she said. "Uh."

Shane went back to checking out the room. He wasn't really worried. Just careful. Afghanistan had taught him that careful men lived longer than the other kind.

In any case, Shane knew that a really high-tech bug would be beyond the scope of his search. Then again, if their cover was blown so badly that the Harmony already had bugged the room, they were dead no matter what they did.

"Nice of your boss to give you this vacation as a bonus," Dani said.

"Yeah."

"The cabana must cost five hundred a day."

"Eight-fifty," Shane said. "I'll be back in a minute."

"I'll be here," Dani said sweetly, "just hanging on your every 'uh.' "

Shane went to the bedroom door and opened it. He took one look and smiled bitterly. Buddha must have a sharp sense of humor, he thought.

Quickly Shane went over the bedroom and bathroom. He found nothing but what he had already discovered. He flushed the toilet and listened. Everything worked.

Including him.

His body was on full sexual alert. None of the mental exercises that had worked so well in Tibet were doing any good now. The scent of Dani was on his shirt, the taste of her was on his lips, and the memory of how her breasts felt under his hands made his shorts tight.

Damn.

With another silent curse Shane stalked back through the main room of the cabana to the wet bar. He yanked open the refrigerator door, spotted a frosty green bottle of Caribe beer, opened it, and drank deeply.

"What's wrong?" Dani said.

Shane took a second long swallow of beer.

Dani looked at him over the green bottle. His eyes were as clear as midnight and just as unreadable.

He lowered the bottle. Then he smiled.

Uh oh, Dani thought. Somehow, somewhere, somebody has stepped in the yak dung. Deep.

"Nothing's wrong," he said.

"You're not acting like it."

His smile widened but didn't warm one bit.

"Acting," Shane said as though he had never heard the word before. "Yeah."

"Hello?" Dani said. "Are we having the same conversation?"

"Not yet, but we will be."

"What in hell are you talking about?"

Shane tilted his head toward the bedroom.

"See for yourself," he said. "Just remember, honey. You asked for it. In bloody spades."

Giving Shane an odd look, Dani went to the bedroom door and glanced in. The room was cool, shaded by sheer curtains. The closet door stood open. Inside were the resort clothes Gillespie had promised.

Dani didn't bother checking the sizes. She was sure they would fit her perfectly.

The rest of the room looked perfect, too. Someone had unpacked clothes for Shane. A T-shirt was carelessly thrown over a chair. A scarlet nightgown was thrown over another chair.

Dani winced and turned away.

Through the open bathroom doorway toiletries had been laid out on the tile sink. The brands were her own preferences. Several of the bottles were half-full, as though they had been used.

Altogether, the room had a lived-in look, comfortable and homey, right down to the coverlet that had been turned down on the king-size bed.

Then it hit Dani.

One bed.

Two people.

Oh shit, she thought.

Dani spun around. Shane was standing in the living area, just beyond the door to the bedroom. He lifted the beer bottle to her in a silent toast.

"Look at the bright side," he said.

"Point it out to me and I will."

"Before this is over, we'll find out how good an actress you really are."

"Screw you, cowboy," Dani snarled.

"Cowboy, huh? Is that better than a Zen cyborg?"

The bedroom door slammed so hard it almost knocked the beer bottle out of Shane's hand.

Chapter Seventeen

Daylight swept like colored thunder over Aruba.

In a single movement, Shane came up off the floor on "his" side of the bed, grateful for an excuse to get out of the room.

He had never guessed how small a king-size bed could be.

Though Dani had clung to her edge of the bed like a lifeline, it hadn't helped much. Her every breath, every shift of her body, even the soft brush of her hair against the sheets had been like repeated whips of fire licking over him.

Just as well I decided against monkhood, he thought. If I had ever met Dani, I would have spent my life regretting my vows.

As it is, I only have a little while longer to regret them.

Resolutely Shane refused to count the days, hours, and minutes that remained. With quick motions he pulled on shorts and took binoculars from the suitcase that had been provided for him.

There was a square of filtered light on the little porch that faced the ocean. From that spot he could look over Harmony Estate without being seen in turn.

Shane spent the next half-hour with the binoculars, staring through greenery. The fence that separated him from the estate was his target.

At first glance, and even at second, the fence looked formidable.

It was ten feet tall, constructed of closely spaced, vertical wrought-iron bars, and topped with coils of razor wire. The deadly wire was stainless steel, glittering fiercely in the morning sun.

The wrought iron hadn't fared so well in the intense salt air. Trade winds and sea spray had subtly corroded the metal beneath the black paint.

"What are you doing?"

The soft voice coming from just behind Shane made him start. It also made him irritated.

He couldn't remember the last time someone had been able to sneak up on him.

"Looking at the scenery," he said.

Dani bit back a slicing retort. Things were tense enough between them without adding to the problem. Even winning five hundred dollars at the blackjack table last night hadn't cheered him up.

"Are you dressed?" Shane asked tersely, without turning around.

"I'm not wearing the butt-floss bikini someone thoughtfully provided for me, if that's what you mean."

"That's what I mean."

Shane would be a long time forgetting what Dani had looked like yesterday afternoon in the few moments after she dropped her beach towel, dove into the pool, and began doing determined laps. There were better built women all around the resort, some of them spectacularly so, but none of them appealed to his senses the way Dani did.

Lowering the glasses, Shane looked over his shoulder. Dani's dark hair was tousled from bed and her skin was flushed with recent sleep. She was covered from collarbone to heels in a white terrycloth hotel robe.

Her feet were bare, narrow, and elegantly arched. Her toes played idly in the silky sand at the edge of the patio, as though she were teasing a sleeping lover.

Heat slid through Shane's blood at the thought. Abruptly he turned away and went back to studying the Harmony's barrier against the rest of the world.

"Nice fence, huh?" Dani said. "Real neighborly."

"Yeah."

"Wonder if they have the same problem here with iron that they do in Florida."

"What do you mean?" Shane asked.

"Sleazy contractors and really salty air," Dani said succinctly.

Shane smiled like a shark. "I was wondering the same thing."

"And?" Dani prodded.

"Looks like some of those wrought-iron posts aren't solid all the way through. A few are really rusted. How do you know about Florida?"

"My ex had parents there. They had to replace their fancy wrought-iron security fence after two years."

Shane looked back at Dani again, intrigued.

"The second time," she said, "they had the contractor saw through a few bars at random before the fence was installed, just to prove he was using solid iron rather than a shell wrapped around cardboard."

Laughing, Shane turned back to scanning the fence through binoculars. "At least they learned."

"Yeah. Too bad they didn't pass on that ability to their one and only son."

"Dumb, huh?"

"Nope," Dani said. "He just didn't give a damn about anything that wasn't stronger or meaner than he was."

Shane's hands tightened on the binoculars. There was a flatness in Dani's voice that told him of unhealed wounds just beneath the surface of her smile.

No wonder she doesn't trust men, Shane thought. Sounds like she married a real prince.

"I've seen the type," Shane said casually. "But not in my shaving mirror."

Dani drew half a breath, laughed without meaning to, and spoke without thinking.

"I know that," she admitted. "If I didn't, I would have locked the bedroom door instead of just slamming it."

Shane kept on studying the fence.

"You don't have to sleep on the floor," Dani said. "That bed is the size of a hockey rink."

"I got used to floors in the monastery."

"How long were you with the Azures?"

"Long enough for Prasam to know I wasn't one of them," Shane said.

"Wrong race?"

"Wrong temperament."

For a time there was silence while Dani watched Shane watching the fence.

"What—" she began.

"Not now," he interrupted.

Dani went back to watching Shane. As he scanned the fence through the binoculars, the small motions of his muscles beneath the skin of his back fascinated her. It was rather like watching light move over finely woven silk. She was tempted to trace the outlines of the shifting masculine flesh, as though sensing with her fingertips the invisible weaving of life beneath.

"Just as I thought," Shane said.

Dani's fingers jerked back when she realized she was within inches of touching him. She put her hands behind her back.

"What is?" she asked guiltily.

"The closed-circuit television cameras aren't quite in sync," Shane said.

Dani gave out a silent breath of relief. He hadn't noticed her straying fingers.

"What does that mean?" she asked.

"Brine and laziness."

"Oh, well, that explains it," Dani said with languid sarcasm. "Why didn't I figure that out?"

Shane looked back over his shoulder at her.

"See those cameras?" he asked.

"I saw them yesterday."

"They're supposed to provide continuous, overlapping coverage of the fence."

Dani watched the slowly sweeping cameras.

"Looks like they're doing the job," she said after a few moments.

"Not quite. Every three minutes they don't overlap."

Dani frowned. "For how long?"

"Twenty-nine seconds."

"How big is the gap in coverage?"

"Big enough for a man to get through," Shane said.

"You aren't thinking—" she began.

"I sure as hell am," he interrupted. "Every three minutes, the part of the fence next to the resort's sand volleyball courts is invisible to the Harmony's control center."

"Gillie said we're going to meet our contact *off* the grounds."

"Uh huh."

Shane's agreement didn't reassure Dani. If anything, it did the opposite.

"The razor wire doesn't look a bit rusty," she pointed out.

"Sure doesn't. Reminds me. I'd better shave. We're due at the museum after breakfast."

Dani started to say something, then gave up. Shane was already on his feet again, headed for the bathroom.

At least, she thought, he's wearing shorts instead of the *cache-sex* bikini that was in his luggage. My God. Being bare-assed nude would be less revealing.

And less unsettling.

By the time Shane and Dani were on the road at midmorning, heavy clouds had boiled up, giving Aruba an unearthly look. Old Town's waterfront with its orange and blue stucco buildings had an eerie radiance against the clouds. The Dutch windmills seemed both more fitting against gray skies and completely out of place next to the swaying palms.

Shane had raised the top of the blue rental convertible before they left the hotel. Even with air-conditioning, the interior of the car was oppressive.

They parked on a quiet street in back of Aruba's open-air market and set off on foot.

"That's the place," Shane said.

Dani glanced across the narrow street as they passed the building Shane had indicated with a subtle movement of his head.

"Keep walking," Shane said. "I want to check out the neighborhood before we go inside."

"Museo Numismatico," Dani said, reading the sign. "A money museum?"

"Money fuels this little island paradise. Three hundred and fifty banks and damn near that many casinos."

"A fitting place to meet a spy," Dani said under her breath. "I assume your man Boston is well paid for infiltrating the Harmony?"

"How much is a human life worth?"

"Frighteningly little in some places," she retorted.

Shane didn't disagree. He had spent most of his adult life in just those places.

"Boston is from an old Aruban family," Shane said. "His father died just before he was due to become prime minister."

"Natural causes?"

"If you call greed natural."

"What happened?" Dani asked.

"The Colombians killed him ten years ago, when they needed a place to set up their crooked banks."

"He didn't want them on Aruba?"

"No, but the new prime minister couldn't take their bribes fast enough. Hand over fist is his chosen style," Shane said.

"Why am I not surprised?"

"Boston despises money," Shane said. "He thinks it's responsible for destroying the island."

"The *love* of money is the root of all evil," Dani corrected. "Money is just that. Money."

Shane smiled swiftly, coldly.

"Boston doesn't share your academic approach to the subject," he said. "He's old-fashioned. He wants to annihilate the people who turned Aruba into the cesspool of the financial world."

"Is that why he joined Risk Limited?"

"No. That's why we contacted him. Boston is the chief of household staff on Katya's estate."

Dani shook her head slowly. "From what Gillie told me about Katya, Boston should get combat pay."

"She's a real bitch to work for, but Boston has a dream."

"Of what?"

"Sinking a knife in Katya's back all the way to the bloody hilt."

Dani stumbled slightly. Shane caught her arm and steadied her.

"Sorry," she said. "The world keeps shifting under my feet."

"Is this when I say 'I told you so'?"

"No."

"You're sure?"

"Drop off," Dani said in perfect imitation of Gillie's British accent.

Shane laughed and kept holding her arm. Not that Dani needed it any longer. It was just that her skin felt good beneath his fingers.

"Where did Boston take his training?" Dani asked.

Shane gave her a blank look. "Training?"

"You know. How to be a covert operative in enemy territory, that sort of thing."

"Boston is a smart, well-connected civilian with a grudge. That's his entire training."

"Katya isn't a civilian."

"So far Boston hasn't found any sign that he's under any more suspicion than anyone else in the household."

Shane stopped and inspected a shop window.

Dani waited, wondering just which of the window's dusty offerings had attracted his attention.

Then she realized that Shane wasn't looking through the glass at all. He was using it as a mirror to check their back trail.

A fat drop of rain splashed on the broken sidewalk in front of them. Dani looked at the threatening sky.

"The travel brochures didn't talk about rain," Dani said.

"Every November, just like clockwork."

The satisfaction in Shane's voice was unmistakable. He watched as the people around them looked up at the black clouds and then began looking around for places to hide.

"Here she comes," Shane said.

Another fat drop smacked a tattered canvas awning above their heads. Then another drop and another. Suddenly the air turned to water. Vendors in the open-air market closed up as their customers ran for the nearest cover.

"Come on," Shane said. "Here's where we make like tourists trying to get in out of the rain."

Grabbing Dani's hand, he led her back down the street at a trot. Soon they were at the front door of the museum. A thin, well-dressed black man in a tropical suit and a white straw hat entered just ahead of them. The man paid no attention while Shane bought two tickets and dragged Dani inside after him.

The only other person in sight was a sleepy-looking guard. He was holding up the door frame of the first gallery with his back. It looked like a job he was used to.

The first gallery was filled with displays of Central and South American currency. All Dani got was a fast look, for Shane kept tugging on her hand.

"Forget the pretty paper," Shane said. "The good stuff is up ahead.

"Good stuff?"

"Gold."

"The love of which is the root of all evil, right?"

"Whatever you say, professor."

"Actually, I'm only an associate professor. If I'm a good girl, my promotion will come through before Christmas."

Shane said nothing. He had just spotted Boston who was examining a display of Spanish *reales* and gold doubloons.

A quick glance around assured Shane that there was no one else in the gallery or the doorways.

"Here we are," Shane said. "The real twenty-four carat thing."

For a few moments the three people stood side by side yet distant, like strangers admiring the display.

Dani didn't know what the men were doing, but she was listening with every pore in her body for the sound of approaching footsteps.

There were none.

After a bit longer, Boston swept off his white hat and bowed slightly to Dani and Shane.

"You must forgive my poor island," he said. "The sun will soon return."

"That's all right," Shane said. "I like gold."

"There is much gold on Aruba."

Boston smiled broadly, showing a full set of bright white teeth.

Dani noticed his eyes were anything but servile. He was assessing her with a swift intelligence he didn't bother to disguise.

"Is this the only place we can talk?" Shane asked in a low voice.

"The guard is my brother," Boston said.

Shane still didn't look happy.

"He is one of the last surviving members of the Aruban Liberation Front," Boston said in a low voice. "He is no more lured by money than I am."

Shane looked around swiftly. They were still alone

"You are Miss Danielle Warren?" Boston asked.

"Dani," she corrected.

Boston gestured toward the displays.

"Once this was the Happy Island," he said. "Aruba was the one place in the Caribbean that was never tainted by African slavery."

Dani nodded. Gillie's briefing had been thorough.

"Yet now our people are surrendering their freedom willingly to monsters in the name of greed," Boston said bitterly.

"They won't be the first," Shane said, "or the last. Which of the Harmony's monsters are here at the moment?"

"Only the chief dragon, Katya."

"Good. Less security that way."

Boston nodded. "Delegates from the constituent organizations intend to gather again, soon."

"Here?" Shane asked.

"No. The Pacific Coast of the United States."

"That's a long way from Sicily or Chicago," Shane said.

"It is for the convenience of the Chinese representatives."

A stillness came over Shane.

"Katya has finally lured them in?" he asked.

"I fear Tony Liu is the Harmony's newest member," Boston said.

"Bloody hell. Are you certain?"

Boston shrugged fluidly.

"Katya presented Liu's Christmas stocking to him with her own white hands," Boston said. "She and Liu talked privately for some time—long enough to make de la Pena restless."

"Do you know what was in the stocking?" Shane asked.

"I cannot be certain. It appeared to be a passport."

"American?" Shane asked skeptically.

"Possibly. From what I saw at a distance, it was blue."

"So are Canadian passports," Dani pointed out.

"What about the Japanese?" Shane asked.

"That remains to be seen," Boston said. "Katya has great expectations for the Yakuza. She is courting several, but mostly Kojimura and Ishida."

"It would be too much to hope that Ishida joins instead of Kojimura," Shane muttered.

"Why?" asked Dani.

"Ishida's life expectancy can be measured in weeks. Kojimura has a knife just waiting."

"A short life but a happy one," Dani said sardonically.

"The shorter the better," Shane said. He turned to Boston. "When and where is the meeting?"

Boston shook his head unhappily.

"Katya, the honeyed bitch," Boston said, "trusts me with nothing beyond household chores."

"She even makes her own travel arrangements?" Shane asked.

"She keeps records, travel plans and the like, in her personal computer."

"Coded?"

"I do not know." Boston shrugged eloquently. "Most certainly she works in Russian, of which I am ignorant."

"Do you know her access code?" Shane asked.

"I do not understand."

"Some computers are programmed so that only a person with the correct code can use it."

"The computer itself is a code so far as I am concerned," Boston said. "I know nothing about such machines other than the name I managed to send to your superior. Nor does anyone else on the staff. Katya is most careful in such things."

"Where is her computer?" Shane asked.

"In her personal quarters."

"Locked away?"

"Why lock up an enigma?" Boston asked. "The machine is on a desk in the sitting room of her private wing. It is always turned on. She has great contempt for Arubans, myself most of all."

"Or vodka is finally affecting her judgment," Shane said.

"The devil would not be so kind," Boston murmured, "and God has abandoned His corrupt Eden."

Though Boston's voice was calm, the tension in his body promised the kind of violence that hell would understand.

"There is a safe in the Czarina's room," Boston said. "Though I have never used it, I have obtained the combination."

Surprised, Dani looked at Shane. He had no expression on his face, but she sensed that he already knew about the safe and its combination.

"What I need from you," Shane said to Boston, "is more about this meeting with the Asians. Anything you've overheard might be helpful."

"I know only that Katya has been working on it for many months. She is obsessed with bringing all of Asia into the Harmony."

"China isn't a bad start," Dani said dryly.

"It's not enough," Shane said. "Too much of China is still in the nineteenth century—if they're lucky. Katya needs Japan's twenty-first-century access to the Pacific Rim's financial levers."

"She should make a run at the United Nations."

"Why bother?" Shane said. "All they do is talk. The Harmony's members wash blood off their hands long enough to shake and make deals before they go back to bloodletting."

Boston smiled slightly.

Dani thought of a knife in Katya's back.

"I believe the Japanese whom Katya is courting are powerful

men in their own country," Boston said, "but they almost certainly have criminal records."

"Why?" Dani asked. "Simply because they're associated with her?"

"The men had great difficulty in securing entry papers into the United States," Boston said. "Katya spent many thousands of dollars smoothing the way."

"Interesting," Shane murmured. "Where is Katya right now?"

"At home."

"What about Kasatonin?"

"He left this morning."

"Good. I'd hate to stumble over him in the dark."

"I, on the other hand," Boston said, "pray for his swift return. Without him, Katya is as pleasant as a cat in heat."

"Did Kasatonin bring anything unusual with him?" Dani asked. "A metallic tube about a meter long, or a glass tube with a piece of cloth inside?"

Boston shook his head. "He arrived, as always, with no more than a passport and much cash."

"Damn," Dani said. "Maybe he stashed it at the airport."

"More likely he hasn't seen it since Tibet," Shane said. "That's what I would have done in his shoes—get as far away from it as possible until the heat dies down."

"It?" Boston asked.

When Dani would have answered, Shane cut her off.

"It's safer for Boston if he doesn't know," Shane said bluntly.

"But if I see such an odd item as a metal tube or a glass tube . . . ?" Boston asked.

"Grab it, get the hell off the estate, and get in touch with Risk Limited as fast as you can," Shane said.' 'Don't even stop to kill Katya. Understand?"

Boston hesitated, then nodded.

"When Katya is sleeping alone, what are her habits?" Shane asked. "When does she get up, when does she go to bed?"

"If Katya is not entertaining," Boston said, "she goes to

her quarters around nine. Often she will work on the computer or the telephones until midnight."

"How do you know? Do you listen in?"

"The light from the computer reflects on the window," Boston said. "When she works, the light is different."

Shane nodded.

"As for listening in," Boston continued. "I have not done that yet. Nor will I, until I am ready to die. Katya has ways of finding out who listens and who does not."

Shane wasn't surprised.

"After she works on the computer or the phones," he said. "What then?"

"If Kasatonin is not available, Katya drinks until she can sleep without nightmares."

"How long does that take?" Dani asked curiously.

"An hour, no more. Katya is not subtle when she addresses her bottle of vodka."

"So by one A.M. she's out cold?" Shane asked.

Boston shrugged. "It seems that way. The few times I interrupted her for urgent messages, I had to shake her awake."

"When does she get up?"

"Dawn. Always."

Shane whistled softly. "That's one tough female."

"Yes," Boston agreed. "She has great discipline, great ambition, and a fertile, corrupt mind."

"What is Katya doing tonight?" Shane asked.

"She is giving an intimate dinner party for a dozen bankers from Oranjestad and Medellin."

"Will that keep her in the main house, away from her private quarters?" Shane asked.

Boston hesitated.

"Usually Katya will be occupied until midnight, perhaps even one o'clock, by such a party," the man said slowly. "She must make certain her male guests are . . . satisfied."

"Does she amuse them herself?" Dani asked.

"Katya?" Boston smiled coldly. "Never. She accepts a man only under threat of death and will not satisfy him. Kasatonin takes her by force but can do nothing about it."

Dani thought of the photograph she had seen of Kasatonin.

"A rather, er, unique arrangement," she said.

"It works for them," Shane said laconically. "So, Katya will be away from her quarters most of the evening. What about the rest of the staff? The guards?"

"The staff is much less alert when Kasatonin is away," Boston said.

"Including the gate guards?"

"Sadly, no. They are Turks. But the rest of the security force is made up of island people. They are too gentle to make good watchdogs."

"Not all of them," Shane said, looking pointedly at Boston.

"Ah, yes. But I have hired all the men except the gate guards."

"Including the maintenance men, no doubt."

Boston's smile reminded Dani of a shark.

"What's the perimeter security like?" Shane asked.

"Unless Kasatonin is in residence, there is but one man watching the monitors. He spends most of the evening with his television monitors tuned to the commercial stations in Caracas."

"Kasatonin would have a litter of green lizards," Shane said. "He's a gung-ho bastard."

"He shares Katya's contempt for Arubans. Why should he not? The Harmony has bought everyone on the island who matters."

"Does the guard ever get hungry during his lonely watch?" Shane asked.

"He is courting a pastry cook."

"Good. See that she—or he—takes up a snack at ten-thirty tonight."

"A snack?" Boston asked, smiling. "Perhaps a bowl of galina sopi well seasoned with chloral hydrate?"

"Nothing that direct. Just make sure he's distracted from his screens at exactly ten-thirty."

"Is that all?"

"It will be enough," Shane said.

At least, he added silently, I hope to hell it will be.

Chapter Eighteen

Washington, D.C.
November

The music is all wrong for a high-quality bookstore, Cassandra Redpath thought irritably. Bookstores need Baroque or Renaissance concerti, or even medieval chants.

But in DuPont Circle, dissonance and cacophony reigned.

Redpath glared at the loudspeaker behind the service counter. A group that sounded like pigs mating during a rocket launch had been thumping out of the speakers for the past twenty minutes.

As though in response to Redpath's ire, a new disc slid into place. A rap anthem came over the speakers in machine-gun bursts of urban hatred.

On the whole, Redpath decided, I'll take rutting swine.

The girl at the cash register was anorexic. Except for a purple bandanna tied around her head like a sweat band, she was clad entirely in black. The metal studs piercing her ears, eyebrows, and nostrils were numerous enough to set off a metal detector.

The clerk didn't notice Redpath standing on the other side

of the cash register. She was too busy scowling down at an open biology textbook on the counter in front of her.

Redpath put the books she had selected on the counter. The thump was enough to lift a few pages of the biology text.

The clerk looked up with a total lack of interest.

"Canihelpya."

Redpath ran the sounds through the language computer in her brain. Twice. Finally she decided it was English.

"*Canihelpya,*" the clerk repeated with emphasis.

"Yes, you may help me," Redpath enunciated carefully. "I would like to pay for these books."

"Yah?"

"Yah," Redpath said.

"You read this stuff?"

"No, I use it for weight-lifting."

"Cool."

The clerk looked at the books and then at the cash register as though trying to remember the connection.

"The noise makes it difficult to concentrate," Redpath suggested.

"I can't concentrate, like, anywhere?" the girl said. "It's way bad here? All these books, like, string me out?"

Her voice lifted into a higher note at the final word of every sentence, turning what should have been statements into tentative questions. So far as Redpath was concerned, it was the most annoying linguistic tic to come into vogue since *ya know?*

"Do you read?" Redpath asked with mild interest.

"Huh?"

"Words. Sentences. Perhaps even entire paragraphs."

"Oh, sure thing," the girl said with a shrug. "They said I had to read to get the job."

"But *do* you read?"

"You mean, like, books?"

Redpath nodded.

"Uh, no," the girl said. "I'm more a listening person?"

"Thank God there are books on tape," Redpath muttered.

The girl blinked. "I meant CDs?"

"Of course," Redpath said. "Whatever was I thinking of?"

She slid a hundred dollar bill across the counter to pay for the three books.

"Cool," the clerk said. "Is it real?"

Redpath thought of pointing out that people who read often have access to more real money than those who don't, but decided it wasn't worth the effort.

"It's real," Redpath said.

The clerk moved her lips slowly, reading each title as she punched numbers into the machine: *Chinese Triads and the Opium Wars, Silk and the Asian Mind, The New Russian Mafias.*

"You really gonna read this stuff?" the girl asked.

"Tonight? No. But over time, yes."

A look of sympathy went over the clerk's face as she rang up the sales.

"You need a life, ya know?" she whispered.

Redpath laughed. "Last time I checked, I had one."

"No, I mean a real one?"

"So did I."

Shaking her head, the clerk counted change and handed it over, along with a plastic bag which contained Redpath's books.

"Haveaniceday," the clerk said automatically, even though it was almost nine p.m.

Redpath slipped the books into her leather bag, shouldered it, and pushed open the bookstore's front door. For a moment she hesitated, trying to decide whether to walk or hail a cab.

A harvest moon was rising gold over the trees of Rock Creek Park. The sweet-sharp tang of burning leaves hung in the air.

Cold but invigorating, Redpath decided.

She had just come from a tai chi chuan session conducted by an instructor from the People's Republic interest section. Her body felt alive and her concentration was heightened. She wore slacks, a jacket, and comfortable shoes.

A walk will be tickety-boo, as Gillie would say, Redpath thought, smiling.

The smile faded at the thought of what Gillespie would say if he knew she was walking alone in the dark.

On the other hand, Gillespie wasn't due back until after midnight. He would be tired, but he would need food and a chance to decompress. Redpath had ordered a light supper for him before they retired to their connecting rooms.

As long as I get home before Gillie does, Redpath told herself silently, I won't have to listen to a lecture about security and going out after dark without him.

Their worst and most long-standing argument revolved around Redpath's refusal to have any bodyguard but Gillespie invade her personal space. On that, she had been adamant.

Redpath turned south, choosing the well-lighted route down Connecticut.

A short time later a large man stepped out of the shadows of a doorway. He wasn't quite close enough to threaten her.

"Good evening, Ambassador," he said in a pleasant voice.

Redpath half-turned. She knew him instantly.

Ilya Kasatonin.

Kasatonin saw Redpath's pupils expand as she recognized him.

"Be calm and nothing will happen to you," he said softly. "Understand, though, that I hold Sergeant-Major Gillespie's life in my hands."

"I doubt that," Redpath said.

Kasatonin held up a small cellular telephone in his right hand. The small red status light glowed urgently, showing that the device was in use.

"I would have spoken to you sooner," Kasatonin said, "but we lost the sergeant major earlier today."

"An elusive man, the sergeant major," Redpath said casually. "I doubt that you found him at all."

Then she waited, trying not to show the ice that had formed in her gut when Kasatonin stepped out of the night and spoke Gillespie's name.

"We have found him," Kasatonin said. "He is in Miami at the moment."

"So are a lot of people."

"Not all of them are waiting for a flight back to Washington, D.C."

Redpath merely lifted her auburn eyebrows and waited.

"You are skeptical," Kasatonin said. "But of course. Let me tell you exactly what he is doing."

Kasatonin lifted the telephone to his ear and spoke in Russian.

Although Redpath didn't show it, she understood every word. He was asking someone to describe what Gillespie was doing at the moment.

"They tell me," Kasatonin said in English to Redpath, "that he just purchased a soft pretzel at a kiosk. Something yellow—mustard, perhaps?—is on the pretzel."

Redpath devoutly hoped that her expression gave away nothing. As a vegetarian, Gillespie found little to eat at airports other than pretzels.

"He is reading a soft book," Kasatonin continued. "Paperback, is that the word?"

Redpath simply stared at him.

"The title of the book is . . ." Kasatonin stopped.

He growled a short question into the phone.

"Culloden?" Kasatonin repeated to Redpath. "Is there such a book?"

For an instant Redpath's heart stopped in her chest. She nodded her head curtly.

"A book by John Prebble," Redpath said, hoping her voice sounded normal. "It's about the Scottish Highlanders' last stand against England."

Redpath didn't add that she had seen Gillespie pack the book ten hours before, when he had left the townhouse.

Kasatonin's smile was strangely sad.

"Culloden," he said quietly. "Would I enjoy it? Sergeant-Major Gillespie and I share many interests, as you know."

"Not the kind that matter."

The odd smile vanished, leaving Kasatonin's face blank. It was the face of a man whom nothing touched. Whatever life he had enjoyed, whatever death he had delivered, whatever agony he had taken or given; none of it truly had touched him.

As Redpath watched Kasatonin's face, she wondered if the Afghanis had excised more than his genitals.

"This phone," Kasatonin said, "is my link to someone who holds your sergeant major's life in his hands. If you signal your bodyguards or do anything that would attract attention, he is dead. Do you understand this?''

Redpath didn't trust her voice not to reveal her anger and her fear. She simply nodded.

Bodyguards, Redpath thought. Ah, Gillie, you were right. But who guards you when I'm not there?

The people walking by on the sidewalk showed no curiosity about the man standing just inside a shadowed portico and the woman who had paused nearby. There were no gun in sight. Kasatonin wasn't standing close enough to Redpath to appear threatening. To any passing pedestrian, it appeared she had stopped to talk to an acquaintance.

Cautious man, Redpath thought bitterly. Since he didn't kill me outright, he must have some use for me.

The thought wasn't reassuring.

Kasatonin's eyes constantly probed the shadows across the street and the automobiles that cruised slowly by.

Thank God he believes that I've got a bodyguard or two stashed just out of sight, Redpath thought.

Next time I'll listen to you, Gillie.

If there is a next time for either of us.

Deliberately Redpath took her mind off of Gillespie. He had been stalked by killers before. He had done his share of stalking in turn. All she could do was keep her head and buy time.

For both of them.

"What do you want?" Redpath asked distinctly.

"I would like to discuss a business proposition," Kasatonin said. "It is something that will be of much benefit to both of us."

Redpath waited, watching Kasatonin with eyes that showed glints of emerald even in the darkness of night.

"The bus bench," Kasatonin said. "If you please?"

As he spoke, he gestured toward a bench about fifteen yards down the street.

Redpath turned and went to the bench without a word. When she sat down, she held the book bag against her torso. She doubted that three hardback books would be enough to stop a bullet. On the other hand, it was the best armor she had, other than Kasatonin's belief that she wasn't as alone as she appeared.

Kasatonin held the phone to his ear and spoke in Russian, asking about Gillespie's scheduled departure from the airport. Then he reminded the man on the other end of the line that Gillespie was an accomplished assassin. He repeated the fact twice, apparently unsatisfied with his comrade's response.

Silently Redpath wished Gillespie good hunting.

"I want to know," Kasatonin said, lowering the phone, "that we have the greatest respect for you and your organization."

His smile was bland. His eyes never left Redpath's hands, as though he thought her dangerous despite the threat to Gillespie's life.

"We?" Redpath asked.

"Come, Ambassador. You recognized me."

"Ilya Kasatonin?" she asked.

He tilted his head in a sardonic bow.

"In that case," Redpath said crisply, "the 'we' to which you refer is a mongrel assembly known as the Harmony. It is presided over by a whoremistress called Katya Pilenkova."

Kasatonin's thin lips shifted into a smile that might have been truly amused.

"The Harmony," he said. "Katya's little joke. We are simply a shifting confederation of individuals who share common interests."

Redpath said nothing.

Kasatonin watched her hands very carefully.

"As a matter of fact," he said, "your organization shares many of the Harmony's interests."

"That surpasses belief," Redpath said flatly.

"Not at all. You and the people of your organization are intelligent, aggressive human beings who are willing to gamble much—sometimes even life itself—to pursue your interests."

"Our interests are not those of the Harmony."

"You have a global vision," Kasatonin continued as though Redpath hadn't spoken. "Such clarity is rare in a world that is spiraling down into clan warfare and the tyranny of barbarous warlords."

"The process you describe is being hastened by every member of the Harmony and fought by every member of Risk Limited," Redpath said. "I fail to see where our interests coincide."

"You have extraordinary resources," Kasatonin said. "No organization except the former KGB or the CIA of twenty years ago could summon up so many diverse assets around the world with a phone call."

"How flattering and how untrue. Have you considered a job in advertising, lobbying, or selling snake oil?"

Kasatonin laughed once, more surprised than amused.

"You are too modest," he said.

"I am a realist."

"No organization save your own was able to penetrate the Sicilian's heroin apparatus, and to cause such damage that they are still repairing it."

Redpath stared at Kasatonin without expression.

"I was unaware of such a coup," she said. "I salute whichever group managed it."

"Salute yourself, Ambassador. Someone informed the Italian police about that shipment. Then that same informant passed the word to the Americans in order to force Italian action. Thus, the shipment was confiscated."

"Amazing."

"We know this happened, because the informant then sold the same information to us."

"An active person, especially in regard to imagination," Redpath said.

"Informing the Americans was a brilliant idea," Kasatonin said. "I must congratulate you. Nothing else would have persuaded the Italian government to move against the Mafia."

"Assuming what you say is true, which it isn't, how would that make our interests coincide?" Redpath asked. "The Sicilians are first among equals in the Harmony."

"That confiscation was a double stroke against us," Kasatonin said matter-of-factly.

"Delightful."

"The shipment was financed by Russian money," he said.

"As you know, Western currency is a precious commodity in my country. Several heads rolled when the merchandise was lost. I mean that literally, of course."

"That's of no interest to me," Redpath said briskly. "Risk Limited is a private corporation that offers advice on security issues to American and foreign clients. We are neither policemen nor security guards. We advise and, on occasion, we assist."

"Advise? Assist?" Kasatonin asked coldly. "That darkhaired bastard who almost put a bullet through my head in Lhasa last month—tell me, was that advice or assistance he was dispensing?"

"You'll have to ask him. I don't know what you're talking about." Redpath smiled slightly. "But if you find him, do pass his name along to me. We're always interested in people who can operate in Asia."

Kasatonin glanced at his watch. When he looked at Redpath again, she knew that whatever time she and Gillespie had left was running out.

"Enough fencing," Kasatonin said curtly. "We know much about your operation. It is very impressive. That is why we are offering you an opportunity to join the Harmony."

Unable to disguise her shock, Redpath simply stared at Kasatonin.

"If you know anything about Risk Limited at all," she said finally, "you know we detest everything the Harmony represents."

"Power and money are universal goals. You make that point time and again in your writings. The Harmony offers a direct route to both."

"I'll take the long way around," Redpath said.

"Do not be hasty. We live now in a world where superpowers have collapsed, where nations such as the United States no longer have the will to act, and where lesser powers are interested only in maintaining civil order. To summarize, there is an international power vacuum."

"Succinctly put."

"Thank you. I took it from one of your articles."

"I doubt that you needed to."

Kasatonin's smile was as coldly intelligent as his eyes.

"You are correct," he said. "The power vacuum will be filled by the Harmony. We will then crush our enemies." He lifted the telephone in his hand.

"If you choose to disregard our offer, "we will begin our retribution, right here, right now, tonight."

Gillespie.

Cold swirled inside Redpath. Kasatonin was shrewd. So was the whoremistress who stood behind him.

Why are they pushing so hard right now? Redpath asked herself silently.

Then the answer came.

The silk.

For some reason that scrap of cloth was so precious to the Harmony that they would rather recruit the opposition than gamble on losing the silk.

Recruit us or kill us, Redpath thought. No difference really.

A garbled sound emerged from the cellular phone. Kasatonin put the telephone to his ear.

"Yes, sack of shit," he said in harsh Russian, "follow him by all means. Remember! Do not get too close. He may be an aging lion, yet his teeth are still sharp."

Kasatonin lowered the phone.

"You see," he said, "I respect men such as Gillespie. The range of his talents is rare and very valuable. In the shifting alliances known as the Harmony, such a man would be useful to me."

"Gillie is the last person in the world who would cast his lot with the Harmony."

"That is why we did not make our offer to him. He is a guard dog loyal only to you."

Redpath sat very still.

"You," Kasatonin said, "are a commodity worth guarding. When it comes to international power, you have a profoundly inventive and insightful mind."

"So does your boss," Redpath pointed out.

"She is not in your league. Katya is a woman of splendid

criminal instincts. She is perfect for the dogs of the Harmony who pant after her.''

Redpath raised her eyebrows and said not one word. She hadn't been recruited by the enemy for many years, but she hadn't forgotten the first rule: get away alive.

"When the power of a criminal group surpasses a certain point," Kasatonin said, "the group either falls apart into warring units, or it finds a leader clever enough to take the gang into the world of 'legitimate' power. The world of stocks and bonds, lobbyists and governments. Katya cannot take the Harmony there. You can."

"Remarkable," Redpath said, meaning it. "What about you?"

He shrugged. "I have no patience for toadying to fools. You will advise me."

"I would lose my contacts very rapidly when word got out that I was advising the Harmony."

"No one need ever know except the two of us."

"Katya isn't a fool."

"Katya is a beautiful, lethal weapon made of ice. Vodka melts her."

"Not noticeably," Redpath retorted.

"It will become noticeable. She will miscalculate. You will step into her place."

Redpath didn't notice the cold of the bench seeping into her body, nor the cold wind blowing down the neck of her coat. She was thinking on many levels at once.

Kasatonin's offer could be real.

It could be as false as his smile.

It could be both, depending on the circumstances.

In any case, Gillespie's life and Redpath's own depended on what she said in the next few moments.

Silently Redpath saluted the inventiveness of the Harmony's approach. Given his choice, Kasatonin probably would have killed Gillespie as a warning to Redpath and Risk Limited. But this tactic had elegance and finesse.

Collaboration rather than blunt force.

Katya Pilenkova is more subtle than I would have guessed, Redpath thought. Or Kasatonin is.

The second thought was more chilling than the first.

"Suppose I were interested in pursuing your offer," Redpath said slowly. "How would we proceed?"

"It is quite simple. We must establish a basis of mutual trust between us."

Redpath managed not to smile. Kasatonin spoke the words as though he had just thought of them, as though he had never gone to other people and corrupted them with bribes or threats or flattery or beatings.

As though he didn't hold Gillespie's life in his callused hand.

"Someone must make the first step toward trust," Kasatonin said.

The cellular made another garbled sound. He lifted it to his ear, listened, and frowned.

"Yes, of course," Redpath said quickly, praying hard and fast in the depths of her soul. "What did you have in mind?"

Kasatonin hesitated, listening. His mouth hardened.

Redpath shifted on the bench like she had just realized that she was talking to the enemy and was having second thoughts about the whole matter.

As Kasatonin and she both knew, recruitment was a delicate process. An interruption at the wrong moment, a wrong look or word, and the fish slipped the hook before he—or she— was in the net.

Deliberately Redpath began fussing with her handbag, shifting her feet, and looking around for approaching people. She was the very picture of a woman becoming more and more ill-at-ease with her situation.

"Xepa," Kasatonin snarled.

He lowered the phone and concentrated on Redpath.

"The name of your informant within the Harmony," Kasatonin said, "would be an appropriate gesture of unity with your new associates."

"You're assuming that I have such an informant."

"You must. No one could have done us so much damage over the past few years without a source of information."

Redpath fussed with her bag some more, a woman thinking, weighing matters carefully.

"If there were such an informant," she said finally, slowly, "it would be a very valuable asset. What do I get in return?"

"Another valuable asset. The sergeant major."

"Even if I did have an asset inside your organization," Redpath said, "I couldn't spend it in the way you suggest and still be useful to you."

"Why not?" Kasatonin demanded bluntly.

"Risk Limited relies on the voluntary cooperation of our assets. If word spread that I had disclosed an asset's identity, I would have none left in the field."

Kasatonin shook his head.

"I am surprised at you, Ambassador," he said. "To protect a minor pawn—probably one of Katya's whores—you would sacrifice a knight such as Gillespie."

"Gillespie is far more valuable than a knight," Redpath said. "That's why I want to make a counteroffer."

"You are not in a position to bargain."

Kasatonin lifted the phone to his ear.

"Wait!" Redpath said urgently. "You can always kill a man, but you can't resurrect him. Hear me out."

The conviction in her voice stopped Kasatonin.

"Speak, then," he said curtly.

"I would be willing to withdraw any assets I might have inside the Harmony and to promise that I won't seek to employ any more."

Kasatonin looked thoughtful.

"In return," Redpath continued, "you will agree to several conditions. The most important would be that I must deal, face to face, with Katya Pilenkova."

Kasatonin shook his head.

"Impossible," he said. "Katya might be willing to meet you, but before such a move could be considered, I must know the name of the informer."

"Why?" Redpath asked blandly.

"A simple matter of discipline."

"But you agree to the second condition?"

''Katya Pilenkova is a friendly woman,'' Kasatonin said indifferently. ''She is always pleased to meet people.''

''Have her come see me,'' Redpath suggested quickly. ''There are things I would tell her and only her.''

''There is one thing you must tell me immediately. Who is your spy? A whore? A member of the household staff? For the past week I've had them all under close surveillance, but I must be certain.''

Boston. Shane. Dani.

Despite the names ricocheting through Redpath's mind, she didn't so much as flinch.

''Or is it one of those verminous bankers in Oranjestad?'' Kasatonin demanded. ''I must know!''

''I didn't say there was an informant,'' Redpath reminded him calmly. ''I simply said I have some information that Katya could use profitably.''

''The name,'' Kasatonin said. *''Now.''*

Redpath drew a deep breath and played her trump.

''I will cooperate,'' she said, ''but first I must be sure you speak for the Harmony and are not using this simply as a ploy for your own purposes. Let me speak to Pilenkova.''

''No,'' Kasatonin said.

He put the phone to his ear.

''Do you have him in your sights?'' he demanded.

Redpath froze, caught between ugly choices.

Gillespie was the most physically and mentally resourceful man she knew, yet the Harmony had access to the world's most skillful killers.

Then, too, there was her informant. She owed Boston a moral debt.

''Let me talk to Katya,'' Redpath pleaded. ''Where is the harm in that? Let me be certain you're acting with her approval.''

''No.''

In calm Russian, Kasatonin ordered his man to kill Gillespie at the first clean opportunity.

''If you listen carefully,'' Kasatonin said, holding out the phone to Redpath, "you might hear the shot that kills Sergeant-Major Gillespie."

"No!"

"Then tell me the name!" he snarled. "It is not too late. Yet."

Gillie!

Redpath heard a faint noise from the phone. It was someone announcing a final boarding call in Spanish.

Then she heard a scrambling sound and a choked groan of pain. More vague noises crossed a thousand miles of telephone connection.

Feral sounds. The kind that came from extreme exertion.

Redpath had heard those same sounds from Gillespie as he worked out hour after hour with Shane and with other men and women similarly skilled in martial arts.

Good hunting, Gillie.

Kasatonin clamped the phone to his own ear and began speaking in rapid Russian.

"Chechin. Chechin! What is happening? Answer me!"

Redpath yearned to rip the phone from Kasatonin's hand and listen for herself.

The Russian's face was unreadable. Then a faint smile played across his lips. Silently he held the phone out to Redpath.

She snatched it and turned partially away, afraid of what Kasatonin might read in her own expression.

"Yes?" Redpath said, her voice husky.

"Hello, pet. What in the name of God are you doing at the other end of this line?"

The sound of Gillespie's voice sent a wave of relief through her so great that she felt light-headed.

"Are you all right?" she asked.

"Bugger me. What about you?"

"Good question."

She turned to look at Kasatonin.

The bus bench was deserted. So was the sidewalk. It was as though Kasatonin had never existed.

For an instant Redpath thought she heard the faint brush of

footfalls drifting back from a nearby alley. Then the night was hers again.

She was alone.

"I'm all right," she said. "Are you sure you aren't hurt, Gillie?"

"Nothing permanent, which is more than I can say about the two wankers who just tried to kill me. What in hell is going on?"

Gillespie was breathing lightly, quickly, as though he had just run a fifty-yard dash and was now catching his breath.

"Later," Redpath said. "First we have to contact Shane. I'm afraid they've been compromised."

"Bloody hell," Gillespie said. "Get on it, guv. I'll keep."

Quickly she started punching in the numbers that would connect her to Risk Limited, and through that network to Shane Crowe.

As she worked over the phone, Redpath prayed that she wasn't calling a dead man.

Chapter Nineteen

Aruba
November

Tropical rain hammered down on the slanted roof of the bungalow in a steady drum roll of sound. Except for the rain, the hotel room had been silent for some time.

With eyes as brooding as the night, Dani watched Shane.

If he noticed her stare, he ignored it. He was at the small dining table, working with the tools he had purchased that afternoon in Oranjestad.

"I still think this is a piss poor idea," she said bluntly.

"Gillie didn't. That's why he packed a hard drive and cables along with the butt-floss bikinis."

"We're supposed to be a team."

"It's too dangerous for you inside the estate," he said curtly.

"But not for you?" Dani retorted.

"Right."

"Wrong!"

Shane looked up. His face was expressionless, his dark eyes calm.

"All I need is five minutes with Katya's computer," he said.

"Is that all?" Dani asked sarcastically. "Why don't you just ask for a fairy godmother and a golden carriage while you're at it?"

"Too noticeable."

"Damn it, this isn't a joke!"

"Am I laughing?"

"Shane, that computer could be wired into the whole security system."

"It isn't."

"How do you know?"

"Boston."

"What if he's wrong?" Dani demanded.

"What if he isn't?"

Dani made a sound of exasperation, shot out of the chair, and began pacing. While she did, she watched Shane.

Without looking at her, he wrapped plastic around a square, metal box the size of a loaf of bread. He stuffed the package into a dark backpack.

The rest of Shane was dark, too. Dark, long-sleeved shirt, dark slacks, dark hair. His feet were covered by flexible black reef-walker shoes. A dark rain poncho hung over a nearby chair.

At first glance his clothes looked like fashionable, tropical-weight resort wear. A closer look revealed an unusual number of pockets. And even more careful scrutiny exposed an odd fact. None of his clothes were truly black. Instead, they were shades of darkness flowing together in random patterns.

Night camouflage, Dani realized, startled.

"No matter what Boston said, I can't believe Katya doesn't code her files," Dani said.

"I don't need to read them, all I need to do is copy them."

"But—"

"But nothing," Shane interrupted impatiently. "Cassandra has hackers on retainer. In their younger days, they once stole the monthly accounts receivable of American Express, just for the hell of it."

"This is supposed to reassure me?"

"It works for me. Those boys could unscramble a commercially encrypted file with a rusty nail."

"Then why haven't they hacked their way into Katya's computer?"

"She's too clever to hook it up to a modem. No modem, no access, no way to hack in. Except the old-fashioned way."

Smiling, Shane held up a hacksaw. It vanished into the backpack along with the hard drive. He added a few more tools, leaving only the bolt cutter on the table.

Dani stalked over to the table as Shane shrugged into the backpack.

"Let me go with you," she said. "I know more about computers than you do."

"I know enough to get the job done."

Shane picked up the bolt cutters and stowed them in a side pocket of his black pants.

"What am I supposed to do, *partner?*" Dani asked coldly. "Wring my hands and pray?"

"I'd rather you watch the back door."

"What?"

Shane dug a cellular phone out of his pocket. It was specially modified to vibrate rather than ring when there was an incoming call.

"Once I'm inside I won't be able to see the cameras," he explained. "You'll have to let me know when the fence is clear so I can come out."

Dani gave him a skeptical look.

Shane smiled blandly.

"You don't want me to walk out of the bushes and become the star of Aruba's Ugliest Home Videos, do you?" he asked.

With tightly controlled motions Dani went to the window and jerked the curtains aside.

"Both cameras are on high poles," she said. "Even in this cloudburst you'll be able to see them."

"You don't miss much, do you?"

"Something about nearly being killed sharpens the senses," Dani said sweetly.

There was a long silence while both of them listened to the thunder of rain on the roof.

As Dani watched Shane, she hoped against hope that he was finally listening to her.

After a time he came to her and put his hands on her cheeks. Gently, relentlessly, his thumbs tilted her face up until she could see his eyes.

Dani went very still. It was as though he had taken off a mask. The hunger she saw in him was as shocking as it was exhilarating.

"I'm not a Zen cyborg," Shane said. "When I look at you, I want you. All of you. As hard and deep as I can get."

He felt the shiver that went through her.

"Frightened?" he asked.

"No," she whispered.

"You should be. It scares the hell out of me. I'm a lone wolf. I always have been. I wasn't a part of anyone's life. But with you . . ."

Shane's voice faded. His hands tightened momentarily on Dani's cheeks while his thumbs caressed the line of her chin and the pulse beating rapidly in her throat.

"You're different," Shane said simply. "You cut through me right to the soul."

For a moment Dani simply looked at him. His eyes were like his words; clear, honest, ruthless. They left no place to hide.

For either of them.

I could love this man, Dani thought. If I let myself.

If he lets me.

A shiver of awareness went through her.

Shane felt it, too. A current was flowing between them that was as real as electricity.

He jerked his hands away from Dani's skin.

"You see what I mean?" he asked softly. "I have to go out alone tonight."

"But—"

"Listen to me," Shane interrupted fiercely. "I can't think

about you without wanting to touch you. I can't touch you without forgetting everything except how much I want you.''

Abruptly Shane turned away from Dani. He stared out the window at the black fence with its glistening top of razor wire. Silently he counted the sweeps of the cameras, watching for the moment they wouldn't overlap.

"The other night," Shane said, "I kissed you because I thought it would drive you away."

"What?"

"You're afraid of big men," he said simply.

"Not of you."

"Why?"

Dani hesitated, then shrugged.

"The whole time in that damned box coming out of Tibet," she said. "You didn't . . .''

She shrugged again.

"Take advantage?" Shane suggested dryly.

Dani nodded.

"That doesn't explain why you trust me," Shane said. "In that alley with Feng dead at your feet, I held out my hand and you took it. Why?"

"I'd seen you earlier."

"You'd seen Kasatonin earlier, too. Would you have taken his hand?"

"No," she said instantly.

"Why, Dani?"

"He wasn't you."

She heard Shane draw a quick breath. Then there was nothing but the drumming of rain on the roof.

"Do you always trust your gut instincts?" he asked after a few moments.

Dani hesitated, then shook her head.

"When I was younger," she said, "I didn't listen to that still, small voice deep inside me, telling me something was right or wrong."

"Your ex-husband?" Shane guessed.

"My ex," Dani agreed. "He was big, handsome, and charming in company. He wasn't bright, but he wasn't stupid. I told myself that no man is perfect, I'm certainly not perfect, all brides have second thoughts, and that sort of garbage."

The thunder of rain filled the silence.

"After that spectacular mistake," Dani said, "I decided to listen to my gut and to hell with so-called rationality."

Shane smiled faintly. "Spoken like a true Buddhist."

Dani would have laughed but was afraid it would sound more hysterical than humorous.

"Both my gut and my mind," Shane said, "tell me that I can't work if I have to keep looking over my shoulder to make sure you're all right. A man could get killed looking over his shoulder."

"A man could get killed leaving his back unguarded," Dani pointed out.

"I know. So stay behind and guard my back."

Dani closed her eyes and fought the fear that was growing in her like a living thing.

"I'm afraid for you," she said starkly.

Shane's laugh was as sharp and bitter as almond shells.

"I feel the same about you," he said.

"Then don't leave me behind!"

"I have a lifetime of experience in protecting myself. You don't. That's why I'm the boss and you aren't. Stay behind, Dani. Promise me."

She didn't speak.

"Dani? Can I count on you?"

Abruptly the whole stance of her body changed. Before she even spoke, Shane read her answer in the defeated line of her shoulders.

"I'll stay," Dani said.

Shane wanted to go to her, to touch her, to reassure her.

But he didn't trust himself to stop with a touch.

Hell of a mess, Shane told himself harshly. You'd think I never wanted a woman before.

Then he realized it was the simple truth. He hadn't wanted a woman before. Not like he wanted Danielle Warren.

Shane glanced at his watch. Time to go.

Quickly Shane grabbed the poncho, threw it over himself,

and zipped it up. The hood masked his face in shadow. Saying nothing, he pushed open one of the patio doors.

Without looking back he stepped into the storm-swept night. Moving like a shadow to the fence, he stopped at the base of a tall palm and merged with its outline.

Wind drove silvery curtains of rain across the estate's security lights. Shane didn't have to look at the cameras to check their positions. The rhythm of their routine was engraved on his mind.

Soon the cameras would scan past the palm, creating a gap in the security zone. Until then, Shane had to wait with the immobility of a stone.

Stillness was one of the many disciplines he had learned from the Azure monks. Prasam Dhamsa had been a fine teacher. He had seen in Shane what Shane had never seen in himself— patience, dedication, intelligence, a consuming hunger for something that was not death.

Dhamsa had also seen what Shane had only reluctantly concluded. The path of a monk wasn't Shane's path.

Now he understood.

How did you know, Prasam? Shane silently asked his old teacher. It was the last thing I would have guessed. Celibacy wasn't that difficult once I made up my mind.

Then Danielle Warren put her hand in mine, trusting me to pull her out of death into life. Or is it the other way around? Did she pull me into a new kind of life?

I'll have to ask Prasam when I see him again.

If I see him again.

Like Dani, I don't have a real good feeling about this. Too many amateurs. Too little time. Too much we don't know.

Heavy drops drummed on the soft rubberized fabric of Shane's poncho and fell in steady rivulets from its edge. He was already wet below the hips. But the computer hard drive in the pack was still dry.

Tickety-boo, as Gillie would say, Shane thought grimly. In this case, the man is simply a way to get the machine in and out the door of the Harmony. If the man gets wet, tough. Just keep the machine dry.

The seconds until the security window would open clicked by with the precision of a metronome in Shane's mind. Though nothing in his posture changed, a kind of elation began sliding through his blood as the countdown approached zero.

As always, Shane relished the freedom of the night. He was eager for the coming challenge, the certainty that he was doing something he knew, something he was good at, something he loved.

Something that mattered.

Yet even as his awareness of his own heightened senses came, he knew it was different this time than it had been in the past. His definition of freedom had changed. Part of him was impatient within the disciplined stillness. Part of him wanted it all to be over so that he could go back to the woman who waited for him because he had asked her to.

Just that. Asked.

Yet Dani was about as meek and submissive as a panther guarding her young. She was as unassuming as a wild tropical sunset. She had a mind like a razor blade and sometimes a tongue to match.

Yet she trusted him in a way no one ever had.

Not even himself.

Rain poured down with no rhythm at all. Random lightning scored the sky. Thunder rolled behind. Only the cameras and Shane's heartbeats were predictable.

He counted down the last seconds and stepped away from the palm's rain-soaked trunk. He didn't hurry. The gray-black shades of the poncho provided effective camouflage in the rain, but quick movement always drew attention. While he approached the wrought-iron fence, he slowly eased the bolt cutters from a pocket along his thigh.

A few careful scrapes on the painted metal told Shane he was in luck. Either before or after Katya had bought the property, someone had covered over the corroded state of the iron bars with a coat of black paint. The paint had quickly pitted. Salt air had been at work on the soft iron beneath for years.

The bars hadn't corroded evenly. Some of them were weaker

than others. Rapidly Shane inspected several bars, selected one, and went to work.

At first the bolt cutters bit easily through the rusty bar. Then metal met uncorroded metal. Shane closed both hands on the tool and pushed relentlessly. Sweat sprang on his forehead and spine, yet he made no noise of exertion.

There was a satisfying snap as the cutting jaws met. Kneeling, Shane swiftly made another cut a few inches above the ground. A three-foot section of vertical bar fell onto the sand.

He started to repeat the cuts on the adjacent bar. He wasn't as lucky this time. The bar was less corroded. He had to lever the bolt cutters up and down, up and down, up and down, and still the jaws didn't meet.

Seconds ticked off in his mind but he didn't rush. He simply ground the jaws of the bolt cutter together while muscles stood out on his neck and sweat ran freely down his spine beneath the poncho.

Finally another section of bar fell into the sand. He put away the bolt cutters, scooped up both severed sections of iron, and crawled through the fence.

Within seconds he was in waist-high bushes, tall flowers, and the shadow of a graceful tulip tree. The lush plantings ensured that the Harmony wouldn't have to watch tourists grunt and flail on the sand volleyball courts that bordered the estate.

The foliage also hid intruders quite nicely. Before the camera closest to the water completed its circuit and began to swing back toward the unprotected fence, Shane was completely hidden.

Gillie would have heads on a pike if he was running this operation, Shane thought. Boston has done a subtle job of trashing security for his beloved boss.

Shane eased the cut sections of fence beneath a bush and set out across the grounds. The security lighting system was like the fence. It needed maintenance. He moved easily from shadow to shadow.

The only lights that were fully functional were around the swimming pools. Shane bypassed a place where he would have been outlined against the bright lights of one pool. Then he belly-crawled across a pathway that led down to the cabanas and the white sand beach.

A voice came from one of the cabanas.

Shane froze, fearing discovery.

The voice continued unchanged.

A quick glance through the window of the nearest cabana told Shane he was safe. A dinner guest, Venezuelan by his accent, was grunting drunkenly into the cleavage of a young Aruban woman. She watched the wall above the bed and rode him with mechanical motions of her hips. From her expression, she could have been polishing silverware.

Ride 'em, cowgirl, Shane thought. That's one guest I won't have to worry about tripping over.

Rain lashed against the land. Lightning burst and thunder rumbled around the estate.

The storm was a mixed blessing. On the one hand, it covered all sounds and kept people indoors. On the other hand, an inconvenient flare of lightning could give away his presence as surely as a spotlight on a dark stage.

Shane eased away from the cabana, pushed into a small forest of chin-high poinsettia bushes, and headed for the big white stone and stucco house. As he moved, he searched for guards. No matter how lax security became in Kasatonin's absence, Shane knew there had to be men assigned to the grounds.

One of the guards was sitting on a lawn chair beneath a cabana's porch, protected from the storm. As Shane slipped past, the man snored loud enough to be heard above the rain.

A second guard was playing slap-and-tickle with a housemaid in the dark shelter of another cabana. Unlike the couple in the first cabana, both the man and the woman seemed fully involved in the fun.

Shane left them to it.

Wind swirled around the big house, bending the palms and rattling the thin branches of the divi-divi trees like bones. Soundlessly Shane slipped through shadows until he located the guards manning the front gate.

The men were huddled together beneath a front veranda, smoking something that didn't smell like tobacco.

La mota, Shane thought. Suck hard, boys, and pleasant dreams.

Katya might be hell on wheels when it came to the household staff, but it took a cold-rolled bastard like Kasatonin to keep security troops in line.

Shane moved on, making no more noise than a shadow. Bright lights poured through a first-floor window. Screened by shrubbery, he stayed well back from the glass and looked inside.

Katya Pilenkova was the only woman at a table full of well-upholstered and largely drunken men.

Bankers or money launderers? Shane wondered silently. Not that there's much difference on Aruba, thanks to the Harmony.

Katya wore a flame-red dress that emphasized her pale, bare shoulders. Despite the hot color she looked like an ice sculpture—aloof, glittering, chill.

It was obvious to Shane that the meal had progressed through many courses of wine and food. Liqueur, brandy, and tiny cups of coffee sat before the men. Ashtrays were full. Neckties were loose. The men were flushed and sweaty. Several leaned heavily to the side in their chairs, glassy-eyed.

The whores will have their work cut out for them tonight, Shane thought. Half of those men couldn't get it up with a splint.

Katya herself sat with a decanter of brandy at her elbow and a snifter in her hand. She knocked back a slug of the clear brown liquor as though it was iced tea.

Maybe it is, Shane thought. She sure doesn't look like she's spent the night slamming shots of brandy.

Katya smiled at first one man, then another. She bent forward to a third, giving him a pale flash of cleavage. A fourth man earned a light touch and a sideways glance that promised everything. Other men leaned closer, lured by the icy brilliance of their hostess.

Promises, promises, Shane thought cynically. Is it money talk or her tits that turns on the bankers? Either way, she has them eating out of her ice-cold little crotch.

Shane faded back into the night to complete his reconnoiter of the main house. The security control center was in the back. Through a rainy window, Shane saw a wall of small screens. The televisions showed a montage of deserted fence line and wind-whipped palm trees, rain, swimming pools, cabanas, and areas of the main house.

None of the screens showed Katya's private quarters.

Boston was right, Shane thought with satisfaction. The spy master doesn't want anyone spying on her, even in the name of security.

Of all the monitors in the central security room, only the one playing a commercial South American TV channel held the guard's attention. At the moment, the show was featuring the artificially lusty coupling of two Mexican soap-opera stars.

A glance was enough to tell Shane that they were better actors than the whore he had glimpsed in a guest cabana.

Shane turned away and circled the servant's quarters before he cut back through the poinsettias to Katya's cabana. Her isolated rooms were dark, apparently empty. No guard waited in the lanai or watched from the main house.

Just to be certain, Shane went around Katya's private rooms. Only one area showed the least bit of light. At first he thought Katya had left a TV on. Then the rhythmic, predictable flipping of shadows and lights made Shane decide that it was a compu-ter's screen-saver rather than a TV.

He went to the back patio doors of the cabana. With a burglar's pick and rake, he teased the well-oiled lock like a lover. The surgical plastic gloves he wore didn't get in the way in the least.

The lock turned. Silently the door opened.

Shane stripped off the wet poncho and stuffed it behind a potted plant outside the door. His dirty reef-walker shoes followed.

Barefoot but still wearing gloves, he slipped into the cabana and closed the door behind him.

The air was thick with a sweet perfume that Shane found cloying, an overdose of jasmine and gardenias combined. Standing motionless, he listened intently while his eyes adjusted to the faint illumination offered by the security lights in the garden.

There was no sound of another person breathing. No sound of movement. No intangible sense of another presence.

The bedroom was done entirely in white—white curtains, white carpet, white furniture, and white knickknacks.

Virginal, Shane thought ironically. Katya seduces men by the dozen, but never has sex with them. She is taken only by a rapist who threatens her with death.

Of course she's a virgin.

The corruption in sweet Katya's soul is even deeper than I thought, Shane realized. Some day it will eat her alive. But until then, it will just make her more and more dangerous.

He turned to the living room of the suite. It was gently illuminated by a night light. He stayed low so that he wouldn't cast a moving shadow on the blinds. Circling the room carefully, he approached the computer that sat on a low work table next to the bar.

The machine was exactly what Boston had led him to expect, a state-of-the-art Apple. The machine was switched on and running. Its screen-saver was unusual, consisting of graphic couplings by unusually limber lovers.

Shane touched the keyboard. The screen blossomed with a white illumination that made him wince. He turned down the light gain. The screen glowed more discreetly.

Quickly he punched up a screen menu and started scanning the files. They were in Russian, as he had expected. The numbers in the directory, however, were quite understandable.

There was too much data for his hard drive.

As Shane scanned the directory, he cursed in the silence of his mind. Though the file names weren't encrypted, they were unreadable to him.

Other than an impressive command of Russian invective, Shane's familiarity with Russian wasn't good enough for him to make truly informed choices as to what to copy and what to leave behind. He might copy something only to find out it was simply a program available over the counter in any computer store in the world.

Abruptly a Russian word caught Shane's eye. He knew what it meant: eaters of pig excrement.

Curious, Shane called up the folder, opened it, and scanned the files within. Non-Cyrillic names leaped out at him.

De la Pena.

Liu.

Spagnolini.

The list went on, some in the Cyrillic alphabet, some not.

Tong.

Yakuza.

Cartel.

There were other linked files and documents under each master file, and other Russian phrases that were repeated in the main directory.

Shane let out a silent breath of amusement and relief.

Katya, you are truly warped, he thought. I'll start with Eaters of Pig Excrement. Then I'll stuff whatever else has an obscene heading into the drive until it burps and refuses to eat any more. Cassandra's cybernuts can sort out the mess.

It took only a minute to remove the hard drive from his backpack and connect the communications cord to the output port in the back of Katya's machine.

He went through the directory while the clock in his mind counted off seconds. A click, a drag on the mouse, a release over the slave hard drive icon, and a new file was dropped off to be copied. With impressive speed the computer began duplicating entire blocks of data onto the slaved hard drive.

If any alarms went off anywhere, Shane neither saw nor heard any sign of them.

With a silent prayer, he held down the shift key and began gathering file after file as he scanned the computer directory.

The pager in his pocket went off, vibrating subtly against his leg.

Shane ignored Dani's summons. He was focused only on the computer and the priceless information it contained about the Harmony. He knew that the window between camera sweeps had come and gone, but the hard drive was still working to swallow the huge chunks of data he had lined up for it to copy.

While the two computers mated, he went to the huge, old-fashioned safe that loomed in one corner of the room like a cast-iron stove. As Boston had said, the safe was strictly nineteenth century. It relied on sheer weight rather than sophistication to keep out thieves.

But then, who would steal from the Queen of Thieves when she was guarded by the Prince of Darkness?

Shane went to work on the safe. Tumblers clicked and fell, clicked and fell. The door swung open.

No alarms sounded.

He pulled out a tiny flashlight and played its pencil beam around the safe's interior. Boxes of gold coins, packets of what looked like loose diamonds, and stacks of various currencies filled a long vertical row of cubbyholes.

Getaway money? Shane wondered. Or bribes?

Impatiently he dismissed the portable fortune and turned to the inner door of the safe. Behind it was the only compartment big enough to hold the glass capsule containing the silk.

A quick movement of his hand on the lever opened the compartment.

The pager vibrated again.

Ignoring it, Shane reached for the three-foot tall, porcelain-headed doll that was stuffed into the compartment. She was dressed in a baptismal gown of very old lace. Her hair was real, and as red as Katya's. The body was soft, flimsy, unable to conceal anything as rigid as a glass capsule.

The doll's eyes had been carefully scratched out. A dark stain spread out from the crotch of the gown, as though the doll had been violated and the blood had dried long, long ago.

The bottom of the compartment was covered with photographs of a girl in various stages of growth. Baby pictures, photos of a toddler in a lacy dress, snapshots of a coltish, beautiful girl with Katya's empty eyes and cold smile.

The pager vibrated continuously against Shane legs. He noted it, but only at a distance. The tiny beam of his flashlight picked out photo after photo.

In each of them, the child was being held by an older man. Her eyes had been scratched out. His were intact, but his crotch was not. It had been mutilated as thoroughly as Kasatonin's was.

Very gently Shane put the doll back in its compartment and closed the door. As he did, he remembered the teaching of Ngon tok gyen, who said that wherever any person drew breath, there the Buddha would be, compassion incarnate.

Shane wondered if even the Buddha could live in the sad, twisted midnight of Katya's soul.

He closed the safe, spun the dial and went back to the computer. The hard drive was still ingesting files. He lined up a batch more, dropped them on the slave icon and went to collect others.

Suddenly Shane heard the *shack-a-shack* sound of poinsettia pods being disturbed by something nearby. It could have been the wind.

Or it could have been someone pushing through the shrubbery for a peek in the window.

Shane dropped a big load of files over the slave icon and jerked the mouse pointer sharply off the screen. Instantly the screen saver came back on.

As he pushed away from the table, he turned the light gain back to high. Making no noise in his bare feet, he crossed the plush carpet of the suite.

Shack-a-shack. Shack-a-shack

The sound came from the patio just outside the sliding bedroom doors.

Standing motionless to one side, Shane peered into the darkness.

He saw nothing.

Don't trust your eyes, he told himself. What is your gut telling you?

The answer came instantly.

There's someone out there—someone who knows that I'm in *here*.

Swiftly Shane weighed his options. The computer was still working obediently in the other room, copying files onto the hard drive. He wanted every bit of information he could cram onto it. Then he needed time to disconnect the drive, stuff it in his backpack, and get the hell out.

He listened to the night sounds. Wind shook trees and shrubbery tapped against windows. Rain drummed steadily. Thunder came erratically.

No voices.

No gentle trying of the door's lock.

Maybe it's just another randy pair of servants looking for a place out of the wind, Shane thought. If so, they'll move on. No matter how horny they are, they won't go at it in the Czarina's private quarters.

He eased up to one side of the door, slid it open an inch, and listened with every sense. Wind and rain masked sounds, but the damp air made up for it by enhancing all smells.

He breathed in softly, deeply. The scent of rain and vegetation filled his nostrils. And beneath those other scents, there was something else, something . . . feminine.

It can't be Katya, Shane told himself, breathing out carefully. I could smell her at a hundred yards in a slaughterhouse.

Unless she only uses the jasmine-gardenia perfume in her bedroom. Then I'm up to my lips in yak shit. She might have come back, sensed an intruder, and took off.

If I stay here, I'm trapped.

On the other hand, it might just be a guard poking around. If so . . .

Like a shadow, Shane opened the door, closed it soundlessly behind him, and slipped out into the night. As he eased into the underbrush, he pulled a folding knife from his pants pocket. The locking blade made no sound as he opened it with a quick motion of his thumb.

The knife was no match for the assault rifles the gate guards carried, but Shane wasn't particularly worried. Afghanistan— and Gillie—had taught him that brains, silence, and a knife often were all a trained man needed to survive.

Cool, intense, relentless, the rain washed over him. It soaked through his dark clothing and ran down his skin. He crouched in the brush and did a full-circle check.

Nothing.

He was starting to straighten up when a flicker of movement

caught his eye. He froze in the crouch, ready to spring up like a tiger from ambush.

A figure slipped out from behind a nearby tree and advanced on Shane. He could see size but little else, except that the person carried something in his right hand.

Then the scent came more clearly to him on the wind and rain, a scent that had haunted even his dreams.

Shane eased up behind the figure, clamped his hand over its mouth, and pulled it down into the shrubbery.

"What the hell are you doing here?" he demanded in a soft, savage voice. "You promised you'd wait for me!"

Dani's stiff body sagged against him when she realized who her captor was. She touched his mouth with one hand. Her other hand held a cellular phone.

Shane put the phone to his ear but he didn't remove his hand from Dani's mouth.

"What?" he snarled softly.

Cassandra's voice came back. "Get off the island immediately."

"But—"

"*Get out.*"

Chapter Twenty

"I'm inside the Harmony," Shane said into the phone.

"Warn Boston and get out," Cassandra said urgently.

"You're sure he isn't a double agent?"

"Yes. Dani will explain. *Move.*"

Shane was left swearing under his breath with a dead cellular in his hand. He pulled Dani closer. Rain had plastered her clothes against her body like a second, colder skin. Slowly he removed his hand.

"She said you would explain," Shane said quietly. "But keep your voice low. Don't whisper. Whispers carry."

"Kasatonin has had the staff under hard surveillance for the past week."

"Shit."

Shane thought quickly. He hadn't seen anyone following Boston, but that was no guarantee. Not if Kasatonin somehow had been forewarned.

"If Boston was followed," Dani said softly, "Kasatonin's people may have spotted us."

"Or photographed us."

"That's what Gillie said. One picture is all it would take. Kasatonin would recognize either of us instantly."

"I'll get the hard drive. Then I'll warn Boston," Shane said.

"Cassandra said to cut our losses and run. The chopper is standing by."

"Negative. I have more raw intelligence on that hard drive than Risk Limited has been able to gather in years."

"But—"

Shane's rubber-covered hand came over Dani's lips again.

"Do you remember Boston's number?" Shane asked tersely.

Dani nodded.

"Go to the hole in the fence," he said. "Stay under cover. Call Boston. Do you remember the message?"

Dani nodded. The code was engraved in her brain: *Au revoir, mon cher.*

"Wait in the shrubs by the fence until I come," Shane said against her ear. "Got that?"

Again she nodded.

"If you hear any noise from Katya's quarters," Shane murmured, "don't wait for me. Get the hell out."

Dani's whole body stiffened in silent rebellion.

Shane kept talking.

"Take the car to the rendezvous point," he said, "set off the signal, and hide at least one hundred yards away from the car until the chopper lands. Got it?"

Dani didn't move.

"Listen to me," Shane said urgently, softly. "I know how to go to ground in enemy territory. You don't. Remember what Gillie said?"

Reluctantly Dani nodded. She hadn't liked the instruction then. She hated it now.

If there is any question, obey Shane and do it without arguing.

Shane did a full-circle head check of the area.

Nothing had changed.

He turned Dani and looked at her. She was shivering with a combination of cold and adrenaline, but her eyes were clear, alert. She was biting her lower lip to keep her teeth from chattering.

There was something extraordinarily sexy about the way she did it. He tried to look away but couldn't. It was all he could do not to kiss her right there, one last hot taste of life before he went back into Katya's frigid, dangerous quarters.

Abruptly he started to straighten up.

Dani's hands clamped hard around his wrist, silently telling him not to move. Even as her fingernails dug into his skin, he caught the movement that Dani had already seen.

Katya was strolling down the path from the main house beneath a large black umbrella. She carried the hem of her gown in one hand. The flame red sequins of the dress flashed and glittered in the light of the pathway lamps.

She was walking just a bit too carefully, like a drunk trying to appear sober.

Maybe that wasn't iced tea she was sucking up after all, Shane thought. If I had to go back to that room and that safe, I'd try to numb myself all the way to my soul.

Motionless, so close that they breathed one another's breath, Shane and Dani froze in the underbrush. Katya passed less than twenty feet away from them.

If Shane could be certain, absolutely certain, that he could kill Katya without making a sound, he knew he should do it, if only to insure that he pillaged her files undiscovered.

But he couldn't believe that Katya was as unguarded as she appeared. There were too many shadows on the garden path behind her, shadows that could have been a man or men following her at a discreet distance.

It was an old trick for drawing an enemy out of cover. One of the oldest.

Because it worked.

Dangle the bait and then gaff the fish that lunged out of the darkness.

He would risk his own neck on the gambit, but not Dani's.

Even as Shane listened to his own thoughts, he was appalled. He should be worrying about the hard drive, not Dani.

But I am worrying about her, he told himself, and that's the way it is. Deal with it. Stop being surprised. A lot of men die with a surprised look on their face.

In any case, no matter how much Katya has earned killing, remember what Cassandra says—information you have that the enemy doesn't know you have is *always* the most valuable kind.

If I kill the lovely Katya, Kasatonin will consider the whole operation compromised and begin damage control.

Starting with the silk.

Shane dismissed the thought of killing Katya except as a last resort, and settled in to wait with the patience of a man who had spent days meditating in the icy winds of Tibet.

As Katya approached the door, she dropped the hem of her gown. Slowly she fished the cabana key from her tiny sequined purse. Then she put down the umbrella to work the lock. Her lustrous hair began to darken and droop in the relentless rain.

She muttered a curse in Russian and tried the lock again. After fumbling with key and lock and swearing some more, she finally managed to open it.

"Get ready," Shane said very softly. "She'll take one look at the cables and hard drive and all hell will be let loose."

The door closed behind Katya.

Shane watched the windows carefully. He caught a faint glimpse of Katya as she passed through the living room without turning on the lights.

A few seconds later Katya was in the bedroom. A rather dim bedside lamp came on. Silhouetted against it, Katya pulled down the zipper of her dress. She stepped out of the glittering scarlet cloth and kicked it aside. Her bra and pantyhose followed.

Dani looked at Shane.

He was systematically looking everywhere but at the window where Katya was undressing. He already knew what was inside the rooms. It was what might be outside that worried him.

Leaning to one side, Dani breathed words very softly into Shane's ear.

"You sure know how to show a girl a good time. I've never been to a strip show before."

Shane didn't know whether to laugh or to strangle Dani for making him want to laugh when he should have every sense alert, ready for whatever the situation might demand—killing or dying or anything in between.

He shook his head and placed his fingers over Dani's mouth. Through the thin rubber gloves, her lips were cool. Her breath was not. The heat of her life flowed through to his skin.

Katya stalked across the bedroom into the bathroom. She emerged a moment later with a large towel. Vigorously she dried herself before she fashioned the towel into a turban for her wet hair. She pulled a bathrobe out of the closet and disappeared back into the living area.

Shane took his hand off Dani's lips and got ready to yank her to her feet and flee.

The good news, he told himself, is that I haven't seen any guards lying in wait.

Yet.

To Shane's profound relief, the living room lights remained off. He relaxed slightly.

Looks like Katya has taken on enough of a load that bright light hurts her eyes, he decided.

Waiting, waiting, waiting, he marked Katya's progress across the room, past the computer terminal, to the wet bar. She took a glass off the shelf, opened the freezer, and poured herself a stiff shot of vodka.

The glass barely had a chance to form frost on the bottom before Katya drank the vodka in one long, ecstatic swallow.

"She must have a problem sleeping," Dani murmured.

"She has a problem, period."

Katya poured another generous shot of vodka into her glass and walked carefully back to the bedroom. When she came to the sliding glass door Shane had used, she stopped as though something had caught her interest.

Bloody hell, Shane thought. Even barefoot, did I leave smudges on her virginal white rug?

Katya came to the doorway. After a moment, she pulled back the thin curtain and stared out into the black, wild night. Lightning flashed, revealing her face for a stark instant.

Her skin was the color of a white marble tombstone. Her eyes gleamed eerily. She had a look of madness about her.

Shane and Dani froze. Katya was only a few feet away and she was staring directly at them.

Then Shane realized Katya was seeing nothing but her own thoughts.

Slowly Katya's expression changed. The vicious smile that came over her face made Dani want to turn and run.

Katya lifted the frosty glass in her hand as though in derisive toast to a world so easily corrupted. Then she tilted her head and drank her chosen poison to the last frigid drop.

The curtain fell from her fingers. She turned unsteadily and started toward her bed. The glass slipped from her hand and bounced on the carpet.

As though traversing uneven ground, Katya changed her course twice. Finally she collapsed onto the bed. Even the mild illumination of the bedside lamp was too much for her alcohol-dilated eyes. She fumbled for the switch, but it eluded her. The electrical cord was easier to handle. She yanked it out of the wall.

Darkness descended.

"May all your dreams be nightmares," Shane murmured.

Dani shivered.

"I wouldn't take a million bucks for her hangover in the morning," Dani said. "She must miss her demon lover."

"Love isn't a word I'd use with either her or Kasatonin."

"Somehow demon fornicator lacks a certain—"

Shane's hand closed over Dani's mouth even as he bit back laughter.

"Woman," he murmured, "that quick little tongue of yours is going to be the death of us."

A muffled sound came from beneath Shane's hand. He didn't know if it was protest or agreement. He didn't really care.

"Can you get back to the hole in the fence alone?" he asked very softly against Dani's ear."

She nodded vigorously.

"Go to the fence," he said. "Wait there for me in the underbrush."

Another muffled sound came. Shane ignored it.

"When you're there," he said, "buzz me once. If you get into trouble, buzz me twice or scream your head off."

She nodded.

"Go to the fence, Dani. I will assume that anything between me and the hole is an enemy. I could kill you and never know until it was too late. Do you understand?"

Dani shuddered even as she nodded.

Shane lifted his hand.

"Go," he said softly. "I'll be along as soon as I get the hard drive."

"Cassandra said—" Dani began.

Shane's hand came back down over her mouth. He did a quick yet thorough check, listening with every sense he had, including the nameless one that had saved his life in Afghanistan more than once.

Nothing was around them but the Caribbean storm. Like Katya, it had settled in for the night.

Shane lifted his hand.

"Go."

Dani took one look at Shane's eyes and decided that she wasn't going to win this one.

She went.

Shane drew the night and the silver-black rain around him like a cloak of darkness and waited, motionless.

Nothing moved inside Katya's suite.

Nothing moved outside but the storm.

Shane waited, listening, reaching out into the darkness with his senses.

Finally the pager vibrated against his skin. Once.

Breathing a silent prayer of thanks, Shane went to the patio door. He didn't need his burglar's rake and pick. Katya hadn't managed to lock the door.

Shane cleaned his bare feet on his poncho as best he could before he opened the door. Once he was inside, he went straight to the computer. With one hand he turned down the light gain. With the other, he tapped a key.

Instantly the screen displayed a message telling him that there wasn't enough space on the hard drive for all the documents he had selected.

Shane canceled the copy order. Deftly, quietly, he removed the cables and hard drive and stuffed them into his backpack.

It was damp from the rain, but not enough to damage the hard drive.

The screen saver returned. Acrobatic figures coupled and uncoupled with the mechanical regularity of a piston.

Shane turned up the light gain on the computer to its previous level. Without hesitating he eased open the patio door and stepped out, closing it softly behind him. He stripped off his gloves and picked up his reef shoes and poncho. He didn't put the shoes on until he merged with the underbrush.

With every second Shane counted off in his mind, he wondered if Dani would be discovered before he got to her.

Rain and drenched leaves slithered over Shane's poncho, but lightning and thunder came only once. The violent edge of the storm had passed on, leaving only a steady drumming rain in its wake.

Shane sensed Dani before he saw her, crouched in the midst of thick bushes. The shivering of her body was covered by the trembling of the leaves beneath the downpour.

Despite her obvious discomfort, she was watching the cameras.

He went in behind her. Again, his hand came over her mouth to prevent a cry of surprise. Again, her body stiffened and then relaxed when she realized who was touching her.

Shane lifted his hand.

"How long before the gap?" he breathed against Dani's ear.

"Nine seconds. Did you get the hard drive?"

"Yes. Head straight for the car but don't touch it."

"What about you?" she asked.

"I'll be right on your heels."

An instant later Dani went through the gap in the fence. As promised, Shane was barely a step behind her. Before they got to the car, he was a hundred feet ahead of her.

Dani watched while Shane went over the car. Nothing seemed to have been disturbed. He turned back to Dani, only to find that she was already reaching for the door, ignition key in hand.

"What the—" Shane began.

"Stand back at a safe distance," Dani said, interrupting him.

"Give me those keys," he demanded.

"No. As you pointed out, you have a better chance of surviving in enemy territory with that hard drive than I do. *Back off.*"

Shane struggled with himself. Dani was right and his mind knew it. His emotions were in flat out rebellion.

After a few moments, discipline won.

"No lights and no noise," Shane warned.

Dani laughed rather raggedly.

"I'll do my best," she promised.

Cursing silently every step of the way, Shane backed off and waited.

Dani turned the key in the door lock and then in the ignition itself.

No manmade lightning and thunder tore the night apart.

Relief poured through Shane in a wave of adrenaline that left his heart hammering harder than the rain. He ran to the car.

Dani was already scrambling over the center console into the passenger seat. Wet poncho, backpack, and all, Shane slammed into the driver's seat, yet he closed the door behind him with little noise at all.

He didn't turn on the headlights until the car was beyond the hotel grounds and had mixed in with the traffic on the way to the hotel casinos.

"Did you get through to Boston?" Shane asked.

"Y-yes."

Belatedly Shane realized that although the air temperature was in the seventies, Dani was thoroughly chilled. He turned on the heater.

After a few minutes Dani let out a long sigh of relief. Heat seeped into flesh that had been chilled by rain, wind, and fear.

"I hope Boston doesn't try to kill Katya on his way out," Shane said.

"Why?"

"Same reason I didn't. The information on that hard drive is more valuable if the Harmony doesn't know we have it."

"Oh."

The shiver that went through Dani had little to do with cold.

"Do you do that sort of thing often?" she asked after a time.

"Kill people?"

"Yes."

"No," Shane said. "I got a gut full of killing in Afghanistan."

"Is that why you decided to become a monk?"

Without answering, Shane checked the car's mirrors. No matter how many turns he made or how unexpectedly he veered off into a hotel or casino parking lot, no car darted out of line to follow him.

Satisfied, Shane headed for the back road. No headlights appeared behind the car. None appeared in front.

"Is it?" Dani asked, as though no time had passed since her question.

Shane shot her a sideways glance.

"Did your ex-husband slap you around?" Shane asked coolly. "Is that why you walked out on him?"

Dani made a startled sound. She was on the edge of telling Shane that it was none of his business when she realized that his question was no more personal than hers had been.

"I didn't mean to pry," Dani said. Then, distinctly, she added, "Yes to both questions. I don't break my vows any more lightly than you do."

"I'm glad you understand about vows," Shane muttered.

"Why?"

"Because it's going to be damned cold waiting for the helicopter."

"What does that mean?"

"You'll see. Wait here until I come back for you."

With that Shane turned off the road into the underbrush, shut off the lights and engine, and got out. Through the pouring rain, Dani could just make out his shape as he opened and closed the trunk. Then he vanished into the rain and night, carrying the electronic signal that would call down the helicopter.

Dani waited in the increasing coolness of the car and wondered how long it would be. Already, her clothes were clinging coldly to her body.

The passenger door opened. Cool rain and wind washed over her.

"Out," Shane said.

"But—"

"Yes, I know," Shane interrupted. "It's dry here. It's also the first place someone would look for us."

Dani got out and followed Shane into the mixture of palms and underbrush and relentless rain. She almost walked into him when he stopped, knelt, and finally sat with his back against a palm tree.

Rain ran from Dani's hair down her neck. She didn't really notice. She was so wet she might as well have been swimming. Shivering, she settled on the ground near Shane, wrapped her arms around her knees and hugged herself.

She didn't ask for the poncho. She knew keeping the hard drive dry was more important than keeping herself warm.

"C-can a helicopter fly in this s-storm?" Dani asked.

Her teeth weren't chattering. Not quite. But they would be soon.

"I've flown in worse," Shane said tersely.

"How long will it b-be before the helicopter c-comes?" Dani asked.

Shane stifled a curse at the gods who had chosen to torment him with the very thing he wanted more than breath itself and couldn't have.

Not yet.

Not without breaking his vow.

"Too long," Shane said with grim certainty. "And not long enough by far."

"You s-sound like one of those Zen enigmas the masters use to t-teach acolytes."

"First a cyborg, now an enigma. Is that a promotion?"

Dani laughed despite her discomfort.

Listening to the laughter, Shane didn't know how long he would be able to resist kissing her, touching her, probing the satin heat of her body.

He was afraid he was going to find out. Soon.

Too soon.

Damn.

With a swift jerk of his hand, Shane unzipped the neck of the poncho as far as it went. It wasn't far enough.

He pulled the knife out his pocket. A flick of his thumb opened the blade. Steel sliced easily through the poncho's soft material.

"What are you d-doing?" Dani asked.

"Making room for two heads."

"But the hard d-drive—"

"Is just fine," Shane interrupted.

Hard drive, he repeated sardonically in his mind. Now there's a phrase worth meditating on.

"Come here," Shane said.

Dani didn't need a second invitation. Kneeling, she ducked beneath the poncho. The scent of vegetation and wet clothing and sheer male warmth swept over her. It was a heady combination. She wanted to stay there and simply breathe.

Reluctantly Dani shoved her head through the newly enlarged opening of the poncho and tried to get comfortable on her knees.

"Quit squirming and sit with your back to me," he said curtly.

Dani stopped squirming, turned around, and sat.

Instantly she found herself surrounded by Shane. His torso covered her back, his legs rose on either side of hers, and his arms wrapped around her.

The blunt reality of his desire prodded her hip.

"Ulp," Dani said.

Shane almost laughed. But that would have rubbed his body against Dani's. He told himself he didn't want that.

He lied.

"Don't panic," he said. "I'm not going to rape you."

"I know. It j-just startled m-me, that's all."

For a few minutes the two of them huddled together while rain beat down over the poncho. Shane's heat radiated through Dani like a Caribbean sun. Slowly her teeth stopped chattering. With a long sigh she relaxed against him.

"Better?" Shane asked.

His mouth was so close to Dani's ear that she felt the warmth of his breath. The shiver that went over her had nothing to do with cold.

"Yes," she said, biting her lower lip. "Thank you."

"My pleasure. Two bodies together are warmer than two apart."

"You don't feel a bit cold."

Shane laughed.

Dani heard her own words and wanted to groan.

"I didn't mean that," she said.

"I know."

Shane's breath washed over Dani's ear. With a hunger she was just admitting to herself, she put her hands on Shane's forearms. The high-tech cloth he wore felt cool, but the man beneath wasn't.

Arms crossed over her own chest, Dani smoothed her hands over Shane's arms from wrist to shoulder and back. Her palms drank his heat. In a silence broken only by rain, she traced the outline of his biceps with her fingers again and again, measuring his strength.

For the first time since her ex-husband had betrayed her trust, Dani found herself enjoying the difference in physical power between men and women. Slowly she began caressing the bunched muscles that were so unlike her own.

Shane's arms flexed, hardening beneath Dani's touch as he drew her closer. When he pulled her still closer, his forearms lifted the soft weight of her breasts in a slow caress.

A shiver of desire went through Dani. Her nipples tightened and filled in a response that was as involuntary as the blunt length of Shane's arousal pressing against her hip.

He leaned forward a little and brushed his lips against the soft, damp skin of her neck. Then he tasted her with the thoroughness and delicacy of a cat licking cream from a spoon.

"Shane?" Dani whispered.

"I'm right here."

"Is this a good idea?"

"No," he said. "Want me to stop?"

"No."

Shane went completely still for a moment.

"Two bodies together are better than two bodies apart," Dani said, repeating his words.

"Warmer," he corrected.

"That too."

Shane laughed softly.

Closing her eyes, Dani tilted her head to one side, offering him more skin to kiss. His lips found the lobe of her ear. He sipped the rain dripping from the cool, sensitive flesh.

"Wine," Shane said.

Dani's laugh had a catch in it.

"Just rain," she said.

"Just you."

Shane's arms shifted and his hands slid across Dani's ribs. Her blouse was still cool with rain, but the heat of the woman beneath called to him with a siren song as old as male and female.

Gently, inevitably, Shane's hands moved beneath Dani's breasts and then curled upward, surrounding her, savoring the soft flesh that was so different from his own. He hungered to test the hardness of her nipples but didn't trust himself.

Then Dani shifted and the choice was taken from him. Her taut nipples nudged against his fingers. She arched her back and moved slowly, luxuriantly, increasing the pressure of the caress.

Shane bit back a curse of pleasure and regret. Her nipples were like his own body, aroused, hard, hungry to be stroked.

She moved again, dragging her breasts over his hands in unspoken plea. Her hands came over his, squeezing, urging. After a moment her fingers lifted.

For an instant he wondered if she had changed her mind. Then he felt cloth parting beneath his hands as she unbuttoned her blouse and the front fastening of her bra. She pulled his hands over her breasts with frank sensuality, arching against him.

Raw hunger slammed through Shane, shaking him. He wanted nothing more than to rip off the rest of Dani's clothes and bury himself in her.

Wrong time, he reminded himself fiercely. Wrong place.
Right woman.

With a throttled groan, Shane took what Dani offered so
honestly. He caressed her breasts and plucked at her nipples
until she was whimpering with pleasure. Each sound she made
was a thin, fiery whip laid across the aching body of his own
need.

"I can feel your heart beneath my hand," he said. "It's
beating harder than the rain. I like that."

"I can feel how much you want me," Dani said. "I never
thought I would like that again, but I do."

Arching her back, Dani twisted gently, increasing the pressure of her hips against the insides of Shane's thighs.

"I want you, too," Dani admitted huskily. "I've never
wanted a man the way I want you."

For an instant Shane's arms tightened until she could barely
breathe. He held her hard, straining against her with his hips.
Abruptly he loosened his grip, buried his face against her neck,
and groaned.

There was nothing Shane would do about his own hunger,
but Dani's . . . that was different.

"Is this uncomfortable for you?" Dani asked quickly, turning
her head toward him. "I can move."

Shane took her mouth in a kiss that left her in no doubt as
to the depth of his own hunger. His fingers trembled slightly
as he touched the brass button that fastened the waistband
of her jeans. Then he traced the cold roundness, as though
anticipating another, far warmer button beneath.

The waistband of Dani's jeans went slack. Slowly Shane
drew the metal tongue of the zipper down her belly. The knuckle
of his thumb brushed intimately against her. Then his long
fingers were inside her briefs.

Dani made a sound deep in her throat and arched to give
Shane more of herself. He teased the warm, sleek flesh until
she twisted against him. Then he plucked the tight nub he had
drawn from her softness.

She made a ragged sound and tried to turn in his arms. She
couldn't. He was holding her too close. Her hand reached

behind her hips, trying to caress him. He caught her fingers and held them tightly against her hip.

"Let me—" Dani began.

"No," he interrupted huskily.

"I want to touch you."

"I know."

"Don't you want—"

Dani's words ended in a gasp as Shane probed the slick heat of her body. She shivered and another, much hotter kind of rain slid over Shane.

"Hell, yes, I want," he said fiercely. "But I won't."

Sanity returned to Dani.

"Dammit," she said fiercely. "You're right. I'm not taking anything. I could get pregnant."

The thought sent a shaft of pure excitement through Shane. His reaction startled him.

"You won't," he promised.

"A Boy Scout, huh? Always prepared."

"No. A vow."

Shane's hand moved, savoring Dani's readiness for him and pleasuring her at the same time.

A wave of pleasure burst in Dani, shocking in its unexpected, piercing sweetness.

"What—vow?" Dani asked on a breaking breath.

Shane's hand probed and retreated, probed and retreated in a rhythm that made Dani wild. She bit her lip against crying out as waves of pleasure she had never known coursed through her.

"Celibacy," Shane said against her ear.

"What?"

"I swore off sexual gratification for three years. But don't worry. Only one of us will regret it."

Dani shook her head, dazed by Shane's words and the shocking pleasure he was giving her even as he spoke.

"You can't mean that," she said raggedly.

Shane didn't answer. He simply caught Dani's mouth beneath his and caressed her until she was arched like a drawn bow against him, shivering and twisting as pleasure ravished her with every stroke of his hand.

Finally, feeling as though he was tearing away his own skin, Shane forced himself to release Dani's mouth and her slick, hot flesh. He couldn't tell if it was rain or tears of ecstasy that streaked her face. He only knew that he would have sold his soul to taste her and find out.

But if he tasted tears instead of rain, he would break his vow.

Very carefully Shane shrugged out of the backpack, ducked out from under the poncho, and went to stand alone in the rain.

Chapter Twenty-one

Washington, D.C.
November

Forget it, Dani told herself. It didn't happen.

Even after three days, embarrassment flushed Dani's cheeks when she remembered how she had all but demanded that Shane make love to her.

No wonder he walked off without a backward look, she thought. The only surprising thing is that he didn't just dump me out in the rain to cool off.

But he didn't. He gave me more in a few minutes than I'd had in a lifetime from men.

The printouts swam and blurred in front of her eyes. She tried to remember the last time she had slept for more than an hour or two.

She couldn't.

She looked up from the stack of printouts on her desk and focused instead on her campus office. Her glance slid from the framed silk-screens to tapestries hanging on the wall. The various cloths had been faded by time, but to her each was oddly vibrant, almost alive.

She loved the ancient fabrics. They had been created by human hands for human pleasure. Each style of weaving spoke of a different culture, a different weaver's touch. Each color came from herbs or minerals or mollusks that were distinctive to certain areas of the world and no other.

There was also a modern Italian silk shawl that had taken its design from a painted panel in one of the monasteries along the Silk Road. Next to it was a glass box holding a delicate fragment of cotton cloth found cast aside in a looted Anasazi ruin. A modern Japanese kimono of vivid greens, blues, and whites shimmered in a case along one wall.

Opposite it, a fine *k'ossu* tapestry from the late Ming period showed the flight of a phoenix. The colors were still as vivid as a rainbow. The silk had cost six months' salary. Dani considered it a bargain at three times the price.

Silent, voiceless, the collection of fabrics nonetheless sang to Dani of millennia of women spinning, weaving, talking, laughing while they created something that would outlast themselves, their children, their grandchildren, their great-grandchildren . . . generations of humanity making cloth from single fibers twisted one upon the other, beauty created where nothing had existed before.

Like those few moments in Aruba, Dani thought.

Wearily she rubbed her dry eyes and wondered why it was her fate to choose the wrong man.

Celibacy.

Anger and shame rippled through Dani.

He could have told me sooner. I wouldn't have made such an ass of myself. *Damn him.*

And damn me, too. *Fool.*

Deliberately she turned her attention to the present. Seasonal change had swept through Washington while she was in the tropics. An icy gray rain from Appalachia was drenching the city. Winter was settling in, austere as a monastery.

The thought of monks made Dani wince.

The phone rang, breaking into her thoughts. Relieved, she picked it up before the second ring.

"Danielle Warren," she said.

"Still at it, lass?"

Gillespie's deep voice made Dani glance guiltily at the stack of briefing papers in front of her.

"I'm working on it," she said. "What a mountain."

"It's not a patch on what Shane brought back. Cassandra and four other translators are still working around the clock."

"Have they found the silk?" Dani asked, her voice eager.

"No."

"Bloody hell," she said wearily.

"Amen. What about your own network of textile enthusiasts?"

"No one has heard about an ancient, extraordinary piece of Indian or Tibetan or Chinese silk for sale. Or if they've heard, they aren't talking."

"Bloody hell."

"Is this where I say 'amen'?" Dani asked.

Gillespie laughed.

"Shane was right about that, too," he said.

"What?"

"He said that no matter how tight it got, you could get him to smile."

Dani simply closed her eyes and fought against the flush she knew was climbing up her cheeks.

"Do you know he died a thousand deaths watching you turn the key on that rental car?" Gillespie asked.

Dani's breath caught, but she said only, "It didn't show."

"You're one hell of a trooper. Shane has nothing but praise for your level head."

"Yeah. Sure. That's why I felt like an albatross around Mr. Crowe's stiff neck."

Gillespie cleared his throat. Or it could have been laughter. Dani wasn't certain.

"Is Boston out yet?" she asked.

"We picked him up night before last."

Dani let out a long breath.

"Good," she said. "Shane was afraid he would go after Katya."

"He almost did," Gillespie said. "His brother didn't make it."

"What?"

"The museum guard. The Harmony got to him before we did."

Dani stared at the rain and tried to think of nothing at all.

"Dani? You still on?"

"Yes."

"Good. There's another package on the way to you. Let us know what you think of it. It's the latest stuff our boys pulled off the Internet."

Dani couldn't suppress a groan.

"For three days I've fielded memos, queries, and rude questions from scholars, art merchants, and 'assets,' " she said. "Now the cybernuts get in the act."

"The guv appreciates it."

"Really? Does 'the guv' appreciate that not everyone can get by on three hours of sleep per night?"

Gillespie laughed. "And here I thought we had handled you with kid gloves."

"Was that before or after the marathon?"

"Marathon?"

"My debriefing," Dani retorted. "Surely you remember the thirteen-hour coffee klatch we had?"

"We put Shane through the wringer for twenty."

"Should I be comforted?"

"Only if you're a sadist," Gillespie said cheerfully.

"No. Nor am I a masochist. Do keep it in mind."

"Getting close to the edge?"

Dani thought about it, sighed, and looked at the rain some more.

"Not that close," she said. "But, damn it, Gillie, it makes me crazy that after all we risked in Aruba we still don't know where the silk is or why the Harmony took it!"

"We accept educated guesses."

"I doubt that mine would be more educated than Shane's."

"His view is Eastern. Yours isn't."

"Eastern? As in the Orient?"

Gillespie made a sound of agreement.

"Gillie," Dani said calmly, "do you have any idea what a difficult task you've given me?"

"Tell me."

"You've asked for a modern monograph in three days."

The sound that came from Gillespie might have been sympathetic.

Dani chose to believe it was.

"Monographs," she said distinctly, "usually take years."

"Good job you're so bright."

She ignored the flattery.

"My previous monographs were written after the fact," Dani said. "Hundreds of years after. Sometimes thousands."

Gillespie made a sound that was definitely encouraging and questioning at the same time.

"It was all over," Dani said, trying to make him understand. "It was a static situation rather than a dynamic one. I could take my time picking through the dust and sift out patterns, trends, explanations."

"Exactly. Cassandra says you're brilliant at patterns. That's why she wants you to analyze all the Harmony information, plus the political and economic projections for Asia, depending on the strength of the Free Tibet movement and the power of the Harmony with or without various members."

"Gillie," Dani said in a ragged voice, "nobody ever lived or died because of my monographs."

"Makes a difference, doesn't it? As heady as straight Scotch."

"Yes," she admitted. "But what about the hangover?"

"Ask Shane. He's been a right bastard for the past few days. Finally sent him off to the Azures to work it out on that Parakeet fellow."

"Poor man."

"Shane?"

"Pakit," Dani said.

"Bugger him. He's trying to talk the lama into taking Risk Limited off the investigation and hiring some other firm."

"Any particular reason?"

"Parakeet claims that Shane lost the silk twice," Gillespie said, his voice rich with disgust.

"What?"

"Once in Lhasa when he saved you instead of the silk and again in Aruba."

"There isn't a shred of evidence that the silk was in Aruba," Dani said. "Boston made it clear that Kasatonin arrived empty-handed."

"Parakeet says we can't prove the silk *wasn't* there."

"Lovely."

"If you say so," Gillespie retorted. "From here, it looks more like a real Charlie Foxtrot."

"You ought to see my office. Charlie Foxtrot in a broom closet."

Gillespie laughed. "Call if you need anything, love."

"More time!"

"If working twenty-four hours a day doesn't get it done—"

"—try working nights," Dani finished dryly. "Thanks, Gillie. Remind me to do you a favor sometime. Salt in your coffee comes to mind."

Dani hung up while Gillespie was still laughing. To her surprise she was smiling, too. Talking with Gillespie had energized her.

It's a good thing, Dani said to herself. I'll need every bit of stamina I have.

Her office desk and work tables were piled with documents, catalogues, and stacks of clippings. Some of it came from the computer databanks of Risk Limited. But most of the research materials were from Dani's own collection—art show catalogues and auction programs, books that were out of print, and esoteric academic journals that had print runs in the hundreds of copies yet contained information compiled nowhere else in the world.

In the days before and after Aruba that Dani had spent sorting and summarizing the material, she had slowly realized that she herself was a unique library of information.

Other people had often regarded her interest in ancient textiles as at least peculiar, if not outright silly. Now Dani understood that she could be more than the sum of her monographs. She was bound not only to the dead past, but to the living present and to the unsettled future. What she did mattered not only to a handful of academics but to politicians and tribal people living all over the world.

Not to mention the crooks and murderers, she reminded herself.

Even after summers spent in the relative anarchy along the Silk Trail, Aruba had been a revelation for Dani. It was like the difference between reading a travel brochure and a coroner's report.

The average Caribbean tourist saw sunshine and beaches and colorful lights at night. Yet there was another, much darker reality just beneath the sand and neon surface of Aruba. People lived and died by that reality. To deny the darkness was to trivialize the good that did exist.

But we could use a lot more light, Dani thought, pulling a document from the pile. A few campfires burning against the Harmony's night just aren't enough.

Seemingly at random, she selected more documents. Once she would have questioned why she chose those papers from among so many. She no longer did. She had learned that the rational level of her mind wasn't always the most useful level. Patterns came from somewhere else, where instinct and intelligence merged.

I'll go home to work, Dani decided as she stuffed documents into her leather shoulder bag. I'll make minestrone soup. While it's simmering, I'll put on a Gregorian chant and give my whole mind room to work.

She hesitated, then put the remainder of the Risk Limited documents into her leather bag along with the other papers. After seeing the burglar's tools Shane used so deftly, she no longer put much faith in locks.

The rational part of Dani's mind scoffed at the worry that the Harmony somehow could reach out into her academic office, riffle her documents, and know that the Harmony's own security had been badly compromised.

But the instinctive part of Dani's mind told her to quit dithering and stuff the last Risk Limited document in her bag. She did just that, vigorously.

Someone knocked on the door. Before she could say anything, the door opened.

Henley Cage, chairman of the archaeology department, stuck his head in. One of America's top experts on the archaeology of the Chinese interior, he was a tall, thin Ivy Leaguer who had a penchant for corduroy coats with leather arm patches and haircuts that were neither long nor short.

"Hi, there, stranger," Cage said easily.

"Hi, Henley," Dani said, smiling. "What's up?"

"I'm glad I finally caught you in your office. I've been looking for you for days."

Cage was usually a tolerant chairman, within limits. Apparently Dani was pushing those limits.

"Sorry," Dani said. "Things have been hectic."

"So I see," Cage said.

He walked in, glancing speculatively at the piles of books and articles scattered around. Like many Washington academics, Cage was no stranger to the place where the bright peaks of scholarly thought merged with the dark canyons of political reality.

Without thinking, Dani closed the flap on her bag over the sheaf of Risk Limited documents. Such secrecy was a new impulse for her. She felt rather silly. Paranoid, even.

But the primitive level of Dani's mind kept remembering how surprised Feng had looked when he died.

Cage picked up a book and thumbed through it idly.

"Since when are you interested in Caribbean archaeology?" he asked.

"I'm not. I'm interested in a vacation. Since you approved that outside consulting job for Cassandra Redpath, I've been as busy as a one-legged man in an ass-kicking contest."

"Oh, yes," Cage muttered. "Ms. Redpath. I did give you the go-ahead on that, didn't I?"

"You sure did."

Cage dropped the book on the Caribbean and moved on to a monograph that discussed the differences in silk thrown by wild Indian moths versus the early domesticated version in 2000 B.C. China.

"I find it hard to believe that particular special project has kept you out of the office so much in the past few weeks," Henley said.

Tension, tiredness, and a desire to be home making minestrone soup put an edge on Dani's tongue.

"Is this an official departmental inquiry, Chairman Cage?" she asked.

"Oh, er—"

"If it is," Dani interrupted calmly, "I would like to point out that I have a very light teaching load this semester."

"One evening seminar," Cage agreed. Then he added, "Which you neglected to attend last week."

"Ms. Samms covered for me. Her credentials—particularly in the area of Renaissance silks—are equal if not superior to mine."

"Of course," Cage began, "but—"

"Otherwise," Dani continued, giving him no chance to speak, "I've been available for office hours in addition to working overtime on the project *you* recommended me for."

"You know I've always regarded you as one of the department's stars," he said.

"Thank you."

"It's just that I thought the Redpath consultation was a short-term one. Can you give me an end date?"

"You'll be the first to know."

"That's not what I asked," Cage said.

"I'm sorry, I can't give you an end date."

He frowned.

"Do you think neglecting your academic work at this time for an open-ended project is a good idea?" Cage asked.

"My work for Ms. Redpath is firmly based in my area of academic expertise. I consider this a unique opportunity for professional growth."

"You sound like a high school grad selling Daddy on a university education."

Dani reminded herself that Cage, while sometimes more a

professional rival than a colleague, was still her boss. He respected her work. Although his specialty was in Ch'in Dynasty bronzes and hers was in Asian fabrics, he often came to Dani with suggestions or questions.

"Cassandra Redpath is brilliant," Dani said evenly. "Her mentorship is an extraordinary opportunity for me."

Cage's frown deepened.

"I was afraid it was something like that," he said.

"Like what?"

"Ms. Redpath can be very charismatic. But . . ."

Dani waited.

". . . but her genius," Cage said carefully, "is sometimes applied in a retrograde manner."

"I beg your pardon?"

Cage sighed. "May I be frank?"

"Of course."

"Through the years Ms. Redpath has kicked over some bee-hives in this town. Some very big ones. She is widely regarded as retrograde if not renegade."

"Really? By whom?"

Cage made a noncommittal gesture with his hands. His look was that of a man who knew more than he was prepared to say.

"While I approved your involvement with Risk Limited in principle several weeks ago," he continued, "I didn't expect Redpath to preempt you to this extent."

"I—" Dani began, but he gave her no chance to talk.

"You're an academic. Your first loyalty must be to this university."

Coolness slid down Dani's spine.

"Has there been a particular complaint about my work?" she asked.

Again, the chairman made a noncommittal gesture.

The back of Dani's neck prickled. She didn't know what was wrong, but she had no doubt that something was.

"If someone has been trying to poison my well," she said carefully, "I'd like to know who it is."

Cage met her gaze with chilly gray eyes.

"Nothing so dramatic," he said, smiling. "This is just a friendly little chat to remind you that you were hired to teach, not to worship at Ms. Redpath's rather tarnished altar."

"Not to worry," Dani said, showing Cage two rows of clean white teeth. "I gave up hero worship along with Santa Claus."

She picked up her leather bag and threw the strap over her shoulder.

"Then you'll be back at work full time?" Cage asked.

"Just as soon as I've finished the project *you* committed me to. Unless, of course, you give me written instructions otherwise."

Still smiling, Dani waited for Cage to put the contents of his "little chat" into a formal memo.

In the end, he shrugged.

"I don't want to drag the Academic Senate into the matter at this point," Cage said.

"At what point will you be willing?" Dani asked.

"Final exams are in ten days. I would hate to see your excellent reputation eroded by a failure to administer adequate examinations to your students."

"I would hate for that to happen, too," she said evenly.

"Is that likely?"

"Not at all. No matter what I do in on my own time, my academic duties won't be neglected.

Cage hesitated, then shrugged. "I hope you know what you're doing, Dani."

"Spell it out for me, Henley. Off the record."

"Academic duties are broad and hard to define."

"Meaning?"

"You're up for tenure."

"What does—"

"That's my last word on the subject," Cage interrupted. "It's more than I should have said."

Cage opened the door, went out, and pulled it shut behind him.

For a long time, Dani stared at the blank door. Her rational mind and her gut were in full agreement on this one.

She turned, picked up the phone, punched in Redpath's private, direct number, and waited.

She didn't wait long. The phone was picked up on the first ring.

"Yes," Redpath said.

Her voice sounded slightly frayed, as though she were feeling the strain even more than Dani.

"I still don't know how many cards there are in this deck," Dani said, "but I can safely tell you there is at least one joker."

"We'll be expecting you."

The line went dead.

So much for homemade minestrone soup, Dani thought, sighing.

Chapter Twenty-two

Seattle
November

Through Ilya Kasatonin's binoculars, the yellow, blue, and red horizontal stripes of the Colombian flag on the *Esmeralda* showed vividly against the gray sky over Elliot Bay. Trim, muscular green and white Foss tugboats maneuvered the rusty container ship toward the berth at Pier 43. The tugs looked like chorus dancers circling an aging, ponderous prima ballerina.

"Can you see it?" Katya asked Kasatonin.

"Not yet."

Restlessly Katya shifted on the seat of the sedan and smoothed her cashmere coat down her long thighs. She would have preferred to wear sable, but hadn't wanted to attract attention. Americans were so tiresome about turning small furry animals into warm coats.

Kasatonin moved the binoculars slightly, peering between the rows of containers that awaited further transport.

Two hundred yards offshore, a small long-line troller dragged baited hooks back and forth through the commercial and tugboat traffic. The troller was piloted by a wizened Vietnamese refugee named Huang Khe.

Huang had been a deep cover Viet Cong operative in Saigon. Now he performed the same kind of work in Seattle, except that he reported to Ilya Kasatonin instead of to Ho Chi Minh. At the moment Huang was doing the same thing his boss was—looking for a certain container amid the bounty of containers in Elliot Bay.

Carefully Huang examined the rusty checkerboard pattern of steel shipping containers the size of box cars that were stacked on the deck of the Colombian ship. At first he didn't see any blue containers bearing the four-letter designation of a Taiwanese shipping company.

Kasatonin, watching at a distance, saw nothing useful.

"Anything?" Katya asked in Russian.

"Be patient, little mink. It is early."

Katya's full lips thinned, but she said nothing. She knew Kasatonin had a spy out there somewhere. She just wasn't certain where.

Tony Liu was hunched in the front passenger seat of the sedan like a monk in meditation. He gave no sign that he could hear every word spoken behind the smoked glass that separated passenger and driver from the Russians in back.

Not that Liu had learned anything useful. Katya and Kasatonin were hardly innocents. Undoubtedly, they knew they could be overheard, for they spoke most of the time in Russian. Later, Liu would have the recording translated.

A man who was foolish enough to overlook the obvious didn't last long in the unsubtle world of the Harmony. Tony Liu wasn't a foolish man.

"Containers," Kasatonin said, scanning the troller rather than the rusty ship, "are the perfect smuggling tool. Anonymous as eggs in a hen house."

"Which is why they are inspected," Katya said. "How else to know computers from pickled Asian vegetables?"

"Not every container is inspected."

"Still, the risk . . ."

"We have done all we can. Global shipping has done the rest. So many countries. So many boxes."

"So many spies," Katya retorted.

Kasatonin shrugged.

"We deal with spies," he said.

"When we find them. But what if we haven't found all of them?"

Kasatonin didn't answer. His attention was fastened on the troller that was just barely visible between the rows of containers.

Huang was pulling up his lines as though weary of the unproductive fishing. He went to a box on deck, pulled out a big blue rag, and shook it seven times. Then he wiped off his hands and replaced the rag in the box.

"It is here," Kasatonin said in Russian.

"Are you certain?" Katya asked in the same language.

"Yes."

Katya strained toward the window closest to her. The portion of the Foss tug that she could see looked unreasonably elegant against the rusty container ship. Smoke poured from the sleek, raked stack as the tug nudged the huge ship into a berth.

Even through the car's smoked glass, Kasatonin could see the distinctive blue boxes on the ship's cargo deck. Three of the containers were in the stack immediately behind the wheelhouse. Four more were in the top rank at the bow.

All seven of the boxes belonged to the shipping company controlled by Tony Liu's Earth and Sky Tong.

Kasatonin laughed aloud at the thought of what must be going on among the American customs officers.

"What is so amusing?" Katya demanded in Russian.

"Your Mr. Liu is a clever man," Kasatonin said in English.

"Of course. I don't align myself with fools."

"Liu is more clever than most," Kasatonin said, switching back to Russian. "As the English would say, he gives the customs officers an annoyance of riches."

Katya barely controlled her desire to pinch him.

"Tell me," she demanded.

"American customs officers have a world-wide intelligence

system that monitors shipments from known narcotics source countries. Bangkok, in particular.''

"That is why I did not want the containers to come from Bangkok. But no, you said to trust Liu to know how to smuggle in the silk.''

"Liu has sent seven containers on this ship. All blue. All from the Earth and Sky's captive shipping system.'' Kasatonin laughed. "The Americans will be as busy as flies on shit.''

"Ahhh,'' Katya purred. "Clever indeed. Only Liu will know which one carries contraband.''

"You and I know,'' Kasatonin said.

"But of course. We paid well for the information.''

"We should have had it for the asking.''

Katya smiled slightly.

"Liu is clever indeed,'' she said. "No one in the Harmony knows the details of his smuggling networks.''

"Except us, this time.''

Kasatonin fell silent as he strained to read the identification numbers off the blunt ends of the blue containers. It was difficult, but the binoculars were powerful and the sedan provided a stable platform.

"Eight-nine-three-three-five,'' Kasatonin said in Russian.

"Which one? Where?''

Excitement and impatience thinned Katya's voice. Close, so close, to the coup of her dreams—power and wealth so great that nothing could ever threaten her again.

Safe.

Finally.

She could almost touch it.

"The box in the top rank behind the foremast,'' Kasatonin said.

"Will it be first off?''

"Probably.''

Katya frowned. "I would have put it elsewhere.''

"So would I. Customs officers are more vigilant at the beginning of an inspection than at the end.''

Kasatonin lowered the binoculars and looked at Katya. She grimaced.

"If we object," Katya said, "we will betray our knowledge."

Silence was Kasatonin's answer.

It was all Katya needed. Both of them knew that the Harmony was an intricately balanced structure composed of trust and mistrust.

But the Buddha's Robe was too important to entrust to anyone. All Liu knew was that he had been asked to smuggle something in a glass bottle. Only Katya and Kasatonin knew what was in the cylinder, for the man who had created it and placed the silk within was now dead.

At least, that was how Kasatonin had planned it. He assumed that Liu had somehow discovered what was in the glass, just as Kasatonin had discovered the smuggling route.

"Such trouble for a rag," Kasatonin said in Russian.

"To you, a rag. To Kojimura it is the Shroud of Turin and the Holy Grail in one."

"Foolishness."

"If people were not fools, where would we be?" Katya asked.

"Dead or very poor, which is the same thing."

Katya laughed.

"The unloading has begun," Kasatonin muttered.

Instantly Katya looked toward the dock.

Overhead cranes on rolling gantries slid into position with oiled ease. Long-legged, eight-wheeled container tractors gathered like gigantic steel locusts. Once the signal was given, they would pick the container ship clean with breathtaking speed.

Katya knocked on the window that separated her from the driver and Tony Liu.

The window slid down. A wall of smoke spread out into the luxurious passenger compartment. Outwardly Tony Liu might look calm, but he had been chain-smoking harsh Asian cigarettes for an hour.

Katya lowered the smoked glass side window of the dark Cadillac sedan.

"Katya," Kasatonin said warningly.

"I cannot abide Chinese tobacco," she said in curt Russian. "In any case, no one is near."

A cold wind whipped in off the bay. The *Esmeralda* was less than a hundred yards distant. From where they sat in the parking lot of the shipping company, the ship was visible in sections as it loomed above columns of neatly stacked, colorful containers.

"Which container is ours?" Katya asked Liu in English.

"The one on the outside, just behind the wheelhouse."

"How is the capsule concealed?"

Liu coughed softly, rolled down his own side window, and spat through it.

Katya barely controlled her expression of distaste. The man's manners were even more offensive than usual.

"Rice," Liu said. "A bag of Thai Basmati rice."

"Will that not be conspicuous?" Katya asked. "Americans export rice, not import it."

Liu smiled. "Basmati is favored by American gourmets. There are two hundred bags in the container box."

"The cylinder? It is there, too?" Kasatonin asked.

"Yes."

"Glass is fragile."

"Do not worry, Mr. Kasatonin. I know my business."

"Of course," Katya said quickly. "Your tong is without peer in smuggling."

It wasn't flattery. It was the simple truth. Liu nodded very slightly in acknowledgment.

"I am less worried about glass than I am about spies," Katya said.

Tony Liu sucked air between the gap in his front teeth, a sign of annoyance.

"The Earth and Sky Tong commands great loyalty," he said.

Knowing how much Liu disliked casual physical intimacy, Katya reached into the front of the limousine and stroked his cheek.

"I meant no insult to your tong," Katya said gently. "Yet we are adults here. We know that loyalty is always for sale in our trade."

More air whistled noisily through the gap in Liu's teeth.

Katya smiled and withdrew her hand.

The mechanical army of container handlers went to work on the *Esmeralda*. There was a flurry of shifting boxes and equipment moving into position. Without fanfare an overhead crane swung toward shore the three blue containers behind the wheelhouse. Gently the containers were lowered to the pavement.

The crew forward of the wheelhouse seemed less efficient. The first of their four containers, eight-nine-three-three-five, was still suspended beneath the forward crane when a dark blue helicopter roared in over Elliot Bay. The chopper traced the length of the *Esmeralda*, then whirled nimbly and came back to the stack of containers behind the wheelhouse.

Simultaneously, sirens wailed from the public street beyond the parking lot's fence. Three sedans roared past startled gate guards and into the container yard.

The cars were the same dark blue as the helicopter. Tires squealing and sirens screaming, the sedans dodged around tractors and stacks of containers, heading for the blue containers that had just been off-loaded from the *Esmeralda*.

When the cars roared past, Katya drew back so as not to be seen. The decals on the sides of the cars were unmistakable.

Adrenaline flooded through her body, shaking her.

"United States Customs," Katya said starkly.

The crane operator began to lower the precious container onto the land—and into the waiting arms of the U.S. Customs.

Liu watched the scene with complete indifference. His driver lounged in the front seat of the limo with his cap drawn over his face. For all the movement either man made, they could have been dead.

"What is this?" Katya demanded in English.

Liu reached out and patted Katya's cheek.

"The United States Customs, as expected," Liu said.

"What are you talking about?"

"Watch," Liu said. "You will learn."

With that he turned back to watch the raid.

Kasatonin made a sudden motion toward Liu, but Katya held her deadly lover in place with a curt gesture.

"Wait," she said in Russian.

"If he has betrayed us—" Kasatonin said in the same language.

"Yes," Katya interrupted. "Then you will kill him."

"It may be too late."

"There is always time for death."

Through slitted eyes, Kasatonin watched the wharf.

Like the unloading of the container ships, the raid was efficient and well orchestrated. A dozen agents rushed out of the sedans dressed in blue coveralls and carrying shotguns and pistols. The men swarmed over the docks, securing the area.

More vehicles poured in. Two canine units arrived in separate trucks. Dogs and handlers leaped out. German shepherds danced at the end of their leashes, excited and ready for work.

Katya looked at Tony Liu.

He was as calm as a lotus blossom. He watched while the container with modern rice and ancient silk dangled from the crane and swung toward shore. Slowly the box was lowered toward the hardtop where agents swarmed.

Kasatonin's hand closed around the lapels of Liu's beige silk suit.

"Stop the unloading, you fool," Kasatonin snarled. "The container with the capsule is not yet touching American soil. The customs officers have no right to search it!"

Anger followed surprise as Liu realized that Kasatonin knew which container held the silk.

Kasatonin shook him roughly.

"Yes, fool, we know where it is," he said. "Stop the unloading before it is too late!"

The grin that spread across Liu's face exposed all of his tobacco-stained teeth. He laughed in Kasatonin's face.

"Fool? Not I," Liu said. "Just wait. You will see."

"If we lose that capsule, you are a dead fool."

Liu just laughed harder.

"Ilya," Katya said. "Look!"

Without loosening his grip on the laughing Chinese, Kasatonin turned and stared through the open window.

The Customs team had descended on the three blue containers that were on the ground. Members of the *Esmeralda*'s crew and a crowd of longshoremen gathered to watch. An agent jammed a crowbar through the seals of one container's inspection door. The thin metal strips popped apart easily.

When two agents opened the door, one of the dogs charged past and lunged at a cardboard box that was now exposed. The box shredded beneath the dogs' attack. Plastic bags fell out and tumbled to the ground.

Both dogs attacked the bags, ripping them apart with their jaws. White powder exploded into the air before the handlers could drag their dogs off.

Customs agents and more longshoremen gathered around the spilled cargo. The helicopter landed on the hardtop nearby. Air from the rotor whipped white powder aloft and scattered loose bags everywhere.

Search dogs tore at the bags, snapping and lunging. Everyone but the handlers scrambled out of the way. Several of the bags dropped into the water between the *Esmeralda* and the pier.

Liu laughed and laughed.

"Why are you laughing?" Katya demanded. "This is a disaster!"

Shaking his head, Liu kept on laughing.

"The dogs," he finally gasped. "They are so finely trained. A whiff of heroin and they go mad."

Katya simply stared at Liu as though he, too, had gone mad.

"Container eight-nine-three-three-five," Kasatonin said suddenly. "Look, Katya!"

As the circus on the wharf swirled outward, attracting work crews from other ships, the crane operator kept on unloading container eight-nine-three-three-five. He finished swinging the big blue box ashore, then carefully lowered it to the wharf.

Freight handlers broke away from the turmoil around the first blue containers. They went immediately to the box that concealed the ancient silk. A container tractor maneuvered quickly into position.

While every other eye was trained on the narcotics bust, the tractor picked up the container. The long-legged rig wheeled away with container eight-nine-three-three-five hanging from it like a baby kangaroo from its mother's pouch.

An instant later the box disappeared behind a three-tiered bank of containers that covered most of a city block.

Kasatonin released Liu's suit coat.

"Clever little man," Kasatonin said. "How much heroin did that cost you?"

"A kilo."

Liu snickered, still watching the farce he had arranged.

"It looked like more than a few pounds from here," Katya said.

"The heroin was heavily cut," Liu explained. "Dogs only know the scent. They have no way of knowing quantity."

Deliberately Liu turned and stared at Kasatonin for a long time.

"So," Liu said, sucking air through his teeth, "you do not trust me? You spy on me?"

"Of course," Kasatonin said flatly. "The capsule has great value."

"The People's Republic of China put a high bounty on it," Liu agreed. "I chose not to accept."

Kasatonin didn't respond.

"Who in my tong sold information to you?" Liu asked in a calm tone.

Kasatonin shrugged.

"It is to your benefit to tell me," Liu pointed out. "What you have purchased from him, others may also buy."

"Tell him," Katya murmured. "He is right."

Kasatonin didn't hesitate any longer. He had been waiting for Katya's cue, for they had discussed this contingency.

Better to have Liu do the dirty work. The Harmony's members would get restless if they believed they were at immediate risk from Kasatonin.

"Ricky Po," Kasatonin said. "I believe he is your 'red pole,' your enforcer, in Bangkok."

Liu nodded again. As he did, a faint smile of disappointment changed the lines of his face.

"Ricky, Ricky, Ricky," Liu said sadly. "Yes, he is my red pole. Now I will be forced to bring someone in from Hong Kong to kill him. What a nuisance."

"I can arrange something, if you wish," Kasatonin said.

"Thank you, no."

"As long as he dies," Kasatonin said. "Anyone who sells secrets for a mere ten thousand Canadian dollars is a fool."

"You would kill the traitor you yourself seduced," Liu murmured.

"As you pointed out, what one buys, another could also buy."

Liu glanced at Katya.

"Your own red pole must have some Chinese blood in him. He understands the necessity of ruthlessness. Do you trust him?"

Katya smiled at Kasatonin.

"Ah, my red pole," she murmured. "Of course I trust him. He is the only one I have ever known who is as remorseless as I."

Katya was still smiling when Liu turned and spoke sharply in Mandarin to his driver.

The anonymous sedan sped away, leaving chaos behind.

Chapter Twenty-three

By the time a cab deposited Dani in front of the Georgetown townhouse of Risk Limited, she was questioning her suspicions of Henley.

But the memories of danger in Lhasa and Aruba were very fresh in her mind. She couldn't shake the feeling that there was much more to her world than its peaceful surface.

Two gardeners were working along the walk to Risk Limited's townhouse. Dani looked at the men very closely as they methodically spaded the half-frozen dirt in the flower beds. Both men were wearing miniature earphones of the kind Gillespie had taught her went with two-way radios.

A partially concealed Uzi lay within reach of one man, stowed in his workman's tote along with more ordinary gardening tools.

Was there this much security here last time and I just didn't notice it? Dani asked herself as she went up the walkway.

Probably, she admitted silently. Six weeks ago, I wouldn't have spotted the gun and the earphones. The gardeners would have been just gardeners planting next spring's tulips.

Henley would have been just a jerk flexing his institutional muscle.

The gardeners inspected Dani discreetly and thoroughly.

Dani nodded politely to each of them.

One smiled slightly in return. The other was muttering into a hidden microphone.

Cassandra Redpath opened the door before Dani could set off the chimes.

"Come in," Redpath said. "Gillie is serving tea in the conference room. We'll talk there."

"Yak butter tea?"

Redpath grimaced at Dani's hopeful expression and shut the door behind them.

"You and Shane," she muttered, shaking her head. "As a diplomat I had to consume more than my share of international 'delicacies.' Yak butter tea is among the worst swill I've ever encountered."

"I'd trade it for some minestrone soup," Dani said wistfully.

Redpath smiled. "I've had a yen for that myself. Gillie and I started making some at dawn. I'm sure there's some left."

"Is there a Gregorian chant to go with it?"

"Feeling in the need of some mental space?"

"Yes," Dani said bluntly.

"That can be arranged."

"Bliss."

"Most people's requirement for bliss are a little more complex," Redpath said, leading Dani through the house.

"Lhasa had a clarifying effect on my needs," Dani said dryly. "I'm into smelling all the flowers I can whenever the chance comes along."

Together the two women walked through the last of the public rooms in the house. A specially constructed door shut behind them.

"All right," Redpath said. "We're free from any eavesdropping. What happened?"

"Remember Henley Cage?"

"Yes. He was one of my most ambitious, least academic students. He is now the chairman of your department. He approved of our borrowing your expertise."

"Not anymore."

Redpath turned and looked at Dani with vivid green eyes. For Dani, it was rather like being scanned by emerald lasers.

"Off the record," Dani said, "Henley told me that if I insisted on slighting my academic duties to work with you, my tenure was in doubt."

Redpath's auburn eyebrows lifted in surprise.

"When I invited him to put it in writing," Dani said, "he declined."

As though somehow disappointed, Redpath shook her head and kept walking. Dani followed.

"I knew Henley wasn't a particular friend, but I didn't think he was an enemy," Redpath said.

"I'm not sure he is in the way that you mean," Dani said. "The more I think about it, the more I believe that Henley was the messenger rather than the bad news itself."

"Interesting," Redpath said, pausing by a closed door. "What makes you think that?"

"Henley has done a lot of work in Xi'an and the Chinese interior. He has extensive contacts in the culture ministry in Beijing. He depends on their good will for nearly all his original research."

"PRC."

Dani nodded. "Or maybe I'm just paranoid."

"Even paranoids—"

"—have real enemies," Dani finished wryly. Then she shivered. "I brought every Risk Limited document with me when I left the office."

Redpath looked at the younger woman's taut, pale face.

"It's not too late, Dani. You can leave the documents with us, go back to your office, and tell Henley you've seen the light."

Slowly Dani shook her head.

"It's not light that I've seen," Dani whispered. "It's the kind of cultural night that makes the Dark Ages look bright."

Gently Redpath touched the younger woman's shoulder.

"Think carefully," she said. "You've been a great deal of help to us, but the situation has become frankly dangerous."

"Has something else gone wrong? Is it Shane?" Dani asked urgently. "Is he all right?"

"He's just beyond this door," Redpath said.

Dani let out a slow breath of relief.

"I was afraid he was back in Lhasa or Aruba or someplace even worse," she admitted. "I didn't even know where he was, if he was in danger or hurt or . . ."

Compassion softened the lines of Redpath's face.

"Shane has been locked up with the Harmony's computer files, trying new variants of code breaker as our hackers devise them," she said. "He has barely slept at all. Don't expect much from him."

Dani's face became expressionless. "Why should I expect anything from Shane?"

"A guess, nothing more," Redpath said. "Gillie and I have never seen Shane in quite this mood."

"Does a saint have moods?" Dani asked with faint bitterness.

"Shane is no saint."

"You couldn't prove it by me."

Redpath smiled briefly. "So that's it. I wondered."

Dani shut up.

"If it helps," Redpath said, "Gillie has been thinking of taking Shane to the gym and beating the hell out of him."

"He would have his hands full."

"They both would."

Dani managed to smile. "Never mind. I've survived worse mistakes than Shane Crowe."

"Are you certain he's a mistake?"

"He's certain *I* am."

Silence settled while Redpath chose her words with the care of the diplomat she had once been.

"In the old world," she said slowly, "the one we're all leaving behind, warriors and women usually walked separate paths. No longer. Now some women go to war beside the men they love. The men hate it, but . . ." She shrugged. "We all adjust. Painfully."

Dani looked at Redpath and realized how tired and yet how

very much alive the other woman was. There was a vital force in her that was almost tangible.

Charisma, Dani thought. Henley was right about that. He was dead wrong about the renegade part.

"What happened?" Dani asked. "And don't try to tell me nothing did."

"Kasatonin tried to exchange Gillespie's life for my agreement to conspire with the Harmony."

"What? When?"

"While you were in Aruba, Kasatonin caught me on the street. We talked while his men tried to kill Gillie in Miami."

"My God."

"Gillie took care of the assassins. The only reason I'm alive," Redpath added, "is that Kasatonin didn't believe I was as vulnerable as I appeared to be."

A sound that could have been a laugh or a curse was Dani's only answer.

"Katya got lucky that way, too," Dani said. "Shane could have killed her."

"He told us. I'm glad he didn't. For his sake as well as ours. What he found in her safe made her all too human to him. A lost child . . ."

Redpath's voice died. She shook her head slowly.

"All Shane told me was that he didn't find the silk," Dani said.

"He was protecting you. There is nothing in Katya's safe that would enhance your life."

While Dani thought about that, Redpath opened the door to the conference room and gently urged her inside.

The room couldn't have been more unlike Redpath's stately private library. There were books, yes, but the room was dominated by six computer terminals, twice as many multi-line phones, and other less readily identifiable electronic apparatus set up in carrels throughout the area.

Swiftly Dani looked for Shane.

He had his back to her. The headset he was wearing was the kind worn by air traffic controllers—lightweight, high-tech, and discreet.

The computer screen in front of Shane was filled with non-sense combinations of numbers, symbols, and letters. He stared at them as though his will alone could break the code.

"Anyone else for minestrone soup?" Redpath asked.

Gillespie looked up from a stack of printouts. Next to him was an elegant, modern silver tea service with the requisite cookies and biscuits, milk and sugar.

He was wearing half-glasses. He looked angry and weary at the same time, like a man who had seen too much greed and stupidity, death and pain.

"No thanks," Gillespie said, "but I'll ring the kitchen for you."

"I'll take care of it," Redpath said.

Shane didn't even glance away from the screen. The encrypted files stared back at him with the eyes of a thousand dead men.

He highlighted everything and hit some keys.

The cursor became a tiny blue globe, spinning. Spinning. Spinning. It was meant to reassure the operator that the computer was at work, despite the lack of visible results on the screen.

"Dani just got a veiled warning, compliments of the PRC," Redpath said.

Shane spun around. His eyes went over Dani like hands, checking for injury. Then he switched his bleak gaze to Redpath.

"Do they know about Aruba?" Shane asked.

Redpath turned to Dani.

"Henley saw a book on the Caribbean in my office," Dani said. "I told him I was hunting up a vacation."

"Did he buy it?" Shane asked.

"He seemed to. He moved on to a monograph about silk moths."

Shane looked at Gillespie.

"Nothing here, mate," Gillespie said. "Not so much as a hint that you or Dani were identified in Aruba, much less that part of the Czarina's computer is spilling its guts to us."

"Somebody in the PRC knew about Dani," Shane said flatly.

"Lhasa," Redpath said.

"Maybe. And maybe a lot closer to home."

"I doubt that it's Henley Cage," Redpath said.

"He's a more likely leak than the Azures," Shane said. "I'll give him a thorough vetting. Real thorough."

Redpath and Gillespie traded looks that were readable only to them.

"Not you," Redpath said. "I'll put Walker on it."

"You do that," Shane retorted.

He looked at Dani.

"I hope you brought some clothes," Shane said. "You're staying. If you set foot outside, you go with bodyguards."

Without waiting for a response, he turned back to the computer screen. The tiny blue globe was still spinning, spinning, as the computer worked to break the coded file.

"Any luck?" Redpath asked.

It was Gillespie who answered.

"The encryption system is Soviet. A relic from the Cold War. A sodding tough one."

"What do our hackers say?" Redpath asked.

"Nothing worth repeating. They're putting bells and whistles on a decoding program they filched from a National Security Administration computer."

The spinning globe on Shane's screen stopped. Everyone stared at the computer screen.

An unholy alphabet soup stared back.

"Crap," Shane said. "So much for version nine."

"They just sent version ten by modem," Gillespie said. "Same file, point ten. They said it might work for some files but likely won't work for all. Katya's a tricky bitch."

Shane highlighted everything, punched in letters and numbers, and waited.

The little blue globe spun while the computer chewed through permutations and combinations of the new decoding instructions.

Abruptly twenty lines of gibberish appeared.

Shane studied the characters on the screen for an instant, highlighted everything, and punched in a translation request.

The screen snapped into readable words and sentences.

"Bingo," Shane said softly.

Gillespie was up and out of his seat in a startlingly fast movement. His black eyes scanned the screen over Shane's shoulder.

"Fifty-one down, one hundred thirty to go," Shane said.

"What is it?" Redpath said.

"Good question," Gillie muttered.

"Some kind of memorandum," Shane said.

As one, Redpath and Dani came to look over Shane's shoulder. They saw acronyms and abbreviations and groups of numbers.

"Might as well still be in Russian," Shane growled.

He picked up a nearby phone and punched the intercom.

"Front and center," Shane said. "We've got one more for you."

Moments later Boston walked into the room. His face had aged years in the days since Dani had seen him.

"I was sorry to hear about . . . your brother," Dani said.

The quality of her voice conveyed all that words couldn't. What she said wasn't simply a polite response to grief. She meant every word.

"Thank you," he said softly. "He will be avenged."

Looking at Boston, Dani didn't doubt it.

"What do you make of this?" Shane asked.

Gillespie made way for Boston.

The Aruban leaned forward and studied the screen intently.

"Yes," Boston said.

There was a world of satisfaction in the simple word. He pointed at a set of letters and numbers.

AA491 AR-MIA

"That," Boston said, "is American Airlines' daily flight from Aruba to Miami."

"Are you certain?" Shane asked.

"I have put many passengers on it."

"What about the rest?" Shane asked.

Boston hit the cursor to run through the document.

"The Czarina gave me lists in this form when arriving mafiosi needed to be met," Boston said.

Shane took the cursor up to the top of the document and went through it again, quickly.

"A travel itinerary," Shane said. "No, a set of them."

He read them off—flight numbers, airline and airport abbreviations, itineraries for ten passengers.

"Two from Moscow on Aeroflot," Shane summarized. "One each from Europe, Rome, Paris, and London. They came through New York and connected to U.S. domestic carriers."

Redpath and Gillespie looked at one another, but neither spoke.

"Three more came to Miami from three points in the Caribbean," Shane said slowly. "They boarded the same connecting flight."

He pointed to the tenth entry in the document. The acronyms were unfamiliar to him.

"ANA 511," Shane said. "Do you recognize it?"

"All Nippon Airlines," Dani said before Boston could.

"Of course," Shane said. He shook his head as though to clear it. "I should have thought of that."

"You should have thought of sleep," Redpath said.

Shane ignored his boss.

"These itineraries all have the same date," Dani said. "Everyone will be in the air tonight."

"Yes, but why?" Shane asked.

No one had an answer.

"Boston?" Redpath asked.

"I don't know. I'm sorry."

The Aruban stared intently at the screen, as though he could make the acronyms and tangled numbers yield knowledge solely with the force of his own desire for revenge.

"Someone with access to airline ticketing systems could tell us who these travelers are, where they are going, and when they'll get there," Shane said.

"I'm on it," Gillespie said.

He went to another computer, copied the file from Shane's screen, and dialed a number.

"Right," Gillespie said after a moment. "Sending."

A few strokes of the keys sent the document to another computer on the Risk Limited network.

Shane called up another document on the computer. Gibberish. He set de-coding program number ten to work.

The little blue globe spun. And spun.

"Boston," Redpath said. "Try to rest. If you're hungry, the kitchen is warming some minestrone soup for Dani. There's more than enough for two."

"If you need me—" Boston began.

"We'll call for you," Shane interrupted, his voice surprisingly gentle. "Until then, rest."

What Shane didn't say was that Boston looked like death walking.

Boston nodded wearily and left the room.

"Did you learn anything new about the silk while I was gone?" Redpath asked Shane.

"You were only gone a few minutes," Shane said.

Redpath gave him a narrow look.

"Next time you can get the door," she said.

"Only if Kasatonin is on the other side," Shane retorted.

"He belongs to me," Gillespie said flatly. "Don't you forget it, mate."

Shane looked at Gillespie and decided not to argue the point.

"There's no mention of silk in any of the documents we've managed to break," Gillespie said.

"I think that operation was run out of Kasatonin's hip pocket," Shane said. "He works alone."

"That's something you ought to understand," Dani said without thinking.

"Meaning?" Shane asked coolly.

"You've made it clear that you prefer to work alone. What would you do in Kasatonin's shoes?"

"I'd hate like hell to turn the silk over to Tony Liu."

"Yet you would, if you had no better way of moving it," Redpath said.

Shane shrugged. "Then I'd watch that slime-oozing son of a bitch the whole time."

"That's the biggest problem with being a crook," Redpath

said. "The minute you step outside the social contract, you can't rely on anyone but yourself."

"It's amazing the Harmony hasn't ripped itself apart by now," Dani said.

"Katya," Shane said simply.

"Or Kasatonin," Redpath corrected. "The offer he made me was ambiguous and provocative, to say the least."

Gillespie let out a blood-freezing sound that would have been at home on a highland battlefield.

Dani spun toward him, astonished.

"We've got them!" Gillespie said, looking at his computer screen.

"Where?" demanded Shane.

"Seattle," Gillespie said. "Pack your bags, boys and girls. We're going hunting."

"Dani isn't," Shane said. "She's staying here, under guard."

"Think again," Dani retorted.

"I don't need to."

"The hell you don't," Dani said. "I'm still the only one who can recognize the silk in the dark. Remember?"

Shane remembered.

He didn't like it one bit.

Chapter Twenty-four

"Printout, Gillie," Redpath said curtly, ending the possibility of an argument between Dani and Shane. "And Katya's file as well, please."

Very quickly the laser printer began spitting out sheets of paper. Redpath hovered over the machine like an eagle at a spawning stream, picking off the sheets as soon as they showed enough white for her to grab.

Shane loomed over her shoulder, scanning the sheets as they appeared.

"I'll bet the travel agent loves Katya," he said after a few sheets.

"Why?" Dani asked, peering around Shane's shoulder.

His nostrils flared as he took in Dani's unique scent. The maddening response he couldn't control slid hotly through his veins.

Two days and counting.

"There's a better commission on first class bookings," he said in a clipped voice.

"I don't recognize the names," Dani said.

"False documents," Redpath said absently. "Without

Katya's computer list, we wouldn't know who was doing what and with which and to whom.''

"That must be Spagnolini booked on Alitalia from Milano tomorrow,'' Shane said. "He's traveling under the name Buttafuco.''

Redpath grabbed a legal tablet. She began writing quickly as she identified various aliases by their country of origin.

"But what are—'' Shane started to ask.

Redpath held up her hand, commanding silence.

A few moments later she began reading from the list she had drawn up.

"The head of the Union Corse is traveling as Jacques Revel, direct from Marseilles,'' Redpath said.

Shane glanced at the illuminated wall map that was divided into time zones.

"He'll be in the air in four hours,'' Shane said.

"Katya and Kasatonin have already left,'' Redpath said, glancing at the clock, "as has our friend Tony Liu, who came in to . . . let me see . . . yes, there it is. Vancouver, British Columbia.''

"Vancouver? I thought the others went to Seattle,'' Shane said.

"They did. Tony Liu flew down this morning on a commuter flight,'' Redpath said.

"That fits,'' Gillespie said. "We just heard that Liu acquired Canadian travel papers. He uses them to visit his tong chapter in Vancouver. Looks like he goes to the states, as well.''

"Isn't he shit-listed with Customs and Immigration?'' Shane asked.

"I thought he was,'' Gillespie said. "I'll put someone on it.''

"Quietly,'' Redpath added. "Let the fish run before we reel him in.''

"Quietly it is, guv.''

Gillespie picked up a phone and began punching in numbers.

"Where is Liu now?'' Dani asked.

Redpath scanned Katya's decoded memorandum.

"The Four Seasons in Seattle," Redpath said. "Lovely bit of work getting this document, Shane."

"I'd rather have the silk and to hell with the memorandum," he said.

"We have the means, now. It's more than we had before." Dani looked over Redpath's shoulder.

"They're all staying at the Four Seasons?" Dani asked.

"So it seems," Redpath said. "There's a private dinner arranged at one of Seattle's better-known steak houses on the day after tomorrow."

"The Seattle Steak Summit," Dani said wryly. "Wonder if they'll slit each other's throats over the vodka-tomato sorbet?"

Shane gave a crack of laughter.

"Too much to hope for," Gillespie said, standing up. "This is the biggest gathering of international criminal bosses in history. It makes that Appalachia summit in 1957 look like a grammar school reunion."

"That means we'll be tripping over the FBI," Shane said.

"Not bloody likely," Gillespie retorted. "This is the type of thing that falls somewhere between the Bureau and the Agency."

"In other words," Redpath said, "nobody is responsible so nobody cares."

"Too right," Gillespie muttered.

"It doesn't matter," Redpath said. "These men won't be sitting on bags of heroin and using Uzis for calling cards."

"Every one of them will be as clean as a surgeon's fingernails," Gillespie agreed. "Just a quiet little rainbow coalition getting together for a chat about global crime opportunities."

"They're all traveling under false names," Shane pointed out. "That's still a felony in the United States."

"Immigration law violation," Gillespie said disdainfully. "They would post a ten-thousand-dollar bond and walk."

"Does that mean we can't do anything?" Dani asked.

"Not through channels," Redpath said. "The Harmony's members have isolated themselves magnificently from the dirty work."

Shane went back to studying the lists.

"Yukio Koyama," he said. "Is that Kojimura under a false name?"

"No," Redpath said. "He's traveling as Fujiwara."

Frowning, Shane and Redpath began cross-matching names and schedules.

"He's a wild card," Shane said finally. "Do you think he's traveling under his own name?"

"Gillie, do we have Yukio Koyama in our database?" Redpath asked.

Gillespie punched in a set of search instructions and waited.

"Nothing in the black files," he said after a moment.

"Fascinating," Redpath said. "Keep after it."

Gillespie's lean mahogany fingers danced across the keyboard again, shifting databases.

"Here he is, in the open files," Gillespie said.

Redpath waited.

Gillespie whistled softly. "He's a big one, guv. Legal to his back teeth."

Shane switched his attention to Gillespie's computer screen.

"Japanese industrialist," Shane read aloud.

"President of one of the biggest financial holding companies in Tokyo and an adviser to the leadership of several recent prime ministers," Gillespie added.

"If Koyama is such a fine specimen of citizenship, what's he doing hanging around with the Harmony?" Shane asked.

"Good question," Redpath said. "Gillie?"

He bent to the computer again.

A few minutes later he looked up. "No answer yet, guv. The Archbishop of Canterbury looks like a thug next to this Koyama chap."

"Well, we can't just sit on our thumbs and spin," Shane said savagely. "If we don't recover the silk there will be bloody hell to pay, and everybody from Tibetan tribesmen to Risk Limited will be paying it!"

The raw anger in his voice made Dani wince. The Zen cyborg of Aruba was gone. Shane was a man riding the eroding edge of his patience.

He saved me instead of the silk in Lhasa, Dani thought

unhappily. Is that why he can barely bring himself to look at me?

"I have a contact who might be able to help us," Dani said before she had time to think better of it.

"Who?" Shane demanded. "Not that chickenshit Henley?"

"No. But this man is in an . . . exceedingly sensitive position."

"Discretion isn't new to us," Redpath said simply.

Dani pulled a notebook from her purse, found a number, and went to one of the nearby phones.

Everybody in the room made it a point not to listen in.

Dani talked in a low voice to several people, longer to someone else, and hung up.

"Tom will meet me at the Renwick Gallery in fifteen minutes," Dani said.

"Like bloody—" began Shane.

"Go with her," Gillespie interrupted. "I'll cover Cassandra."

Shane didn't look happy, but he didn't object anymore. While Gillespie called up a car, Shane turned to Dani.

"Are you sure he can't come here?" Shane asked.

"Quite. He has an impeccable reason to be at the Renwick."

"Move it, then. Time is on the Harmony's side."

"Wait," Dani said. "This time *I'm* in charge. Tom is a friend. I know how to approach him."

For an instant Dani thought Shane would refuse. Then he smiled and gestured toward the door.

"After you, boss," Shane said.

Dani would have felt better if his smile had had less teeth in it.

Quickly she walked past him. No sooner were they out of the town house and into the car than Shane turned on Dani with another barrage of questions.

"Excuse me," interrupted the driver, "but Cassandra said Ms. Warren was supposed to have some soup before you grilled her."

"Soup? Walker, what the hell are you talking about?" Shane asked bitingly.

"Minestrone," Walker said, deadpan. "In the holder beside your seat."

"Aren't you supposed to be vetting Henley?" Shane asked.

"Gillie told me to put someone else on it. Someone who hadn't scored perfect hundreds in target practice."

Dani looked more closely at the driver. He had a two-way radio in his ear.

She wondered if he still had dirt under his fingernails.

A gently steaming cup of minestrone soup appeared under her nose, wrapped in Shane's big hand.

"Eat," he said curtly. "You look like hell on the half-shell."

"Thanks. You look wonderful, too."

"Eat or I'll feed it to you."

"Promises, promises," Dani muttered.

Then she started in on the soup with the speed and efficiency of a woman used to eating hot liquids in cold tents in Tibet.

Shane watched Dani spooning soup past her lips and tried not to remember the feel of her mouth under his.

Then she started licking the plastic spoon.

Abruptly Shane looked away.

"Who is this source of yours?" he asked curtly.

Instead of answering, Dani licked the spoon as though it wasn't already shiny clean.

"I'm not sure I have the right to bring you along," she said finally. "Tom didn't ask for any of this."

"Assassins don't worry about rights."

For a time there was only the sound of plastic scraping cup as Dani dug out the last delicious drops of soup and licked them from the spoon. Several times.

Shane tried not to watch. It was like trying to sneak dawn past the night. Impossible.

"Dani—" Shane began. His voice was almost hoarse.

"Tom," Dani interrupted quickly. "Call him 'Tom.' "

"Tom who?"

"Tomohide Noda," Dani said reluctantly.

The car slid to a stop in front of the Renwick Gallery. The building stood like a dowdy sentinel next to Blair House, across Pennsylvania Avenue from the White House.

The red sandstone Victorian of the Renwick was as quiet as an empty church. As a museum, the Renwick prided itself on housing only the most esoteric shows in Washington, D.C. Only true devotees of obscure arts and crafts—or the cold and homeless—spent much time at the Renwick.

"Nobody followed us," Walker said.

"Run up the glass," Shane said.

A bullet-proof privacy screen went up, separating the sedan's driver from his passengers.

"What's the problem?" Shane asked Dani bluntly. "Are you afraid I'm going to question your buddy with a gun?"

"You're in a mood to blow up things. Tom hasn't earned your anger, even if I have."

"What does that mean?"

"First I lost the silk for you, then I . . ." Dani flushed. "Your bloody vow, damn it. Anyway, don't take it out on him."

"I'm not angry with you on either subject, silk or celibacy."

"Forget it."

"Sure thing," Shane said dryly. "Just as soon as I stop breathing."

Dani bit her lower lip.

Shane looked away.

"Listen," he said after a moment. "I'll let you take the lead with good old Tom, but I won't let you go in alone. Deal?"

She hesitated, then sighed. "Deal."

"Wait until I open your door."

Shane got out, came around the car, and opened Dani's door. His wool jacket was unbuttoned halfway to his waist. As they walked toward the building, the wind gusted. For an instant the shoulder harness he wore for his pistol showed clearly.

Again, Dani questioned her right to bring Tomohide Noda into such a potentially dangerous situation.

But it was too late to change her mind. Shane had already opened the door to the foyer. With a silent prayer, Dani stepped inside.

"Let's do the main gallery first," she said clearly.

"Whatever you say, honey."

Dani leaned close to Shane.

"Remember," she said in a low voice, "Tom is meeting me as a personal favor. Nobody is paying him to stick his neck out."

Silently Shane wondered just how personal the favor was, but he knew better than to say anything aloud.

"Good friend?" Shane asked matter-of-factly.

"He's a cultural attaché at the Japanese embassy. I've known him for several years."

Shane's dark glance ran down the rows of glass cases in the main gallery. Each of the cases contained an elaborately embroidered silk garment with its multiple hems fanned for display. The range of colors was extraordinary. The quality of the workmanship transcended mere decoration and became art.

"Is he responsible for this exhibit of kimonos?" Shane asked.

"Yes. It's the best collection of contemporary silk the Japanese have ever allowed to leave their country."

"Impressive."

"Remember," Dani said in a low, urgent voice, "Tom has a lot to lose if somebody as powerful as Koyama thinks that he's helping Risk Limited."

Shane didn't answer. He simply inhaled the fresh scent from Dani's hair.

"This exhibit gives Tom a plausible excuse to get away from the embassy to meet us," she said, "so show a real interest in it."

"How close is your relationship with him?"

"Is that a personal question or a professional one?"

"There's no distinction in Japan," Shane said. "Diplomats have their own agendas. Does Tom think there could be something in this for himself and his government?"

"Tom was raised in San Francisco. He's as American as he is Japanese."

Leaning down, Shane brushed his mouth against Dani's mouth, clean hair.

"Be careful what you reveal," he said softly against her ear. "The same government that pays your friend's salary kowtows to Koyama. Good old Tom might already have his nuts in a cracker."

"He's an artist at heart, not a diplomat interested in power games."

"Unless artists have the luxury of civilization's armor, they have to be interested in power games," Shane said. "That's where people like you and me come in. We're their armor."

Dani laughed almost helplessly.

"You're a strange one, Shane Crowe," she whispered. "You truly see your strength as a shield."

"There's no other use for it except to dig ditches."

"Some men see strength as a weapon, not a shield or a tool."

Before Shane could say anything, he heard approaching footsteps. He turned swiftly, stepping between Dani and whoever was coming toward them.

"It's Tom," Dani said softly.

Shane moved aside.

The Japanese attaché bounced up the stone steps with the lithe grace of a gymnast. Tomohide Noda was five feet six and exceptionally well-proportioned.

"Danielle, it's been too long," he said, holding out his arms.

He took Dani's shoulders and drew her close for a moment. She responded with a quick hug.

Shane let out a long, secret breath. Their mutual body language told him there was respect and affection between them, but nothing sexual.

"Did you finally come to see the show?" Noda asked.

"I've seen this show once a week since it opened, but Shane hasn't," Dani said. "I thought it would be valuable for him to see it through your eyes."

Tom measured Shane with a swift, intelligent glance.

"Tom, this is Shane Crowe," Dani said quickly. "Shane, Tomohide Noda."

Noda shook hands like an American, firm and brisk.

"I'm always glad to meet a friend of Danielle's," Noda said.

Dani smiled thinly.

"Shane and I are, uh, consulting on a rare piece of Tibetan silk that has been stolen," she said.

"Dani has spoken of you and your work with great respect," Shane said. "What little I've seen in this gallery suggests she understated your skill and esthetic judgment."

Noda smiled. "Such a polite, gently Asian approach. Your size made me underestimate your subtlety, Mr. Crowe."

Shane smiled and bowed slightly. "You wouldn't have been the first, Mr. Noda."

"Nor the last, I'll bet." Noda turned to Dani. "Are you sure you know what you're doing?"

"Yes," Dani said simply.

Noda's eyes narrowed.

"All right," he said. "The name you mentioned to me over the phone is very, very well known to anybody in the business."

Shane waited, but with little real hope. Noda's tone wasn't encouraging.

"I'm not asking for official secrets," Dani said. "Anything you can tell me about that person from public files could help save one of the most valuable silk artifacts in the world today."

For a time Noda studied Dani. Then he looked at Shane. Then Noda looked at no one.

"Your advice on salvaging the peony tapestries was invaluable," Noda said softly. "Japanese culture is in your debt."

"No, I—" Dani began.

"The least I can do is show you the glory of our kimonos," Noda continued, not allowing any interruption. "You will see things among the silks that will delight and enlighten you."

With that, Noda strode quickly toward the rows of cases.

Dani looked at Shane, shrugged, and followed.

"I myself prefer the modern garments," Noda said.

He pointed to the loose, flowing creations that looked more like Western gowns than kimonos.

"The heavy hand of tradition needs to be lifted from Japan," Noda said, "just as it was lifted here in America a century ago."

Dani made a polite sound.

Shane made no sound at all.

"Japanese artists must learn to make use of the bold, innovative weaves and dyes that push their art in new directions,"

Noda said. "This show is an effort to encourage such artistic freedom."

The slight stress on the word *freedom* focused Shane's attention on the man. He started listening to Noda with the same intensity he had used when sitting at the feet of Zen masters.

And for the same reason. Noda had something to say, something that could only be taught indirectly.

"My modernist impulses don't prevent me from appreciating some elements of traditional workmanship," Noda said, "particularly when tradition is wedded to contemporary change."

"Would you show me an example?" Shane asked quietly.

Dani glanced sideways. The focused intelligence in Shane was almost tangible.

Like Lhasa, she thought. Like Aruba. I wonder what he senses in Tom that I don't?

Noda stopped in front of a large, free-standing glass case. Inside was a brilliant blue silk kimono. The cloth was vibrant with gold and green embroidery.

"This," Noda said, "is the most famous single garment in the recent history of Japanese textile arts."

Dani didn't need to read the plaque.

"The Boss's Kimono," she said. "A marvelous achievement."

"It was created by Norhige Tanaka," Noda said to Shane. "She is one of the best young fabric artists in Japan today. She is, in truth, brilliant. There is much to learn from her."

Again, the faint stress on a single word, *learn*, alerted Shane to look for more than one level of meaning in Noda's words.

When Dani circled the case, Shane followed. Both looked intently at the extraordinary artifact inside.

"Notice the patterns on the side panels," Noda said. "They are abstract and traditional at the same time."

"Ancient, sacred cranes in tangles of blue and white ocean waves," Dani said, slowly. "Yet there is a fluid feeling of motion that is new."

"Exactly," Noda said. "Now, examine the back."

The back of the kimono was spread in a graceful fan to

display a gold and black carp swimming among gently waving strands of river weed.

"The design is traditional," Dani said, "taken directly from Edo period garments."

"But unlike traditional Edo work," Noda said, "the carp is very contemporary. He has an almost postmodern self-consciousness. You can see it in his eyes and in his canny, bearded expression."

Shane studied the fish. Its whiskers did indeed look like the wispy beard of a Japanese patriarch.

"The carp is very well done," Dani said carefully, "but I'm not sure I understand your point."

"To understand that, you have to understand the traditional significance of the carp," Noda said.

"The carp is a symbol of patience or steadfastness," Shane said.

Noda smiled, not surprised by Shane's knowledge.

"In this case," Noda said, "you might think of the carp as a businessman, slowly making his way against the tide, waiting for his patience to pay off."

"That's definitely the traditional view of Japanese businessmen," Dani said.

"But this fish seems more smug than usual," Noda said, "as though he is certain the tide will soon be running his way."

"Interesting," murmured Shane.

"In truth," Noda said, "this particular carp is a finely drawn and beautifully executed commentary on the nature of Japanese business today."

"All that from the back panel?" Dani asked.

"See the silken under kimono?" Noda asked. "It comes from classic Noh theater costuming. One of the most common Noh characters is a young virgin who seeks entry to the temple."

"I remember," Dani said. "The audience knows she isn't a maiden."

"Yes," Noda said. "They know she is a sorceress, because they can see the gleam of silver triangles on the white silk of her underdress. They know it is the shimmer of a snake's scales."

Silently Dani studied the kimono, waiting and hoping that Noda would be less cryptic and more helpful.

Shane looked at the display card inside the case. In Japanese characters and in English, the card identified the designer of the kimono and credited the owner for allowing the silk to be shown.

The owner was Yukio Koyama.

Silently Shane drew Dani's eye to the card.

"The Japanese," Noda said, "have an odd view of the way polite society and the underworld interact. Some of Japan's business practices would strike an American as frankly devious."

"How so?" Dani asked.

"For example," Noda said, "there are the *sokaiya,* the financial gangsters who disrupt corporate stockholder meetings and extort protection money from large companies. Most Japanese believe them to be members of various Yakuzas, Japanese organized crime families."

"In that case," Dani said, "the businessman-carp should be worried, not smug."

"Unless the carp is connected to the *sokaiya,*" Shane said.

Noda smiled again.

"I believe that this one is the, er, godfather of all carp," Noda said, gesturing to the garment. "It controls the *sokaiya,* the interface, if you will, between organized crime and the legitimate establishment in Japan."

"No wonder Kojimura started collecting silk. Gives them something to talk about in public."

"Art is like life itself," Noda said, "full of subtleties, secrets, and surprises."

Noda looked around, assuring himself they were alone in the gallery. Then he drew a blank envelope from his breast pocket and handed it to Dani.

"Let's not go so long between meetings," Noda said. He glanced at Shane. "Mr. Crowe, perhaps I shall call on you in the future."

"Dani has my number," Shane said. "Feel free to use it anytime."

"Thank you. I will."

Noda turned and walked out of the gallery without looking back.

Dani stared at the envelope Noda had left with her. There was nothing to indicate its origin or its destination.

"May I," Shane asked, holding out his hand.

"Why not?" Dani asked sardonically. "You and Tom seem to have reached an understanding."

Shane took the envelope and broke the seal with his finger.

"Tom knows you weren't asking about the silk for yourself," Shane said. "So he was pointing out politely that I now owe him a favor."

"Tom never seemed particularly devious to me."

"Who said anything about devious?"

Dani threw up her hands.

The envelope contained a single sheet of paper, a photocopy of a newspaper clipping. The narrow columns and the tombstone headline suggested the clipping was old.

Five Japanese Industrialists Convicted of War Crimes

Shane held the clipping so that Dani could read it as he did. Both of them were drawn immediately to a name that had been underlined.

Yukio Koyama.

The story was a straightforward recitation of allegations made against Koyama and other Japanese businessmen by the military tribunal charged with trying war criminals after World War II. The offenses were comparatively minor. They had yielded short prison sentences from a government eager to put the shame of a lost war behind them.

Shane made the satisfied sound of a hunter who finally has his prey in sight.

"Koyama is a war criminal," Shane said quietly. "A minor-league war criminal compared with the Nazis, but a war criminal nonetheless."

"The same could be said of half the leaders of that era," Dani pointed out. "Besides, it was over fifty years ago."

Shane read the clipping again.

"There's no mention of the possibility of official pardons," he said.

"So?" Dani asked.

"So it just might be enough to keep the godfather of all carp out of the U.S. Provided the right people know in advance."

"And you know the right people."

Shane smiled. "Cassandra does."

"What good will that do?"

"It might give us what we're running out of. Time."

Chapter Twenty-five

Seattle
November

Katya lay in a daze that was partly sleep and mostly sexual surfeit. Her arms were thrown back over her head. There was a rare expression of relaxation on her face.

Kasatonin traced the soft lines of Katya's arms with a blunt, powerful finger.

"Be careful, oaf," she muttered without opening her eyes. "I do not enjoy being tickled."

Saying nothing, he traced the bridge of her shoulder and dropped down to her collarbone.

Katya's eyes remained closed.

His finger slid off her collarbone. He dragged his nail across Katya's breast.

"You hate being tickled," Kasatonin said. "Is that why I cannot remember ever hearing you truly laugh?"

His finger circled in toward Katya's nipple.

She captured his hand, stalling the advance. He shook off her grip easily.

"Neither of us has much to laugh about," Katya pointed out.

"So morose. So very Russian. Next you will start looking for your balalaika and sobbing old ballads."

While he spoke, Kasatonin's fingers strummed Katya's ribs like a musical instrument.

Her eyes snapped open. They were clear and dark at the same time, their pupils dilated by vodka.

"You are unusually playful tonight," she said.

"And that does not please you."

Without answering, Katya got out of bed, pulled on a robe, and stalked across the suite to the bar. She stared at her pale reflection in the long, gold-marbled mirror behind the bar.

The suite was the most expensive in the Four Seasons Hotel. It was filled with what Katya regarded as small, cheap touches of the sort that appealed to Japanese businessmen but offended her.

"I am not like others," she said calmly. "I never feel good."

"Except after sex."

She shrugged. "Like a breath, it is here and gone."

Katya pulled a bottle of vodka out of the ice bucket and poured a small glass half full. She drank, then grimaced.

"It is *not* cold enough. Why do Americans make hotel freezers so tiny?"

"Poor, sad little mink," Kasatonin said mockingly. "Never happy."

"Happiness is for fools. I prefer control."

Kasatonin sat up and scratched a small round scar on his belly. Then he stretched until the tendons in his shoulders cracked audibly.

"Do you feel in control now?" he asked.

The only answer Katya gave was an irritable shrug.

"You should," he said, yawning. "Even Tony Liu finally understands that he would be a fool to trifle with us."

"Does he?" she asked.

"If he does not, he is a dead man. He knows it."

Katya knocked back the vodka as though it was a particularly bitter medicine.

"I am most edgy when things seem to be going well," she said curtly.

"What is the American proverb—you cannot abide prosperity?"

"It is impossible to smile when the Harmony's monsters gather together. Only Satan knows what they could be planning behind their hands."

Kasatonin laughed out loud and flung back the sheets. Naked, he padded across the room toward Katya. His whole body was a lithe, muscular weapon.

"If they do anything stupid," he said casually, "I will just kill them. That is the first thing you keep me for, is it not? Or is it the second, mink?"

In the mirror Katya watched Kasatonin stalk her. She was always amazed that she could control that much masculine power with only her lips and agile tongue. Such control made the pain worthwhile.

No, Katya admitted silently to herself. It makes pain an aphrodisiac.

And he knows, damn him. He knows.

Kasatonin whipped his arms around Katya and pulled her against the ungiving wall of his flesh.

"My poor, poor little waif," Kasatonin mocked. "Always thinking, always worrying, always afraid. You are about to become the most powerful woman since Cleopatra, yet you mope."

Through half-closed eyes, Kasatonin studied Katya's face in the mirror. Earlier, during dinner with the first arriving members of the Harmony, she had seemed so vital and alive. No man could keep his eyes off her, including Kasatonin himself.

Now, as much at rest as she ever allowed herself to be, Katya wore a death mask. Her eyes were hollow and her skin looked brittle, almost mottled in its transparency.

When she reached for the vodka bottle, his hand flashed out. He held her fingers just short of their goal.

"You have had enough," he said almost gently. "Vodka no longer agrees with you."

With startling savagery, Katya tore free of Kasatonin and snatched the bottle from him.

"You are not my father!" she shouted.

Rage burned in her eyes, making their color more intense.

Fear brushed cold claws over Kasatonin's nape.

She is too close to the chasm, he thought. Closer even than I believed.

He needed a bridge across that chasm, a way to hold onto the global power that was slipping from Katya's grasp. Cassandra Redpath would have provided that bridge.

For a moment he cursed Gillespie's skill in eluding his Russian assassins.

So close, he told himself bitterly. So close to having another, even more clever Katya.

Idly Kasatonin wondered if Redpath would be like Katya in sex, releasing control only at the highest peak of pain and orgasm.

But that was something Kasatonin wasn't likely to discover before he found a way past Redpath's new defenses. Until then, he must make do with what he had.

Katya.

"You spoke of control," Kasatonin said coldly. "Vodka takes it from you."

"No."

"*Yes*. I saw it in the Russian army, the moods and sudden rages. Vodka is not good for you anymore."

"Good. Bad. Words, Ilya. Sound without meaning. The world is evil. Do you deny it?"

"Vodka does not change evil into good."

"No. It simply makes the evil more tolerable."

He moved so suddenly that Katya never saw the hand that snatched the vodka bottle from her grasp. His arm came around her body, forcing a gasp of air from her lungs as he pulled her back against him so viciously that her shoulderblades slammed against his chest.

"It is amusing to hear Katya Pilenkova talk of good and evil," he said.

Her body went rigid. She fought her captivity for a few seconds, but it was futile.

It always had been futile.

"I have no illusions," Katya said tonelessly. "Only men such as you can afford them."

"Men such as I? What kind is that?"

"Cruel. Quick. Strong. Evil."

Kasatonin chuckled. "A good match for a shrewd little mink, yes?"

"Give me the vodka!"

"No."

Katya fought more violently.

Laughing, Kasatonin easily controlled her. This was familiar sexual territory to him; the stalk, the capture, the sense of his own masculinity heightened by her struggles.

Without warning Katya sank her teeth into the hard muscle of his forearm.

That wasn't familiar. Not since the first time Kasatonin had taken her had Katya drawn blood. He thought he had taught her not to do it again.

Apparently she needed another lesson.

Kasatonin slammed the vodka bottle back into the ice bucket and hooked his right arm around Katya's neck. Effortlessly he snapped her head back and clamped a vise around her windpipe.

Only then did he raise his left arm and look at the wound. Crimson welled up in the slashing marks her teeth had left in his muscle.

"Bitch," Kasatonin growled. "Look what you have done."

Katya's only response was a strangled gasp. She fought to breathe around the rigid bar of his arm across her windpipe.

With one arm, Kasatonin lifted Katya until her toes dangled a few inches above the carpet. Her arms and legs flailed uselessly. After a minute, her struggles slowed, then stopped. She made an odd sound. Her eyes rolled up and she went limp.

After a few moments longer, Kasatonin shifted his grip, supporting Katya and loosening the bar across her throat at the same time.

She sucked air in great, choking gulps.

"You made me bleed," he said in her ear. "Should I make you bleed?"

Katya was too consumed with the simple act of breathing to reply. She gasped repeatedly, dragging air into a body that was starved for it.

Subtly Kasatonin tightened his grip on her again.

"Should I make you bleed?" he repeated gently.

Katya floated on the edge of consciousness. The sensation was oddly pleasant. She clung to it as she clung to the heady haze that came from just the right number of drinks, the amount of vodka that put her on the edge of death without killing her awareness of being alive and in control of her emotions.

"Do you have any idea how slowly a human bite heals?" Kasatonin asked.

Unable to speak, Katya shook her head.

"A long time, mink. And it always leaves scars. Remember the scars I left on you?"

Katya shuddered.

"Where shall I bite you?" Kasatonin asked.

He shifted his grip. His blunt hand thrust inside her robe. His fingers clenched around her breast in a caress that was pain and pleasure combined.

"There?" he asked. "Would you like to be bitten there?"

Katya stiffened against Kasatonin's callused hand. A sound came from her throat that had nothing to do with a need for air.

It was impossible for him to tell whether the noise was pleasure or pain or both mingled. That was why Katya excited him as no woman ever had.

Each time, she pushed both of them closer to the death that waited.

Perhaps this time, Kasatonin thought with a combination of reluctance and blood lust. Perhaps . . .

He spun Katya so that she was facing him. The movement tore her robe open. He lifted his left arm. Blood flowed freely from the gashes left by her teeth.

He jerked the wound across her pale cheek. The resulting smear was like red wine on snow.

"Perhaps I should bite you on this shoulder?" Kasatonin asked.

He yanked Katya's robe down her arm. Then he grabbed the muscle above her collarbone between his thumb and forefinger.

Though Katya made no sound, pain stiffened her body even as a feral excitement snaked through her belly.

This game was not new to her. Kasatonin would hurt her, perhaps badly, but there would be no marks.

"Or here?" he asked softly.

Kasatonin shoved his hand between Katya's thighs.

Air hissed between her clenched teeth as pain, pleasure, and sexual anticipation combined, electrifying her body as nothing else could, not even vodka.

"No," Kasatonin said. "I will not bite you there. You like it too well."

He loosened his grip on Katya's shoulder and sawed back and forth between her legs with the outer edge of his hand. It was his killing hand. Its edge was rough and calloused.

Katya had seen him break bricks with that hand. She knew he could break necks much more easily.

Slowly she gave herself to the hand that was also a weapon, thinking about the death it had brought to so many people. The same death would someday come to her, if she misjudged and pushed him too hard.

The thought was unbearably exciting.

"Ah, my sweet death," Katya said, her voice oddly childish. "I promise I will be a good little girl for you."

"Good? You?"

Kasatonin's hand twisted, tearing a cry from Katya's lips. She shuddered and ran like blood over his hand, hot and wet.

He laughed as the remnants of his sexuality stirred into life. Only Katya was able to give him the dregs of hellish pleasure that were all that the Afghanis had left him. Only Katya, because she reveled in the pain he had been through. His mutilation excited her as an intact man never could have.

"You are good for one thing only," Kasatonin said, moving his hand rapidly, harshly. "That is pain. You crave it even more than you crave vodka. I shall give it to you, mink. Perhaps . . .''

Katya's breath began to come more quickly. Despite her reluctance to give way to Kasatonin, she knew she was losing control of her body.

The pain was exquisite, perfect.

The phone sounded twice before the noise penetrated Katya's sexual daze. Her body stiffened as though the current that rang the phone passed through her.

''It's not the hotel phone,'' Katya gasped. ''It's my cellular.''

''Then go to work, mink.''

Before the phone rang a third time, Kasatonin released her, wiped the edge of his hand against her robe, and picked up the bottle of vodka from the bar.

Katya shook her head twice, sharply. She straightened her robe as she walked across the room to her attaché case. Impatiently she picked up the phone and punched a button.

''Yes,'' she said.

Her voice was cold, controlled.

It excited Kasatonin.

He took a swallow of vodka straight from the bottle. Then he sneered at himself and his pathetic cock. It was his weakness. He knew it.

He suspected that Katya might have guessed his vulnerability to her. If he became certain that she knew, her life would be even shorter than either of them had anticipated.

Vodka slid down his throat, as cold and hot as Katya herself.

''Speak more clearly,'' Katya said. ''I do not understand.''

From the background at the other end of the line came a high-pitched voice speaking an Asian language. After a moment another voice began talking into the phone in heavily accented English.

''Honored guest not permit maintain plans his,'' the voice said.

Katya recognized Miuro Tama, chief aide to Yukio Koyama, before she sorted out the meaning of the words. A fear that had nothing to do with pleasure and death rushed through her.

All the work, all the planning, all the killing, and now this! Katya thought savagely. Years, I have worked. *Years*.

"I regret to hear that," she said, her voice controlled. "My associates and I anticipated the meeting with great pleasure."

"Impossible, impossible," Tama intoned. "Impossible!"

Katya snapped her fingers lightly to catch Kasatonin's attention. When he looked at her, she held out her hand for the vodka bottle.

He crossed the room and gave it to her. She took it, but didn't drink yet. She was thinking quickly, trying to get the information she needed without giving away the game to any eavesdroppers.

Tama was calling in the clear, unscrambled. Their conversation could be overheard by anyone who had a cellular phone.

"Is there a particular reason for this change of plans?" Katya asked.

A flurry of Japanese came from the other end of the line as Tama conferred with someone.

Then Koyama himself took the phone. Anger vibrated in his voice.

"The Americans," he said distinctly. "They have withdrawn my visa."

"What? *Your* visa?"

Shocked, Katya tried to imagine what could have prompted such an insult from American bureaucrats. She took a drink of vodka and swallowed as though it were merely ice water.

"A newspaper reporter found some old information," Koyama said, his voice clipped. "He called me a war criminal."

"Which paper?"

"The New York *Times*. They called me a criminal!"

Outrage vibrated in Koyama's voice.

"I will have their apology," he said distinctly, "if I have to buy Manhattan and sell it to Koreans."

"It does little good to anger powerful interests," Katya said soothingly. "I can assure you, the paper you name is a very powerful interest."

The Japanese wasn't interested in being reasonable.

"First the dog turd questioned the American immigration

bureau," Koyama said. "Then he called me directly and asked me about 'crimes' that occurred in a war nobody remembers!"

"Where did the reporter's information come from?" Katya asked.

"I don't know."

"Do you know his name?"

"Tolliver," Koyama said. "Find him. Find his source. Then do what civilized people do with dog turds."

"The American press enjoys a special immunity," Katya said. "It is insulated from responsibility for its acts."

"I thought you and your associates had well-placed 'friends'. Obviously that is not true. I will not bother with our discussions any longer."

"You misunderstood me," Katya said quickly.

"Excellent. I will expect to leave on schedule."

"Please be patient. It may take longer than eighteen hours."

Koyama made a sound that suggested he wasn't feeling patient.

When Katya spoke again, her voice was warm, husky, infinitely feminine.

Kasatonin almost laughed out loud.

"Trust me, my friend," Katya murmured. "My colleagues and I have a gift that will show our great respect for you."

Koyama grunted as though he would expect no less.

"Our gift is like nothing else you have ever seen," Katya said. "Men have died to obtain it. Others have spent their entire lives preserving it."

"What is this thing you tempt me with?"

Katya laughed softly, seductively, inviting the old man at the other end of the line to respond to her as a male, rather than as an insulted crime lord.

"That would spoil the surprise," she said.

"There will be no surprise for me in the United States."

"If you will be patient, I—"

"I am an important person," Koyama interrupted coldly. "I will enter through the front door or not at all."

Katya thought for a moment, then smiled.

"But of course," she said huskily. "I will personally rearrange your ticket and our whole party, as well."

"What does that mean?"

"We will all meet you in Canada. There we will give you the gift that proves how valuable our collaboration will be."

"When?"

"Within two days."

"See to it."

The connection vanished.

Katya looked at the cellular phone in her hand. Her expression was as cold as her voice had been warm.

"Trouble?" Kasatonin asked.

"Nothing that cannot be cured. But the next time you have Ms. Redpath's throat within reach, crush it."

Chapter Twenty-six

Washington State
November

The Risk Limited jet bored through the air east of Spokane. Beyond the portholes the sky was indigo shading into twilight. Below, clouds blazed with reflected fire from the setting sun.

Dani came awake slowly and glanced at her watch. She had slept more than three hours.

Shane Crowe was slumped in the seat across from her. His eyes were shut and his body appeared relaxed. But not until she saw that his hands were also relaxed was Dani certain that he was truly asleep.

Trying not to awaken him, she moved slightly, stretching the tension out of her shoulders. The adrenaline ride since Lhasa had been as exhausting as it had been exhilarating.

And the worst—or best—is yet to come, Dani reminded herself. God, I could sleep for a week.

How does Shane stand it? Maybe that's why he went into the Buddhist monastery. A simple need for peace.

The plane altered course slightly, angling south a few degrees. A shaft of sunlight flooded through the round window.

The light touched Shane's face like an artist's brush, revealing every line, every shadow, every texture.

Dani fought an urge to brush the raw silk of Shane's hair back from his forehead, to touch the masculine roughness of beard stubble, to trace his lips with her fingers and then her tongue.

Adrenaline, she told herself. Just adrenaline. In the calm of everyday life, Shane wouldn't be half as sexy to me, half as attractive, half as fascinating.

And if I tell myself that often enough, maybe I'll begin to believe it.

Light across his eyelids awakened Shane. Slowly he moved his head. When the light didn't dim, he opened his eyes irritably.

He saw Dani watching him. Irritation vanished. A slow, lazy smile spread over his mouth. He shifted his long legs until his knee touched hers.

"Didn't expect to see you here," he said. "You've been avoiding me."

His voice was husky with sleep and something more, something that made Dani remember Aruba and sultry rain and a kind of pleasure she hadn't believed existed.

"Just trying to make life easier," she said.

"For you?"

"For both of us."

Restlessly Dani straightened in the seat. She stretched her arms above her head, trying to release the tension in her back and shoulders.

She didn't intend for her actions to be sexy, but they were. Her blouse drew tight across breasts, whose sensitivity had been heightened just by looking at Shane and remembering Aruba.

Belatedly Dani saw that the top buttons of her sand-washed black silk blouse had come open. The cloth had fallen aside, revealing a soft white bra and the swell of her breasts. Automatically she reached down to button the blouse.

At the same instant Dani's fingers touched the first button, she realized that Shane was watching her with an unmistakable male intensity. Her fingers trembled. A process that should have been simple became impossible. The buttons refused to go through the slippery silk holes.

Gently Shane brushed aside her hands and fastened the buttons. Dani felt the faint caress of his fingertips over silk and her taut nipples while he straightened the blouse.

"There," he said. "All buttoned up, just the way you wanted it. Or did you?"

Dani looked away from the frank hunger in his eyes. She studied her hands and silently cursed the fingers that had betrayed her feelings.

"Sorry," she said tightly. "I'm not trying to come on to you."

"I know."

"Do you?"

As Dani spoke, she met Shane's eyes squarely.

"Yes," he said. "The time between sleeping and waking is when basic emotions are the strongest."

For a moment, their eyes locked. Dani fought to breathe through the grip of her hunger for this one man.

Shane fought in the same way, even while he savored the knowledge that Dani wanted him as deeply as he wanted her.

Soon, he promised himself. Very soon.

Yet it seemed like forever to Shane before his vow would be fulfilled. Then, finally, he would be free to fully explore an aspect of his humanity that he had once thought he could live better without.

Prasam Dhamsa had thought differently. Not for the first time, Shane wondered what the lama had seen in Shane that Shane had overlooked in himself.

The bulkhead door opened, interrupting the charged silence. Lea Rubin, Risk Limited's chief pilot, came into the passenger cabin.

Shane looked at the pilot. She was neither large nor small, fat nor skinny, nor anything but dead bright, with the quickest reflexes Shane had ever found in man or woman.

"SeaTac or Boeing Field?" Rubin asked. "The ground party needs to know."

"Boeing," Shane said. "This is a downtown kind of operation. Who's waiting?"

"Gelmann. He came in yesterday from Los Angeles."

"Does he know Seattle?"

"He called up a local asset named Flanders."

"Flanders?" Shane asked.

"A former U.S. Customs agent. He's worked this part of the world for a long time."

"Should I know him?"

"He's not famous, if that's what you mean," Rubin said. "More like infamous."

A corner of Shane's mouth turned up.

"I'm familiar with the problem," he said, glancing at Dani. "What happened?"

"He was cashiered last year," Rubin said bluntly.

"Why?"

"Officially he took early retirement."

"Unofficially?" Shane asked.

"Flanders made life too difficult for the Native American smugglers trying to get around cigarette taxes," Rubin said. "He also knows a lot about Fukien Chinese operations."

"Our kind of guy," Shane said. "An equal opportunity cop. Too stubborn to be politically correct."

Dani grimaced.

"It's not too late," he said, watching her. "You can always go back to campus."

"Why do I hear 'ivory tower' echoing in your voice—"

"Sorry. Reflex, I guess."

"—as though a Buddhist monastery is somehow less sheltered than a campus?" Dani continued without pause.

Rubin laughed out loud.

"I may not like knowing all the bloody details about tongs and mafias and drug cartels and assassins," Dani said, "but I'm not going to run away and hide, either."

For an instant Rubin examined Dani thoroughly, then winked at Shane.

"An idealist and a realist," Rubin said. "I told you Redpath and I weren't the only women who combined those traits."

"Go fly your plane," Shane growled.

"Yes, my lord and master." Rubin bowed mockingly. "Notice, Dani, that he likes women who take orders well."

"Life's a bitch and then you die," Dani said sweetly.

Rubin was still laughing when the bulkhead door closed behind her.

"Zen philosophy?" Shane asked.

"Compliments of Shane Crowe, Zen monk."

"Not much longer," he said, glancing at his watch. "Good thing, too. You'll like Juan."

Dani shook her head, making her dark, glossy hair fly.

"Am I part of this conversation?" she asked.

"The centerpiece. Trust me."

"I'm clueless in Seattle," Dani muttered.

"Juan Gelmann is a sociologist who wrote his thesis on L.A. street gangs. Then he decided to apply his knowledge in more direct, non-academic ways."

"Like you?"

"I never wrote a thesis," Shane said.

"No, you *lived* it. Big difference."

"You lived yours, too. How many academics spend time in the field like you do?"

"Not enough," Dani said succinctly.

"Perhaps. And perhaps universities provide a necessary sanctuary."

"Necessary?"

"Not everyone is as resilient as you, Dani. Damned few are as beautiful."

"Beautiful?" Dani said, startled. "Yeah. Sure."

"I'm glad we agree on something."

"Wrong. I own several mirrors. I could safely be described as average in the looks department."

"We see differently," Shane said. "In my eyes, you are . . . beautiful."

Dani didn't know what to say, for she knew that he was telling the truth.

As he saw it.

Smiling slightly, Shane closed his eyes, leaving Dani to think about different ways of seeing the world. He didn't open his eyes again until the plane touched down fifteen minutes later.

Dani and Shane were met by Juan Gelmann, a slim, black-haired Latino with sad eyes behind round, wire-rimmed glasses. He looked more like a schoolteacher than a Risk Limited operator. Gelmann introduced them to his companion, Bill Flanders.

Dani put on her academic-tea smile and shook hands all around while sizing up Flanders.

He was a hulking, middle-aged Caucasian, with a face flushed from sun and wind and whiskey. His mouth was set in the cynical lines of a man who had spent his lifetime rummaging in society's garbage heaps, human and otherwise.

Wind gusted, lifting the tails of his Pendleton wool shirt. A pistol the shirt no longer concealed was stuffed into the waistband of his jeans.

He looked like the kind of man who would be uncomfortable without a gun close at hand.

Given what Dani had been through in the past weeks, she wasn't as harsh in her judgment of Flanders as she once would have been. She was willing to wait and see if he was as rock-stupid as he looked.

"How are you?" Flanders said to Shane and to Dani in turn.

He had a flat Sunbelt accent, Texas smoothed by the West Coast.

Dani had expected to be ignored or given the usual male once-over. She was pleasantly surprised when neither happened.

Flanders pointed across the tarmac to a waiting van. From the outside the van looked like a dirty recreational vehicle with heavily smoked glass windows.

"Your chariot awaits, lords and lady," he said.

"Ever heard of a car wash?" Shane asked as they walked to the van.

"Clean stuff is too glittery," Flanders said. "Hurts my poor old eyes."

Shane laughed and ducked to get in the van's door.

"Nice," Shane said after a quick once-over. "A rolling surveillance platform."

"Everything but satellite TV," Flanders agreed. "Damned antenna is too flashy."

Dani climbed in and saw what Shane was talking about. There were comfortable chairs, a two-way radio console, binoculars, and night-viewing scopes.

"Early retirement, huh?" Dani said to no one in particular.

"Some habits are hard to break," Flanders replied cheerfully.

"Gelmann climbed into the front passenger seat of the van and closed the door.

"The nice thing about Customs laws," Flanders said, "is that there are rewards for catching the bad guys."

"Really?" Dani asked, surprised.

"Yes, ma'am. I make just about as much as I did when I worked for the government. And now there's no Constitutional rights paper-pushing to do as unpaid overtime."

"Good work, Juan," Shane said, approving his choice of Flanders.

"I thought so," Gelmann said quietly.

Shane scanned the van again, looked at its owner for the space of several breaths, and made a decision.

"If this works out," Shane said to Flanders, "there might be other consulting jobs for you. Interested?"

"Is a frog's ass waterproof?"

Dani snickered.

With an agility that belied the gray in his shaggy hair, Flanders climbed into the driver's seat. He headed out of the airport on back roads. No matter how many twists, turns, and crossroads appeared, he never checked a map or a street sign.

"Was our information good?" Shane asked Gelmann.

"The hotel and the rest of the reservation information has proven out," he said.

"Visual confirmation?"

Gelmann removed his glasses, polished them on the sleeve of his corduroy coat, and replaced them.

"Cassandra told me not to work in close," Gelmann said.

"How close is too close?" Shane asked.

A smile changed Gelmann's sad face into a puckish one.

"I got a table next to the Sicilian gentleman and his French cohort at the hotel bar last night,'' Gelmann said. "Positive ID on both.''

Shane made a satisfied sound.

"They sat all night drinking expensive brandy and trading lies about their successes with money and women,'' Gelmann added.

"Anything useful?'' Shane asked.

"They were speaking in French, the only language they share comfortably, so they were fairly open, but I didn't hear anything I didn't already know.''

"You speak French?'' Dani asked.

"He speaks ten languages,'' Shane said.

"Twelve, actually, if you count isolates like Basque and Finnish,'' Gelmann said, "but who's counting?''

"And here I thought you were nothing but an overeducated Messican,'' Flanders said.

"And here I thought you were just another dumb Texican,'' Gelmann retorted.

Flanders said something in machine-gun Spanish. Gelmann fired it right back, with interest. Both men laughed.

"Sounds like they're pretty well-matched in a thirteenth language,'' Shane said dryly.

"Which one?'' Dani asked.

"Gutter Spanglish.''

"If you say so. The only really good bad words I know are in English, and some obscure tribal languages.''

"I could teach you,'' Gelmann offered, turning around.

"I'll take care of Dani's education,'' Shane said.

Gelmann looked at Shane and then faced the front again without a word.

"What about Pilenkova and Kasatonin?'' Shane asked.

"They're registered at the Four Seasons, in the biggest suite available,'' Gelmann said.

"Any luck getting close?'' Shane asked.

"Bill has an old contact on the security staff,'' Gelmann said.

"The two of them have kept a pretty low profile,'' Flanders said, "except for a little blood on the linens.''

"Whose?"

"No visible bandages today," Flanders said. "It looked like someone had a cut and wiped off the blood on the sheets."

"For some people," Dani said quietly, "sex is a blood sport."

Shane gave Dani a quick, sideways glance.

"Knowing those two," Shane said, "it wouldn't surprise me."

"Other than that," Flanders said, "they've been there two nights and have powered through three fifths of Stolichnaya."

Flanders glanced at Shane in the rearview mirror.

"That's serious drinking, son," he said. "Take it from one who knows."

"Been there, done that?" Shane asked.

"You bet I have," Flanders said easily. "Got the scars to prove it."

"Katya's scars only show in her eyes," Dani said.

"So she drinks herself blind," Flanders said. "Figures."

Silently Shane worked with a pair of binoculars, adjusting the fine focus on the eyecup. He studied Mt. Rainier in the distance.

"Any sign that the pressure increased on Katya between yesterday and today?" Shane asked.

"I didn't see any," Gelmann said, "but I'm working the Russians at a distance. Why?"

"Dani and I turned up the heat last night, or at least we tried to," Shane said. "I was hoping there would be some immediate results."

"Nothing struck me," Gelmann said. "Bill?"

"I don't know anything about your Russians," Flanders said, "so I can't help much there. But . . ."

Shane waited while Flanders slid the van between two delivery trucks. He drove with the abandon of a man who had plenty of traffic cops for friends.

". . . a guy from the Earth and Sky Tong was supposed to meet me early this morning," Flanders continued. "He was a no-show."

"One of Tony Liu's men?" Shane asked.

Flanders nodded.

"He's what they call the 'incense master' of the local chapter," Flanders said, "but he'd like to be the Hill Chief. Once in a while, when he figures it will help him, he passes me information."

"Is he reliable when he sets up a meet?" Shane asked.

"This is the first time he's stiffed me. Maybe he got hit by the five thunderbolts they're always talking about."

"It happens," Shane said.

"It happened a lot down on the Mexican border where I grew up."

"Are there tongs there?" Dani asked.

"Just across the line is a Mexican town that has the biggest tong temple south of San Francisco," Flanders said. "In fact—"

"What do your instincts tell you?" Shane interrupted.

Flanders shot Shane a quick look in the rearview mirror. "Instincts, huh?"

"If you didn't have them, you would be dead by now."

"Not many folks appreciate that. They're all shot in the ass with paper trails and such."

"I'm not," Shane said.

Flanders smiled. "Well, there was a really weird dope bust on the container docks at Elliott Bay yesterday."

"Was it a trip-over bust or did the cops have a snitch?" Shane asked.

"Oh, it wasn't no accident," drawled Flanders. "One of the DEA boys in Seattle got a tip about a stash of heroin in a container from Bangkok."

"What's weird about that?" Dani asked.

"Nothing, at first," Flanders said. "Customs and DEA nailed the container right away."

"A whole container of heroin?" Dani asked, shocked.

"Nah, just twenty kilos of white powder. Made all the papers and the six o'clock news," Flanders said. "A real big triumph in the ongoing international war against dope."

"What's the punch line?" Shane asked.

"The dope turned out to be less than five-percent pure,"

Flanders said. "Well mixed, well blended, and about as worthless as tits on a boar hog."

"You're right," Shane said. "That's weird."

"Why?" Dani asked.

"No righteous smuggler would haul forty-two pounds of talcum powder and two pounds of smack," Flanders said.

"Certainly no Chinese smuggler," Shane said. "The tongs value efficiency just slightly below loyalty."

"So?" Dani asked.

"So somebody went to a shit-pot of trouble and expense to stage a circus on the docks at Elliott Bay yesterday," Flanders said.

"You think it was Tony Liu's group?" Shane asked.

"Let's put it this way," Flanders said. "The tip to DEA came from a low-level street dealer who runs a restaurant up in Bellingham. That's just south of the Canadian border."

"A Chinese restaurant?" Shane asked blandly.

"Give the boy a prize."

"Which restaurant?" Shane asked.

"The Shanghai Inn," Flanders said.

"That's an Earth and Sky cover," Gelmann said. "They have a whole chain of Chinese restaurants. The tong distributes bok choy, bean sprouts, and Number Four white heroin, all on the same trucks."

"So someone in the Earth and Sky fingered their own load," Shane said. "Why? Are they fighting among themselves?"

"Nope, them babies are as tight as lice on a wino's scalp," Flanders said, shaking his head. "If they gave up their own smack, they were protecting something more valuable."

"The silk," Dani said.

"The silk," Shane agreed.

"That would be a mighty fancy piece of silk to be worth all the fuss," Flanders said.

"It is," Dani said.

"So the silk is here," Shane said. "Now, the only question is how the Harmony will finesse the fact that their honored guest isn't."

"Isn't?" Flanders asked.

''Here,'' Shane said. ''Can you drive faster? We're on a very short clock.''

Flanders looked up at the rearview mirror to see if Shane was joking.

He wasn't.

Flanders settled into the seat and drove. Fast.

Chapter Twenty-seven

Except for the gap between Tony Liu's front teeth, he would have done credit to the Cheshire Cat. Liu's smile gleamed with a sly sheen in the harsh lights that hung from the old wooden beams of the warehouse.

The Buddha gleamed, too, but differently.

Slightly more than life size, the statue was made of fine teak. The carving transcended craft to become art. The seated Buddha's arms and torso were that of a man at the height of his physical strength, giving the statue an aura that combined the sensual with the sublime.

But it was in the face that the artist's greatness was most evident. The Buddha's expression was both serene and vastly powerful, evoking the peace that surpasses understanding.

Liu buffed the gleaming arm of the statue with his sleeve.

"Nice, yes?" Liu said.

Kasatonin nodded. "More like a soldier than a god," he said slowly. "Is that not so, Katya?"

She merely shrugged and looked away. Anything having to do with religion made her uneasy.

"The statue was made in Bangkok," Liu said. "It will be

the centerpiece of a grand new temple the Buddhists are building here in Seattle.''

Impatiently Katya turned and faced the Chinese man. Liu had been subtly goading her for the past hour, hinting at the silk's presence without actually revealing it.

''Amazing, isn't it,'' Liu said, ''how religious icons such as this have a power to make us feel small, even if we are not of any particular faith or belief?''

''If you say so,'' Katya muttered.

Kasatonin watched Liu with blank blue eyes.

''Even government officials and bureaucrats show reverence,'' Liu said.

''Is there a point to this?'' Katya asked with a thin smile.

Liu nodded slightly, enjoying her impatience.

''There is always a point,'' the Chinese murmured.

''Then explain. Please,'' Katya added.

''It would be unthinkable for some lowly customs inspector to examine an expensive, artistically worthy religious icon such as this too closely,'' Liu said.

While Kasatonin watched with the unblinking interest of a blue-eyed snake, Liu picked up a hammer that had been used to uncrate the statue. He hefted the tool, testing its balance and weight.

''It would be unthinkable, for instance, to do this,'' Liu said.

As he spoke, he swung the hammer.

The movement was as quick as it was unexpected. Steel slammed into teak. The unearthly, beautiful face shattered. Pieces flew in all directions.

Shocked, Katya drew a sharp breath. Despite her outward indifference to the statue, she was still a Russian schoolgirl at heart, with a schoolgirl's fear of icons.

Liu laughed out loud at Katya's reaction, and gestured to one of his assistants.

The man opened a box and removed a Buddha's head that was as extraordinary as the one Liu had just smashed.

''Never fear,'' Liu said. ''The Buddha will not go headless to its new temple. I have a replacement from the same artist.''

"You have done exceptionally well for such short notice," Kasatonin said.

Liu's nod was also a tiny bow of self-congratulation.

"I have been saving my beautiful two-headed statue for some time," he said. "I knew someday I would find a piece of contraband that was worthy of the Buddha's protection."

"The Harmony thanks you," Katya said.

"It is but a small repayment for the gift of my grandson," Liu replied.

He circled around behind the Buddha and reached down into the body of the statue. With a slight flourish, he produced a package that resembled an oversized football. He slit the tape that sealed the package with a pocket knife.

As he unwound the cushioning material, a glass cylinder slowly emerged. It was about eighteen inches long and four in diameter. The base was a simple cork. Packets of silica gel insured that whatever air got past the dense cork wouldn't be moist. The tiny vent that had been used to remove the air was plugged with a piece of ebony.

"The silk," Liu said simply, "safe and whole. As beautiful as the day it was stolen from the monastery in Lhasa."

Katya looked closely at the glass. There were no cracks, no chips. More importantly, there was no sign of condensation on the inside of the glass. Though rather crudely done, the seal had worked.

"You will note that there is no sign of moisture inside," Liu said carefully.

"For your sake, that is good," Kasatonin muttered. "Let me see it."

The glass cylinder looked almost frail in the Russian's big, blunt hands. He rolled the capsule over and over, letting the light play across the interior.

Only a small corner of the azure silk showed between the protective covering of dense white outer silk that shielded the frail textile within. Ancient gold thread gleamed against an ethereal blue.

With a shrug, Kasatonin held the cylinder out to Katya.

"It has not changed," he said. "It is still a faded blue rag.

The gold in it is not worth a ruble. I clean my boots with better cloth.''

Liu smiled widely, almost generously. For an instant he had been afraid that Kasatonin was going to cause trouble over the silk fragment.

With both hands, Katya took the glass from Kasatonin. She stared at the silk with a small smile on her face.

''It does not look worth the trouble it cost,'' Kasatonin added. ''But I am merely a soldier, not a general.''

''History, not beauty, is what we are giving to Mr. Koyama,'' Katya said. ''I believe he will be suitably pleased.''

''He is coming, then?'' Liu asked, his voice rough.

''Of course he is coming,'' she said. ''Why would he not?''

''The Japanese Yakuza are not known for their desire to collaborate,'' Liu said.

''Koyama needs us more than we need him,'' Kasatonin said.

Liu looked dubious.

''The need is *equal*,'' Katya stressed. ''We are both Koyama's peers and his competitors. Whether we are friends or enemies is the choice he must make. We trust he will make the profitable one.''

''Of course,'' Liu said impatiently. ''But how will you fix Koyama's visa problem?''

Katya's eyes kept seeking the corner of ancient silk as she turned the cold glass cylinder over and over in her hands.

''No government decision is final,'' she said. ''There is always a higher official who will take an appeal . . . for a price.''

Liu's eyelids lowered until his eyes were gleaming black slits.

''Ah,'' he murmured. ''Some American immigration bureaucrat will soon have a retirement home in Florida.''

''Not this time,'' Katya said. ''We already have an immigration officer under our control—the woman who signed your entry papers.''

''She is in Ottawa,'' Liu said. ''She is Canadian. What use is she to Koyama?''

Katya smiled.

"How far is it from Seattle to Canada?" she asked. "To the city of Vancouver?"

"A hundred twenty miles," Liu said, "but—"

"The arrangements were being made while we wasted time here," Kasatonin interrupted.

Katya gave her lover a warning look.

"We are moving our meeting to the Four Seasons Hotel in downtown Vancouver," Katya said.

"When?" Liu demanded.

Irritated by Liu's attitude, Kasatonin took a half-step forward. A touch from Katya's thin hand stopped him.

"Koyama flies in to Vancouver tonight," Katya said calmly. "The meeting will be tomorrow."

"Ah," Liu sighed. "If you need a secure place for the meeting, the Earth and Sky Tong has many to offer."

"Thank you, but that will not be necessary this time."

"What do you have in mind?" Liu asked sharply.

Again, Kasatonin made a motion toward the smaller man.

Again, Katya held her assassin in check with a touch.

"We are chartering a yacht for those who are in Seattle now," she said. "We will cruise the San Juan Islands on our way to Vancouver."

Liu grunted.

"You, of course," Katya added pleasantly, "will not be on the cruise with us."

Fear showed on Liu's face in the instant before he controlled his expression.

"Why not?" he asked bluntly.

"You will be much, much too busy," she said.

Smiling, Katya handed the glass cylinder back to Liu.

"It will be your job to smuggle the rag for us again," Kasatonin explained.

Liu hid his relief even more quickly than he had hidden his initial fear.

"I trust you will have no difficulty," Kasatonin said. "From what I have seen, the border between the United States and Canada is as easy to penetrate as a whore."

"Yes, yes, I expect no trouble," Liu said, smiling and nodding his head rapidly.

"How will you do it?" Kasatonin demanded.

"The fewer people who know a route, the better off we all will be," Liu said.

"No good, little man," Kasatonin snarled.

"You trusted the Earth and Sky with the silk bef—"

"Trust?" interrupted Kasatonin, laughing. "I followed the silk along its route more closely than you did."

Alarm went across Liu's face.

"Tell me the route to Vancouver," Kasatonin said, "tell me now, and tell me in detail."

While he spoke, the Russian pulled a folded map from the pocket of his leather jacket. He opened the map until the route from Seattle to the city of Vancouver could be seen in detail.

Angrily Tony Liu drew himself up to his full five-feet four-inch height. He looked like a terrier snarling at a wolfhound.

"Please, tell him," Katya said, smiling and touching Liu's arm delicately. "The Harmony exists because cooperation is more profitable than war."

Liu knew he had no choice. He had known it from the instant he saw the Canadian passport that both gave him his grandson and put the baby under subtle threat.

Even so, Liu didn't like being ordered around by Katya's hellhound. He sucked air through the gap in his teeth, noisily showing his displeasure.

Then Liu took the map and spread it out over a crate.

"There are several possibilities," Liu said curtly.

Kasatonin and Katya flanked the tong leader, towering over him.

"For example?" Katya asked.

"There is a local commuter lane at the port of entry in Blaine," Liu said. "Cars with the proper decals are allowed to pass through with minimal inspection."

"Good," Katya said. "The silk could be in Vancouver in three hours, correct?"

Liu moved his head in a sharp negative.

"Few Asians have such decals on their cars," Liu said. "We

would have to enlist a Caucasian to do the driving. Perhaps Mr. Kasatonin would—''

"No," Katya interrupted. "Ilya stays with me. Always."

Liu wasn't surprised. It was common knowledge among Harmony members that Kasatonin was Katya's bodyguard as well as her pet assassin.

"Someone else, then," Liu said.

Katya looked at Kasatonin. Next to killing, he was most useful for tactics and logistics.

"No," Kasatonin said. "No outsiders at this point unless it cannot be done any other way."

"What about fishing boats?" Katya asked. "Do they not use the sheltered water route to Alaska?"

She pointed to the Inside Passage between Vancouver Island and mainland Canada.

"It would be easy to hide the capsule in a bilge," Kasatonin said.

"Fishing boats move with the seasons," Liu said. "Now is not a good time."

"What route, then?" Kasatonin asked impatiently.

"The dead-drop," Liu said. "It's probably the best choice in any case. It's easier to control. That's what you want, isn't it—control?"

"Explain," Kasatonin said. "I know the term, but not in relation to the smuggling trade."

"As you pointed out, this is a very loose border," Liu said. "Earth and Sky crosses it often, but usually from the other direction."

"How?" Kasatonin said.

"We bring heroin into a little Canadian town on Vancouver Island, then ship it south on a ferry route through the San Juan Islands."

Katya frowned. "What of customs inspections?"

"They exist on the direct international runs," Liu said. "But there are other, inter-island ferries that go back and forth without inspection."

"Truly?" Katya asked. "Even for the Americans, I find that astonishing."

Liu smiled and sucked air noisily.

"The islands are a maze of ferry lines and schedules," he said. "It's possible for someone to take a shipment out to, say, San Juan Island and leave it in a dead-drop."

Kasatonin saw where Liu was leading. He began nodding in agreement even as Liu finished explaining.

"Someone from the Canadian side comes down on an inter-island run, clears the drop, and returns to Victoria," Liu said. "From there, it's a few minutes by seaplane to Vancouver. There is, of course, no customs inspection between Canadian islands and the mainland of Canada."

"Why San Juan Island?" Kasatonin asked, looking at the map. "There is a small city there. Friday Harbor."

Liu shrugged. "So?"

"Why not one of these other islands, where there are fewer people, less chance of being observed?"

"Because, my friend," Liu said ironically, "there is a safe place to store the contraband in Friday Harbor."

"Where?" Katya asked.

"A restaurant called the China Girl." Liu grimaced. "I despise the name, but it appeals to tourists."

"This China Girl," Kasatonin said. "It belongs to the Earth and Sky Tong?"

Liu gave them his gap-toothed Cheshire grin, but at the moment he looked less like a cat than a waterfront rat.

"It's as secure as a bank vault," Liu said.

Katya glanced at Kasatonin, waiting for his approval or veto of Liu's plan.

For a few moments there was no sound at all in the warehouse while Kasatonin considered the plan from all angles. Then he nodded curtly, accepting it.

"The silk must be in Vancouver by tomorrow morning at ten o'clock," Katya said. "Can you do that with your dead-drop?"

"Of course, Czarina," Liu said.

His smile challenged Katya to object to his use of her nick-name.

"Then do so," Katya said.

As she smiled at him, she began planning the revenge she would have on the arrogant Chinese. The thought gave her a thrill of anticipation that was almost sexual.

But first, she reminded herself, Liu must fulfill his part in my silk strategy.

Chapter Twenty-eight

In the decaying warehouse district that once had been the home of Seattle's Chinatown, shattered timbers and broken brick walls were piled like burial mounds. Despite the many vacant lots, there was a distinct Cantonese flavor to the century-old buildings that remained.

Dani had spent the last twenty minutes trying to visualize the place as it once had been. The mental exercise was her way to deal with a combination of anxiety and plain boredom.

There was no doubt that suveillance, which so far had been nothing more than sitting and watching nothing at all, was monotonous.

"Is surveillance always this, uh, exciting?" Dani asked sardonically.

"Yes," Shane said.

"Then the adrenaline quotient in this line of work is vastly overrated."

"It's only boring when you set up half a mile away from your target," Flanders said under his breath.

"What?" Dani asked.

Flanders looked up from his task, which was cleaning and polishing a large pistol.

''If you get closer,'' he said, looking at Shane, ''surveillance is a hell of a lot more interesting than watching paint dry.''

Ignoring Flanders, Shane sat motionless, a shadow tiger hidden in the mottled darkness of the jungle, staring out the smoked glass windows of the van.

Flanders muttered something in gutter Spanish and started shoving bullets into the pistol.

''It is not boring and it is boring,'' Shane said softly. ''It is neither and it is both.''

''Try it in English,'' Dani said.

''Compared to staring at a spot on the wall of a stone cell in a freezing monastery and thinking of the infinite varieties of infinity,'' Shane said, ''surveillance is incredibly stimulating.''

''The Zen of surveillance,'' Flanders said. ''I always heard you Risk Limited types were cerebral, but I didn't know there were any Zen warriors left in this business.''

''He's a monk,'' Dani countered with faint bitterness. ''There's a difference.''

''A seeker,'' Shane corrected them both. ''Just that. No more, no less.''

''Seeking anything in particular?'' Flanders asked innocently. ''Seattle's a big town. We've got most everything here.''

Shane laughed. In the few hours they had spent in the van, he had come to appreciate the dour, burned-out customs cop.

Prasam Dhamsa would enjoy Flanders, Shane thought. He would see the stubborn quest for a better world that lies beneath the cop's cynicism.

''Peace is what I'm seeking,'' Shane said. ''That's what everyone seeks, down underneath.''

''Speak for yourself,'' Dani said. ''The only piece I'm looking for is tangible—a piece of the Buddha's robe.''

''That would give me peace,'' Shane agreed. ''It would give me a whole lot of peace.''

Flanders gestured with his pistol toward the warehouse they had been watching for an hour, ever since Katya and Kasatonin entered.

''Doesn't it bother you that you're probably staring right at it?'' Flanders asked.

"We don't know that," Shane said.

"We could kick in the door and find out."

"But you can't unkick the door if the silk's not there," Shane said dryly.

"How about a little parabolic microphone, maybe a nail transmitter in the warehouse wall?" Flanders suggested.

"Too dangerous. They're sure to have guards watching."

"I do a great impression of a homeless drunk."

Shane shook his head.

"Shit Marie," Flanders muttered. "Just so I understand the home park rules, does Risk Limited have a problem with dirty tricks?"

"It varies," Shane said.

"It's not like you're trying to make a case for federal court, right?" Flanders asked. "All you want is information."

"Anonymous information," Shane corrected. "Untraceable."

"That's the nice thing about a parabolic mike," Flanders retorted.

Shane shook his head again.

"We're not dealing with home-boy crack merchants," Shane said. "Kasatonin has a sixth sense for danger."

"So do you," Dani pointed out.

"It didn't keep both of us from taking a real hot burn in Lhasa the last time we were in the same block with Kasatonin," Shane said.

Flanders looked up. "How hot?"

"How cold is a grave?" Shane asked.

"That's a real close burn you took, son."

"Yes," Shane said simply. "I don't want Dani in that kind of danger again. She's a civilian."

"Whatever you say," Flanders replied. "You're paying the freight."

"How long are we going to watch?" Dani asked Shane.

"Until we see something."

"Would you be doing that if I weren't here?" Dani pressed.

"Probably," he said.

Flanders snorted.

"We can still afford patience," Shane said. "Our Tokyo operatives are watching Koyama. There's time for us to do it right the first time instead of doing it over."

"But—" Dani began.

"Wait," Shane interrupted curtly.

Dani stared. Shane had changed in a heartbeat from the shadow of a jungle tiger to the tiger itself.

Flanders came alive an instant later. He sat upright in his chair, shoved the pistol into a holster on his belt, and clapped a pair of binoculars to his eyes.

Shane was already using his own binoculars.

Across the rubble-strewn lot, a tan pickup truck with a camper shell pulled up in front of the Earth and Sky warehouse door. The driver got out, walked to the door, and knocked.

"Chen Li Hwan," Flanders said, recognizing the Chinese man. "Hot damn! Five thousand dollars on the hoof. I didn't think he'd ever show his scrawny beard and skinny ass on my side of the border again."

The warehouse door slid up to let the man in.

Shane cataloged the contents of the interior with a single sweeping glance through the binoculars.

"Eight, maybe ten people inside," Shane said. "Kasatonin. Katya. Liu. Looks like a seated Buddha, a temple statue. The head is missing."

"Now you know how they smuggled the contraband," Flanders said.

"What are we waiting for?" Dani demanded, excitement rising in her voice.

"Better odds," Shane said succinctly.

Flanders pulled a cellular phone from a bag at his feet.

"Ever hear of nine-one-one?" he asked Shane.

"Yes. And no, don't call."

"Chen's a federal fugitive," Flanders said. "An anonymous tip to the Seattle PD could bring a full-scale special weapons alert down around here in five minutes."

Shane watched the warehouse door slide down behind the camper before he answered.

"Put the phone away," Shane said.

"Do you want the goddamn silk or not?" Flanders demanded, exasperated.

"That silk is as fragile as a spiderweb," Shane said. "We have to wait until we can be sure of getting it intact. Special weapons teams aren't noted for their subtlety."

In addition, there was another problem—one only he, Redpath, Gillespie, and an anonymous weaver knew about. If Shane's plan worked, not only would the silk be safe, the Harmony would be in shreds.

Flanders drew a deep breath and shook his head in disbelief.

"You're the boss," he said. "But we have to take a chance sometime or you'll never get close enough to do any good."

"We need to get ahead of the Harmony and set up . . . an ambush," Shane said without looking away from the closed warehouse door. "Who is Chen Li Hwan?"

"A smack smuggler," Flanders said. "He's a customs fugitive. His family runs a noodle shop in Victoria's Chinatown. It's probably the stash house for half the smack coming in from Asia, but nobody's been able to catch the family dirty."

"Is Chen Earth and Sky?" Shane asked.

"Looks that way," Flanders said dryly. "No strangers are getting in the front door of that warehouse, or we'd just stroll on in ourselves."

The two men watched the warehouse for several more long minutes.

Nothing changed.

Suddenly there was a soft, rhythmic tapping on the metal side of the van. Shane turned as the door slid back and Gelmann stepped inside. His satisfied expression suggested that the operative had news.

Shane lifted the binoculars and resumed watching the warehouse.

"Tell us," he said to Gelmann.

"The concierge at the hotel is a lovely young Latina, born and partly raised in Guadalajara, just like me," Gelmann said.

"You told me you were born in Guanajuato," Flanders said.

Gelmann shrugged elaborately.

"The concierge had a very busy morning," he said. "She's

setting up a luxury yacht charter for a party of very rich foreigners who are staying at the Four Seasons.''

"This matters?" Dani asked.

"Patience, *chica*," Gelmann said, grinning. "Two days into their five-day reservation, the rich ones of the Harmony decide to leave the hotel and cruise though the islands to Vancouver. The city, not the island.''

"When do they leave?" Shane asked.

"A few hours.''

"What vessel?" Shane's voice was crisp, unmistakable in its command.

"Something called the M.V. *Party Tyme*," Gelmann said. "Katya set up an overnight charter that arrives in Vancouver tomorrow morning. The Harmony is set up for a few nights at the Four Seasons Hotel on Georgia Street.''

"Who will be on board?" Shane asked.

"Everyone except Tony Liu.''

Shane grinned. "Good work." Damned good.''

"Vancouver," Dani said. "Could Koyama get a visa for Canada?''

"Sure," Flanders said. "The Canadians are a lot more liberal in their immigration and visitor requirements. They'd probably offer political asylum to Tojo himself, if he was still around.''

"Then all this has been for nothing," Dani said bleakly. "The Harmony will have their Japanese connection, Koyama will have the silk, and the rest of the world will be shit out of luck.''

"Hey," Shane said softly.

He set aside the binoculars and put his hands on Dani's shoulders. She was tight, fairly vibrating with anger.

"It's all right," Shane said. "This is our chance to get a little ahead of them.''

"Ahead? For God's sake, Shane! They've probably got guards all over the new hotel already. Not to mention the chartered yacht. What are we going to do—swim along in their wake?''

"It's called the sheepdog tactic," Shane said.

"It's called getting skunked," she shot back.

"We've got them going in a new direction," Shane said, "a direction they haven't anticipated. That's when mistakes happen. We'll get our chance, Dani."

"Sounds like it's a hell of a lot more risky than marching in there right now and grabbing the silk," Flanders muttered.

Shane's head swung toward Flanders.

"Think," Shane said. "Is the Harmony likely to take the silk with them on the yacht?"

The former customs agent thought about it for a moment, then shook his head.

"This time of year, there's damned little pleasure-boat traffic headed north through the San Juans," Flanders said. "If we made a phone call, the Mounties would be all over that yacht like white on rice."

"The Russians are paranoid," Gelmann said. "They won't chance getting caught with the silk."

"That's why Tony Liu isn't going," Shane said. "He's the smuggling expert. If you were Liu, how would you move the silk?"

"Chen Li Hwan," Flanders said instantly. "He's as slick as they come."

"Isn't he Canadian?" Dani asked.

"Pipelines work both ways," Shane said. "Pass me the cellular with the scrambler."

Flanders pulled an unusually large cellular phone from the bag at his feet and fired it at Shane. With a quickness that made Flanders blink, Shane snatched the phone out of the air and started punching in numbers.

Seconds later, the connection was made. The decoder changed Redpath's voice, but it was still recognizable.

"Hi, Cassandra," Shane said. "Is Gillie around?"

"Yes."

"Good. Put this on the speaker."

Breath held, Dani watched Shane, drawn by the tangible intensity in him as he waited for Redpath to switch the phone to the speaker on her desk.

"We're virtually certain that the silk is in a warehouse in the International District of Seattle," Shane said.

"How did it get there?" Redpath asked.

"In the belly of a Buddha."

"Can you get to it without sending up a balloon?" Gillespie asked.

"Negative. They have it under close guard. Has that fat Japanese carp left yet?"

"Hold," Redpath said. "Gillie is calling Japan."

Thirty seconds later, Shane had his answer. He relayed it to the impatient listeners in the van.

"The Tokyo operatives followed Koyama to Narita Airport," Shane said. "He's in duty-free at the moment, carrying a boarding pass for an Air Canada flight. They can't get in tight enough to figure out which flight."

"If it ain't tight, it ain't no damn good," Flanders said to no one in particular.

"Tell them to check the departure board," Shane said into the phone. "I'm betting there's a flight to Vancouver, Canada in the next twenty minutes."

Shane waited while the message was relayed, answered, and relayed back to him.

"You're brilliant," Redpath said.

"Yeah, right," Shane said with a grim smile. "That's why I let the silk get away in the first place."

"Bullshit," Redpath said distinctly. "If you had made any other choice, I would have fired you."

Shane's smile softened. "Is Gillie still there?"

"Yo," Gillespie answered.

"It's Plan B now. Did the techs get that bug?"

"Tickety-boo."

"Good," Shane said. "Uh-oh. Gotta go. Chen is on the move. We'll keep you posted."

Flanders lunged into the driver's seat as Shane hit the disconnect button on the cellular.

"Take Chen down once he's clear of the area," Shane said.

"I thought we were trying to keep a low profile," Gelmann objected.

"I'm sure Flanders can think of a way to keep Chen's mouth

shut," Shane said blandly. "Advising him of his constitutional right to cooperate would be my personal choice."

Gelmann looked puzzled.

Flanders laughed out loud. "You saw it, huh?"

"Hard to miss along with all the metal," Shane said.

"What are you talking about?" Dani demanded.

Shane's long leg snaked out. He hooked his foot through a loop in the heavy leather bag that belonged to Flanders and dragged it within arm's reach.

"This," Shane said, reaching into the bag.

He dragged out a dark blue windbreaker and shook it out. **U.S. CUSTOMS** was written in big white block letters on the jacket.

"You have a badge, too?" Shane asked Flanders.

"Fake, but nobody's ever complained."

"Maybe they were too busy looking at your big gun to notice," Dani said.

"Yeah, that old pistol has a real distracting effect on bad boys," Flanders drawled.

Beyond the smoked windows of the van, Chen's pickup pulled away from the curb and headed downhill toward the Kingdome.

Flanders reversed out of their hiding spot. He took up station a discreet block behind the truck and stayed there for a mile. Then Chen made a turn onto a small side street in the waterfront area.

"He's headed for the Asian produce market," Flanders said. "We always figured he hid his loads in the bok choy."

"Nail him," Shane said. "Fast."

The van lunged forward with surprising speed. Very quickly Flanders caught up with and got slightly ahead of Chen's pickup. Giving no warning, Flanders cramped the wheel of the van to the right and braked hard.

Predictably Chen stood on the brakes and swerved to the right to avoid a collision. By the time he realized his mistake, it was too late. Chen's pickup was pinned against the curb by the van.

Flanders jammed the van into park and bailed out the driver's door. An instant later he appeared beside Chen's door.

When Chen saw the blue Customs raid jacket, he tried to shift into reverse, missed, and tried again.

"Don't move, asshole," Flanders snarled.

The words carried clearly through the closed window, but it was the bore of the big pistol that got the point across.

Chen sat very still.

"Stay put," Shane said to Dani. "You don't know the drill."

"Why am I not surprised?" she retorted. "The first excitement in hours and I have to play spectator."

Dani was talking to herself. Shane and Gelmann had already leaped out through the side door of the van. Together they hauled Chen out of his seat, threw him across the hood of his truck, and frisked him.

"Howdy, Chen Li Hwan," Flanders said. "You are in deep, deep kim chee. You should have stayed underground in Victoria or Canton. Lot safer there. Not so close to U.S. federal prison."

"No, no, no," the Chinese objected, still spreadeagled across the hood. "You got wrong Chen. You want 'nother Chen."

"Just before that Vancouver load came through, I spent a week living in your hip pocket," Flanders said cheerfully. "I know my Chens when I see them. And I'm seeing *you,* asshole."

"No, no, not me, not me. Some other Chinaman, not me."

"Fingerprints never lie," Shane said calmly. "If you're the wrong Chen, we'll apologize. If you're the right one, you'll call your wife and tell her you'll be late for dinner. For the next twenty years."

Shane grabbed one of the wiry man's wrists and twisted it around as though preparing to apply handcuffs.

"What fingerprints?" Chen demanded.

Shane looked at Flanders.

"There were prints all over the plastic wrapping," Flanders lied easily. "I watched you handle the bags myself."

Chen looked puzzled, as though he couldn't remember handling the contraband so carelessly.

Flanders knew better than to let Chen think things over. He

grabbed a handful of the smaller man's jacket and straightened him up forcefully.

"The U.S. government don't care much for smugglers," Flanders drawled, towering over his captive. "Dumb of you to come back on this side of the line, Chen. Real dumb."

"I no smuggler," he said. "Own restaurant, that's all."

"Yeah yeah yeah," Flanders said with a total lack of interest. "That's what they all say. What's a little heroin mixed in with the bok choy, right?"

"No! No smuggler!"

"Cut the crap," Shane snarled, his voice like a lash, "or we'll add another five years for the insult."

Chen's mouth set into a thin line.

"No smuggler," Chen insisted.

"Twenty-five years," Gelmann said. "Want to go for thirty?"

"Sure," Shane said. "I hate liars."

"Think about it," Flanders said gently to Chen. "Your ass is ours. We can make it easy or we can make it hard. It's up to you if you get home on time tonight."

For a moment Chen looked confused. Then he looked relieved, almost euphoric.

"You want somebody else, yes?" Chen asked eagerly. "I can give you somebody else, big man, real big."

Flanders managed to look shocked and bored at the same time.

"Are you offering to roll over on your brothers in the Earth and Sky Tong," he asked, "the tong you swore to uphold with the last drop of your own blood?"

Chen smiled. "These not tong brothers. They pale like you. Big Russian gangster, sure bet."

"Keep talking," Shane said. Then he added very gently, "Don't lie, Chen. You won't like what happens when we find out. And we will find out."

"You catch Russian real easy, boss," Chen said. "He say he right behind me every step. You want?"

Shane's fist slammed down on the hood of the pickup.

"Damn," Shane snarled.

''What's wrong?'' Flanders asked.

''If Kasatonin is right behind Chen,'' Shane said, ''he's right behind *us*, too.''

''Shit Marie.''

''Amen. Move it, children,'' Shane said. ''The ass flapping in the breeze could be ours.''

Chapter Twenty-nine

The master of the M.V. *Party Tyme* was a big, ruddy-faced man. He was sixty years old, trying to look forty and act twenty. Binoculars to his eyes, he leered as he watched the group of brightly dressed young women crossing the gangplank. Their heels were almost as high as their skirts were short.

"Not much, as sailors go," the captain said, "but I'd sure like to have one of them come down on me in a good blow."

Ilya Kasatonin stood a few feet away, inspecting the ship's log book. When he finished, he deliberately dropped the book on the compass table.

Annoyed at the loud noise, the captain lowered his binoculars and looked around.

Ignoring the captain, Kasatonin studied the compass as though it was of great interest.

The captain picked up the glasses again.

Again, the log book thumped onto the compass table.

"Young man," the captain said, "if you can't hang onto things, don't handle them in the first place.

"You have a keen appreciation of female flesh, Captain," Kasatonin said, still studying the compass.

"I'm a man," the captain retorted.

"The women are not here for you or your crew."

Suddenly Kasatonin looked up, pinning the captain with the blank glance of an assassin.

"The entire crew will stay in their quarters when not on duty," Kasatonin said. "That includes you."

The ship's master smiled thinly, but still politely.

"Don't worry," the captain said. "This is an experienced charter crew. Your guests will have privacy, as requested."

Kasatonin freed the captain from his glance and went back to studying the compass.

"On the other hand," the captain said, "if any of your young ladies want a little taste of the seafarer's life, just send them up to the bridge. Never had a single complaint about the, er, view."

The quick movement of Kasatonin's head was like a snake striking.

The captain took one look at Kasatonin and flinched before he could prevent the betraying action. Though both men were of equal height and build, the reptilian coldness of Kasatonin's eyes was intimidating.

"You have not listened to me," Kasatonin said distinctly. "When your men are not at their duty stations, they are to be invisible."

"Some guests enjoy being on the bridge, that's all," the captain muttered. "We try to accommodate them."

"I will not be on board for the first part of the voyage."

The captain tried not to show his relief.

He failed.

"I will rejoin you in Victoria," Kasatonin said. "If any of the guests have been disturbed in any way, you will answer to me. Have you any questions?"

The captain's face became a darker shade of red. He wasn't used to taking orders from anyone.

"Apparently you don't understand the law of the sea," the captain said gruffly. "Once we're underway, I'm in charge, not you. If there are problems, I'll deal with them, not you."

Kasatonin moved as though to turn away, then whirled back. With one hand he seized the captain's throat.

"You are the captain of a floating whorehouse, not a ship of the line," Kasatonin said calmly.

The captain stood at rigid attention. It wasn't a gesture of respect so much as an attempt to escape the steel fingers squeezing his windpipe.

"This is a pleasure vessel in the strongest sense of that word," Kasatonin said. "If you or your men do anything that interferes with the pleasure of the passengers, I will castrate you. Do we understand one another, *Captain?*"

The captain made a throttled sound and nodded.

Kasatonin relaxed a bit of the pressure on the other man's neck.

"You will be in Victoria by midnight," the Russian said.

The captain nodded again.

"Where?" Kasatonin asked.

"There's a private wharf at the foot of Government Street," the captain whispered around the vise on his windpipe. "I have a space reserved."

"Do not plan on staying long," Kasatonin said. "We must be at the inner harbor of Vancouver for breakfast. We will disembark in time for me to meet a flight at Vancouver airport in almost exactly eighteen hours. Do you have any questions?"

"No," the captain said hoarsely.

"Be ready to sail in an hour."

Kasatonin released the captain's neck as swiftly as he had grabbed it in the first place.

Without looking at the man again, Kasatonin left the bridge. He went down the ladder to the main deck with the speed and coordination of the athlete he once had been.

Katya was checking through a pile of boxes and bags that had just been delivered on board. They all bore the trademark of a cold-weather outfitter in downtown Seattle.

"You were a long time," Katya said. "Was there a problem?"

"Nothing worthy of your attention."

Katya searched Kasatonin's eyes.

"If the captain gives you the least difficulty," Kasatonin

said, "remind him that I will be waiting for this floating whorehouse at the foot of Government Street in Victoria."

Smiling, Katya made a feline sound of contentment. She relished the fact that she held the leash on a man as lethal as Kasatonin.

"I will be certain to do that, pet," she murmured.

Katya bent over and pulled a heavy down parka from one of the boxes. Gracefully she shrugged into the warm jacket.

"There are more," she said, gesturing to the box. "Most of the men were not prepared for a late autumn cruise."

"Let the whores keep them warm."

As Kasatonin spoke, he glanced without interest at the women. They were gathered at the head of the gangplank, smoking and talking like shop girls waiting for the front doors to open and the day's work to begin.

"Do they all have travel papers?" he asked.

"Yes."

With a grunt of disdain, Kasatonin turned away from the brightly dressed whores.

"Be certain of it," he said. "The Canadians might have some absurd laws about importing women for prostitution."

"A la Cosa Nostra whoremaster in Los Angeles sent the girls up by chartered jet," Katya said. "They are all Americans. They can enter Canada without visas."

"What about supplies? Did you check the galley? Do you have the proper stimulants?"

"Of course," Katya said, yawning. "I know my work. Stop worrying."

Kasatonin didn't answer. Deep in his gut, he felt uneasy. He had felt that way since Chen drove out of the warehouse.

"Relax, my pet," Katya murmured. "This will truly be a pleasure cruise."

Kasatonin grunted.

"Tony Liu and his people will see that Koyama's gift arrives safely in Victoria," Katya added. "Let us take this time to rest before we begin fencing with Koyama."

The tension in Kasatonin's body didn't diminish one bit.

Katya sighed. She had hoped to spend the voyage playing sexy, dangerous games with her assassin.

"Look," Katya said, holding up a heavy sweater. "I bought this just for you. It will make you feel like you are home in Estonia."

Wind gusted across the salt water, lifting Kasatonin's pale, silky hair. Katya's own hair whipped around her cheeks.

"This country is so cold and clean," Katya said, inhaling deeply. "It makes me long for what once was."

"What once was is dead."

Katya grimaced at Kasatonin's mood.

"Wear this," she said softly, holding out the sweater. "It will make you even more handsome."

Kasatonin pushed the gift aside.

"We have come too far to be diverted now," he said.

"But who will get in our way?" Katya asked.

If Kasatonin could have answered, he would have. But all he had were the instincts of a predator who had also been prey. Those instincts were pricking him like a hair shirt.

"The Canadians are interested only in preventing cigarette smuggling from the United States," Katya said. "We are not using people who are in that trade. The silk is safe."

When Kasatonin still didn't answer, Katya held the sweater up to his broad shoulders. Then she smoothed one sleeve down his thick arm, checking the length.

Her fingers touched the spot where his long-sleeved shirt covered a thin bandage. She remembered the fear and excitement of seeing blood welling from his hard flesh and knowing she had caused it.

Katya brushed her lips over the sleeve that hid the wound.

"Please, my darling, come with me," she said huskily. "Let me atone for hurting you."

Still holding the sweater against his chest, Katya stepped closer. Deliberately she rubbed her breasts against him.

Kasatonin caught her by the shoulders and held her harshly between his hands. The smell of vodka and sexuality rose from Katya, tempting him.

It also made him even more uneasy.

"Why are you so eager to have me with you now?" Kasatonin demanded. "Usually you are pleased only to send me off to fight your wars. Are you planning something you have not told me?"

Surprise showed on Katya's face, but not alarm.

"Of course not!" she said.

"Then why do you want me to stay? Has something frightened you, mink?"

Katya moved against Kasatonin with more pressure, but he didn't ease his grip on her shoulders. She looked away, not wanting him to see the little girl's fear in her eyes.

"Yes," she whispered. "I do not want to wait alone with these beasts. I sense I cannot trust them now."

"You never could," Kasatonin said. "They would eat you for a snack and never need a toothpick, were it not for the Russian wolfhound at your side."

A whiplash of fear went through Katya, making her shiver.

"I know," she said. "Stay with me. Please."

Laughing, Kasatonin held her away as she tried to burrow into his arms.

"So you finally understand your need of me," he said. "That is good. It will make you more eager."

He straightened his arms completely, pushing Katya away.

"Ilya?"

Kasatonin gave her an oddly weary smile.

"We will discuss this after the silk is safe," he said. "If you truly recognize my value . . ."

Katya stood tensely, waiting for him to finish.

Saying nothing, Kasatonin stared out across the cold, wind-whipped water of Elliot Bay toward the ragged peaks of Hurricane Ridge.

"What is it?" Katya asked finally. "What do you want?"

"An equal partnership. It is only fair, yes?"

"You want half of what I have worked my whole life to build?" Katya asked softly. "You want half of what I have allowed myself to be raped and beaten to acquire?"

"Did you do it all alone?" Kasatonin asked sharply.

"Yes!"

"I think not."

Anger, fear, and vodka combined to send Katya into a rage.

"I dug you out of the scrap heap of the Soviet Army," she snarled. "I saved you from a lifetime of drinking cheap vodka with your aging comrades, whining about the good old days, and now you claim you have earned half of what I own?"

"I have been your assassin. Without me, you would have nothing. I thought you had finally realized that." Kasatonin shrugged. "But no, you still live in the world of a wounded child."

"Without me, you—"

"Do you think your fierce tongue keeps the Italian at bay?" Kasatonin interrupted.

"At bay? Ha! He crowds me like a bull after a cow."

"Has he touched you? Ever?"

Katya started to say yes, but caught herself. The lie would do no good and much harm.

"No," Katya said through her teeth.

"Why do you think that is?" Kasatonin asked softly.

"He knows you will kill him, just as you killed that informer in his mob in Calabria last year."

"And he knows I would kill him with a knife, slowly, not with a car bomb."

Katya didn't doubt it. Neither did any of the men of the Harmony.

"If you like," Kasatonin said, smiling slightly, "consider my offer a marriage proposal."

Shock showed on Katya's pale face.

"Or consider it a business proposition," he said, "if you wish to keep our fucking on that basis. But consider my offer well before you refuse it. I will not make another."

For the space of many breaths Katya simply stared at him. Then a small, quiet smile that was the mirror image of his own spread across her face.

"And if I do not accept?" she asked, knowing the answer but needing it in a way she didn't understand.

"I will do what I always do," Kasatonin said. "I will threaten to kill you. But this time I will not let your beauty distract me. Then I will have all instead of half."

"You would have nothing," Katya snapped. "Without me, you would have a very difficult time controlling the Harmony."

"Probably," he agreed.

"So we have a stalemate," Katya said.

Kasatonin's smile broadened.

"Perhaps we should call it a marriage of convenience," he said sardonically.

Katya's smile faded.

"Or a marriage made in hell?" she suggested.

"There is little to be accomplished in heaven," Kasatonin said. "Hell, on the other hand, offers much for people such as us."

"Does it?" Katya whispered.

Kasatonin laughed again. Then he pulled her hard against him and gave her a kiss that left blood on her mouth.

"Oh, yes," he said, watching Katya lick her lips. "You will like hell very much, my mink. It is your natural home."

Chapter Thirty

A late November sunset gilded the brightwork and the teak decks of the long white yacht. For a moment the handsome couple on the deck—the massive Russian soldier and the willowy, exquisite blonde temptress—seemed frozen in golden radiance, like insects in amber.

"Kind of sweet, isn't it?" Dani said.

"Kasatonin and Katya?" Shane asked.

"Yes."

"Only from a distance. Once you see their eyes, the illusion is lost."

Dani looked out at the chartered yacht again. She and Shane were sitting well back from a window in a restaurant on Pier 57. From their vantage point they could watch the yacht without fear of being seen themselves.

"But they look as though they might be in love," Dani said stubbornly.

Shane made a strangled sound of surprise, laughter, and disbelief.

"Stranger things have happened," Dani muttered.

"Not in recorded history."

"You don't believe that love exists?"

"For those two? No way. A complex form of hatred is what they share."

"Then why are they still together? Greed?"

"Maybe," Shane said. "And maybe it's as simple as the fact that hate can be as binding as love."

"Not for me."

"No, not for you. You're as different from Katya as a diamond is from shit."

Dani gave Shane a startled look. His attention was still focused on the yacht.

Three gleaming limousines pulled up to the curb on Alaska Way. Doors opened with appropriate flourishes. Eight passengers, all men, emerged into the golden light. Each man was expensively dressed. Each moved with the confidence of a prince.

"Ah, more members of the badly named Harmony," Shane said. "I don't think you want to know what they 'love.'"

"Power," Dani said succinctly.

"Of course. But how they express that love ..." Shane shook his head. "That's what you don't want to know."

"You know."

"I have no choice. The first rule of war is to know your enemy."

Silently Dani watched while crewmen from the yacht trotted down the gangplank and began unloading luggage from the limousines.

The eight godfathers of the world's most powerful crime syndicates milled about, admired the yacht, and joked like tourists on a vacation.

The scene was absolutely ordinary, even mundane.

"They look so normal," Dani said. "They're my enemies and I don't know them at all."

"You don't want to."

"What does wanting have to do with it?" Dani challenged. "Did you want to know or did you simply understand the need?"

Shane hesitated, then began talking so softly that Dani could barely hear him.

"There's no need for you to know," he said. "It can't help you."

"Shane, listen to me," Dani said, leaning close to him. "Ever since Lhasa I've been fighting a battle with my intellect, which has been taught that evil is an archaic idea, and my gut, which suspects there are greater devils in man than there ever were in hell."

For a moment Shane was absolutely still.

"It was the same for me," he said in a low voice. "I ended up in a monastery. You ended up in a university."

"And we both ended up in Lhasa."

Shane closed his eyes.

"Help me so I don't make the wrong choice at the worst possible instant," Dani said. *"I need to know."*

Shane let out a long breath and opened his eyes. When he spoke, his voice was deliberately light, almost flippant.

But his eyes were as dark as what he was describing.

"Let's see now, who do we have?" Shane asked idly.

He shifted his chair for a better view of the eight men.

"Do you see the tall, handsome devil with the dark hair and the thin mustache?" Shane asked.

"Yes. Jose Gabriel de la Pena of the Medellin Cartel," Dani recited, remembering her briefings. "Drug lord."

"He's also a fashion innovator," Shane said.

Dani made a startled sound. "That wasn't in his file."

"Gillie vetted those files rather carefully before he showed them to you."

"Why?"

"No point in panicking an innocent."

"I'm less innocent than I was in Lhasa," Dani said.

"Yes," Shane said. "I regret that, Dani."

"I don't. Tell me about de la Pena and fashion innovation."

"He created something called the Colombian necktie," Shane said. "I won't trouble you with all the details, but it has to do with slitting throats vertically and pulling tongues down and out through the open wound."

Dani's eyelids flickered. It was her only reaction.

"He's really a nice guy to his mother, though," Shane said. "Keeps her and her local Catholic church awash in money."

"How can the priests take her money?"

"How can they not? Think of all the good they'll do with it."

The irony in Shane's voice made Dani wish she had never brought up the subject.

But she had. Now she had to live with the results.

"There's Sallie Spagnolini, the one wearing the black silk shirt with white polka dots," Shane said. "He's going to be cold out on the water, but that getup is his trademark."

Dani nodded.

"Sallie is from Chicago but he spends lots of time in Vegas," Shane said.

"The file Gillie showed me didn't mention that Spagnolini is a gambler."

"He isn't. In Vegas they call him 'Sallie the Stallion.'"

Dani shrugged. "No news there."

"Sallie goes through several showgirls a night," Shane said. "And I mean he uses them up. He has yet to find one that can go the distance. As you pointed out, for some men sex is a blood sport."

Again Dani's eyelids flickered.

Again she said nothing.

"A few months ago Sallie overheard one of the girls criticizing his sexual technique," Shane continued. "Her pimp got her tongue, tits, and a few other spare parts in the mail. They never found the rest of her."

Dani's mouth flattened. Her whole body was tight, both with distaste for what she was hearing and for the fact that Shane was angry.

He wanted to protect her.

Know your enemies.

"Sallie dotes on his kids," Shane continued. "They have more junk than any fifty kids could play with."

Shane paused, but Dani made no comment.

"Sallie raises show horses, too," Shane continued. "The

ones that win are kept in marble-walled luxury. The others he kills for the insurance money.''

Dani didn't say a word.

''Recognize Giovanni Scarfo?'' Shane asked.

''Yes,'' she said. ''It's hard to miss that mane of silver hair.''

''You'll be happy to know he's not like the rest of the Harmony's men. Scarfo is a good family man with a mistress on the side, the picture of a good Calabrian citizen.''

Dani waited for the rest. She knew it wouldn't be good. She just didn't know how bad it would be.

''Scarfo is such a good citizen,'' Shane said, ''that when he's not pumping three-quarters of a ton of eighty-five percent pure heroin into the U.S. every year, he collects orphans.''

''Orphans?'' Dani asked faintly.

''Yeah. Little girls. Really little. Seven and under. Want to guess why?''

''He must be popular on the Internet,'' Dani said, trying to be as ironic as Shane.

But her voice blurred, ruining the effect.

''Had enough?'' Shane asked.

''I had enough the first time I went through the vetted version of the files.''

''Then why ask for more? Are you a closet masochist?''

''If I was, I'd still be married,'' Dani said tightly. ''But, dammit, standing around out there, the men look so bloody ordinary.''

''They work hard on it.''

''Why bother? They own half the world and are taking out options on the rest.''

''If the crooks went around in horns and tails, it would be harder to ignore them,'' Shane said dryly. ''They want people to think the only difference between the Harmony and any other multi-national corporation is that 'recreational' drugs are illegal.''

Dani grimaced but she didn't look away from the men who were bathed in golden light.

''Some recreation, huh?'' Shane asked, turning on her. ''Ever been in a crack house, Dani? Or in ER when someone sucks up too much cocaine? Boy, are they ever having fun.''

"Why are you so angry with me?" Dani asked. "Do you still blame me for costing you the silk?"

"It was my choice, not yours."

"Then why are you hammering on me? And don't deny it. Your voice could fillet sharks."

Shane opened his mouth, closed it, and looked at Dani.

"I'm afraid you still don't understand," he said.

"What?"

"Those men would kill you in a heartbeat if they so much as suspected you were trying to get in their way."

"I was in Lhasa, remember?" Dani asked. "I'm sure Kasatonin does."

"Lhasa was just a chance encounter."

"Some chance. Some encounter."

"It was nothing compared to what you're doing now," Shane said. "If my plan works—and if the Harmony finds out you're still involved—you might never be able to go back to a normal life again."

Dani gave Shane a sharp look.

"What *do* you have planned?" she asked.

He shook his head.

"You don't need to know," he said. "I didn't even want you here."

"Now there's a surprise," Dani said sarcastically. "But I'm here anyway. Why? You haven't let me do a damn thing but look through windows."

Shane's eyes narrowed with an anger he no longer tried to conceal from her, or himself.

Dani stared right back at him.

"Not afraid of me, huh?" he asked.

"No."

"Doesn't speak highly of your intelligence."

"I'm a gut person, myself," she retorted.

Despite himself, Shane smiled.

Then he glanced around casually. No one was close enough to overhear.

"I'm trying to get close enough to that glass capsule to switch it," Shane said bluntly.

Dani's mouth opened. Nothing came out. She cleared her throat.

"With what? Did the Azures have another piece of old silk lying around?" she asked finally.

"Remember that debriefing you complained about?" Shane asked.

"Hard to forget. I didn't realize how much I knew about ancient silk textile techniques."

"Our, er, consultant was very impressed," Shane agreed. "She wove a substitute for us."

"Using what?"

"Raw hand-thrown Tussah silk, plus a variant of Bombyx moth silk, just as you said."

"Just like that, huh?"

"Well, we had a hell of a time finding gold wire fine enough for the weave, but we finally did it. Then we turned the piece over to a lab to 'age' it."

"Is it done?"

"Just. Gillie is sending it Risk Limited Express." Shane glanced at his watch. "Any time now."

"That's why you didn't want to grab the silk sooner," Dani said. "You don't want the Harmony to know they've been had."

The smile that crossed Shane's face was frankly wolfish.

"That's the general idea," he said.

"General, huh? What are the particulars?"

"You don't—"

"—need to know," Dani interrupted.

"Glad you understand."

She grimaced. "Then why did you bring me?"

"Cassandra insisted."

"Why?"

"Because you can recognize the real silk with a touch," Shane said. "No one else can."

Dani started to say something, paused, then understood.

"You're afraid the silk has already been switched, aren't you?" she asked.

"Tony Liu had the motive, opportunity, time, and means."

"I thought he was part of the Harmony."

"That doesn't mean he can't have his own agenda."

"No honor among thieves," Dani said.

"Honor has less meaning to the Harmony than a dog fart."

"What a lovely world you—we—live in."

"It was your choice," Shane said. "I tried to keep you out of it."

"No. You tried to keep me ignorant."

"Ignorance is bliss."

"Really?" Dani asked. "Then why are there so many unhappy people in the world?"

Shane smiled wearily. "You and Cassandra are quite a pair."

"Meaning?"

"She said the same thing."

"What about Gillie?"

"He's like me," Shane said. "Still trying to protect his woman despite hell, high water, and modernism."

"Maybe," Dani said, "she's trying to protect him, too, by not being a bloody helpless albatross around his neck."

Startled at the idea of Redpath trying to protect the very lethal sergeant major, Shane laughed. Then his laughter faded. He focused on Dani with an intensity that was tangible.

"Is that what you're doing?" he asked. "Trying to protect me?"

"Do I look crazy?" Dani asked.

But her voice wasn't as steady as her eyes.

"All right, damn it," she said tiredly. "I'm a fool. That shouldn't come as news to you."

Shane's fingertips brushed Dani's cheek, then her mouth. He felt the warm rush of her breath between his fingers.

"I wasn't laughing at you," he said softly. "No one as gentle as you has ever tried to protect me. It surprised me, that's all."

Dani flushed and looked away from Shane's clear black eyes.

"Forget it," she muttered. "I know you need about as much protection as the average avalanche."

"Before Afghanistan, I would have agreed with you. Then I learned."

The haunted quality of his voice made Dani look at him again. The combination of anger and grief in his eyes caught her, held her, made her cry as he once must have cried— silently, invisibly.

A grief that was all the more terrible because it had no sound.

"There are wounds," Shane said quietly, "and then there are wounds. I thought I had healed. Then I saw you trying to make a deal with a devil for a piece of sacred silk . . ."

The gentleness of Shane's smile made Dani's throat ache with unshed tears.

"I wish you hadn't been . . . hurt," she said huskily.

"I could say the same of you. But pain is a great teacher. We just have to be careful not to learn too well."

"What do you mean?"

Shane's only answer was another brushing caress across Dani's cheek.

"If something should go wrong," he said, "stay low and stay out of it."

"But—" Dani began.

Shane kept talking.

"Then you can go back to your classroom and your research with nobody but Risk Limited the wiser," he said.

"What about you?"

"If I get lucky, the Harmony will be history."

"And if you don't, you'll be dead, is that it?" Dani asked starkly.

"The Harmony will do its best. So will I."

"Shane—"

The touch of his fingertips on Dani's lips stopped her words.

"No arguments," he said. "Just promise me you'll stay low."

"If I can."

"Dani—"

"I'm not going to save my neck at the cost of yours," she interrupted angrily, "so don't even bother saying the words!"

Shane raked his fingers through his hair, but no bright ideas emerged to counter the determination in Dani's hazel eyes. With a muttered curse, he looked at his watch.

"Gillie's package should be here by now," Shane said.

He looked out at the yacht tied up alongside the pier. The crew was loading the last of the provisions. Soon the yacht would be ready to sail.

"Look!" Dani said softly.

Kasatonin was climbing up the gangway to street level. Katya stood and watched until he disappeared into the late afternoon pedestrian traffic along the waterfront.

Dani glanced at Shane. He looked neither surprised nor unhappy. The implications of that made her stomach clench in fear.

"You're going to switch the silk right under that killer's nose?" she asked tightly.

"If I have to," Shane said. "But if that damned plane ever lands with our silk, I'll do it in Seattle before Kasatonin gets into a position to guard the real silk."

Shane caught motion from the corner of his eye and his head snapped around with predatory speed.

Gelmann was striding across the restaurant toward them. He sat down and began talking in a low voice.

"Bad news," Gelmann said.

"We're sitting down," Shane said.

"The flight crew just called," Gelmann muttered. "They lost a boost pump, had to set down in Boise. They'll be an hour late, probably two."

"Shit," was Shane's only comment.

He looked out at the yacht. A dock hand was just casting off the last of the lines. Black smoke roiled up out of the diesel stack. Dirty seawater at the stern of the boat started to boil.

"It's going to be tight," Gelmann said.

"How bad?" Dani asked.

"Chen is supposed to leave the warehouse in the next ten minutes."

"That fast?" Shane asked. "Bloody hell. What a time to lose a pump."

"In two hours Chen will drive aboard a ferry out of Anacortes, headed for Victoria," Gelmann said.

"Anacortes?" Shane asked.

Silently he ran through the map of Washington in his mind.

"It takes ninety minutes by car on a good day," Gelmann said before Shane could ask. "That doesn't leave many windows of opportunity for us."

"One little window is all I need," Shane said, "but the damned thing has to be open."

"What are we waiting for?" Dani asked the men. "Let's get off our butts and start opening windows."

Gelmann gave her a startled look.

Shane was already up and heading for the door.

Chapter Thirty-one

Anacortes
November

As the last lemon-yellow autumn color faded from the western sky, the Washington state ferry *Winomish* slid into the Anacortes dock. A dozen foot passengers filed off. When the pedestrians were out of the way, the deck crew signaled cars coming in from Canada to disembark.

There weren't many cars parked in the land lanes, waiting for their turn to get aboard the rapidly emptying ship. Fewer than sixty vehicles were lined up to be ferried to Victoria, Canada, via a stopover at Friday Harbor, Washington.

Chen Li Hwan's truck was second from the front in the second row of vehicles. Kasatonin was five cars behind. The Risk Limited surveillance van was a cautious ten cars behind Kasatonin.

Dani had become accustomed to living in the shadow of her enemy and quarry. She had spent the last hour stretched out on the bench across the back of the van, half asleep from a combination of boredom and a grueling kind of tension.

The only break in the routine of waiting came when she

permitted herself to lift the side curtain of the van an inch. That allowed her to look out across the parking lot to the steely blue water of Rosario Strait.

At the moment, two oceangoing tugboats were passing by. They were headed north with flat log barges in tow. Dani knew the barges were headed west, into Canadian waters, because she had spent her spare time looking at maps.

Surveillance gave a person a lot of spare time. By now Dani felt qualified to lead tours through the San Juan Islands.

I wonder how long it will take the *Party Tyme* to get to Victoria? she thought.

She didn't say anything aloud. The leashed tension in the van told her that the subject wouldn't be appreciated.

Time was running out.

"Chen is a real piece of work," Flanders muttered.

Dani glanced to the front of the van, where Flanders waited alone.

"Why do you say that?" she asked without real interest.

"He knows he's towing a convoy a mile long and he's sitting up there like he's asleep," Flanders said.

Shane made a sound that could have meant anything. He was in the back of the van near Dani, concealed behind the van's curtains. He had tilted one of the seats back and was lounging like a cat in sunshine.

What irritated Dani was that his ease wasn't a pose. Somehow he was able to shut down and save energy until it was needed.

Zen cyborg, she thought.

Then she remembered Aruba. Heat shot through her.

Well, Dani told herself sourly, he's a Zen cyborg *now*. I wish I could be one, too.

But she didn't have the knack. She couldn't shut off her mind. It kept jumping from the boring present to the frightening future or the unnerving past when she had discovered passion in the arms of a celibate man.

Unhurriedly, Shane straightened up. He stirred the curtain with his fingertip. The movement was just enough to make a crack. Kasatonin's car was caught in the viewing slit like a bear in the crosshairs on a sniper scope.

"Chen has a smuggler's nerves and burglar's balls," Shane said. "A dangerous combination."

"Your Russian friend looks a little edgy," Flanders said. "He's been sitting like he's got a poker up his ass ever since we left Seattle. You'd think he was carrying the silk himself."

"He always looks like that," Dani said.

"The guy better learn to relax," Flanders said. "Your average customs inspector can read body language like a billboard."

"They can vet him to the back teeth," Shane said. "They won't find anything. He may be Katya's pet wolf, but he's damned smart."

"Is she really in charge?" Dani asked.

"She's the glue that holds the Harmony together," Shane said.

Flanders snorted. "Makes sense, I suppose. Big crooks are like big bulls. It takes a cow to bring them in line."

"Redpath would slit your throat for that statement," Shane said.

"I'd help her," Dani said.

"Your boss?" Flanders asked Shane, ignoring Dani.

"Yep," Shane said cheerfully.

"What's it like, working for a woman?" Flanders asked. "I got out of the business before the skirts got promoted over me."

"Are women really that different when it comes to business?" Dani asked before Shane could say anything.

Shane grinned. "Have you ever read Sun Tzu on war?"

"Until the last few months, I never needed that particular skill," Dani said.

"It might be a good exercise," Shane said. "Sun has an outlook that is almost feminine, from a Western cultural viewpoint."

Flanders yawned.

"For instance?" Dani challenged.

"Sun believed it was better to win *without* a battle," Shane said. "Most men would rather fight and lose than use finesse and win."

"You have to know when to attack and when to wait," Dani agreed. "But that's only logical."

"Logic has sweet bugger all to do with it," Shane said. "If logic held sway, crystals would rule the universe."

"Who says they don't?" Dani countered.

Shane laughed. "I'd love to sic you on Prasam some time."

"I got the feeling that women were an exotic species for—"

The van's engine started up, interrupting her. The lines of waiting cars had begun to file aboard the ferry.

With a curse, Shane picked up the scrambled cellular phone and punched in a number.

"We're five minutes from departing Anacortes," he said tersely. "Where in hell is the package?"

Dani listened but couldn't hear Gelmann's response.

Shane could hear just fine. He didn't like a word of it.

"Look, I'm sitting in his back pocket," Shane said flatly. "He won't touch the silk until it passes through Canadian customs outside Victoria. After that, school is out. It's plan D all the way. Got that?"

Silently Dani wondered what plan D was. The look in Shane's eyes told her that she probably didn't want to know.

An urge to protect him swept through her, startling her with its intensity. She didn't want Shane to be hurt again, to suffer again, to have to fight to keep balance in his life.

Is this how he feels about me? she wondered. It's not that I think he isn't good enough to do whatever he must . . . but I know it will cost him.

And I don't want him to have to pay.

You need about as much protection as the average avalanche.

Before Afghanistan, I would have agreed with you. Then I learned.

Dani didn't want Shane to learn any more on the subject of physical or mental pain.

But it wasn't her choice to make.

Shane lowered the receiver and looked at Flanders.

"When do we stop at Friday Harbor?" Shane asked.

"About an hour."

"Is there an airport there?"

"You might have to kick some critters off the runway."

"All right," Shane said into the phone. "Charter the fastest helicopter you can find. Do it now. *No.* Just listen."

Dani stiffened at the tone of Shane's voice.

"Have the chopper standing by on the flight line at Boeing, with outbound clearance for Friday Harbor," Shane said. "When our jet gets in, grab the package and get on your high horse. You can come aboard as a foot passenger at Friday Harbor."

Shane made a curt gesture with his hand.

"Of course there's time," he said flatly. "Just get the damn thing to Flanders."

"I'll meet him near the snack bar," Flanders called out.

"Snack bar," Shane repeated into the phone. "Flanders. Got it?"

Gelmann must have understood, because Shane shut off the phone and put it aside before the other man had time to answer.

"Let me meet Juan," Dani said. "A man picking up a woman is a lot less obvious than—"

"No," Shane cut in.

"Why not?" she demanded.

"Kasatonin."

The arguments Dani had lined up died on her lips.

"He'd recognize me," she realized. "And you."

"In a heartbeat," Shane agreed. "Likely our *last* heartbeat."

"How long?" Flanders asked.

"The jet is still ten minutes out of Boeing," Shane said.

"Christ, you're cutting things finer than frog's hair," Flanders said. "What happens if we miss connections in Friday Harbor?"

Shane's eyes narrowed. All he said was, "Put us aboard where we can keep an eye on Chen's truck."

"I'll do what I can without sending up a flare," Flanders grumbled.

He maneuvered the van onto the ferry and parked. Chen's truck was near the bow. Kasatonin's vehicle was one row away and two cars back.

Drivers were getting out of their cars and heading for the

passenger accommodations on the upper deck. Chen emerged from his truck, locked up, and joined the people going upstairs.

A moment later Kasatonin got out, stretched hugely, and locked his door behind him.

"I'm on him," Flanders said. "I'll be back after I meet Juan."

Like a bear just awakened from hibernation, Flanders stepped out of the van, locked up, and shambled off toward the stairway. But he was moving faster than he appeared to be. Soon he caught up with and passed Kasatonin.

Flanders stuck a cigarette into the corner of his mouth and stopped just in front of Kasatonin. Flanders patted his pockets, came up empty, and looked around for a man with a light.

Kasatonin shook his head.

Flanders continued toward the stairway and went through the pantomime again with another passenger. No luck again.

Kasatonin paid him no attention.

"U.S. Customs made a real mistake, turning Flanders loose on the world," Shane said. "He's a genius."

"I imagine Risk Limited could find a use for him," Dani said dryly.

"Hope so. He's too dangerous to allow out without a keeper."

"Look who's talking," Dani said, shaking her head.

Shane gave her a sideways look.

"What's that supposed to mean?" he asked. "I've been quite the gentleman with you. The rest of the world will just have to take its chances."

"That's what I meant. In some ways, you and Flanders are like the people you chase. A wee bit predatory."

"If you're going to hunt sharks, you need sharp teeth."

"But your spiritual skin isn't as thick as a shark's," Dani said softly.

"That's what keeps me human."

"And hurting."

"It's the same thing."

Ferry engines throbbed in a register that was felt as much

as heard. The ungainly white boat backed out of its berth and swung around to head west into the San Juan Islands.

For the first time since Aruba, Dani was aware of being truly alone with Shane. The thought made her breath break in the instant before she remembered.

Celibate.

In an effort to ease the knot of tension in her back, Dani propped herself on her elbow against one armrest and stretched fully out on the bench.

Shane got out of his chair and came toward her.

"Curl those lovely legs up, will you?" he asked. "I have to keep an eye on Chen's truck. You've got the best seat in the house."

Wordlessly Dani shifted toward the center of the bench, making room for Shane. He settled onto the padded bench and stretched his long legs out in front of him.

"Thanks," he said, "I'm too big and too old for this kind of punishment."

Dani laughed helplessly and shook her head.

For a time they sat hip to hip while Shane looked out the window through a gap in the curtains.

Dani was aware of his simple human warmth in every cell of her body. She searched his face for any sign that he was aware of that warmth, or of her, or of the fact that one or both of them could die in the next few hours.

Shane's mouth was relaxed rather than tight. A shadow of stubble showed against his skin. His eyes were narrowed, but only for better focus. He looked half asleep.

He probably was.

"How do you do it?" Dani asked in exasperation.

"Do what?" he said, turning toward her.

"You're so relaxed," she said. "The closer it gets to ground zero, the calmer you are. And I know it's not because you think you're bulletproof."

Shane glanced back at the pickup, then at Dani again.

"I've made my peace with whatever might happen to me," he said. "That way I can do what needs to be done without getting distracted."

''The warrior's code, right?'' she asked, subtly challenging. ''He who accepts his own death masters his own life.''

''Something like that.''

''Is that why you're celibate? No distractions?''

No sooner had the words left Dani's lips than she tried to take them back.

''Never mind,'' she said quickly. ''I have no right.''

''You're the only one who has the right,'' Shane said. ''For me, celibacy was a simple exercise in self-discipline. It least, it *was* simple. Then you came along. Good-bye simplicity.''

''I'm sorry. If I had known, I'd never have—''

Shane's long fingers brushed the words from Dani's lips.

''No,'' he said. ''None of this is your fault. You're the only innocent party on the whole damned boat.''

''Innocent?'' Dani laughed almost wildly. ''You make me sound like a grammar schoolgirl in a pinafore.''

''I meant clean, pure, untainted by . . .'' Shane hesitated.

''Evil?'' she suggested.

Shane shrugged. ''It's as good a word as any.''

''I'm not a plaster saint.''

''You're all woman.'' Shane said. ''Unfortunately.''

There was a grim line to his mouth as he looked at his watch. Twenty-four hours and one minute remained of his vow.

It will be just enough to protect her, Shane thought. Barely. She radiates the kind of tension I know I can do something about. I hope she's not picking up the same signals from me.

I have to stay away from her. Kasatonin knows me—who I am, what I am, what I do. As long as he's alive, Dani can't afford to be linked with me.

Ever.

''Shane?''

''Don't worry, honey. I know what I'm doing.''

''But I don't!''

''Can you trust me?''

''Haven't I always?'' Dani countered. ''And don't ask me why. I don't have an answer.''

''I don't need one.''

Shane turned toward her, slowly settling his big hand on her shoulder. She wore a light down vest over a wool sweater. The heat of her body warmed his palm. The gentle female shape of her lured him as nothing else could.

Flexing his fingers, he enjoyed the sensation of having her shoulder curving beneath his palm. His fingers slid beneath her vest. He felt the faint outline of her bra strap and remembered Lhasa, when he had gone through her luggage and felt like a Peeping Tom.

No black lace fantasy here, Shane thought once more. She doesn't need it. The heat of her is enough to burn any man.

Especially me.

The tension in Dani's muscles made them unnaturally hard. Gently Shane kneaded with his fingers.

"You're like a rock," he said.

Dani closed her eyes and fought against the instant response of her body to his touch.

"I'm scared," she said tightly.

"Of me?"

"I've never been in a—a war like this."

It was part of the truth, but not the part that mattered to either of them.

Shane knew it. He wondered if Dani did.

Silently, gently, insistently, he kneaded her flesh, working to loosen the tension in her body.

"You're not scared," he said after a time. "Not of the war, anyway."

He caught the glint of unshed tears before Dani twisted out from under his hands. She sat with her back to him, as stiff as a ramrod.

"What are you afraid of?" Shane asked, knowing he shouldn't.

Yet he needed to hear what he already sensed—that she wanted him as much as he wanted her.

Dani shook her head. She drew a deep breath.

"Hadn't you better get back to your post?" she asked with false calm and an echo of bitterness. "If something goes wrong, I don't want to feel responsible for *distracting* a Zen cy— warrior."

Saying nothing, Shane put both hands on Dani's shoulders. For a time he tried to massage away the tension that had bunched her muscles into knots.

The vest kept getting in his way. He unzipped it and slid the cloth partway down her arms.

"Shane—"

"It's all right," he said across Dani's protest. "You trust me, remember? It won't help anyone if you're tied up in knots."

His fingers curled over her shoulders and rested lightly on her collarbone. Gently he worked his thumbs into her clenched muscles.

Though Dani tried not to, she shivered at the gentle power of Shane's hands. Biting her lip, she steeled herself against the dizzying sensations that cascaded through her body with each movement of his fingers.

But in the end Dani couldn't fight what she needed more than air. Both the tension and the strength slowly ebbed from her body. Her head slumped forward as Shane bore in tenderly, relentlessly.

He shifted his thumbs and slowly began probing the muscles along her spine. Without thinking, Dani lifted her head and rotated it slowly, luxuriating in the narrow, intense universe that was Shane's hands and her body.

"You're so tough," Shane said, "So strong. I don't think I've ever felt so much strength in a woman."

Dani laughed sadly.

"Strong?" she asked, her voice low. "Hardly. I couldn't bench press two hundred pounds if I tried for the rest of my life."

"That wasn't the kind of strength I meant."

Her only answer was a shaky kind of breath.

"Right now I don't feel very strong in any way at all," she said. "I feel like wax in front of a fire."

Shane's eyes closed in a sensual reflex as old as passion. His fingers hesitated on her spine as they encountered the band of her bra.

Before Dani could object, Shane's fingers were beneath her vest, under her wool sweater, against her bare skin. With a quick movement he released the catch of her bra. The resilient band parted, freeing her breasts.

Part of Dani longed to turn toward Shane, to capture the hands that were both gentle and calloused, to hold them against her breasts.

Celibate.

Angrily Dani closed her eyes and forced herself to think about something else. Anything else. She didn't want to put Shane through another gauntlet of half-finished passion.

His hands slid from beneath Dani's clothes. The powerful, impersonal massage began again.

She wanted to jerk away from the maddening contact, but she was afraid the motion would be as revealing as the nipples that had tightened into hard peaks.

"You chose to live in the beauty of the best of human creation," Shane said quietly.

"Is that an accusation?"

"No. A fact. Your life is dedicated to preserving whatever beautiful fragments of the past have survived."

"And you chose to live in the ugliness of the worst of human creation," Dani said.

"Not quite. I chose to try to change the worst. To do that, I have to get close enough to be effective."

"You're at a terrible disadvantage when you work in close," Dani said huskily. "You care about life. People like Kasatonin don't."

"And you have more of life's magic in you than I've ever found in any human being. When I think about you . . . I lose my focus on everything else."

Dani stiffened as though she had been slapped.

"Then don't touch me," she said through her teeth.

"You're too tight. You need—"

"Another mercy fuck?" Dani interrupted bitterly. "But it wasn't even that, was it? Just what do you call it when a man—"

Dani's words ended in a startled sound when Shane turned her toward him so swiftly that her hair swirled out.

"You call it making love," Shane said in a soft voice.

But there was nothing soft about his eyes. He was furious. So was Dani.

"Lovemaking requires two," she said distinctly. "As a solo act, it lacks a lot. And don't tell me you didn't notice!"

"I noticed."

"Then why in hell are you tormenting both of us again?"

"I . . . can't help it," Shane whispered. "I would rather touch you and suffer than not touch you and suffer anyway."

"I wouldn't! How do you think it makes me feel to take everything and give nothing? How would *you* feel if you were me?"

"Trapped. Frustrated. Ready to explode."

"Bingo."

"I'm trying to protect you, Dani."

"From what?"

"Me."

For an instant Dani was too shocked to speak.

"You would never hurt me," she said.

"Sexually? No. I'd love you from your forehead to your heels and back again. And again. And—"

Shane gave an odd crack of laughter.

Dani flinched.

"Forget that line of thought," Shane said, his voice almost rough.

But neither one of them could.

"You have to let go of me," Dani said. "Your vow."

Shane looked at his watch.

"If it was tomorrow at this time," he said in a low voice, "nothing could keep me away from you."

"But it's today."

"Yes. Be grateful, Dani. I've never wanted a woman the way I want you. I'm not a here-and-gone kind of man."

"All or nothing at all?"

"Yes," he said simply.

"Then you're the one who should be grateful it isn't tomorrow. I'm not a here-and-gone kind of woman."

Shane searched Dani's hazel eyes and shook his head sadly.

"I'm not the right man for you," he whispered.

"What you're saying is that I'm not the right woman for you."

"Dani." Shane's voice broke. "I'm trying to spare you."

"When I want to be spared, I'll be the first to say it."

"You don't understand. I've seen things . . . done things."
Shane took a ragged breath.

"So?" Dani asked.

"Dammit! You aren't listening! I'm not the man you think I am!"

"Zen cyborg?"

"I'm too damned human," Shane said savagely. "I've been broken in ways you can't imagine."

"I know. Just as I know that true strength is in healing, not in never breaking."

Shane's eyelids flickered as though Dani's words had touched a raw wound with salt.

There was a long silence followed by the slow, whispering sound of Shane letting out his breath. Willing his body to relax, he settled back onto the seat.

Then he held out his arms.

"Will you let me hold you?" Shane asked. "Just that. Hold you."

"This isn't a good idea," Dani whispered.

But before the words were out of her mouth, she was moving toward Shane's open arms.

He looked down at Dani's lips. They were trembling between sadness and a smile.

"It's a wonderful idea," Shane said. "Come and curl up with me. It's all we can do. After this is over, you can't see me again."

Although Dani said nothing, her instant refusal to accept his words was written in the renewed stiffness of her body.

"Kasatonin," Shane said. "Not celibacy."

"What?"

"Kasatonin has no doubt that I'm a player. If he finds you with me again, you'll be marked for death. I won't let that happen. So hold me now, Dani. Just . . . hold me."

With a broken sound Dani gave herself to the torment and

shelter of Shane's arms. Slowly, carefully, she lowered her head until she lay against his chest as she once had in the belly of a Tibetan truck.

Again Dani breathed in the combination of heat and man that was Shane Crowe. Again she measured the difference in their individual strength.

But this time she wasn't afraid of his physical power. She sought it as inevitably as a river seeks the sea.

Slowly Dani's eyes closed. With a long sigh, she let herself relax into Shane's strength, into him. For a moment she felt complete with him in a way she couldn't put into words.

In some ways it was better than making love. It was like loving and being loved in return.

"What a beautiful smile," he whispered.

"I've made a beautiful discovery."

"What's that?"

"In some men, physical strength can be a gift and a joy. Men like you, Shane."

His arms tightened for a heartbeat, shifting Dani even closer. Then his grip gentled again.

But it was too late. Dani had felt the rigid proof of Shane's hunger for her. She pushed away from his chest, trying to sit up.

His arms held her gently, unbreakably. He breathed a kiss against her neck.

"No," Dani said. "I don't want to be the woman who made you break your vow. You'd hate me for it."

"I can't imagine hating you."

"Then you'd hate yourself!"

Shane said nothing. Nor did he release Dani. He needed to explore her complex hunger for him as much as he needed to breathe.

Why didn't I make my vow one day sooner? he asked himself futilely. *Just one damned day.*

But he hadn't. Now there was no guarantee that he would survive today to test tomorrow's promise.

Too bad the international date line doesn't run through Puget Sound, Shane thought.

Then he laughed out loud.

It was true laughter, not bitterness.

"Shane?" Dani asked warily.

"The international date line," he said.

"What about it?"

"For better or for worse, it's tomorrow in Tibet."

Dani started to ask what Shane meant, but couldn't speak. A swift movement of his hands had slid her sweater up to reveal her breasts. The sound he made when he saw her took her breath away.

The hot caress of his tongue drew back her breath in a ragged gasp of pleasure.

"Shane? Are you sure?"

The thick sound he made was laughter and passion combined. He drew one of her hands down his body until she could measure his need for her.

"What about you?" he asked. "Are you sure?"

Dani started to answer, but all that came from her lips was a sound of pleasure as Shane's mouth caressed first one breast, then the other. The only word she could say was his name.

Then she felt her jeans loosen, felt the hard glide of his hand between her legs, and answered him, lifting to him. With sultry ease she accepted his probing, pleasuring touch until her need pooled like liquid silk in his hand.

Shane bit off a reverent curse, lifted her, and stripped away her jeans and underwear in a single movement. Then he watched her unfasten his jeans, freeing him even as she caressed him.

"I can't protect you," he said.

"Did I ask you to?"

Jaw clenched, Shane fought for control. It slipped further away with each breath, each touch, the scent of desire curling up between them.

"I wanted to take forever," he said roughly.

"Next time," Dani said. "Next time. This time I—"

Her words unraveled in a rippling sound of ecstasy as Shane pulled her onto his lap and joined their bodies seamlessly. For a timeless instant they simply held each other, savoring the knowledge of sharing one need, one hunger, one body.

Then his hips moved and stripped the world away from Dani, leaving only pleasure. She moaned and gave herself to him without reservation, moving in counterpoint, doubling and redoubling the sleek tension of their dance.

He made a deep, primitive noise in his throat. She answered with a hoarse cry and tiny, silky convulsions that shredded Shane's control. He called her name and gave himself to her deeply, repeatedly.

Ecstasy transformed Dani. Wave after wave of pleasure slammed through her until she couldn't breathe, couldn't see, couldn't speak. She could only cling to Shane and know at some primal level that she was both lost and entirely found.

Shane held Dani in the same way, for the same reason; both lost and finally, completely, found.

They didn't let go of each other until they heard the sound of a powerful helicopter flying low and fast over the water.

"Juan?" Dani asked.

"If we're lucky."

Or unlucky.

Then each wondered if the thought had been spoken aloud.

Chapter Thirty-two

Fully clothed again, Dani was curled up in Shane's lap when the ferry pulled out of Friday Harbor. He had his chin on her head, watching Chen's car through the slit in the window curtains.

Dani's eyes were closed. She was breathing in Shane's presence and trying to think of new arguments to undermine his certainty that being seen with her was a death warrant as long as Kasatonin was alive.

Or maybe it's not that simple, Dani admitted unhappily. Maybe Shane doesn't want to see me again because I made him break his vow.

The thought made Dani ache. Celibacy—or more importantly, its lack—was the one thing she didn't want to debate with Shane. He had said nothing about the subject after his enigmatic statement about it being tomorrow in Tibet.

Tomorrow, Dani thought, touching the pulse in Shane's neck with her lips. He's determined that I won't have any tomorrows with him.

Only today.

The sound of a key turning in the van's front door was very

loud in the silence. The lock popped open. Gelmann slid into the driver's seat.

"Rise and shine, boys and girls," he sang out softly through the drawn curtains.

Dani felt the subtle tension that changed Shane's body.

"Showtime?" Shane asked.

"I'm leaving the box on the front seat and heading back up to the passenger deck," Gelmann said.

"Why?" Shane asked.

"Flanders is going nuts trying to keep an eye on Chen and Kasatonin at the same time."

"Are they together?" Shane asked sharply.

"Negative," Gelmann said. "They act like they're on different planets."

Gently Shane lifted Dani off his lap, brushed a kiss over her lips, and put her on the bench next to him.

"What's Chen doing?" Shane asked. "He hasn't come back to his truck."

"He snuck off just before the ferry docked in Friday Harbor. Acted like he was going to the men's room, but he met another Asian instead, a guy dressed as a ferry steward."

"Standard," Shane said, unimpressed. "Anything else?"

"Flanders couldn't get in close enough to be certain, but it looked like Chen handed off a locker key or maybe an ignition key."

"What?" Dani asked, sitting up straight. "Is Chen trying to double-cross us?"

"If not us, maybe Kasatonin," Gelmann said. "Probably both. From what Flanders said, Chen could teach slippery to an eel."

"No matter who Chen is betraying, we'll have to move fast," Shane said. "Go back upstairs. You and Flanders can keep an eye on all three of the bastards."

"On my way," Gelmann said, reaching for the door handle.

"If anyone heads down here, give us a call on the cellular," Shane added as the van door opened.

"No can do," Gelmann said softly. "We're out of cellular

range here. Besides, it's going to be tough enough as it is. There are two of us and three of them.''

"Do the best you can, but whatever happens, give us a shout,'' Shane said. "I don't want to turn around and find Kasatonin's knife in my back.''

"Gotcha.''

Gelmann slid out and closed the door behind him.

After checking to see that they were alone on the car deck, Shane reached through the curtains that divided the back of the van from the front. His fingers found a hard-shelled Halliburton case. He pulled it back through the curtains.

"What did Juan leave for us?'' Dani asked.

"You tell me.''

Shane laid the case across his knees and snapped the latches open. The inside of the aluminum shell was lined on both sides with deep foam rubber. The foam had been cut away to form a protected hollow for a glass cylinder.

A corner of fragile blue cloth shot through with gold threads gleamed against the thick white protection of heavier, surrounding cloth.

"It's the silk!'' Dani whispered.

"So far, so good.''

The end of the capsule was a cork with an ebony toothpick to seal the hole where the air had been drawn out by a vacuum pump. Three packets of silica gel had been sealed in with the silk.

Shane dug a small flashlight out of his kit and played the beam across the capsule.

No moisture had condensed.

"How well do you like it?'' he asked Dani.

"Is this a multiple choice question?'' she retorted.

"As many answers as you need,'' he said, "but only one matters.''

"Then I have to look at it more closely.''

Shane's hand shot out, preventing Dani from touching the glass container.

"Wait,'' he said. "They can pull fingerprints the same as we can. I don't want you associated with this at all.''

He took a pair of lightweight black gloves from his hip pocket and put them on. They were the kind of gloves worn by city people on cold days.

Dani stared at the gloves.

"Kasatonin is wearing gloves that look like those," she said.

"A lot of people do. That's why he chose them. If you go around wearing rubber surgical gloves, you get a lot of odd looks."

Carefully Shane picked up the glass capsule. He held it out so that Dani could inspect the roll of silk inside as closely as she could without actually opening the capsule and touching the silk.

"It looks good," she said after a moment. "But there's something . . ."

She made a frustrated sound, grabbed a flashlight from a wall bracket, and shone the light through the glass from back to front.

"Damn," Dani said beneath her breath.

"What's wrong?"

"Somebody should have listened better."

"What do you mean?" Shane asked.

"The weave. It's the right technique, but it's just not the same rhythm. Not quite."

"So?"

"So anyone with real expertise will spot the difference," Dani said.

"How quickly?"

"What?"

"How many people other than you would know, and how fast would they know it? At first glance?"

Dani hesitated, then shook her head.

"I doubt it," she said. "I've been told I have an exquisite eye."

"Both of them always looked gorgeous to me," Shane said, "from the first time I saw them in Lhasa."

"My sense of touch is even better," Dani said, ignoring him.

"Amen."

The gleam in his eyes told Dani that he was remembering the wild moments when the only thing that mattered was the feel of skin on skin, then a joining so deep that echoes of it would carry through Dani's life.

She laughed almost brokenly.

"You're not listening," she said. "Sooner or later—probably later—this silk will be spotted as a fraud. A very good one, to be sure, but still a fraud."

Surprisingly, Shane smiled.

"That's what Cassandra hoped for," he said. "A good but not a great fraud."

"But—"

"No time now," Shane said over Dani's words. "I've got to make the switch."

He parted the curtains slightly and checked Chen's truck.

Nobody in sight.

Shane pulled an ignition key from the watch pocket of his jeans and took two screwdrivers from his kit bag.

"Stay here," Shane said. "Just a few minutes and I'll be done."

"I want to go with you," Dani said. "If my help can cut even ten seconds off your exposure—"

"No," Shane interrupted. "Someone has to be here if Gelmann sends up a flare. Besides, your job is to save beautiful things, not to risk your neck on a nasty piece of business like Kasatonin."

Dani drew a breath and started to argue again. Then she realized that every moment she delayed Shane meant more danger for him.

"Hurry back," she said tightly.

Shane's kiss was so quick that Dani didn't have time to respond. Then he was out the van's door and walking calmly across the cold steel deck of the ferry.

"Soul of a poet, balls of a burglar," she muttered to herself, remembering Flanders' words. *"Hurry, damn you."*

With a maddening lack of urgency, Shane strolled between the rows of cars all the way to the front of the ferry. A raw, cold wind wailed in across the open bow. The winter sea was no more than forty-five degrees.

Shane was glad he didn't have to swim to his objective. Paddling around without the right gear in that water would kill even a strong man in less than fifteen minutes.

When Shane reached the pickup, the key was already in his gloved hand. He looked around casually yet thoroughly.

No one else was on the deck.

He slid the key into the lock on the passenger side. The lock turned smoothly. The door opened without noise or hesitation.

Shane jackknifed himself into the passenger seat, closed the door, and pulled the glass capsule out from under his jacket.

Another quick look around assured Shane that he was still alone on the deck. He pulled the ashtray out of the dashboard and disappeared from view by cramming himself into the foot well on the passenger side. Counting the seconds in the back of his mind, he went to work on a retaining bracket inside the dashboard itself.

In less than forty seconds, Shane undid the three screws. The bracket swiveled to one side, revealing a surprisingly large secret compartment. A glass container was inside.

A corner of azure silk beckoned.

Shane pulled the capsule out of hiding. The cork, ebony stopper, and gel packs were as the Risk Limited spy had described.

But the ancient silk was wrapped in rich white satin brocade rather than in the plain, heavy silk Dani and the spy had both described.

Damn, Shane thought savagely. *I'll have to rewrap our version.*

Swiftly he pried off the bottom of Chen's capsule. To his relief, there was no significant rush of air. The vacuum seal hadn't been perfect, which meant that he could finish the job here rather than hauling everything back to the vacuum pump he had brought in the van, just in case.

Quickly, delicately, Shane opened his own container and switched the outer covering of the silk pieces. As he finished putting each silk and cork back into its separate container, he shot a quick look toward the stairwell that led down from the passenger deck.

A small man dressed in a steward's uniform had just come down the stairs. He glanced around the car deck, spotted the vehicle he wanted, and started toward it.

The steward passed under an overhead light. Its bulb was grimy from car exhausts and coated with salt spray, but there was more than enough illumination for Shane to see that the man was Asian.

He had a set of car keys in his hand. He carried a package wrapped in a towel under one arm. The package was exactly the size of the one Shane had carried.

The "steward" was heading for Chen's vehicle.

Button, button, who's got the button? Shane asked silently, savagely.

There was only one way to find out.

Shane pressed down the door lock, shoved himself even deeper into the foot well, and waited.

The steward unlocked the driver's door, bent down to get in, and was unconscious before he ever saw the edge of Shane's hand lashing out from the interior gloom.

Shane pulled the steward inside and closed the door behind him. Keeping an eye on the unconscious man, Shane put the Risk Limited silk into the smuggling compartment, screwed the concealing bracket into place, and replaced the ashtray.

The steward moaned. With one hand Shane shut down the man's carotid arteries, sending him spinning into unconsciousness again. With his other hand Shane unwrapped the package the steward was carrying.

He stared at first one capsule and then the other.

Identical.

Right down to the wrapping of the brocade.

"Bloody, *bloody* hell," Shane whispered.

The steward made sounds of returning consciousness.

Carefully Shane turned the steward's head. A brief chopping motion of Shane's hand sent the man under again. He propped the steward behind the wheel as though he were sleeping.

Shane hoped the steward's sleep wasn't permanent, but he

was in no position to be choosy about the outcome. It was enough that the steward wasn't getting in the way anymore.

Quickly Shane grabbed the two glass containers and the towel the steward had carried, stuffed it all under his jacket, and checked around.

Someone was walking out onto the car deck from the stairway. A woman with gray hair, pink pants, and a purple jacket. In her hand was a greasy bag.

A civilian, Shane thought impatiently. Hope she's not coming down here for a nap.

The woman opened a car door four vehicles down and one line over. Instantly a rat-sized dog began yapping and dancing. She held the furry, wriggling creature in her arms and offered tidbits from the bag.

If she's feeding that mutt leftover ferry food, Shane thought, it would do better scrounging with the rats in Lhasa.

The woman cooed over her purse pet for a moment or two longer, then locked it up again and hurried back to the warmth of the passenger lounge.

Shane rolled down the window an inch, listened, and waited to be certain the car deck was empty.

A door opened and closed from somewhere at the back of the ferry. Footsteps approached the truck.

Shane was irritated when he spotted Dani in the side mirror, but he wasn't surprised. He had halfway expected her ever since the steward had appeared.

"Get in," he said, opening the door.

Dani didn't have much choice about it. She was yanked in across Shane's lap and the door was shut behind her before she could do more than make a startled sound.

With swift motions Shane went to work on the two canisters.

"I saw the steward and then you didn't come and—is he dead?" Dani asked, noticing the man for the first time.

"To hell with him," Shane snarled. "Which one of these is the real silk?"

Dani didn't ask for more light. The gloom of the car deck was their best protection. Fiercely she rubbed her fingertips on her sweater sleeve, simultaneously heating, cleaning, drying, and sensitizing them.

Then Dani closed her eyes.

Shane bit off his objections that she could do better with her eyes open. He simply unwrapped a corner of one of the silks and held it so that it was just barely touching Dani's fingertips.

She was holding her breath, but not out of anxiety. She simply didn't want to breathe on the ancient silk if she could avoid it. Her fingertips brushed once lightly, then again, then a third time with slightly more pressure.

"No," she said. "Wrong weave. More Persian than Indian or Chinese. But I'd bet it's old. Very, very old. If it's a fake, it's better than ours was."

"Bloody wonderful," was Shane's only response.

He held out the second silk.

Dani rubbed up her fingertips on her sweater again before she touched the silk. Lightly, gently, she brushed the silk first one way, then at a different angle. The faint, faint rhythm of the long-dead weaver's touch came through. She allowed herself one more lingering, haunting brush against the ancient silk before she lifted her hand.

"Yes," Dani said simply.

Shane didn't ask if she was certain. He simply switched the outer silk wrappings with motions so quick that his hands blurred in the gloomy light. The plain, heavy silk wrapping was transferred to protect the silk Dani preferred. He put it back in the bottle, corked it, and looked around.

No one else was on the car deck.

Shane opened the door, pushed Dani out onto the car deck, and stuffed the capsule beneath her vest.

"Get back to the van," Shane said. "Don't come out again no matter what. Got that?"

"Aren't you com—"

"*Do it.*"

Dani turned and began walking toward the van.

Swiftly Shane wrapped the brocade around the elegant fake, rolled everything up and put it back in the glass bottle. Only after the cork was in did he hesitate.

Common sense told Shane to get out while he could.

On the other hand . . .

Shane worked quickly, precisely. When he was finished, he grabbed the front of the steward's uniform with one hand and felt for a carotid pulse with the other.

The tong member was still alive.

Calmly, repeatedly, Shane slapped the steward's cheeks. After a bit, the man began to moan. Abruptly Shane yanked him face down onto the seat and looked around.

The car deck was empty but for a man-sized shadow next to the passenger stairway.

Hope that's Flanders, Shane thought.

But even if it wasn't, Shane had to get out. Now.

He opened the truck door and climbed out as though he had every right in the world to be where he was. Never letting the man-sized shadow out of his peripheral vision, Shane walked forward as though heading for the stairway.

The shadow detached itself from the darkness.

"Hurry," Flanders growled. "I left Kasatonin taking a crap. He could be on his way down here."

"Gelmann?"

"Watching Chen. You want me to heave that fake steward into the drink?"

"He's more use to us alive."

"Goody Two Shoes," Flanders said in disgust. "I knew it."

Shane laughed softly and walked toward the van.

Moments later, the car deck was deserted once more.

Chapter Thirty-three

Washington, D.C.
December

A dark, anonymous sedan pulled to the curb in front of Risk Limited's D.C. headquarters. From inside the car, Dani looked curiously at the townhouse.

There were no men digging in the frozen ground.

There were no men sweeping the sidewalks or painting the trim or performing any of the other chores that provided a convenient cover for guards.

"Where is everyone?" Dani asked the driver. "The last time I was here, you and your buddies were covering the place like a rash."

"Times change," Walker said.

Dani smiled despite the sadness that had become as much a part of her as her hazel eyes.

"Yes," she agreed. "Times change."

Shane had changed with them.

Once they reached the Four Seasons in Vancouver, Shane walked out of the van and kept walking.

He hadn't looked back.

He hadn't written. He hadn't called.

A new Risk Limited operative had appeared at the door of the van before Shane was out of sight. Since that moment, Walker had all but lived in Dani's hip pocket.

Times changed.

Bodyguards changed.

Emotions were more stubborn.

Why can't I change? Dani asked herself wearily. Years from now, will my heart still jump with hope just at the sight of a tall man with an easy-moving stride?

I'm not the right man for you.

I'm trying to spare you.

Kasatonin has no doubt that I'm a player. If he finds you with me again, you'll be marked for death. I won't let that happen.

And he hadn't. It was as though Shane Crowe had never existed except in Dani's dreams.

The door opened on her side of the sedan. She had learned to wait for the courtesy that was also a security precaution. She gathered her purse and her wits.

"Here you are," Walker said. "She's expecting you."

"Thanks."

When Walker made no move to accompany Dani to the front door, she stopped and looked over her shoulder at him.

"I was told bluntly to stay outside," Walker said with an odd smile. "Real bluntly."

"That's strange."

"I'd say it was overdue."

"I beg your pardon?"

Walker smiled again. A real smile. The kind that made a woman realize that Walker was a good-looking man.

"You're a pleasure to be around, Dani," Walker said. "If you ever get tired of waiting for Crowe to wake up and smell the coffee, let me know."

Sudden tears stung Dani's eyes. She stepped toward the car and gave Walker a quick hug.

"Thanks," she said huskily. "I like you, too."

Dani turned and hurried toward the door to the townhouse.

With every step she felt the bite of late December's icy wind even through her thick wool coat.

The door opened while Dani was climbing the front steps. A man she didn't recognize ushered her in.

"This way, Dr. Warren."

Dani might not have known the man's name, but she had learned to recognize his type—armed, coordinated, highly trained, and far from stupid.

"Is Gillie serving tea in the library?" Dani asked, only half-joking.

"The sergeant major is on vacation."

Dani blinked, startled. "Really? He didn't strike me as the type."

"He got a yen for the Caribbean."

"Beachcombing, huh?"

"Not much else to do on Aruba, unless you like gambling."

For an instant Dani's steps faltered. Memories of Aruba and Shane, rain and ecstasy, went through her like lightning, shaking her.

"Does Gillie like gambling?" Dani asked, forcing herself to act normal.

"Not for money."

The man knocked twice at Redpath's office, then opened the door.

"She's expecting you," he said.

The guard didn't come in with Dani.

The familiarity of the room brought back vivid memories of Shane. Dani had to fight the certainty that he was there somewhere among all the books and works of art, waiting for her, smiling, holding out his hand . . .

Stop it! Dani told herself savagely. It's over. Accept it and get on with your life.

But she could no more stop yearning for Shane than she could stop the beating of her heart. Each night the longing increased. Each morning it was harder to get up and go to work and smile and pretend that she wasn't in love with a man who didn't love her.

"Good afternoon, Dani," Redpath said. "Actually, it's closer to evening, isn't it?"

Dani drew a shaky breath and looked toward the voice.

Cassandra Redpath was sitting in front of the globe that showed the islands and continents as delicate etchings on a transparent crystal sphere. Her green eyes glowed like a cat's in the reflected light. A cup steamed at her elbow and a fat pot of tea waited on a nearby table, along with biscuits and cookies.

"Afternoon, evening," Dani said. "It's all pretty much the same in winter."

Redpath looked intently at Dani, then nodded, as though confirming a private guess.

"Come sit with me," she said, patting the couch. "Tea?"

"Thank you."

"Or dinner, perhaps? You look like you've been working through meals."

"I had a bit of catching up to do," Dani said, forcing herself to smile.

"Did you manage it?"

"I'm making headway."

"You don't look it," Redpath said bluntly.

Dani didn't say anything.

"Noble men are sometimes a noble pain in the ass, aren't they?" Redpath asked. "The vice of their virtue."

The sound Dani made could have been laughter or a stifled sob.

"Do sit down," Redpath said. "I can't put a dent in pig-headed masculine nobility, but I can tell you what happened to the silk you helped us recover."

"I'd like that. Walker was a real clam on the subject."

"Walker is a good man, despite Shane's carping."

Dani hoped her reaction to the name didn't show, but she doubted it. There was very little that Redpath's green eyes and quick mind missed.

Rather grimly Dani walked toward the couch. There were piles of newspapers scattered in front of Redpath. Several of them were in ideograms. One was an English-language version

of a Hong Kong newspaper. One was *The New York Times*.
One looked like a Spanish or Portuguese tabloid.

"Catching up on your reading?" Dani asked.

"You can find the most remarkable bits of information in
newspapers. Rarely on the front pages, of course."

"With some of those newspapers, I couldn't tell front from
back."

Redpath laughed softly, poured Dani tea, and handed the
steaming cup to her.

"Black, correct?" Redpath asked.

Dani nodded. "Thank you."

Politely Redpath put a plate of cookies in front of Dani and
waited for her to eat.

With equal politeness, Dani picked the smallest cookie and
pretended to nibble at it.

"Do you remember Mr. Yukio Koyama?" Redpath asked

"Yes," Dani said starkly. "I remember . . . everything."

"Not surprising. Adrenaline enhances the memory. A survival attribute, I'm told."

Dani made a polite noise and privately wished that adrenaline
hadn't made her memories of Shane so painfully vivid.

"Mr. Koyama seems to have suffered a sea change in his
fortunes," Redpath said blandly.

Dani stopped pretending to be interested in the cookie and
focused on the other woman with intent hazel eyes.

"How so?" Dani asked.

Redpath sifted through the papers in front of her.

"Ah, here it is," she murmured.

Ideograms and photos were mixed on the page. Redpath
began reading aloud, paraphrasing freely.

"Renowned and honored Mr. Yukio Koyama no longer
enjoys the confidence of the business captains and other
important members of society for whom he was a . . ." Redpath
paused. "Bloody hell, we don't have any word for it. Interface.
Intermediary. Go-between. Gray eminence."

"What happened?"

Redpath smiled like a cat.

"Acute loss of face," she murmured. "It's rumored that a very embarrassing incident occurred at a dinner party he gave."

"How embarrassing?"

"Mortally so. A fabulous, ancient piece of silk he had recently acquired turned out to be a modern fake."

"Hard to believe," Dani said blandly.

"Even worse, some diabolical soul had managed to ink an ideogram on the silk. The ink became visible only after a certain amount of exposure to light."

"What did it say?"

"Well, a loose translation would be 'April Fool, Asshole.' "

For the first time in weeks, Dani laughed out loud.

"Koyama was livid, of course," Redpath continued. "He went directly to Katya, who said it must have been Risk Limited that switched the silk on the ferry. She certainly had no reason to humiliate him. She very much wanted Koyama's collaboration in the Harmony."

"Did Koyama believe her?"

"He must have. He didn't kill her."

"In that case I'm surprised you don't have armed guards at each elbow."

"Oh, Koyama has already paid his visit to me," Redpath said blandly.

"What? When?"

"Last week."

"Is he buried in with the spring bulbs?"

"Nothing that drastic," Redpath said, smiling. "I simply explained to him that yes, Risk Limited had knocked out Liu's smuggler on the ferry and switched the silks."

Dani winced. "I'll bet he was thrilled."

"Then I showed him the silk we got in return."

"You showed him the Buddha's silk?" Dani asked faintly.

"No. I showed him a beautiful, very ancient swath of silk that was being passed off as Buddha's robe."

"Was it the silk I saw on the ferry? Chen's fake?"

"Actually," Redpath murmured, "the fake I showed Koyama was one of our back-up efforts. It was a very old piece of Persian silk our labs dyed a rather remarkable shade of faded azure. By now the dye has vanished entirely. Modern chemistry is not perfect, but so useful.''

Dani realized her mouth was open. She shut it.

''I suggested,'' Redpath continued, ''that Koyama look to Tony Liu for his villain. Liu was uneasy with the Harmony's growing power in Asia. He feared for his grandson's life in America. In addition, Liu sold the sacred silk to the People's Republic of China for two million pounds sterling before the silk ever left the Golden Triangle.''

''But he couldn't have,'' Dani protested instantly. ''I touched the Buddha's robe on the ferry. I'm positive of that!''

''So is Prasam Dhamsa. He sends his respect and gratitude to you, by the way. He hopes you will visit him soon. *Very* soon. He has much to tell you.''

''I—but—damn it, who has the real silk?''

''Its real owners. The Azure monks.''

''You're certain?''

''Quite. Koyama, however, believes that Tony Liu betrayed him.'' Redpath shrugged. ''A logical belief. He discovered the weavers Liu had used to create the Earth and Sky's fraud.''

''I can't believe Liu would be that stupid. Making a fake, yes. Rubbing Koyama's nose in it, no.''

Redpath smiled like a cat.

''Liu wasn't a stupid man,'' she said. ''But he's quite dead just the same.''

''Koyama had him killed?''

''Probably. However, the tongs are having a general blood-letting all around the Pacific Rim. Liu could have been killed by any of a number of ambitious thugs. Typical gangster power struggle.''

''*Bon appetit,*'' Dani said sardonically.

''Yes, it really is a rather cheering thought. More cookies? Or aren't you through playing with the one you have?''

Dani looked at the fragmented cookie on her plate, realized her fingers were covered with crumbs and powdered sugar, and shook her head ruefully.

''How did you do it?'' Dani asked. ''And I don't mean the cookies.''

"Actually, I didn't do it. Shane did. The man has a positively brilliant, Byzantine turn of mind."

Dani hid her expression by taking a sip of tea.

"Shane found the real silk hidden in Chen's truck, just as Chen promised. Unfortunately, the silk was wrapped in a brocade rather than in the plain wrapping you described. A plain wrapping that we, of course, had painstakingly imitated."

"Not good."

"Shane wasn't pleased. He switched the coverings, put our best fake in the dashboard hiding place, and was just getting ready to leave when the 'steward' showed up."

A chill went over Dani as she remembered.

"I saw him," Dani whispered. "I felt so helpless. I couldn't warn Shane, I couldn't save him, all I could do was just sit and . . ."

"Yes," Redpath said into the growing silence. "It must have been horrible for you."

Something in Redpath's eyes and voice made Dani think the older woman had been in that unhappy position more than once.

Gillie, Dani thought. Poor Cassandra. But at least he hasn't abandoned her for her own safety.

"At any rate," Redpath said crisply, "Shane knocked out the steward, saw that there was an embarrassment of silks, and availed himself of your expert advice."

"He wasn't thrilled to see me."

"As I said earlier, a noble pain in the ass."

Dani's smile was thin, but real.

"As soon as you left with the real silk in its plain white silk wrapper," Redpath said, "Shane opened up the dashboard again, put in the steward's fake, and then put our fake in the steward's container underneath the towel. All appropriately wrapped, of course."

"I'm getting a headache."

"As I said, Byzantine."

"Who was the steward working for?" Dani asked.

"Liu. When the steward came to, he assumed that whoever had knocked him out was taken in by the fake wrapped in a towel. So he put what he thought was his fake into the dashboard compartment, took what he thought was the real silk with him, and took off.''

"Talk about a shell game," Dani said.

"It was quite amusing while it lasted," Redpath said dryly.

"So Koyama got the doctored silk, Risk Limited style. What happened to Chen's entry in the silk sweepstakes?''

"At present, it's residing in a crate in a Beijing warehouse, along with Tibet's other sacred treasures.''

"How long will the PRC be fooled?''

Redpath glanced at the clock on the wall where a slowly moving curved line marked off night from day around the world.

"Not much longer," Redpath said with satisfaction. "The Earth and Sky Tong's troubles are just beginning. The PRC makes a nasty enemy. But then, so do Tibetans.''

As she spoke, Redpath picked up another newspaper.

"It seems," she continued, "that the Free Tibet movement is more active than ever. Their new rallying cry is 'Sacred Azure.' Something to do with silk, I believe.''

Dani let out a long sigh. "It was worth it, then.''

"There's no guarantee the movement will be successful.''

"No, but at least the Tibetans will still have a piece of their sacred heritage.''

"A rather fabulous piece," Redpath agreed.

"Katya must be furious," Dani said.

"Katya is dead.''

Dani's eyes widened. "You're certain?''

"Quite. Her lover killed her in a fit of rage or sexual passion. The police aren't certain which. Kasatonin committed suicide shortly afterward.''

"I find that . . . hard to believe.''

"Death comes to all of us.''

Dani made an impatient gesture. "I just can't believe that an assassin like Kasatonin would kill himself over a woman.''

"Fortunately the police on Aruba didn't know Kasatonin as well as you did. Officially, it is listed as a murder-suicide.''

"Case closed?''

"Completely."

"Gillie must be relieved," Dani said.

"Gillie is lucky I don't have his beautiful hide for a wall hanging," Redpath retorted, looking past Dani.

"And here I hurried back early," Gillespie said, closing the office door behind him, "just to cook you dinner."

Despite the sergeant major's brisk voice, it was clear that he was tired. There were a few bruises on his face. He walked with a very slight limp.

"Strenuous vacation?" Dani asked him.

"I've had worse."

Redpath's glance went over Gillespie intently, noting every change.

"Sit down," she said softly. "I'll pour you some tea."

"No time. Prasam Dhamsa and his retinue are waiting in the front room."

"You're joking," Redpath said.

"He was impatient," Gillespie said. "Once Kasatonin was out of the way, there was no holding him."

Behind Gillespie the door opened again.

"Prasam Dhamsa doesn't have an impatient bone in his body," Redpath said.

"No," Shane said from the doorway, "but I sure as hell do."

Though the words were for Redpath, Shane never looked away from Dani's face as she came to her feet with a swift movement.

She watched Shane with the same intensity, torn between hope and heartache. He looked as worn as Gillespie, yet never had Shane appeared more wonderful to her.

Prasam Dhamsa stepped around Shane and into the library. His black eyes approved of the room and its contents.

"All gather," Dhamsa said. "Good, this."

"Your holiness," Redpath said, rising quickly. "What an unexpected honor. We were just getting ready to go to Virginia to see you."

"Restless he," Dhamsa said, gesturing to Shane.

Dhamsa started to say more, then switched to Tibetan. Shane translated quickly.

"First the restless one had to find out who stole the silk from its sacred place," Shane translated.

"Restless one?" Dani asked. "Oh, you."

"Yeah. Me. In bloody spades. I went after Pakit like a cat on a snake."

"Pakit," Redpath said. "Then Gillie was correct in his suspicions that an Azure monk stole the silk."

"What made you think that?" Dani asked Gillespie.

"Shane trained the guards," Gillespie said simply. "I've worked with the men he trains. No outsiders would have gotten a step into that room before the balloon went up, so it had to be a monk. An inside job."

"I wasn't as fond of Gillie's theory," Shane said.

Prasam asked a question. Shane answered in the same language. Prasam smiled like a buddha, spoke quickly, and waited.

Shane's smile was less gentle.

"Prasam is reminding me of an old Buddhist saying," Shane said. "When foolish people have a foolish leader, they're all doomed. Pakit thought his lama was a foolish leader and the Tibetans who followed him were fools headed for ruin."

"He thought the PRC was the smart man's future?" Dani asked.

"That's what Pakit told me, finally. His first order of the day was to pry the foolish ones away from the superstitious past."

"The sacred silk," Redpath murmured.

"Yeah," Shane said. "Pakit stole the silk for Kasatonin, then got to thinking about it. He figured Kasatonin would probably slit his throat as soon as the silk traded hands."

Gillespie grunted. "The boy wasn't entirely stupid, was he?"

"He wasn't entirely bright, either," Shane retorted. "He had cold feet all the way to his knees, but he didn't return the silk."

"What did he do?" Redpath asked.

"He gave it to Feng," Shane said. "Then he sicced Feng on Dani and waited for the scandal to break when an American woman was caught buying a stolen religious artifact on the open market. The PRC would look like heroes for rescuing a precious piece of Tibetan history.''

''Which would then be whisked back to Beijing for safe-keeping,'' Redpath suggested dryly.

''That was the plan,'' Shane said. ''But it didn't work out that way. Pakit is collecting frozen yak dung and meditating in an icy hut because the American woman in question had enough grit and intelligence to take a helping hand when it was offered.''

Shane held out his hand to Dani.

''I don't have any Tibetan roofs to climb at the moment,'' he said, ''but I want you with me anyway.''

Dani closed her eyes so that she wouldn't see her dream standing before her, holding out his hand.

''Your vow,'' she said tightly.

''Prasam took back my vow the night he saw us together,'' Shane said.

Dani's eyes snapped open. ''What?''

''It's a Buddhist custom,'' Shane said. ''Vows that become too burdensome can be given back by the person who received them. I gave Prasam my vow of celibacy. He gave it back to me.''

''But—in Aruba—I—you—we didn't—''

Dani gave up trying to talk. She just shook her head.

''I'm not as wise as Prasam,'' Shane said simply. ''I held myself to the full three years. Then on the ferry ride to Vancouver, I realized it was already tomorrow in Tibet. My vow had been kept.''

''The international dateline,'' Dani said, finally understanding.

''Will you take my hand again and share new vows with me?'' Shane asked.

''I won't give any vow back to you,'' Dani said in a shaky voice, ''even if you ask.''

''I'll never ask. I keep my vows, Dani. So do you.''

Dani didn't remember getting up and going to Shane. All she knew was that she was in his arms and he was in hers.

After a minute, Prasam Dhamsa began speaking.

"He has a present for us," Shane said. "A *kata.*"

"What is it?"

"A traditional Tibetan gift. A scarf woven with good wishes."

Gently Shane turned Dani in his arms so that she could see Dhamsa.

Her breath came in with a rushing sound.

The lama was holding out to her an extraordinary piece of silk. Once it had been an indigo as deep as twilight. Now it was a luminous blue.

With shaking fingers, Dani touched the cloth while Redpath slipped it around Shane's and Dani's necks, joining them.

The rhythm of the weave was as familiar to Dani as the sound of her own heartbeat; dip and rise, hesitation, dip and rise.

The Buddha's silk.

Yet the color was wrong. Too deep. And the cloth had been repaired more than once. The repairs were very deft, but they were still different from the main fabric. A long time ago, centuries perhaps, someone had added a soft, creamy silk fringe.

"The weaver," Dani said huskily. *"The weaver is the same one."*

Prasam Dhamsa's smile became even more serene. He spoke quickly.

"There is a legend in Prasam's family," Shane translated, "that one of his ancestors wove the Buddha's robe. He thanks you for once again confirming that all life is one, and we are one with it."

"But I can't take this," Dani said huskily, touching the silk.

Dhamsa bowed and spoke again.

"Prasam is the last of his family," Shane said. "He will die soon. Knowing that he is the guardian of the scarf has been a burden. He wants us to keep the silk, and with it his burden, freeing him from his last ties to the cycle of death and rebirth."

"Shane?" she whispered, searching his eyes.

"It's all right, Dani. Dhamsa knew the first time he saw me."

"I don't understand."

"He knew that I wasn't destined to be a monk. I didn't believe him. Now I see what he saw."

"What?"

"Us. Whether or not you marry me, our lives are woven together. Dhamsa saw that."

Dani smiled through lips that trembled.

"Fate, huh?" she asked huskily.

"Shall we find out?"

"Together?"

"Always. If that's what you want . . .?"

Dani sensed the fragile weight of the scarf around their shoulders, ancient silk joining the past to the present. Then she lifted her head and looked into the eyes of her future.

Shane looked back at her, smiling.

Laughing, Dani held out her arms.